THE TITANIC SECRET

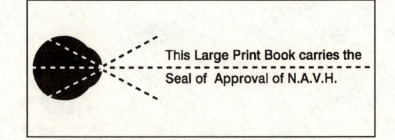

AN ISAAC BELL ADVENTURE

THE TITANIC SECRET

CLIVE CUSSLER
AND
JACK DU BRUL

WHEELER PUBLISHING
A part of Gale, a Cengage Company

GALE
A Cengage Company

Farmington Hills, Mich • San Francisco • New York • Waterville, Maine
Meriden, Conn • Mason, Ohio • Chicago

Copyright © 2019 by Sandecker, RLLLP.
Interior illustrations by Roland Dahlquist.
Mining cart by TTstudio/Shutterstock.com; grunge texture by
STILLFX/Shutterstock.com.
Wheeler Publishing, a part of Gale, a Cengage Company.

Wheeler Publishing Large Print Hardcover.
The text of this Large Print edition is unabridged.
Other aspects of the book may vary from the original edition.
Set in 16 pt. Plantin.

LIBRARY OF CONGRESS CIP DATA ON FILE.
CATALOGUING IN PUBLICATION FOR THIS BOOK
IS AVAILABLE FROM THE LIBRARY OF CONGRESS

ISBN-13: 978-1-4328-6029-5 (hardcover alk. paper)

Published in 2019 by arrangement with G. P. Putnam's Sons, an imprint
of Penguin Publishing Group, a division of Penguin Random House, LLC

Printed in the United States of America
1 2 3 4 5 6 7 23 22 21 20 19

CAST OF CHARACTERS

New York

DIRK PITT Director of NUMA.

THOMAS GWYNN Attorney for the estate of Isaac Bell.

VIN BLANKENSHIP Secret Service agent.

Colorado

ISAAC BELL Detective with the Van Dorn Agency.

JIM PORTER Manager of a Denver post office.

BILLY MCCALLISTER Denver Police.

JACK GAYLORD Denver Police.

BOB NORTHROP Postal inspector.

RUDOLFO LATANG Magician.

HANS BLOESER Banker and co-owner of the Little Angel Mine.

TONY WICKERSHAM Engineer and Bloeser employee.

WILLIAM GIBBS Reporter.

COLIN RHODES Van Dorn agent.

GREGGORY PATMORE U.S. Army Intelligence.

Paris

JOSHUA HAYES BREWSTER Miner and leader of the Coloradans.

VERNON HALL Colorado miner.

WARNER O'DEMING Colorado miner.

ALVIN COULTER Colorado miner.

THOMAS PRICE Colorado miner.

CHARLES WIDNEY Colorado miner.

JOHN CALDWELL Colorado miner.

WALTER SCHMIDT Colorado miner.

JAKE HOBART Colorado miner.

FOSTER GLY Head of special security for the Société des Mines de Lorraine.

YVES MASSARD Assistant to Gly.

THERESA MASSARD Yves's sister-in-law.

HENRI FAVREAU Bell's contact in Paris.

The Arctic

RAGNAR FYRIE Captain of the whaler *Hvalur Batur.*

IVAR IVARSSON Chief engineer of the *Hvalur Batur.*

LARS OLUFSEN 2nd engineer of the *Hvalur Batur.*

MAGNUS Crewman.

ARN Crewman.

PETR Crewman.

THE OTHER PETR Crewman.

GUNNAR Crewman.

England

JOEL WALLACE Van Dorn agent.

DAVIDA BRYER Wallace's assistant.

GEORGE DEVLIN Gangster.

Pitt Trapped in the Turtle

PROLOGUE

New York City
April

The sky over Manhattan was the color of old pewter. The clouds were so low that the tops of some of the tallest buildings vanished into the mist. The air had a biting edge, while the Hudson Hawk, the famed wind that blew along its namesake river, was in full flight. The spring-like weather from a week earlier was but a memory to the city dwellers.

An armored Chevy Suburban with government plates eased up to the midblock curb in a downtown neighborhood. A late-twenties man in a trench coat holding a furled black umbrella and obviously waiting for the vehicle pushed himself from the flower box he'd been leaning against and approached the big SUV as its passenger's-side window whispered down.

The driver, a thirty-year veteran in providing security for government officials, said nothing.

"Greetings," the pedestrian stammered. He peered into the backseat and his mouth flattened into a line when he saw it was unoccupied. "I'm Thomas Gwynn. I'm supposed to meet with the NUMA Director. The National Underwater and Marine Agency. Dirk Pitt."

Back at the beginning of his career, the driver, Vin Blankenship, would have asked to see ID, but he'd checked the website of the law firm where Gwynn worked and recognized the younger man from his online bio. "Mr. Pitt texted me to say his meeting at the UN is running a little long. He asked that I pick you up before I get him, and then we head over to Queens."

"Oh, sure. That's no problem." Gwynn let himself into the back of the big truck. He loosened the belt on his coat. "Nice and warm in here."

Despite the extra weight of its armor and bulletproof glass, the Suburban pulled from the curb with remarkable agility and power. Its throaty V-8 was as heavily modified as her coachwork.

Blankenship soon had the big truck cruising north on the FDR. Had he wanted, he could have hit the sirens and lights, but he figured they had plenty of time.

"Did you drive Mr. Pitt here from Washington?" Gwynn asked, just for something to say.

"No. I'm from the New York office. I was assigned to him while he's here for the UN conference. I picked him up at Penn two days ago, and I'll be dropping him off there after the tour — or whatever it is he wanted to see today."

"FBI?"

"Secret Service."

"Does he need protection like that?"

"C'mon, this is New York. Everyone needs protection." Blankenship laughed at his own joke.

Fifteen minutes later, he wheeled the Suburban onto the plaza in front of the five-hundred-and-five-foot glass monolith that is the United Nations headquarters. He had to present credentials to guards in black tac gear and slalom through concrete barriers to approach the building. He stopped and rolled down his window so he'd be recognized. His wasn't the only government Suburban present.

There were dozens of people milling around on the plaza, huddled in little groups of three and four, all with name tags. Most wore smiles and were shaking hands in self-congratulatory ways. Most were dressed in suits, but there were a few Arabs in white *dishdashas* and some African women in dresses as colorful as tropical bird feathers. This had been a truly international affair. One solitary figure that did not look so pleased spied the idling SUV and its driver. He launched himself across the crowded esplanade with a single-mindedness usually reserved for master jewelers about to make a critical cut.

Dirk Pitt was tall, and rather more lanky than muscular, with a swirl of dark hair and bright green eyes. His mouth was usually held in such a way as to convey a sense that he found life to be pleasantly amusing. Not now, though. His eyes were dark, like the color of a squall at sea, and his mouth was pinched so that his jaw jutted out.

"You look even worse today than after yesterday's meetings," Blankenship said as Pitt neared the Suburban.

Pitt pulled himself up into the passenger's seat next to the driver. This broke security protocol, but the NUMA Director had assured the Secret Service vet that if anything happened he would make sure blame would fall squarely on his own shoulders.

Pitt said, "I may not know how to stem the tide of so much plastic waste entering the world's oceans, but I do know that spending days in a lecture hall with a bunch of overfed and overindulged bureaucrats who decide nothing other than the agenda for the next round of meetings isn't going to solve anything." He gave a little shudder and, just like that, the darkness enveloping him evaporated. He looked over his shoulder with a friendly grin and an outstretched hand. "Thomas Gwynn, I'm Dirk Pitt. Thanks for agreeing to meet in such an unorthodox way. My schedule's tight, and my wife says I have to be back in Washington tonight for a birthday party for her chief of staff."

"This is no problem at all," Gwynn replied. He realized how soft his hand must have felt to Pitt's callused grip. The man ran a massive government agency, but it was clear he was no overfed, overindulged bureaucrat. "Your wife is Congresswoman Loren Smith."

"I'm a lucky man," Pitt said with obvious love. "I will admit that you piqued my interest when you called my office. It was just good luck that I was coming to New York the next day. Most people are aware of the *Titanic* salvage, some may even remember that I headed the raising, but to the best of my knowledge the fact we were hoping to recover the byzanium ore from her holds remains classified. How do you know about that?" Pitt held up a finger to forestall the answer to ask the driver, "You know where we're heading, right?"

"I grew up ten minutes from that old site," Blankenship replied. "I used to fish the East River just upstream."

Pitt grinned. "I hope you didn't eat anything you caught."

The Secret Service man chuckled. "We couldn't even identify half the things we caught."

Turning his attention back to Thom Gwynn, Pitt asked again, "So, how do you know about the byzanium?"

"My law firm kept papers on behalf of the man who recovered it."

Pitt nodded, and stated, "Joshua Hayes Brewster. A Colorado hard-rock miner who first discovered the ore on Novaya Zemlya Island in the Russian Arctic and then returned in 1911 with a group of other men to wrest it from the mountain."

He knew the story as surely as he knew his own.

"No, Mr. Pitt. I'm talking about Isaac Bell."

A shadow of confusion passed over Pitt's eyes. While he couldn't recount the names of the other miners, he did remember none of them were named Bell. "You've lost me."

"I'm not surprised. Are you familiar with the Van Dorn Detective Agency?"

"Yes. I know they were as big and famous as Pinkerton."

"In an age when hotels had their own inhouse detectives, and railways hired armies of guards, Joseph Van Dorn built a thriving business around the motto 'We never give up! Never!' Isaac Bell was the lead investigator. Perhaps the greatest detective of his — or any — generation."

"Okay," Pitt said cautiously. "I don't doubt that, but you need to believe me when I say that he had nothing to do with mining the byzanium or working to smuggle it aboard the *Titanic*. I lived that project for what seemed like the better part of a year. There were no private investigators involved."

"Mr. Bell kept his presence out of all records. He even rewrote Brewster's notes so that his name was expunged."

Pitt's face still showed nothing but confusion.

"Let me explain it this way, Mr. Pitt."

"Dirk," he said absently. "Please."

"Sure, Dirk. Okay. So, Isaac Bell, over the course of his long career, came into posses-

17

sion of a great many secrets. Things that could ruin family dynasties, destroy the credibility of companies and even nations, and reveal hidden motives and behind-the-scenes players of some of the most pivotal events of the first half of the twentieth century. He had all this information, but unlike J. Edgar Hoover, the FBI's first director, Bell had no interest in furthering himself through blackmail or intimidation. He was just a man who knew a lot of secrets.

"When he retired, he decided to record secrets and stories. I must say, had he not been so good as a detective, he could have been a pulp fiction writer. Tales of his exploits read like adventure books. He also knew that while some of what he wrote about must never see the light of day — and those journals were likely burned upon his death — he felt that other stories could be made public at some future date when those most involved were long dead and the legacy had been relegated to the 'dusty corner of history.' Those are his exact words.

"These files he placed in trust with his attorney with detailed instructions as to when and with whom they could be shared. Much of it was straightforward, like 'Thirty years after the death of so-and-so, please see that his surviving children are given this envelope. If they are deceased, please see that it is given to a grandchild.' That sort of thing."

"Sounds reasonable."

"There were other files that he left up to the attorney's discretion as to who to share the information with, although Bell did specify the year in which to make the disbursement, usually some benchmark important to the tale, although I've seen a few that just give a date with no explanation.

"So now, we spring ahead decades after Bell's death, and his attorney built a practice into what is now Gitterman, Shankle, and Capps. My current employer and one of the city's largest law firms. And to this day we continue to honor our commitment in seeing the last few Isaac Bell files find their proper home."

"And you think that's me?" Pitt still didn't quite get the connection.

"Yes, well, when the date on this particular file came due, one of the senior partners had the honor of reading it first. He wasn't sure what to do, but his secretary knew that I was something of a *Titanic* buff. My namesake uncle was part of the recovery operation. He once told me you were the man who raised the *Titanic*. He was a hoist operator on one of the support ships. The

Modoc."

"I'll be damned," Pitt said. "I thought your name rang a bell. Tommy Gwynn. You don't look much like him, I have to say."

"I know. Right? He was huge."

Pitt caught the tense the lawyer used. "Was? What happened?"

"He left NUMA a short time after the *Titanic* operation and worked as a crane operator here in New York. There was an accident at a construction site. Uncle Tommy and two other men were killed. That was eight or nine years ago." Counselor Gwynn paused for a moment, grief darkening his eyes before he thrust it aside. "Back to the story. The senior partners tapped me to find the right person to share this with and I immediately thought of you once I'd read it and did some digging into the lives of Brewster and the rest of his miners —"

"They called themselves the Coloradans," Pitt interjected.

Gwynn nodded eagerly. "Bell mentioned that. There's no family left for any of them, since all but one never married except —"

"Jake Hobart." Now that he was thinking again about that long-ago mission, more and more details were flooding Pitt's mind.

"That's right. Hobart was married, but his wife is long dead, and they didn't have

20

children. Since no one remains from the time the mineral was mined and put aboard the *Titanic,* I figured why not give it to the guy who found it in the end? Bell's journal doesn't change the basic facts, but I thought you might be interested in the backstory of how the events unfolded more than a hundred years ago."

From a deep pocket inside his trench coat, the young attorney withdrew a sheaf of yellowed papers in a sealed plastic bag. The first page just had a simple two-word title. *The Coloradans.* Pitt was about to open the bag when Blankenship interrupted.

"Just so you know, we're only five minutes away."

"Okay," Pitt said, so engrossed in what Gwynn had to tell him, he hadn't realized how swiftly they'd crossed the East River.

Thomas Gwynn said, "I told you I didn't mind meeting on the fly like this, but what's so important about some turtles at a riverside construction site in Queens?"

"Not some turtles," Pitt corrected. "The *Turtle.* In the cargo space behind you is a leather overnight backpack and a waterproof dive bag. Could you hand me the bag?"

Gwynn leaned over the rear bench to recover the bag and handed it to Pitt. Pitt had already slipped off his leather shoes. He

21

held one up so both driver and passenger could see it. "My wife got me these as an expensive practical joke, thinking I would never wear Italian loafers, but they're more comfortable than sneakers."

From the dive bag he removed a pair of shin-high rubber boots and an insulated high-vis windbreaker. He jammed his feet into the galoshes and contorted his way into the jacket while penned in by the Suburban's confines.

"Here's a story for you," Pitt said when he clicked on his seat belt once again. "Following the battles of Lexington and Concord during our Revolutionary War against the British, an inventor living near New Haven named David Bushnell proposed building a submersible craft that could be used to affix mines to the underside of the English ships blockading New York Harbor. None other than George Washington himself liked the proposal and agreed to fund it.

"All that summer, and into the fall, Bushnell and several dedicated woodworkers, metalsmiths, and self-taught engineers built the submarine. About ten feet tall and barrel-shaped — or, as once described, resembling two turtle shells that had been fused together — it was made of iron-banded wood like the staves of a barrel and powered by a pair of hand-cranked screws. It also had an auger that was designed to bore into a ship's hull so an explosive charge could be affixed. It had a foot-pedal bilge pump and windows in a metal . . . Well, I guess conning tower is the best way to describe it. All in all, it was ungainly, awkward, and utterly brilliant.

"And also, a total failure," Pitt added. "In the summer of 1776, after a lot of sea trials and testing, one Sergeant Ezra Lee was selected to be the *Turtle*'s pilot. Finally, in September of that year, Lee launched the *Turtle* at the British flagship HMS *Eagle*, which was at anchor below Governors Island at the mouth of New York Harbor. It took Lee two hours to maneuver the submersible, but no matter how hard he tried, he couldn't get the upward-facing drill to bite deep enough into the *Eagle*'s hull to set the explosives. In retrospect, it's pretty easy to see that maintaining the *Turtle*'s stability while drilling in that exact location was practically impossible given the tides and currents."

"Not to mention the poor guy must have been exhausted," Blankenship said.

Pitt nodded. "The *Turtle* was thought to have only enough air for a half hour. He could replenish his supply by surfacing as he crossed the harbor, but by the end of his attempt at boring into the *Eagle* he would have been delirious from too much carbon dioxide.

"They tried attacking a different ship a month later with the same result. Not long afterward, the British sank the *Turtle*'s support ship on the Jersey side of the harbor. Bushnell claims he salvaged the little sub, but its fate was lost to history."

"Until now?" Thomas Gwynn hazarded.

"Exactly. Interesting, it wouldn't be until almost a hundred years later that a submarine was successful at sinking an enemy warship. That was the Confederate sub *Hunley,* which rammed a torpedo into the USS *Housatonic* during the Civil War."

They were approaching a large construction zone in a commercial section of the city. The ground was mostly broken-up asphalt. The nearby buildings were brick or metal and windowless. Several old smokestacks were silhouetted against the skyline. Dumpsters and rusted equipment littered the alleys between buildings, and most vertical surfaces were desecrated with multiple layers of graffiti, none of which could be considered art. The fine mist that had hung in the air all day became heavier. Not yet a rain, it was a perfect gloomy pall for the forlorn district.

Just ahead, a long corrugated metal fence blocked further access to the neighborhood. A temporary guardhouse had been set up next to an open gate. The metal shack's bank of fluorescent ceiling lights looked especially bright in the gathering murk. Hidden by the fence was a large crane. Its spindly boom was visible as it reached for the sky.

Blankenship braked at the gate. The guard begrudgingly left the warm confines of his little metal hut and stepped out and over to the idling SUV.

The Secret Service agent jerked a thumb toward his passenger. "That's Dirk Pitt, the head of NUMA. He's expected."

"Sec," the guard said. He returned to the guardhouse and consulted a clipboard that he probably should have carried with him but hadn't bothered to. He looked up, caught Blankenship's eye, and nodded.

The worksite was vast, at least ten acres. Much of what had stood here before had been dismantled and carried away, and a huge amount of polluted fill had been hauled out for decontamination. A massive stone and brick seawall held back the waters of the East River, which were flowing by on both the meltwater channeled from the

Hudson via the Harlem River at the very top of Manhattan Island and an ebbing king tide that was escaping through the river from Long Island Sound.

Vic Blankenship looked around. "When I was a kid, this was all warehouses and old manufacturing plants. Smelled awful even on a good day."

"The state archeologist told me," Pitt said, "that from the time of the Civil War until about 1913, there was a plant here to convert coal into gas. The ground was saturated with contaminants that were never removed. The next generation of industry simply capped the old sludge and built anew."

Gwynn asked, rather unnecessarily, "And here's where they found the *Turtle*?"

"As I understand it, an excavator was removing overburden when the bucket hit stone. Not unusual, since all the old foundations were left behind when newer buildings were put up. The operator cleared an area around the granite blocks. It turns out it was a sump below the foundation of a building that had been here around the time of the Revolutionary War. The cavity had a stone lid that the machine slid aside. The inside was filled with fly ash and oil that was still somewhat liquid, and sticking out

26

of it was this brass dome. He managed to open it and peer inside. He didn't know exactly what he'd found, but he told a supervisor, who eventually found someone who recognized the *Turtle* from a replica he'd seen at a museum in Connecticut. Archeologists from the state and city level were brought in."

"And NUMA?" Thomas asked.

"Not really. We heard about the find, naturally. I'm here because, as a lover of archeology, I'm curious. I'm just using my NUMA credentials to get access to what's otherwise a closed site."

"Is anything going to be happening to-day?"

"Absolutely. Today they're going to attempt to pull the *Turtle* out of the hole it's been resting in for nearly two hundred and fifty years."

They parked the Suburban next to several other cars, mostly sedans and pickup trucks. The trucks belonged to the workmen, the cars, no doubt, to the archeologists and techs overseeing the discovery of the nation's first submarine.

The site that had been dug out was easily two football fields long and a hundred feet wide. Some material had been left in place along the old seawall to buttress it against

27

the gray river just beyond. At the bottom of the twenty-foot-deep excavation were large earthmovers, dump trucks, shipping containers for other gear, and dozens of portable pumps with hoses snaking up and out to a separate containment pond that had been purposely dug to store contaminated seepage for later cleanup.

It didn't appear that anyone was working. The site felt abandoned except for the big crane that was maneuvering a large section of steel closer to the seawall. A couple of hard-hatted workers were atop the wall waiting to guide the steel into place. There was a raised platform at the edge of the construction zone. They couldn't see where the *Turtle* lay buried because blue plastic tarps had been erected over the dig to protect the craft from the elements. The tarps rippled in the chilling wind.

The precipitation ratcheted up a notch and now fell as a light rain. The ground at the lip of the site was a muddy morass. Blankenship declined to join Pitt in his trek across to a raised platform holding a half dozen people, but young Gwynn joined him.

As they neared the gathering, Pitt could hear voices rising and tension mounting.

"I don't care who gave you authorization. Until my office is satisfied that this site is

28

secure, no one is going down there. Your toy boat'll just have to wait." The speaker was a man wearing a hard hat and a safety orange vest over a Carhartt coat. Pitt noticed that he was from OSHA, the government watchdog for workplace safety.

Facing off against him were a man and a woman dressed in civilian attire, although they wore proper boots. Pitt correctly guessed that these two were the archeologists, who were doubtless concerned that the submersible needed to be conserved as soon as possible.

It was the woman who spoke for them. "It will only take a few hours. We've excavated the ash and tar from the pit. All that's left is bracing up the hull and rigging the crane."

"Lady, I don't care," the OSHA inspector fired back. From his tone, Pitt could tell that he loved throwing his weight around.

"Excuse me," he said. "Hi. I'm Dirk Pitt. Are you Dr. Lawrence?"

The female academic turned to him. "Susan Lawrence. Yes. I'm sorry, who are you?"

"Dirk Pitt. I spoke to someone in your office about coming today to see the *Turtle.* I'm the Director of the National Underwater and Marine Agency."

She nodded sharply. "Yes, I recall now. I

29

am sorry to say, but it seems you wasted a trip from Washington because our site just got shut down by OSHA."

Pitt didn't mention he was playing hooky on the last day of a UN conference to be here. He turned his attention to the OSHA supervisor. The safety inspector nodded to one of his guys, who, in turn, grabbed two hard hats off a table and handed them to Pitt and Gwynn. "What seems to be the problem?"

"The problem is, the contractor was supposed to leave twenty feet's worth of earth in place next to the seawall, with a sixty percent grade down to the bottom of the pit. As you can see — as you *all* can see," he said with special emphasis, "there's barely ten feet of ground remaining, and its face is perfectly vertical. There isn't enough fill to backstop the seawall and it's in danger of breaching. It looks like they're attempting to shore it up with steel plating, but until I see and go over the engineering specs on that plan, I'm declaring this site too dangerous."

"You must understand," the male archeologist pled, "the *Turtle*'s entire hull is exposed to the air, and every moment we delay could cause irreparable damage." He then remembered another detail and he went ashen. "By

30

God, we left the hatch open. You must let us at least reseal the hatch."

The OSHA inspector said, "Look, I'm not an idiot. I know how these things work. I've been to a lot of sites around the city where you guys are called in, but I can't let you down there until I'm satisfied that it's safe."

Another of the group chimed in. He was dressed like the construction guys but neater, as if he'd never faced the mud and slop found at a typical work zone. He looked like someone from the front office. "Come'n, John. Our engineers sent the changes in the specs to the city three weeks ago. Someone there gave us temporary approval."

"That doesn't give you the right to change anything until a final review. Besides, you dug out the remaining material before you had your steel protection up over the existing seawall."

"Well, okay, that was a screwup," the man admitted. "The contractor dug much faster than we . . ."

Pitt was tuning out the conversation. He knew how this would ultimately end. The jobsite was going to be shut down for the foreseeable future. The *Turtle* would undoubtedly suffer some degradation, but ultimately he didn't think the world's earliest example of an attack submarine would be damaged too severely. And who knew? Depending on the schedule, maybe he could still sneak up to see it hoisted from its two-hundred-fifty-year-old cocoon.

He watched the men working the steel out on the seawall. He would have assumed that the OSHA inspector would have ordered them off the structure, but he had to be enough of a pragmatist to know that placing the heavy metal caps over the existing wall could be done much faster than in-filling the massive excavation to the original design specifications.

The steel structural members were about fifty feet long and L-shaped. The two leaves of metal were each at least an inch thick. The shorter leg would rest atop the seawall, and likely be bolted directly into the cement. The longer section would dangle nearly thirty feet down along its face and well into the riverbank's muck and ooze. Pitt's gut told him, and likely the OSHA guy would agree, that this was an accept-able alternative to leaving twice as much contaminated soil in the work zone to but-tress the old seawall.

The crane was swinging one of the huge steel pieces across the site and over the wall as Pitt watched. Two men in hard hats were on the wall ready to guide the piece into place with ropes hanging from each end. This was a bread-and-butter-type maneuver for ironworkers, something these guys had probably done thousands of times on high-rises and bridges all over the city.

One worker patiently waited for the hundred-foot rope to gently be lowered so he could reach it. His partner might have done the same, had a gust of wind not suddenly hit the plate, twisting his rope so that it started floating away out over the East River.

Pitt never knew why the guy leapt for it. The wind would have died down and the line would have eventually come back to him. He would later come to realize that the workmen had been told to get the job done before the contractor incurred more delays and penalties.

The steelworker managed to grab the rope just before it looped out of reach, but his two hundred pounds was no match for the thirty tons of dangling steel and he was quickly yanked off his feet. The delicately balanced rigging connecting the plate to the crane's forged-steel hook wouldn't have registered such a tiny imbalance had the machine's operator not overreacted. Fearing for the man's safety, that he could fall to the swift current below, the operator snapped back on a lever to reverse the boom's swing. The sudden change in momentum caused the massive steel plate to dip enough to upset its center of gravity. In seconds, what had once been a routine maneuver had spiraled out of control.

The plate twisted and corkscrewed in the air like a bird of prey caught by one foot. The second rigger fled his post, not knowing what was going to happen next. The man clutching the rope was tossed and whipped about like a rag doll and was about to be flung either far out into the river, where his heavy clothes and boots would surely drown him, or, equally deadly, be hurled into the pit, where most of his bones would break upon impact.

The crane operator moved more levers in rapid succession, the jolt of adrenaline making his hands tremble. He timed his action so when the plate dropped from the sky, the iron rigger flopped onto the seawall at the full extension of his rope. He was well clear when the mass of steel slammed into the old concrete like the chisel of a jackhammer.

The crumbly masonry came apart as though it had been hit by an explosive. The clang of the impact echoed painfully across the site as though the Roman god Vulcan had struck his mighty hammer against the anvil of the earth.

Pitt was in motion even before the full effects of the disaster became clear. He turned to Thom Gwynn and said, "Call 911. Make sure they send divers."

Pitt legged over the metal rail that acted as a barrier for the platform overlooking the construction site. The drop to the roof of a container down in the excavation was about ten feet, but Pitt's perception, since he was a tall man, added another five and a half. He didn't hesitate. The wind rushed past his ears and his hard hat was blown from his head. He landed well, letting the big muscles of his legs absorb some of the impact before he dipped a shoulder to collapse his body in order to absorb the rest. He let momentum carry him back up to his feet, and he ran to the edge of the container. He paused to look across the workings to the steel plate that had been rammed into the retaining wall.

Cracks had appeared directly below the impact, and they ran from the top of the wall to where it was buttressed by the dirt left in place. Already, water was burbling through these cracks, frothing and angry and eager to exploit the seams as though it resented being penned up behind such an artificial barrier. In seconds, water was snaking across the dirt berm and cascading down its face. As it fell into the pit the water remained clear for just a moment before its erosive forces started chewing through the ground and it turned a muddy brown. All this was taking place a good hundred yards from the square stone sump that had been the *Turtle*'s home for two and a half centuries.

Pitt had spent his entire career above and below the waters of the world, and few men alive today better understood its undeniable power. He knew what was coming. What he didn't know, what he was betting his life on, was if he had time enough to accomplish what he'd set out to do. He'd done many rash things over the years, putting his life on the line more times than he could count, and while he'd never second-guessed a decision he'd made, he did wonder for a fleeting moment if what he was about to attempt was worth dying for. Realizing the history that was about to be lost, he tore his gaze from the inevitable destruction that was about to be unleashed and focused instead on the ground below the container.

A dark spot appeared on the striated face of the earthworks berm. It quickly spread, opening like an obscene stain. It remained black for a fraction of a second before it turned muddy brown, and the soil became gelatinous and bulged.

Pitt didn't need to see anything further. He started running across the bottom of the site, his rubber boots flopping and splashing through the accumulating rainwater. Drops seared his eyes but didn't slow him at all. His legs pistoned and his arms swung, and his breath came in deep, measured draws, while a few hundred feet away the bulge burst in an explosion of roiling mud. An instant later the entirety of the berm above the hole collapsed into it, the hundreds of tons of dirt and rock and industrial fill vanishing into a cauldron of muck and icy water.

While he didn't turn to see the wave that would now be racing across the floor of the workings, Pitt could hear its sloshing roar and feel the chill wind as it pushed air ahead of it. He might not have been the younger version of himself who'd spearheaded the raising of the *Titanic,* but he'd kept in shape. He was almost to the blue tarpaulin shelter the archeologists had erected around their find when the first of the surge raced past him and almost knocked his feet out from underneath him with its power.

The water hampered his gait, but he fought on, pushing through as fast as he could, actually managing to get ahead of the rising water so what had once swirled around his ankles now fell to an easy half-inch puddle. He saw a seam in one of the tarped walls and rushed through it. The room the scientists had created inside was dim. There were sets of construction lamps on poles, but none were lit, and Pitt didn't have the time to waste.

The *Turtle* was made of wooden staves, like a barrel, and bound with thick wrought iron rings. It had a round conning tower rising from its squat hull that was ringed with glass portholes. Two curled tubes rose from it. These were snorkels for when the *Turtle* was traveling just below the surface. Once it was completely submerged, the operator only had as much air as the volume of the ungainly craft allowed. Next to the conning tower was the hand-cranked vertical propeller. Its blades, like everything else, were blacked with tar pitch, but Pitt guessed they would be bronze. Deeper into the stone-lined sump, he could see the *Turtle*'s larger main prop and a square rudder operated by mechanical levers.

He took in all that detail on the fly because

the water had reached the edge of the sump and would fill it in mere seconds. He leapt across the five feet of open air between the edge of the pit and the *Turtle*'s metal-shod upper deck and threw himself feetfirst down the hatch. His rubber boots landed on a padded seat. The hatch encircled his hips. He blindly felt around with his feet to figure the best way to shoehorn himself into the one-man submersible. The water was a frothing boil as it rose up the filthy walls of the sump. In seconds, Pitt's mad attempt to save the relic would be for naught.

He finally worked his body down into the submersible's dank hull. Just as the water was about to sweep across the rounded upper deck, Pitt slammed the hatch closed. There was a mechanism with a butterfly screw to tighten the seal. Water began spurting in where a cork gasket had long ago rotted away. He worked his fingers to twist the mechanism and eventually turned the nut enough to expand an inner ring that compressed the hull and the hatch together.

He realized his lungs were heaving from his breakneck race to save the *Turtle* and was acutely aware that air had become a precious commodity. He pulled his cell phone from his pocket and activated its flashlight.

The inside of the submersible had an H. G. Wells feel to it, with brightworks mechanisms, gears and cogs made of brass and bronze, as well as rack-and-pinion devices as finely crafted as a Swiss watch. His seat had been padded in leather, although his weight had cracked it apart and pieces had fallen to the floor. By his left knee was a hand-operated pump for clearing out the bilge, which he could hear burbling down below the floorboards. Next to him was a wire rack containing what appeared to be a journal or diary wrapped in oilskin. It looked to be in better shape than the leather seat, but Pitt wisely didn't touch it.

The little light that had shone in through the hatch widows went completely dark as the sump filled and a river began inundating the construction site.

Pitt tried to calculate how long it would take to rescue him. Judging by the torrent of water he'd seen rushing over the seawall, he figured the river would inundate the blocks-long excavation completely in about thirty minutes. By then, police and fire crews would be on hand, as well as divers he'd told Thomas Gwynn to request. There was a crane on-site with more than enough lifting ability, and the divers would be able to rig a sling easy enough. He estimated forty-five minutes, tops, and he'd be able to pop the hatch once again. Unlike the original pilot, Ezra Lee, Pitt had no need to crank the screws in order to propel the *Turtle*. He could sit quietly in his dark little cocoon and wait to be pulled free.

Unseen above Pitt, the upstream breach created by the steel plate continued to widen in fits and starts as the gushing water clawed at more of the concrete and dissolved more of the berm. In all, the excavation was filling, but at a steadily increasing pace. Just as Pitt settled in for his wait, the backflow of water along the inner side of the earthen buttress began to rip away great slabs of dirt and rock that fell into the construction site like ice calving off a glacier. It was the deadweight of the berm that helped the old seawall keep the river from collapsing into the pit, but at a critical tipping point enough of the plug had been dissolved by the flood's scouring action that in a single catastrophic failure a forty-foot-long section of the stone wall and what was left of the inner berm failed spectacularly. A raging wall of seawater exploded into the site, washing against all sides and throwing spume high into the air and sending a wave of water speeding nearly three blocks inland

41

with enough force to shove parked cars away from curbs and topple any pedestrian unlucky enough to be in its way.

For Dirk Pitt, it was like he'd been tossed into an industrial washing machine and it had been set on spin-dry. The colossal surge had created undercurrents in the water already filling the excavation, and like a leaf caught in a gutter the little submersible was yanked from its centuries-old home and borne along like any other bit of flotsam that eventually found itself in New York Harbor.

Freezing cold water from the bilge soaked Pitt to the skin while he braced his arms and legs across the tight cockpit to keep from bashing himself against any of the sharp handles and mechanisms used to propel and steer the craft. Once the initial surge subsided, the weight of water and a ballasted keel righted the submersible. Pitt knew he'd been wrenched from the sump and could now feel the bottom of the *Turtle* scraping ever so slowly along the rocky floor of the excavation. Any chance of a quick rescue was over. The added pressure of the deepening water increased the seepage from around the hatch above Pitt's head. What had been an occasional drip was quickly becoming a steady downpour.

The craft would fill swiftly, but Pitt wasn't ready to throw in the towel just yet.

He reached for the brass handle that operated the bilge pump and gave it a push. The lever moved with relative ease. What didn't was the rubberized canvas bellows that actually created the suction. Like the leather padding for the bench seat, the old material had lost all pliability in the past quarter millennium and turned to so much dust with the slightest pressure.

As a hobby, Pitt restored classic automobiles. He was good with his hands, understood machines, and when he studied the pump with his phone's flashlight he could tell that all it needed to operate properly was some way of building and releasing air pressure. The weave of his rain jacket was too porous to be effective against the water pressure outside the *Turtle*'s hull, but in a flash of inspiration he knew what he had to do.

Pitt wedged his phone into the wire rack so that it shone down on the pumping mechanism and he got to work.

He usually carried a multi-tool in his pocket. It wasn't something the airlines would have let him keep on board, which was why he preferred Amtrak when traveling to New York or Boston. He fished the knife/pliers from his pants and toed off one of his boots. The pliers gave him the leverage he needed to release the tension on the binding ring holding the tattered remains of the old bellows to the pump. Next he cut the uppers from the bottom of the boot. He slipped what was essentially a Croc back onto his foot and was left with a rubber tube more than tall enough to fit the diminutive pump. He trimmed the rubber down a few inches and set the bottom edge in place and clamped it tight with the pliers. He then forced the stiff rubber into the upper part of the pump so that it fit under the pump's metal cap. He ratcheted the binding ring closed with the pliers, creating an airtight seal again.

He began to work the pump handle back and forth. Each time, the hollow leg of his boot sucked flat, then expanded out. In moments he'd built up enough pressure in the system to begin pulling water out of the bilge and through a pipe fitted with a one-way valve that led outside the hull.

Not sure if the pump would allow him to get ahead of the water leaking into the cylindrical compartment, Pitt took an extra minute to slice part of his jacket into strips, then used his multi-tool's knife blade to wedge into the gap between the hatch and the inner ring. The cloth quickly soaked through and water dripped from it, but at one-tenth the previous rate. Pitt was just turning his attention back to the pump when the sound of the *Turtle* rasping against the bottom suddenly stopped and the craft shook violently. Pitt braced himself. He immediately knew that the current had sucked the relic from the excavation and it was now floating in the main channel of the East River. He had no idea how deep the river ran or the crush depth of the ancient craft, and he had no intention of discovering either.

He went to work on the pump like a man abandoned, trying not to dwell on the fact that with all the old tar stuck to its hull the *Turtle* may no longer be buoyant enough to float. He could feel the submersible twist and spin as it was caught in the eddies and current.

Back and forth he moved the pump handle, each stroke taking tiny sips of the mass of water sloshing across the *Turtle*'s floor. For ten solid minutes, changing hands when his arm grew stiff, he sucked the bilge almost dry and was rewarded with the faint aura of weak light coming through the cleanest of the conning tower windows. Pitt

45

couldn't tell if the sub had breached the surface or not. Even turning off his flashlight didn't give him a better perspective. The glass was still dirty and the sun was hidden by storm clouds, but he felt inordinately pleased with his efforts so far.

He turned his flashlight back on.

"Okay, let's see how we're doing," Pitt muttered and reached for the screw stopper of one of the twin snorkel tubes. He couldn't work it with his fingers and attacked it with the pliers. Once he broke the initial seal, the brass plug remained tight. He worked at an awkward angle, and the metal fought him for every degree it turned, and while Pitt wasn't in any immediate danger from asphyxia the air was getting a bit heavy to breathe.

Water sputtered from the tube. Pitt waited a moment to make sure it wasn't just some residue in the line but rather that the snorkel's mouth was still submerged. He retightened the plug. He was definitely still underwater. But judging by the light oozing in from above, the surface was tantalizingly close.

He checked the orange-faced Doxa watch that had been strapped to his wrist for decades. Only twenty minutes had elapsed since he'd raced to save the *Turtle.* Rescue teams would certainly be on the scene by now, though he doubted police divers would have had time to reach the construction site, let alone get into their diving suits and tanks. Pitt figured he still had enough air in the submersible to last long enough for the divers to reach the old sump. His problem came from the fact that he was no longer where they expected to find him, and he doubted anyone saw the underwater craft get swept out of the worksite and into the river. Recalling the speed of the current before the accident, Pitt estimated he was a mile south of where they expected to find him. For all he knew, he could be abreast of Roosevelt Island.

Logic told him he'd gambled and lost and that the right course of action was to let the *Turtle* refill and escape so that, with luck, the antique could be recovered from the river. If he waited too long, it was likely that the little submersible would be borne along until it passed Governors Island and be lost for all time in the lower reaches of the harbor where it widened considerably.

Pitt wasn't one to give in to logic too quickly. Not when he still had options. The vertical propeller hadn't spun in two hundred and fifty years and its blades were encrusted with dried tar that warped their

shape and severely degraded their hydrody-
namics, but Pitt went for it gamely. At first
he couldn't get the prop to crank at all, and
it wasn't until he put both hands on the
knurled wooden handle and braced his feet
against the hull did he succeed in turning it
through one tortured revolution. He kept at
it, turning it a second, and slightly easier,
rotation, and then a third and fourth time,
until he could crank the propeller with one
hand only and could feel through the contraption that the spindly blades were actually biting into the frigid river water.

He cast a hopeful eye on the one viewport
that let some light filter through but
couldn't tell if his efforts had brought the
Turtle closer to the surface. The glass was
just too murky. He knew he had succeeded
at further depleting his air supply. Now he
had to pull air deep into his lungs to feel he
was getting enough oxygen. He did a multi-
plication question in his head to make
certain he wasn't suffering from carbon
dioxide intoxication, which manifested itself
in loss of cognitive function. A quick check
of his watch told him that thirty minutes
had passed since he'd sealed himself inside
the submersible and he'd just about reached
his limit.

One last gamble paid off, however, when

he opened the snorkel valve again. Moist, icy air came in through the inch-wide tube, and Pitt drew it deep into his lungs. He'd managed to surface the *Turtle.* And no sooner had he taken a half dozen deep breaths, water again sluiced from the snorkel's mouth, forcing Pitt to hastily replace the plug. Negatively buoyant even with her bilge dry, the *Turtle* needed the added boost of the vertical screw to stay on the surface. Once it cleared the water, the craft immediately started to sink again.

Pitt turned the screw handle furiously and could tell by how it lost resistance that it had broken the surface. He was ready right away to open the snorkel and let fresh air enter the sub for a few precious seconds before the snorkel again dipped beneath the waves and he had to reseal it.

Because the screw and snorkels were taller than the hatch/conning tower, Pitt knew that it was unlikely the top of the submersible breached too. Still, he put his odds slightly above fifty/fifty that a sharp-eyed captain or crew member working one of the dozens of ships, boats, and ferries that ply the waters of New York Harbor would spot the *Turtle* as it rose and dove repeatedly while it floated ever southward on the tidal current.

49

Forty minutes later, Pitt adjusted his odds downward to zero. He'd felt vibrations through the water twice that indicated a boat of some kind was near, but neither had spotted him. The physical effort to keep the *Turtle* close enough to the surface to draw in even a tiny amount of fresh air had run up against the law of diminishing returns. He wasn't sufficiently replenishing the oxygen he was consuming turning the vertical propeller to raise the submersible. He could keep at it for a while longer, but he also knew that once he escaped the one-man sub, he'd still have to contend with the East River. Always a strong swimmer, Pitt was tiring and had to keep some reserves for a grueling struggle once he hit the water. It didn't help that his core temperature had dropped considerably since his clothes had been soaked by the leaky hatch.

Defeat was a bitter pill to swallow, especially for Pitt, as he was a man who had suffered its pangs far less than most. But defeat was something he must now accept. His gamble hadn't paid off at all. It was time to make his escape. He needed the submersible to fill quickly so he could swim clear of it in as shallow a depth as possible. Pitt would use his knife to remove the strips of fabric he'd wedged around the hatch and again the drips would turn into a steady rain.

He'd just started at it when he felt something through the *Turtle*'s stout wooden hull. It was like the vibrations he'd experienced earlier when a ship had passed close by, but this was somehow deeper, more menacing. He had a quick mental image of a giant vessel, a containership or tanker, bearing down on the submersible on a deadly collision course. He suddenly felt very exposed. The sound and vibration grew until it seemed to fill the submersible, and Pitt finally recognized the noise wasn't a ship's screws at all but the rotor downwash from a helicopter.

Ignoring the water dribbling down on his head from the dislodged jury-rigged gasket, Pitt cranked hard on the vertical prop handle with one hand and furiously worked the bilge pump with the other, gritting his teeth against the sharp pain of muscle fiber pushed to its very limit. His lungs were soon sucking desperately at air that contained less and less of the life-giving oxygen and grew more toxic with his exhaled carbon dioxide.

The chopper had to be directly overhead. He could even hear the screams of its turbines over the hurricane-like downdraft.

The resistance against the screw blades vanished. Pitt had managed to surface the sub one last time. If no one saw him now there was nothing more that he could do.

He waited, knowing the *Turtle* was already starting to sink again. He held out hope against hope, but as the seconds ticked by he had to admit defeat yet again.

Then came two quick taps against the metal hatch that rang Pitt's head like he was in a bell. A second later a gloved hand smeared away some of the grime from a window and a powerful flashlight beam flared in his eyes. The beam came away and the diver's face mask came into view. Pitt had his cell phone lit and gave the man the index-finger-to-thumb diver's okay, but then eagerly jerked his thumb upward to indicate he wanted to surface. The diver returned both gestures and threw a cocky salute as well.

Pitt could just make out through the newly cleaned porthole that there were two men in the water with him and they were rigging a sling around the submersible. He recognized it as the gear the archeologists had planned on using to hoist the *Turtle* from its centuries-old home.

He assumed a workboat with a large crane had been near enough to the accident for the netting to be transferred over to her. The chopper had been the boat's spotter.

It took the divers just a few minutes to sling the sub in the netting. One man tapped the glass again to make sure Pitt was ready and then he vanished into the gloom. Dirk braced his arms and legs just as the crane began lifting the *Turtle* out from its watery tomb. It came up much faster than he expected. He felt like he was being wrenched from the river. And then in a burst of weak sunlight the *Turtle* erupted from the water with white sheets of froth cascading from her rounded hull. Pitt immediately reached overhead to undo the hatch. The submersible turned and danced at the end of the line, spinning as the rigging became unkinked. Pitt put his eye close to the cleaner pane of glass. To his astonishment, he realized that he was a hundred feet in the air and still climbing. There was no workboat or crane.

He managed to finally shove open the hatch. Above him was the massive under hull of a Navy CH-53 Sea Stallion helicopter. Its rear ramp was open, and two men in olive-drab flight suits and helmets were sitting at its edge with their legs dangling into space. When they spotted Pitt poking his head out of the *Turtle,* they waved jauntily as if this was the most normal thing they'd done all day. Pitt craned his head to look back at the receding river below. The two divers who'd secured the submersible in the netting were being picked up by a small police boat with red and blue strobes flashing on its radar arch.

Before the bitterly cold wind forced him back down into the *Turtle,* Pitt noted that he'd floated halfway to the Verrazzano-Narrows Bridge. Considering his level of exhaustion and near hypothermia, he estimated that had he been forced to swim for it he'd have never made it to either shore.

What had taken Pitt over an hour to cover in the submersible took just a few minutes for the jet-propelled transport chopper. Work crews back on the construction site were ready for the helo's payload to be lowered onto a pile of soft sand that had been hastily mounded up by earthmovers. Coordination between the pilot and the loadmaster in the cargo section was precise. The *Turtle* touched down with barely a bump and its weight settled into the sand, so when the netting was hastily unhooked from the winch, the gawky little craft remained upright. The chopper roared off as Pitt emerged from the submersible to the rousing cheers of the construction crew, scientists, and the dozens of firefighters, police, and press that had arrived at the scene.

A ladder was quickly brought, and Pitt's back was slapped black and blue by the time he'd gotten to the ground. An EMT threw a blanket over his shoulders, and someone pressed a paper cup of hot coffee into his hand. He kept repeating that he was fine when nearly everyone thronging around him asked if he was all right. He allowed himself to be escorted to the back of an ambulance but refused the offer of a ride to the hospital. He knew from experience that all he needed was a long shower, three or so shots of Don Julio Blanco tequila, and a soft bed.

Fortunately, the police kept the press back at a respectful distance. At Pitt's insistence, Thomas Gwynn and Vin Blankenship were allowed to join him.

"Hell of a stunt, Mr. Pitt," Blankenship said. "I couldn't imagine the paperwork I'd be doing had you not made it back."

Pitt chuckled at the man's unflappable nature. It reminded him a little of how Al Giordino treated the world. "I am relieved that you've been saved that fate, but somehow I don't think they'd blame you if the guy you're guarding ran off to save an old submarine. Things might have been a lot grimmer if the Navy hadn't gotten here so fast. Any ideas how that happened, by the way?"

Gwynn said, "One of the workers out on the seawall actually saw the sub get flushed out into the river, so the police didn't even bother sending divers down to look for you. They called in the Coast Guard to start scouring the river, and there was a Navy chopper doing search and rescue drills on Long Island Sound."

"Just before they reached Manhattan," Blankenship added, "the crew were directed here to pick up the sling used to pull the sub from the water. It was a police drone that actually spotted you, and its operator vectored in the Navy bird."

"All in all, pretty slick," Thomas Gwynn summed up.

Pitt nodded. "I was just getting ready to pull the plug and swim for it when I heard them. Literally another few seconds later and the *Turtle* would have been lost."

"Was it really worth it?" Blankenship asked.

Had he known Pitt better, he wouldn't have posed the question. Dirk Pitt looked over to where the archeologists were swarming around their prize find. This wasn't something he'd done for them — or even

56

for himself, really — this was about preserving the past so someone in the future could look at the *Turtle* and find inspiration to make the world a better place. Pitt looked him square in the eye. "Absolutely."

Three hours later, Pitt stepped from the hotel bathroom with a plush robe wrapped around his body and splashed more room service tequila into a glass. He'd been interviewed by the police for the better part of two hours. Blankenship had driven Thom Gwynn back to his office and returned with some dry clothes he'd picked up at an outlet store. After the police were done with him, Pitt spoke to a few reporters for no other reason than to get some good press for NUMA, fudging that his presence at the archeological site had been official. He had no desire to spend hours on a train back to D.C., so he'd managed to extend his stay at his hotel near the UN. Outside, the skyline was jeweled by a million lights, as the storm had cleared, leaving the air clean and fresh.

Pitt sat himself in one of the club chairs. Too much adrenaline was still pumping in his blood to sleep. The paperwork generated at the conference held no interest, so instead he removed Isaac Bell's typewritten notes from their plastic sleeve.

Not one to dwell on his own past, he

didn't think about his role in discovering and salvaging the *Titanic*. Instead, he thought about a miner named Joshua Hayes Brewster and how he had driven himself mad in his quest to get his cargo back to the United States. Pitt recalled that when he'd pieced together Brewster's story, there had been some nagging questions about parts of the tale. He remembered thinking it was too fantastic that a miner from Colorado could have pulled off one of the greatest capers in history and yet the evidence of Brewster's success was undeniable. But maybe, Pitt thought, he hadn't sussed out the whole story. Maybe Bell's version would shed some light on what had really taken place more than a hundred years earlier.

Pitt adjusted the lamp and started reading.

1

Denver, Colorado
November 18, 1911

Jim Porter was a big man, thick through the gut and neck, with the florid complexion of a person whose heart is beating far too hard to get blood through his fat body. His doctor repeatedly told him that he had to lose weight or suffer the consequences, but Porter liked food far too much to worry about some potential problem when he was in his sixties or seventies.

He ate most every morning at a small restaurant across from the post office branch where he was the manager. The place was cozy, just six tables, and the husband/wife team that owned it took good care of their customers. For Jim Porter, this meant serving him his bacon extra soft. He was just bringing two pieces speared on a fork to his mouth when the restaurant's front door opened to the tinkling chime of its attached bell. He recognized the first man right away. They had known each other since they were schoolboys. Billy McCallister was a detective now with the Denver Police, and many figured he'd be running the whole department before too long. Behind him and coming in the rear were two men Porter didn't know, and like they were bookends for the two strangers was Billy's partner, Jack Gaylord.

Billy scanned the room and focused in on the heavyset postal worker. Knowing he'd done nothing wrong, Porter was nonplused and finished shoving the limp strips of bacon into his mouth.

"Morning, Jim," the police detective said, removing his hat and taking a seat opposite his old friend.

"Billy," Porter said between bites. "What can I do for you?"

One of the strangers took out official credentials and held them out for Porter's inspection. Porter's eyes widened when he read them, and he suddenly wished he were anyplace other than there. "As you can see," the stranger said, "I'm from the Postmaster General's Office in Washington, D.C. My name is Bob Northrop. And what you can do for us is help end a crime spree."

While the two cops looked like police —

big, grim-faced, and competent — and Northrop had the look of a bureaucrat out of his element but still filled with purpose, it was the fourth man that held Porter's attention. The other three had taken the last chairs at the table, so the stranger stood behind them with his hands clasped in front of him, his long fingers holding his hat by the brim. He wore a suit of good quality and cut and a black overcoat so long it almost swept the ground like a cape. He had bright blond hair and blue eyes with a world-weariness in them that gave him a timeless look. Once Porter had seen those eyes, he recognized that the innocent pose was a disguise and that this man was far more than he seemed.

"Crime spree?" Porter repeated, unsettled and needing to refocus on the conversation.

Detective McCallister replied, "Yes, a crime spree. At least four robberies so far, and, if Mr. Bell is right, a fifth took place last night. Oh, sorry. Jim, this is Isaac Bell of the Van Dorn Agency."

Bell leaned forward with his hand outstretched. "Nice to meet you," he said affably.

Porter wasn't fooled. Bell was probably a nice enough fellow, but there was an edge to him that he did not share with the

outside world. Bell was doubtless a dangerous man, but also one who hid it behind
polish and poise.

Porter suddenly understood what was
happening, and some of his normal flush
waned as his face went a little pale. He
tossed his napkin on the table and was
about to rise.

"Hold on a second," McCallister said.

"You're implying my branch was robbed
last night. Right? That's why you're here
now. We have to go check right away."

"No, Mr. Porter," Bell said, and the
postmaster froze. "There's an accomplice
coming today. It will make everyone's job
easier if we can catch him in the act rather
than having to make a deal with the actual
thief."

Porter looked to his friend for confirmation. McCallister nodded. Porter relaxed
back into his chair.

"There's no rush just yet," Bell continued.
"We want everything to look as normal as
possible when the accomplice comes to pick
up the three trunks he shipped to you yesterday."

Porter knew exactly which three the private detective meant. Two were about the
bulk of large suitcases and quite heavy for
their size. The other was a monogrammed

steamer trunk that looked like it had been around the world several times. "You know who owns them, then?"

"Yes," Bell said. "I watched him mail them yesterday. I had already briefed Mr. Northrop from the Postmaster General's Office and Detective McCallister on my idea of putting an end to the crooks' activities."

McCallister checked the time on a silver half hunter he had chained to his vest pocket. He turned to Bell. "We still have twenty minutes before the branch is to open. I'm sure you told Mr. Northrop here how you broke the case, but do you mind telling me the story from the beginning?"

Bell nodded. "Certainly. The thieves started in Des Moines, where they hit a hotel storage room, before they moved to Omaha, where another hotel was robbed. Next came a railroad depot in Topeka. That's where I was brought in on the case. The railroad's owner is a friend of my boss. During my initial investigation, research informed me of the earlier robberies in Iowa and Nebraska. Next up was a robbery in Cheyenne. This time, they hit another railroad storage depot, though not the same line as my boss's friend.

"Two incidents don't constitute a pattern

for me — nor do three, usually — but this was the fourth job, and I thought I had it figured out. At Cheyenne, I pieced together that the towns these thieves were hitting were getting progressively more westward, so Denver seemed like the logical next step. But the timing of the hits was a mystery. The two hotels appeared to have been robbed sometime four weeks ago. The thing was, the guests didn't realize items had been removed from their stored luggage until days or weeks after the fact. I figure the thieves had cleared out of town long before anyone was onto them. But the railroad jobs were detected the day after the robbery, which didn't give our thieves much time to move on."

Bell paused. He was a natural storyteller and he held the four men rapt. "But the real mystery was how they managed to rob four locked rooms without leaving a bit of evidence that the locks had been tampered with. In addition, the hotel strong rooms were near enough to the reception desk that anyone loitering nearby would be seen and the area around the two depots was guarded by railroad bulls."

"The yard dicks never saw anything?" McCallister's partner, Gaylord, asked.

"And they circled the building all night,"

Bell told him. "The final piece of the puzzle was this."

Bell pulled a sheet of paper from his pocket. It was a garish advertisement for a traveling circus and showed the ringmaster, in top hat and with arms thrown wide, while in the background the artist had drawn roaring lions and a string of elephants performing a trick, all backgrounded by the inside of a brightly colored big top tent with a pair of trapeze artists swinging between the poles. The men all recognized it, for not three days earlier thousands of these flyers had been plastered all over the city because the Fraunhofer & Fraunhofer Circus was soon arriving for their last show of the season before they moved on to their winter-over headquarters outside of Los Angeles.

"Are you saying . . . ?" This from the postal manager, Porter.

"Sure am. Once I realized that this circus had either just played or was about to play the towns where the robberies took place, it all fell into place. I got lucky and caught up with the show in Fort Collins and managed to watch their final performance and stick around to observe them dismantling every-thing."

"And you were able to finger the perpetra-tors by just catching the act?" McCallister seemed incredulous.

"Gentlemen, I have to go," Jim Porter said. "I need to open the branch before the other employees show up for work." He reached into his pocket for money to settle his bill, and since he'd eaten his normal breakfast, he knew the exact charge.

Bell shook his hand once again. "Mr. Porter, all you need to do this morning is to act as though nothing unusual is happening. You needn't tell your staff anything at all. Our mark will come in shortly, no doubt. We are going to watch for him here. We will enter afterward, looking like customers, and accost the thief red-handed."

The man was sweaty and appeared unwell, but Bell suspected that he habitually looked that way. Porter nodded gamely. "Okay."

Bell and Northrop, the man from Washington, moved to a window table once Porter had left. The two police detectives stayed in the back of the little dining room and would take their cue from Isaac Bell.

As he suspected, the wait was a short one. Five minutes after the post office opened for the day, Bell watched a man in a black cape and high black hat make his way down the sidewalk. The day, like most of the month of November, was unseasonably warm, which was no doubt the reason the circus remained on tour this late in the year.

A truck with a chain drive briefly obscured Bell's line of sight, but when it rumbled down the street, trailing dark exhaust, he saw his man again. Like he'd observed at the circus, the man moved with silken ease, as though his joints were fluid. Bell had only really seen him at a distance, but he recognized the jet-black mustache.

The man paused to talk to a drayman, who was feeding his horse stumps of carrots. His wagon was a simple flatbed. Bell surmised that the man had hired the horse and driver and they were setting a time to meet so the man could load up his three pieces of luggage and be on his way. If Bell's guess was right, he wouldn't bother rejoining the circus here in Denver. Bell believed that all the jobs leading up to this one had been practice runs, to hone the plan until it could be executed with military precision. Today was the big score, the one that would be such a payoff that only retirement afterward made sense.

The two men parted company. The driver returned to feeding his draft horse while the man from the circus mounted the three granite steps to the post office. Bell gave it another minute, then waved to McCallister and Gaylord. Bell touched something under his left arm to make certain it was there and then left the restaurant, its little chime on the door tinkling, the D.C. postal inspector at his arm.

Bell crossed the cobbled street, mounted the curb, and climbed the three steps. Through a decorative clear fringe on the otherwise-frosted glass door insert, Bell saw the man from the circus hand over his receipt for the three trunks. There was no sign of Porter, so Bell assumed he was in the back. The clerk who took the ticket acted as though this were any other transaction. The branch manager had kept mum on the impending arrest.

Bell opened the door and started a conversation midpoint with Northrop. ". . . told me it was going to cost twenty-five dollars to fix it and I told him I could buy a new one for that price and left his shop."

"Good for you." Northrop was a veteran of postal stings and played his part even though they hadn't rehearsed anything.

Like many who are forced to wait in a line, the two men let their conversation lapse. Bell smiled at a woman in line ahead of them and got a smile back. Their quarry hadn't turned, instead waited a little way off for his trunks to be brought through from inside the iron-barred cage where they'd spent the night. Moments later, the two detectives also entered the big post office branch. Gaylord got into one of the three lines while McCallister busied himself at a counter filling out an address on an envelope.

The handcart used to move larger items throughout the branch had a wheel badly in need of oil. Its squeak echoed off the tall coffered ceiling. Bell watched his man, sensing the anticipation coming off of him in waves, though outwardly he was the picture of studied nonchalance. Up close, he was handsome enough to star in one of Bell's wife's motion pictures. The clerk was struggling with the trolley because of its weight, and his shoes kept sliding on the polished floor, but eventually he got it through the gate separating postal employees from their customers.

The circus performer was about to place a possessive hand on one of the smaller trunks when Bell said in a clear voice, "Stop." Everyone in the branch turned to face him. The man cast a distrustful look Bell's way.

"Aren't you Rudolfo Latang, the magician?"

The man seemed to release a breath and let his shoulders relax. He smiled charmingly. "I am. Yes." His accent was European but hard to pin down.

He turned back to his luggage to forestall further conversation, but Bell plowed on, playing the act a while longer. "I caught your show in Cheyenne over the weekend. You are one amazing performer. Sawing a woman in half like that. Darnedest thing I ever saw. But I think I figured out how you did it."

Latang looked over his shoulder and said tersely, "I doubt that."

Bell dropped his hayseed persona and said. "Let's just see. Detectives?" At that, McCallister and Gaylord held up their shields and moved in close to the magician, shooing a few customers back so they had control over the suspect and no potential hostages could be taken if he tried something desperate.

"What is the meaning of this?" Latang blustered.

"Depredation of the U.S. mail," Bob Northrop said, holding up his badge and sweeping back his coat so Latang could see the Smith & Wesson .38 caliber six-shooter on his hip.

A look of genuine confusion crossed the magician's face. "Depredation?"

"It means," Bell said, "you've stolen mail from the United States Post Office."

"I've done nothing of the sort. I am here to pick up my trunks."

Bell gave a disappointed tsk. "I find it odd that as a man who travels with a circus, with its own train cars, as well as trucks and autos, that you would mail items to yourself at some expense, given the weight."

Latang had a ready answer. "I so happen to do this quite often, as I work as an advance man for the circus. I arrive at the towns a few days early and put on free demonstrations to build crowd interest for the main show."

"So you've got props and costumes and stuff like that in your trunks?"

"Yes."

"Prove it."

"I will do no such thing," he said, raising his voice.

"May I point out," Northrop interjected, "that you have not taken physical control of your items, so they are technically still under the protective care of the U.S.P.S. and I am a postal inspector." He let the implication hang in the air.

Latang tried to stare down Northrop and then turned his attention to Bell. If anything, he could hold eye contact for even less time before capitulating. He pulled a key from his pocket and handed it to

Northrop. "Fine. Go ahead and search."

The D.C. inspector used his left hand to fit the key into the big trunk's brass lock and release it while his right hovered over the butt of his revolver. The two Denver detectives also looked tensed for the unexpected. Bell looked mildly bored.

Inside the trunk were all manner of magic paraphernalia, like chains, a straitjacket, shiny swords, as well as many smaller boxes that Northrop laboriously removed. In them were macabre costumes, makeup, and smaller little trick items designed to separate the gullible from their money. In moments, the area around the trunk was littered like the floor of some Near Eastern pasha's tent.

Northrop looked to Bell, clearly confused, and more than a little angry that he'd crossed three-quarters of the country to be here and make the arrest and there was no evidence of a crime.

"False bottom," Billy McCallister suggested.

Northrop tapped at the trunk in several places. A postal clerk handed him a wooden yardstick. The D.C. inspector measured the height of the trunk and then set the wooden ruler inside to check its depth. An exact match.

He blew out a defeated breath, and his

eyes shot daggers at Isaac Bell. "My apologies, Mr. Latang. We were clearly misinformed."

The magician began tossing his clothing and equipment back into the trunk with little thought of neatness. He too gave Bell a hard stare. "It is a small matter and only a moment's delay." He closed the lid, shoving hard to compress the contents and managing to latch the lock.

Northrop glared at Isaac Bell, who regarded the D.C. man mildly. Northrop said, "I came all this way because of the reputation of the Van Dorn Agency, and quite frankly, Mr. Bell, I now see that the mystique some hold you in is rather misplaced, to put it mildly."

"Guess this is one time you don't get your man," Detective McCallister said, mocking how the Van Dorns supposedly always got their man and had coined their motto to emphasize that fact.

Everyone in the room subconsciously turned a bit away from Bell. This was instinctive shunning behavior that followed mankind upon his descent from his primitive ape ancestors. Bell had expected it, so he had a moment's privacy even in this crowded space.

Rudolfo Latang was almost out the door,

with the aid of a postal worker, when Bell barked his name in a commanding boom. Everyone turned.

Bell stood with his arm outstretched, his long greatcoat askew from where he'd swept it open to reach for the shoulder holster under his left arm. The gun now in his steady fist was something new, something no one in the room had ever seen, a sleek and lethal amalgam of modern industrial design and brutal form following deadly function. The weapon was still in its development phase, but the Army was eager to begin deploying what they'd already designated as the M1911 automatic pistol but which those that had used it simply called the .45.

Isaac Bell had total command of the room. "Mr. Latang, I am going to fire two shots. One into each of your smaller trunks. One bullet will blow a hole through a stack of cash that had been shipped here from the San Francisco Mint as pay for the mining companies for all the gold and silver they shipped west. The other round will perforate the tender flesh of your stage assistant's twin — and, might I add, one-legged — sister."

"What the blazes are you talking about?" Detective McCallister groused. "Put down that weapon immediately."

"Good God, man, are you daft?" Northrop said. "Those cases are too small for even a child to fit into. Please, Mr. Latang, you are free to go."

Bell used his thumb to draw back the automatic's hammer. The sound was one of finality and inevitability, like a line had just been drawn and a challenge offered. Bell and the magician locked eyes, neither man backing down.

The gun's barrel dropped fractionally and angled ever so slightly farther right. Bell didn't flinch as just a few ounces of pressure against the weapon's internal springs sent one of the big lead slugs roaring down the barrel in a flash of dazzling light and a flat crack of sound that left ears ringing.

A woman's scream, muffled but high-pitched and panicked, filled the silence that followed. A hidden catch inside the suitcase that Bell hadn't shot through clicked open and a woman wearing a skintight black bodysuit of elastic chiffon climbed her way out like a spider. She'd folded herself so tightly that the mind rejected the very idea that someone could have hidden within the valise, so her emergence had a macabre, unsettling feeling. As Bell had mentioned, her left leg was missing from high up on the thigh. Had she not been an amputee, she never would have managed the contortions needed to stow away inside the bag.

Latang made for the door while the police officers were distracted, but then he realized Bell wasn't paying her the slightest attention. He had anticipated this and so was ever vigilant. The gun's aim was centered between the magician's eyes.

The young woman was barely five feet tall and rail thin, with pretty blond hair and a pleasant face, though once she'd gathered her wits, anger flushed her cheeks. She suddenly leapt across the room with amazing speed and slapped Isaac Bell across the face.

"You could have killed me," she said in a thick Cockney accent. "You should be arrested for attempted murder."

She tried to slap him again, but Bell deflected the shot adroitly. And once the contortionist was off balance, her cramped muscles refused to hold her upright and she fell to the floor. She started sobbing.

"How in the devil . . . ?"

Bell holstered his .45. McCallister had moved to restrain Latang while his partner readied a pair of handcuffs.

Bell said, "I figured early on that the thefts were done by someone hiding in the locked rooms, but since I didn't get a look at any of the luggage that had been removed, I was forced to rely on clerks' memories and estimates, which are generally unreliable. Still, it seemed there were few man-sized steamer trunks recalled, so I deduced it was an inside man" — he looked to the crying woman on the floor — "or lady, as it turns out, who was either a child or a contortionist. That is what prompted me to check if any circuses had been in the area of the crimes and, lo and behold, I discover the Fraunhofer & Fraunhofer Circus had been near them all."

The detective turned his attention to the seething mad magician, Latang. "When I watched your performance, I was particularly interested in any tricks you did involving boxes, placing someone in them atop a table. You had an illusion where you saw a lady in half, but your variation was to cut off a leg first. Your regular assistant was the woman who initially stepped into the coffin-sized box in front of the entire audience. All could plainly see she had the proper number of limbs. When you first raised that curtain for a moment, she slipped out the bottom and her twin" — he pointed to the woman on the floor — "crawled in, sticking a realistic-looking foot prosthesis through one hole in the bottom of the box and her own foot through the other.

"Then you used your saw to hack off one leg and allow the box surrounding it to fall to the floor. I noted that the fake foot was kept pointed away from the audience while the woman continued to move her own leg to heighten the effect. While you were distracting the audience by flailing the saws around and shielding the bottom of the box from view, she withdrew her foot, plugged the hole with a second, fake leg, and curled her body into the top portion of the box with her head still exposed. You cut the box in half even higher up than the leg cut, and the audience believes you've just sawn a woman into three pieces.

"Then it's a simple matter of reversing everything, including the sisters switching places under the table, and, presto, you are Rudolfo the Magnificent."

"And you figured this all out by watching his act once?" Northrop was duly impressed.

"I know how the standard illusion is played out. This variation was an intriguing one, but there was only one possible explanation for how it could be executed. Since Latang didn't remove her limb and magically reattach it, it must not have been there in the first place. And since I saw the assistant step into the box on her own two shapely legs, there had to be a second person with only one leg. Confirmation came the next day when I saw the two women working together to help dismantle the circus venue. One walked perfectly normal, the other with a severe limp.

"After that, I followed Latang. I was actually in line at another postal branch when he shipped these trunks here. I managed to chalk an X on the one he hadn't double-checked that he had the key for. That's how I knew to shoot the other one."

"The money," Northrop cried. Previously, he'd implied that he could open Latang's trunks without a warrant, but that wasn't true. Now, considering the circumstances, he felt justified, and he was sure he could square it with a judge. He glowered at the magician. "Give me the key."

"I don't have it," the man replied, his bravado waning with each passing moment. He knew he'd been beaten.

"She has it," Bell said. "She was shipped from the one branch to this one last night stowed away in the larger trunk. Even for her, hiding in the smaller one for more than a few minutes, a half hour tops, would be impossible. The big trunk, though, would be nice and cozy. After the branch closed yesterday afternoon, she let herself out and transferred all the clothes and props from the smaller two steamers into the larger one and relocked it. Then she had all night to find the payroll shipments from San Francisco, remove the cash, and reseal the packages. I suspect she had fake wads of bills to replace the cash with so the weights remained consistent and the robbery wouldn't be discovered until the following payday.

"Just before the post office reopens, she locks up the money trunk and folds herself into the other. I hadn't noticed yesterday when I followed Latang, but I saw this morning that the lock mechanism on her trunk is fake. It can't be locked from the outside, only latched shut from within." Bell held his hand down to the contortionist. She pulled a leather thong up from under her tighter-than-tight body stocking and over her head. Dangling from it was a tiny steamer trunk key. Bell handed it to Northrop. The postal inspector shot Latang a look. Defeated, the magician merely nodded, and the D.C. inspector turned the key. Though the trunk seemed much too small to hold a person, it looked more than sufficiently large to store a million dollars in cash. The dull-green bills were still banded and packed as neatly as sardines in a tin. One stack, though, did have an ugly black hole shot through the middle of it.

Northrop fingered the destroyed legal tender.

Bell gave a little smile. "Van Dorns always get their man. Always. But sometimes there is a cost to doing business."

2

When staying over in Denver, Isaac Bell always roomed at the Brown Palace, the city's premier hotel. While it was already nearing its twentieth year of operation, it had yet to be surpassed in luxury, style, or comfort. And was located just a stone's throw from the state capitol building.

He had finished dining and found himself in the Marble Bar, the site of the infamous murder the previous May of Tony Von Phul and an innocent bystander by Frank Henwood. Von Phul had been carrying on an affair with Isabel Springer, the wife of Henwood's friend John Springer. He had come to confront Von Phul and put an end to the illicit assignation. The sordid matter had the opposite effect and the Springers divorced five days after the double homicide. It was still the talk of the town, Bell had learned.

That, and the deaths of nine miners two days prior out near Central City. He'd read an evening paper about the efforts by Bill Mahoney, the foreman at a nearby mine, to reach the trapped men. He and his fellow rescuers had been turned back by severe flooding. Mahoney had also been the person first informed about the disaster when a mysterious and unsigned note saying there had been an accident was slid under his cabin door. That last detail was something Bell knew well. People were reluctant to come forward with information, especially about something as macabre as a mine accident, or have their name associated with so much death. It was human nature.

He had made reservations for the morning train to Chicago and then on east to New York and was just about to enjoy the last of his drink and call it a night when a middle-aged man in a decent suit came into the bar, swept it once like a searchlight, and made straight for Isaac. He took the stool at Bell's side.

"You wouldn't be Isaac Bell, by chance?"

Wary, Bell said, "Who's asking?"

"Sir, my name is Hans Bloeser." He handed Bell a business card. Bound by etiquette, Bell returned to him one of his own. "I took a chance you were still in town and either at the Oxford Hotel or here. You *are* Bell?"

Bloeser spoke fine English with just a trace of a German accent. In Bell's estimate, he'd come from Germany as a youth and learned English in school but spoke German at home. He had a German's barrel chest, eyes as blue as Bell's own, but his hair was dark and thinning. Bell estimated he was at least fifty years old. And had the smoother hands of someone who worked indoors.

"I am. May I help you with something, Mr. Bloeser?"

The stranger indicated to the barman that he wanted two of whatever Bell had been drinking.

"Your reputation as an investigator is known far and wide, Mr. Bell, but it seems that other than a vague description of your blond hair no one seems to know you. The man at the Van Dorn office here in Denver didn't know you were in town until the arrest this morning at the post office hit the afternoon papers."

"I prefer to keep my anonymity as best I can, Mr. Bloeser. It helps in my line of work. Also, since I wasn't in need of additional agents for this morning's activities, I find it best not to let satellite offices think I'm here checking up on them. As Van Dorn's chief investigator, I find my presence sometimes distracts rather than benefits."

"A wise choice, and one I wish I could follow through on. I own a bank with six branches and I find myself unable to leave them well enough alone. My managers must believe that I think they are incompetent and always need minding. In truth, they are all good men, but I can't help but watch over their shoulders." The man smiled at his own foible.

"If you are in need of Van Dorn agents, I assure you that Charles Post, our man here, is more than qualified, and he has access to additional men as the need arises. For myself, I leave for the east tomorrow morning."

Bloeser leaned in conspiratorially. "Would you be willing to listen to a story that might convince you to remain for a while?"

Bell smiled. He liked Bloeser instinctively. "A man who buys me a drink is entitled to tell me a story."

Bloeser stood and indicated that Bell should follow him to a dark and secluded corner of the bar. He offered Bell a cigar from a leather case. Bell demurred and waited while Bloeser went through the ritual of cutting its tip, warming it with the candle in the center of the table, and puffing the thing to life. The smoke was dense but fragrant.

"Have you heard about the disaster at the Little Angel Mine and the nine fatalities?" When Bell nodded, Bloeser continued. "My brother, Ernst, owns the mine, Mr. Bell. When word reached him in Golden about your presence here in Denver, he cabled me to find you."

"I'm afraid I know little of mining, so I can't imagine why your brother sent you to me."

Bloeser nodded. "But you do know mysteries, sir, and there's a big one surrounding the disaster." The banker saw skepticism on Bell's face. "The papers didn't tell the half of it. For one thing, Joshua Hayes Brewster, the lead miner, claim-jumped the Little Angel."

Bell drew back involuntarily. There was a time that even the accusation of claim jumping resulted in swift and usually fatal justice. It was a crime that miners saw as more loathsome than just about any other. To the men of the Rocky Mountain mining community, calling someone a claim jumper was akin to calling them the murderer of children.

A remembered fact popped into Bell's head that brought into question Bloeser's assertion. "Didn't I read that the mine had shut down back in '81?"

"You did indeed. The mine was a bust from the outset. My brother isn't a miner himself, just the senior partner in our bank, and he invested heavily in the gold rush. The Little Angel was one in which he owned a stake. Many were successful, others were expensive holes that produced nothing at all. However, it doesn't matter if the mine was closed or not, one needs permission from the owner to step one foot into another man's workings. That's the law and Brewster knew it. Brewster also knew that the Little Angel was a worthless bore, and no matter how much he tried to talk up what he was about to do, nothing changed that fact. There wasn't then, and there isn't now, a motherlode waiting to be found up there."

"If all that is true, what was Brewster really doing?" Bell asked.

Bloeser touched the tip of his nose. "That's the mystery, sir. What exactly was he doing up there to get him and eight other men killed? I can tell you plain and true that they weren't looking for silver."

Bell ran a few scenarios, sifting out ideas or trains of thought, but nothing became immediately clear. While part of him balked at the idea of leaving something unknown on the table, the pragmatist in him wasn't intrigued enough to forgo a loving reunion with his wife, Marion.

"That does sound intriguing, Mr. Bloeser, but I'm afraid that I have pressing matters back in New York that need my attention."

"I have yet to tell you the strangest part of my story."

"Very well."

"None of the men were married. No one would miss them if they died in a mining accident. No one other than my brother has the slightest interest in their deaths." Bloeser let that sink in. "One or two bachelors wouldn't be unusual. Heck, even half wouldn't raise an eyebrow. But all? No, Brewster selected these particular men because no one was going to miss them. It was as though they knew they weren't coming out of that shaft. Or . . ."

Bell finished the thought, interest suddenly piqued. ". . . they never went in in the first place."

The banker settled himself deeper into his club chair, a good enough judge of character to know he'd landed his fish.

Like an artist who must paint, or an author who is compelled to write, Isaac Bell couldn't refuse an interesting case. His last cable from Marion said she'd be in Georgia until the twenty-second. Factoring in the time it would take her to get to New York and if Bell upgraded to express trains only, he could buy himself three extra days in Denver.

"If need be," Bloeser added, "my brother said he is willing to double your normal fee."

Bell could hear Joseph Van Dorn in his head telling him to take the extra money, but that wasn't Isaac's style. "That won't be necessary, though I might need to bring in our man here in Denver to do legwork."

"Of course."

"I read in the papers that the mine was completely flooded. How deep is the water?"

"Depth isn't the issue. The Little Angel Mine isn't a vertical shaft dug straight down but rather a gently sloping tunnel drilled into the side of the mountain that's shaped like a flattened V. The very deepest part of the mine is only about thirty feet lower than the adit."

"Adit?"

"Sorry. I've spent too much time around my brother. The adit is the mine's entrance. After the deepest point, the floor of the mine slopes up again. All told, it's a little over a mile long, with a dozen or so smaller side passages dug into what looked like promising quartz veins."

"I see. Can the mine simply be pumped dry?"

"It's possible, but even now water under pressure is still running out of the entrance at a depth of at least a foot. My brother and his mining people tell me this means there is a lot of water still flowing into the mine. It can't be drained until the flow stops. That could be weeks or months, but there's another problem with that. There are some workings down below the Little Angel that are getting inundated with the outflow and they're demanding my brother seal off the tunnel completely. He hasn't agreed yet, but he will eventually."

Bell pictured the scene in his mind. The mouth of the Little Angel perched halfway up a hillside with a slow river of water pouring from it, the water then flowing down and washing through some other mining camps on the lower slopes. He could well imagine that if Bloeser's brother didn't seal the tunnel, the other miners would mete out some frontier justice and do it themselves, consequences be damned.

"As with all investigations," Bell told the banker, "time is always of the essence. I want to see where each of the men lived before they went into that mine. Unfortunately, I suspect many were at boarding-houses. Once news of their deaths reached the lodge owners, it isn't much of a stretch to see that their belongings were sorted through for valuables and the rest discarded."

Bloeser nodded at this grim but practical assessment.

Bell continued. "There is one more avenue to pursue and that is breaching the mine itself."

"But I just explained that it's flooded."

"I understand, but what if I told you that I can breathe underwater?"

"I'd say you'd had one whiskey too many."

Bell smiled at that. "Possibly, but that isn't the source of my boast. Have you ever heard of the Severn Tunnel?"

"In England. Right?"

"Wales, actually. It's a railroad tunnel that was driven beneath the Severn Estuary. In 1880, it had flooded so badly that a diver needed to be sent down to close some watertight doors. He went over a thousand feet into the tunnel and breathed air just as you and I are doing right now."

Bloeser was still trying to process the impossibility of what Bell described when the detective got to his feet. "I need to make some arrangements. How does one get to Central City?"

"The CC," Bloeser said. "The Colorado Central Railroad. It's an old narrow-gauge line that runs right up into the mountains. Not sure of its schedule, but the hotel's deskman should know."

"I will probably need someone up there to help with equipment and who knows the Little Angel Mine."

"Ahead of you on that one. My brother uses an engineer-slash-inspector whenever he invests in a new project. The man's name is Tony Wickersham. He's English and came here as a teenager looking to find his fortune. He has a good head on his shoulders. Ernst trusts him completely."

"Okay. I need you to get word to him that I'm coming tomorrow. What's a good hotel in Central City?"

"The Teller House," Bloeser said without hesitation. "One of the few buildings to survive the fire of 1874. It's a brick four-story place on Eureka Street. You can't miss it. Wickersham is staying there too."

"Excellent."

"I still don't understand how you're going to get into the mine. That much hose to feed a dive helmet would weigh tons. And it would tear on all the sharp rocks."

Bell held out a hand to say his good-bye. "Mr. Bloeser, I myself don't believe how far technology has advanced in the past decade or two. When I first arrived in New York, there were so many horses it reminded me of a rodeo. Now, just a few years later, the Model T Ford is well on its way to replacing them all. We live in amazing times." Bell shrugged off a rare moment of idle contemplation and shook Bloeser's hand. "Our man here will call upon your office tomorrow to sign a contract and discuss the finer details of remuneration. Good night."

3

The locomotive to take Bell higher into the Rocky Mountain foothills wasn't the original from when the tracks were laid in the 1860s at the height of the Pikes Peak Gold Rush, as it had been known, but it hadn't been shipped in until much later. The boiler was oft-patched, and steam hissed from every joint and coupling. It sported an old-fashioned cowcatcher that looked as deadly as a mechanical scythe, and a fluted stack that was shot through with holes. The engineer and his stoker were busy moving around the 2-4-2 engine with oilcans and tins of thick packing grease. Another worker was filling a sand hopper that would dump grit in front of the drive wheels as needed for more traction.

The two carriages behind the coal car were painted in mismatched colors, and Bell could see where the names of their former lines had been crudely painted over with the letters *CC*. The windows were dirty, and clinker burns marred much of the wood-work. Adding the fact that the tracks were only three feet wide, Bell's overall impression was that this resembled a poorly maintained child's toy rather than a working iron horse.

Around him several larger trains, with ornate carriages and occasional private cars, could be seen. One train had just arrived, and passengers were coming down the steps, women in long coats and warm boas, men in suits and sporting homburgs or derby hats. A few children gaped at the size of the sprawling Union Station and its tall central clock tower. Everything smelled of coal smoke and echoed with the sound of industrialization.

Bell handed up his single valise to the conductor and mounted the iron steps to gain access to the compartment of the lead carriage. The seats were worn through in places, the floor gritty, and the few lamps remained unlit even though the day was overcast and the interior gloomy. Unlike on the day before, a fresh chill sharpened the air. Bell suspected that Indian summer was well and truly over and Colorado's notoriously brutal winter was about to set in. He was thankful he'd offered to stay only a couple of days. He had heard stories of travelers stuck in these mountains for weeks on end.

The arrangements he'd made the night before would bear fruit in forty-eight hours, with luck. He'd caught a number of breaks when he'd phoned the Van Dorn office in San Francisco and then reached his old friend Seamus Rourke, a former commercial diver who'd lost a leg in the quake of '06 and turned his experience and skills to designing and building dive equipment. He held five patents already, doubtless with more on the way.

An experienced rider, Bell settled into a seat in the middle of the car so the pounding of the wheels over the rails wasn't directly beneath his body. He had no real interest in watching the landscape as the train ground its way up the mountains and so tipped his hat over his eyes to sleep through the two-plus-hour trip. The locomotive had other ideas, however, and from its rough jerk out of Union Station and up the three-thousand-foot vertical climb, the engine huffed and wheezed and spun its wheels and bellowed such noxious smoke that Bell and many other passengers, all male with the exception of one man's wife, tied a handkerchief over his nose and mouth like a clichéd western bandit. The view wasn't anything dramatic or spectacular, just a long slog up a narrow canyon, and because they had used up so much extra sand, they had a delay in the mining town of Black Hawk, just shy of Central City, for a supply to be located and loaded.

Bell made a mental note to change suits at the Teller House and have the current one thoroughly cleaned.

Central City was much more modern than Bell had expected and he admonished himself for envisioning a ramshackle frontier outpost. Miners had been working the surrounding hills for almost fifty years, and Central City showed off that maturity. The town had wide, straight streets, and all the commercial buildings were brick or stone. There was even an opera house. And like so much of the United States, cars and trucks were rapidly replacing horses. Electrical wires crisscrossed the street on tarred poles. Wood-framed houses dotted the hills above the downtown district.

Stepping from the train at the little depot, Bell noticed the air was markedly colder and all the more difficult to breathe because of the additional altitude. Occasional flakes of snow, like tiny motes of dust, drifted by.

Bell had little trouble finding Eureka

Street or the Teller House. He was running late because of the train delay but still went to his room first to change and make arrangements to clean his laundry. He went into the bar twenty minutes after the predetermined time to meet Tony Wickersham.

The Englishman was seated at a table, immersed in work. Notes and ledgers were spread all across the table's surface, and there was a bag at his feet that Bell could see was filled with more. Wickersham was about thirty, with a handsome face and a mop of curly dark hair. When he sensed Bell approaching, he looked up. His dark eyes were wide-set and inquisitive.

"Mr. Bell?"

"I am indeed." Wickersham stood, and the two men shook hands. "Please, call me Isaac."

"Tony."

"Tony. I am sorry I'm late. There were delays with the train."

"There are most days," Wickersham said. "I heard a rumor that the locomotive had been left abandoned in Mexico before the line bought it and brought it here. True or not, she's not suited for mountain work. Her drive wheels are far too small."

"As long as her brakes are in working order for the journey back . . ." It was a bit early in the day for a whiskey, so Bell ordered two beers, as well as a sliced-beef sandwich with mustard.

Wickersham saluted Bell with his mug before taking a sip. "I'm not sure exactly what you're planning to do up here. I know the Brothers Bloeser think Josh Brewster and the others might not have gone into the mine, but I've got a witness who saw them."

"Some things don't add up," Bell said. "The claim jumping, for one thing, and the fact that they were all unmarried, which means no one would miss them."

"I don't disagree. Brewster's pretty well known up in these hills. People were surprised when he talked about going back into the Little Angel. Had I been here, I would have told him that the mine, though unworked since the 1880s, was still considered an open claim. He might not have known that. Bill Mahoney, foreman of the Satan Mine, just below the Little Angel, was surprised when he learned Mr. Bloeser still retained mining rights. He admitted to using the shaft for storage at times."

"What about them all being bachelors?"

"Coincidence?" Wickersham hazarded.

Bell shook his head. "In my line of work, there's no such thing. It means something. I want to investigate where these men lived, see if it looks like they had planned to come back after the end of their shift or were they leaving permanently. I also want to ask around about equipment. What sorts of gear did they buy to start mining again."

"They would have bought everything in Denver," Wickersham said with confidence. "The stuff you can buy around here is pretty used up and overpriced."

"Okay, thanks, I'll get my investigator on it."

"Have him check Kendry Ironworks and the Thor Forge Company. They're the two major players for mining equipment."

"Does the hotel have a phone?"

"It does."

"Okay, I'll call him when we're done here."

"May I ask your plan to get into the tunnel itself?"

"Ever heard of a rebreather?" When Wickersham's brow furrowed but no thought came, Bell continued. "When we exhale, there is still a great deal of unused oxygen in our breath as well as the carbon dioxide we produce. The idea of reusing expired breath goes back a couple of centuries, but it wasn't until 1879 or '80 that a practical device was built. It was an English firm that made it. Basically, it's a mask with a hose attached to a tank with extra oxygen under pressure and a scrubber chamber that uses a chemical reaction to fix the carbon dioxide. The device was put to the test when flooding halted construction of the Severn Tunnel. A man walked a thousand feet into the flooded tunnel to close some watertight doors to allow the works to be pumped dry."

"I had no idea such a thing had been invented."

"Not exactly standard mining gear," Bell said. "I have a friend in San Francisco that's tinkering with rebreather designs. There's a Van Dorn agent on his way here right now with one of his latest models. He says it'll give me up to four hours underwater. That'll give me more than enough time to see exactly what's been sealed up inside the Little Angel Mine."

Bell's first step following their meal was to head for the town's lone post office. Wickersham had a vehicle, but the office was near the hotel so the two men walked. The single room was bisected by a low counter with prison-like iron bars to offer a measure of security for the off-limits area in the back. Bell could imagine some of the rougher characters who'd lived here over the years blaming the postal workers for late or non-delivered parcels.

He waited until there were no more customers before approaching the clerk, who he could tell was also the postmaster.

"May I help you?" the slight, balding clerk asked. His voice was high-pitched but friendly.

Bell said nothing. He laid a business card on the counter.

The clerk picked it up and pulled the glasses dangling around his neck on a slender silver chain to his eyes. "Wowza! All the way from Washington, D.C."

"There was a certain matter in Denver . . ."

"Oh, the arrest. Yeah, I heard about that. Some cripple woman hiding in a trunk at night to steal money."

"She was missing a leg, but I assure you she was no cripple. Slapped me harder than a mule." Bell turned his head and indeed his cheek was flushed. He took the card back and slid it into his coat pocket.

"What can I do for you, Mr. Northrop?"

"We're here on a separate matter. The Little Angel disaster."

"Terrible shame. These mountains claim their share of men every year, but it's still a shock every time it happens." The clerk suddenly looked suspicious. "There isn't a postal angle to what happened to those men, is there?"

Bell improvised. "There's a question about invoicing for some mining equipment from the Thor Forge Company. They insist the invoices reached Joshua Brewster, but they weren't paid. I wonder if you knew anything about this matter?"

"Can't say I do. Only one of the men killed had an address here. John Caldwell. He rented a room from the Dawson sisters up on Spring Street. The others were spread out too, I imagine, renting rooms or camping up near the mines. None had any business with me."

"What about Brewster? Do you know where he lived?"

"Tent by the mine. Every once in a while, he'd rent a room at the Teller House for a night or two. Up until a few months ago he had a place in Denver, but I know for a fact he sold it to come here."

"Interesting. Any idea why?"

"To open that worthless mine again. Folks that knew him best said he got a little crazy recently. He obsessed over Little Angel. Turned on friends and everything. It happens sometimes. It's like people who drink too much or gamble all their money away. They can't stop themselves. Brewster was like that at the end."

Bell knew he'd gotten as much out of the clerk as he could without rousing more suspicion, so he said, "Well, I thank you for your time. I'll let the folks at the Thor Forge know that unless Brewster had a hidden stash of money with a lawyer or something, they're out of luck getting paid."

He and Tony Wickersham left the post office.

"Isn't impersonating a federal investigator against the law?" the young Englishman asked as they started walking.

"It is," Bell replied. "But I didn't impersonate anyone just now."

"Well, you gave him another man's card and implied that you were Robert Northrop."

"I gave him the wrong card by mistake," Bell said with a knowing smile. "That implied I am Robert Northrop. He was the one who assumed. I just didn't correct him. Cops and judges usually get angry when I pull this trick, but I've never been prosecuted for it."

It took the pair only a few minutes to find Spring Street and the yellow house belonging to the Dawson sisters, a pair of elderly spinsters who supported themselves taking in and feeding lodgers in the large house left to them by their long-dead parents.

There was a wide porch across the front of the clapboard house that would have a swing or chair in the summer months. Gingham curtains were peeking around the edges of the downstairs windows. The roof was slate and appeared to be in good shape despite its age.

A man opened the front door and was backing out just as Bell and Wickersham mounted the porch.

"Excuse me," Bell said with a friendly smile. "Are the Dawson sisters in?"

"Oh, hi," the man said, startled. He wore the threadbare suit of a traveling salesman. In one hand was a leather sample case. Patent medicines, or maybe cosmetics, was Bell's guess. "Miss Emily is in, but Miss Sarah is in Boulder on a buying expedition, as she calls it. It appears that people get snowed in here quite often."

"We've heard," Bell said, and thanked the man, who moved off down the street on his own business.

Bell knocked at the door and waited only a few seconds before it was opened. The woman was young, raven-haired, and beautiful. She smiled at Wickersham, but her gaze lingered longer on Isaac Bell. Her teeth were dazzlingly white. "Well, hello there," she said.

"Miss Emily?" Bell chanced.

"Goodness no," she laughed. "I'm Corinne Johnson. I rent a room. I'm performing at the opera house."

"My apologies," Bell said. "I don't have a description of the Dawson sisters."

"Quite all right, Mr. . . ."

"Bell . . . Isaac Bell."

He shook her hand in a way that showed the gold band around his left ring finger. She gave him a disappointed little look but nevertheless invited them into the home, calling out to the kitchen, "Miss Emily, there are two gentlemen to see you." Her eyes still shone when she turned back. "Mr. Bell, if you're still in town, I'm singing tomorrow night and all through the weekend."

"Not sure our schedule will permit it, but if we can make it, we most certainly will be there."

Corinne Johnson smiled up at him again before climbing the oak stairs to the second floor at the same time an elderly woman came out from the kitchen at the back of the large house. She was wiping her hands on a towel lest she soil her perfectly white apron. She was slender without looking frail, with short-cropped gray hair and wrinkled skin but sharp dark eyes. She was nearer seventy than sixty.

"May I help you gentlemen? Are you looking for lodging?"

"No, ma'am," Bell said, and pulled out one of his business cards with the Van Dorn logo prominent. "I'm a private investigator hired by Mr. Bloeser, the owner of the Little Angel Mine, to look into the tragic events of last week. I understand that you rented a room to one of the miners."

"I did. Poor Mr. Caldwell. Johnny, is what he wanted everyone to call him. He was very young and polite. He would often fix little things around the house that Sarah and I never got around to."

"Did he leave any possessions?"

"Some," Emily Dawson said a little suspiciously. "Why do you ask?"

"Reopening the Little Angel Mine was a rather odd act on the part of Joshua Brewster. The mine's rightful owner, Mr. Bloeser, is hoping to discover why these men went in there. We hope there could be some clues in whatever the poor souls left behind."

"I understand," she replied, satisfied with the answer. "I haven't rented his room yet. And with winter about to set in, it isn't likely we will. Please, follow me."

She led Bell and Wickersham up the stairs

to the second floor. The staircase bisected a long hallway with several closed doors. At each end of the hall were open doors to white tile and marble bathrooms. Given its age, the house had to have been retrofitted with indoor plumbing. Emily Dawson pulled a set of keys from her apron and unlocked one of the doors midway down on the right. She left them alone to return to her kitchen.

Johnny Caldwell's room was small but serviceable. There was a tiny closet and a single bed with a white hand-stitched quilt. The four-drawer dresser matched the night table. Atop the table was a kerosene lamp and an incidentals dish. Usually, such dishes contained spare change, keys, maybe a button off a shirt that needed repair. This one was empty.

Isaac Bell had tossed hundreds of rooms over the course of his career and went about the task quietly and efficiently. He found what he suspected he would — clothing mostly, a couple of books but no Bible, and a cache of dried beef jerky. He also found a silver picture frame that probably stood on the nightstand but was now in one of the drawers. The photograph was missing. What he didn't find, and what told him what he already suspected, was cash or luggage.

Presumably, all of Caldwell's possessions had been brought to the room in a suitcase, but it was now no longer present. Also, miners were paid in cash, and they paid their rent in cash as well. There should have been a rolled-up wad of bills hidden in the back of the drawer or slipped into an envelope taped under the bed. Further suggestive evidence was the lack of shoes in the closet. No doubt Johnny Caldwell wore heavy work boots into the Little Angel Mine that fateful morning, but he didn't wear them exclusively. There were no regular shoes for a night on the town or Sunday service at a church.

"What do you think?" Tony Wickersham asked, Bell standing silently in the middle of the room now that he was finished. Although he had handled every single object in the room, there was no evidence a single thing had been disturbed.

"Evidence suggests that Mr. Caldwell left that morning with no intention of returning home after his shift. He had packed a bag, took some clothes, including a pair of street shoes, and every dime he had to his name. Everything else was left behind."

"So, we know for certain they didn't die in the mine?"

"Not for certain. As I said, the evidence

suggests a scenario different from what the papers reported. This isn't proof. That will only come when I dive into the mine and see for myself. However, this is what we call an evidentiary link. It jibes with what we suspect."

Before leaving the boardinghouse, they thanked Emily Dawson for her help and inquired about other rooming establishments where Caldwell's friends might have stayed. There was no point driving out to the mine until Bell's equipment arrived from San Francisco, so he and Wickersham spent the afternoon asking lodge owners about the other miners. It turned out to be a fruitless endeavor. None of the men lived in the town proper. Like Brewster, they must have camped up near the mine itself.

The one interesting thing Bell did realize as he and the young mine engineer crisscrossed Central City is that their presence had drawn interest.

They had been followed all afternoon.

4

As the sun sank behind the towering Rocky Mountains, Bell and Wickersham headed to their hotel. Bell was aware that their tail was well back, not an amateur, but also not as seasoned as someone with Isaac's abilities. He got an initial impression that it was a slender person, but didn't make it so obvious as to stare at the lurker and let on that he knew the stranger was following them.

They rounded the last corner before the hotel, and Bell pulled Tony Wickersham into the doorway of a boardinghouse so they weren't easily visible from the street. To his credit, Wickersham didn't cry out at the sudden maneuver, though his eyes went wide with unasked questions.

"We're being followed," Bell whispered. "He's going to walk past us in a minute or so. Sport jacket, no overcoat, and a black hat."

The black and boxy Colt .45 was in Bell's hand.

It was less than a minute after that that a figure dressed as Bell had just described ran past the vestibule. He saw the two men out of the corner of his eye and stopped jogging. His shoulders slumped and then went back up again when he saw that one of his quarry not only had detected him but held a pistol on him as well. The man was in his early thirties, dark-haired, with dark eyes behind round metal-framed glasses. He was clean-shaven and rather baby-faced, with an earnestness about him that made Bell think of an academician rather than a laborer. He'd blanched at the sight of the gun, and his mouth fell open slightly. His teeth were tobacco-stained.

Bell could see that neither of the stranger's hands was pocketed or holding anything, so he relaxed and was confident that he had the situation well in hand and there would be no surprises.

"Only one question for you, friend, and I think you know what it is," Bell said, his gun steadily pointed at the man's midriff.

"Ah, Mr. . . . Ah, Mr. B . . . B . . . B . . ." the man stuttered, then stopped.

"Bell," Isaac offered.

"Mr. Bell. I am so sorr . . . sorr . . . sorry."

Bell recognized that the man was truly terrified at having a gun held on him, but the detective wasn't rookie enough to put it away until he knew who the stranger was and why he was tailing him. "Talk."

The stalker took several deep breaths and studiously avoided looking at the gun. "Mr. Bell. My name is William Gibbs. I'm a reporter with the *Rocky Mountain News.* When I heard you were headed here to Central City, I decided to follow you. Just in case you made another important bust like you did at the Denver post office."

"How'd you hear I was coming to Central City?" Bell asked.

"I, ah . . . I have an informant at the Brown Palace Hotel. You were heard speaking with the owner of the Little Angel Mine."

It seemed reasonable, but it was also an annoyance that a hotel with the Brown's reputation would allow staff to discuss the comings and goings of guests with newspapermen.

"Is there a story for me, Mr. Bell?" Gibbs asked.

Bell had always had a love/hate relationship with the press. At times, their ability to reach thousands of households per day made things like manhunts and kidnapping resolutions much easier. But, on the other hand, it made the quiet sleuthing, which was so much of what he did, more difficult. There were no shadows to hide in when the papers were shining lights on everything.

"I'm afraid not, Mr. Gibbs." Bell slid the .45 back into its shoulder holster. "I was asked to look into a few anomalies concerning the accident at the mine, but it appears the only people who know anything died in the collapse." Bell mixed enough truth with the lie to satisfy the reporter.

Gibbs couldn't help but look a little crestfallen. "I doubt my editor will reimburse me for the train fare."

"You're in time to catch the last train back to Denver," Tony Wickersham offered. He checked his pocket watch. "It leaves in a half hour. This way, you're not out the cost of a hotel room as well."

"Thanks for the tip. I guess this was a bust. Sorry if I gave you a scare, Mr. Bell."

Isaac touched the bulge under his arm that was his .45. "Likewise."

Gibbs took off in the direction of Central City's train depot, while Bell and Wickersham returned to their hotel for the night.

5

The following morning dawned clear but very cold. Shaving in the communal bathroom down the hall from his room, Isaac Bell shuddered at the prospect of diving into the icy water that continued to gush from the mouth of the Little Angel Mine. He hoped that his instructions to Alex Hecht, his friend in San Francisco who built rebreathers, had been detailed enough for some extra gear to be sent along with the dive pack.

After their breakfast, Bell and Wickersham made a few stops for provisions before climbing into his new chain-drive REO Model H Power Wagon truck. The vehicle was little more than a flat platform atop a chassis with high sides so cargo wouldn't fall out. It had a gate at the back and a high bench seat for the driver and one passenger. The engine, a nine-horsepower one-cylinder affair, was mounted under the drive compartment. Usually, there was an open-sided canvas cover over the cab to protect the occupants from the elements, but conditions were so harsh up in the Colorado mountains that the minimal protection it afforded wasn't worth the effort of deploying it. The wheels were wood-spoked and sprung on heavy metal leaves, but Bell knew from countless hours behind the wheel of all manner of vehicles that no one other than Rolls and Royce in England had yet developed a smooth-riding suspension.

Tony straddled the steering wheel that rose out of the cab's floor and manipulated the controls springing from the steering shaft. Bell stood in front of the truck, and when the young Englishman nodded, he thrust down on the engine crank. The engine fired immediately and within seconds was running as smoothly as any motor Bell had ever heard.

"Fine piece of machinery," he commented, climbing in next to Wickersham.

"It belongs to Mr. Bloeser, but I'm the only one that uses it. I inspect all the properties he's invested in and investigate others of interest. She's rated to carry fifteen hundred pounds, but in these hills I won't load more than a half ton."

"Still, that's impressive."

"Mr. Olds knows what he's doing."

"Olds, as in Oldsmobile?"

"Yes. He sold that company and started REO. Stands for Ransom E. Olds."

"Learn something new every day."

They raced out of Central City at the truck's top speed of twenty-five miles per hour but soon slowed as the streets became rutted tracks that climbed into the foothills surrounding the old mining town. As they passed, Tony pointed out various abandoned mines. Most were boarded-up portals, with heavy timber lintels, with mounds of waste tailings running down the mountainsides where they had been dumped. He seemed to know the history of each and told Bell how much gold had been pulled from which mines and which mines had turned out to be busts. A few were still actively being worked. Those had a small tent village for the workers, usually with one tent that had smoke coming from a tin chimney, meaning it was the mess hall. The men working the surface stood at impressive machines that utilized water coming down through pipes laid high in the mountains for motivating power to operate the crushing and stamping mills. The crushings were then put through sluice boxes to extract the fine particles of gold from the quartz-veined granite. The higher they climbed into the mountains, the cooler the air and the thicker the patches of snow that lay upon the ground. It wouldn't be long before everything became a sea of white when winter unleashed its full fury.

The Little Angel was an hour outside of town. It differed from the others because the boards once blocking its entrance had been removed, but there was no tent village, just a couple of small two- or three-man canvas structures and an open fire pit with a metal grille that was designed to hold various pots and pans above the flame. The other noticeable difference was the foot-deep gush of water that spewed from the mine's entrance, cutting a deep rut into the sloping hillside and winding down past a mine below.

Wickersham saw the direction of Bell's gaze. "That's Bill Mahoney's workings, the Satan Mine. He's the one that's demanding we cap the entrance up here. Looking at it now, I can't say I blame him. Hell, I think if I were in his shoes, I would've dynamited the Little Angel days ago."

The artificial stream cut right through the Satan Mine, and some of the water even flowed back into its mouth and had to be extracted using a surface-mounted steam pump. Its rocking arms were seesawing away while white smoke and some steam escaped from the boiler. One man stood by in attendance, with cord upon cord of split wood at the ready.

"I think as a sign of goodwill, your Mr. Bloeser should offer to pay Mr. Mahoney something for his troubles."

Wickersham reached into an inside jacket pocket and withdrew a soft felt bag. It jangled with the sound of heavy coins. "Ahead of you on that one, Mr. Bell. Mr. Bloeser said to use my judgment."

Bell searched the camp while Wickersham settled things with the other mine owner. He found nothing of interest in any of the tents. It was clear that since the accident, men had come up and scavenged the site, leaving only the tents behind, as their theft would have been too brazen and obvious. He even dug around under the tents to see if anything had been hidden there, as well as beneath the cold ashes of the fire pit. Nothing of value was found.

Bell had a fire going and had coffee brewing in the time it took Tony to trudge the half mile up from the Satan Mine. There was no milk, but he had brought dark crystals of rock sugar to help ward off the cold. He also added a dash of Irish whiskey to further fortify the insulating effects of the brew.

Finished with his coffee, Bell stood, muttered, "Good a time as any," and began to strip off the overalls he'd bought that morning at a dry goods store. Below, he wore knee-length flannel drawers and a tight flannel shirt that ended at his thickened biceps. Wickersham watched with curiosity, as he had no idea what the detective had planned. Bell then removed his shirt, exposing his skin to the cold wind blowing through the Rockies. He was well muscled yet lean, with just a hint of a summer tan still remaining to give him some color.

Wickersham goggled when Bell opened a jar of lard he'd inexplicably purchased that morning and began smearing the white animal grease across his chest and under his shoulders on his back. "Um?" he said by way of questioning Bell's actions.

"Just read about a bloke who swam the English Channel last September named Burgess. First person to do it since 1875. To keep the water from sapping too much heat from around his heart and vital organs, he smeared on a layer of lard. I plan on exploring the mine for as deep as I can right now, and this should allow me to stay in the water longer."

To protect his feet, Bell slipped on a cheap pair of shoes he'd also purchased that morning. He fetched a D cell–powered flashlight. To help waterproof the cardboard tube, he'd wrapped it with rubberized strips like those used by electricians. The filament was of the new tungsten design, so the light was almost painfully bright when he flicked it on for a test.

"Keep the fire high and the coffee hot. I'll be back in a bit." With that, Bell turned and hiked the last twenty or so feet along the bank of the stream up to the mouth of the Little Angel Mine.

Isaac Bell wasn't a superstitious man nor one to give credence to omens or portents, but he couldn't shake a heavy feeling of dread as he looked into the Stygian mine shaft. He suspected that there were no dead men within whose souls were looking for release. And yet he felt that something of importance had taken place there, something that cast ripples in the fabric of the darkness, amplifying until they could become crushing waves.

All those thoughts ran through his head in an instant and were then cast aside as he flicked the light on again and stepped into the stream without pause. The water was icy cold and it lanced right through to his shins and seemingly made brittle the fine bones of his feet so that with each step he imagined they would shatter like crystal. The current was strong, but only a foot deep, so he wasn't yet offering its flow much resistance. As he went deeper, the going would become considerably slower. His second purpose for making this early foray into the mine was to test whether it would be possible to plumb its depth while lugging the bulky rebreather.

The shaft was roughly square, and along the floor ran parallel train tracks no more than two feet apart. The ties were thin lengths of timber bolted directly into the stone. Bell established a rhythm for walking atop the ties and not slamming his toes into their edges. He felt around with his feet occasionally to detect if anything had been left on the floor, but so far he had turned up nothing. Any light debris would have been swept out with the current, and he couldn't imagine anything heavy being left behind along the rails. The light revealed nothing but bare stone that had been worked with pick, hammer, drill, and explosives.

The downward slope was gentle, but it took only a few minutes of walking for the water to be up around Bell's waist. The cold was so raw that he could picture how blood flowing up from his legs was physically colder than the rest of his circulatory system. His legs moved by effort of sheer will alone. When the water reached the level of his lowest ribs, he felt like he was trudging through the deepest snow these mountains had to offer. It helped a little to turn edge-on to the flow and stick close to one side of the tunnel. Bell knew his lips were blue, and his teeth chattered so hard he had to clamp his jaw shut so his vision remained steady. The lard was protecting his core to a degree, but the agony of being immersed in such icy conditions was sapping both his strength and his considerable will. He forced himself to keep going, vowing only to turn back once he was neck-deep in the numbing water.

His fortunes changed somewhat when he found wires had been bolted into the wall just above head height. They ended at a shattered insulator, and Isaac imagined that scavengers had yanked out the section of the electrical system nearest the surface for its scrap value. It was a telling reminder that life here was a hardscrabble existence and nothing was ever allowed to go to waste. He managed to use his free hand to help pull himself against the current and held on tightly when he needed to rest his failing body.

He had maybe ten more feet of tunnel before the water became too deep when he kicked something under the glittering surface. He groped down for it but he couldn't reach it. Submerging his head was a gamble because he would lose a vast amount of core heat that was already dangerously low, but Bell knew his body, trusted his abilities, and before he could come up with an excuse that was true he plunged below the surface, feeling along the rocky floor until he grasped the object. He burst out of the water with a primal roar of agony, the cold drilling into his temples like railroad spikes.

His makeshift waterproofing had protected his flashlight from the occasional splash, but its full immersion had shorted the circuits. It didn't matter. In the utter blackness he could tell he'd found a miner's pick. He braced the head of the pick against the wall to keep himself from being thrown against it and let the current undo in moments what it had taken him fifteen minutes to gain. He had to start plodding again when the water level was back down around his hips, but going with the current needed much less effort. Moments later, he was back out in the weak sunlight, cold, exhausted, but pleased with his effort.

Tony Wickersham saw him emerge from the inky mine and rushed up with a blanket to toss around Bell's shoulders and helped guide the detective down to their small camp. Bell shook, and his face was so numb he couldn't form words.

The Englishman parked him on a log as close to the fire as he dared and mounded more blankets over his shoulders. Isaac couldn't hold a coffee mug, so Tony held it for him and gave him sips like one would give bouillon to a sick child. It took ten minutes before Bell could even acknowledge the help he was being given and then it was just a weak smile and a tightening of his eyes. Another ten minutes would pass before he could hold the mug, though his hands still trembled.

"Worth it?" Tony asked finally.

"Totally," Bell stammered. "I needed further proof that I'm certifiable."

A half hour later, Bell was dressed properly again and, with a full belly and a couple of pulls at the whiskey, was feeling himself again. "Tell me about this pick I found."

Wickersham grabbed up the miner's tool. He had a deftness in handling the pick that told Bell the young Englishman was more than familiar at using the awkward, top-heavy implement.

"It's a pickax. What do you want to know? This is a fairly large one, more common here than the smaller ones used to chip away inside coal mines. The handle's probably ash and the head is steel, a little rusted, but that's to be expected. And . . . Well, well, well. Interesting."

"What?" Bell asked, hopeful that his freezing sojourn hadn't been for naught.

He showed Isaac the top of the tool where the handle slotted in through a hole in the metal pick itself.

"What am I looking at?"

"See the two nails that have been driven into the wood?" Wickersham asked.

"Yes. And . . . ?"

"It's an old trick to add more tension between the head and the shaft of the pick so the head stays on better. The thing is, you only need to do that with inferior or worn-out tools. This is an old pick."

Bell understood the implication immediately. "And Joshua Brewster was noted for always using the latest and finest equipment."

"The pick was window dressing in case anyone came looking around," Wickersham completed the thought.

"A clever ruse, and one that would doubtless work if we weren't already suspicious about the details of the accident." Bell was more anxious than ever to dive the mine properly and put an end to this mystery. If it turned out that the men had faked their own deaths, it would be up to Hans Bloeser to continue the investigation with Charles Post, Van Dorn's man in Denver, and whoever brings the diving equipment from San Francisco.

6

While awaiting the delivery from California, Bell helped Tony Wickersham prepare the Little Angel Mine for its curtain call. They were going to rig the mouth of the shaft with explosives and collapse the tunnel deeply enough to stanch the flow of water. They'd also hired a couple of Bill Mahoney's men to help drill into the rock to maximize the TNT's effect. They purposely left out the booster charges so there would be no accidental detonations until Bell's explorations were complete.

With just enough time to reach the train from Denver, Bell borrowed Wickersham's REO truck and drove back to Central City to meet his fellow Van Dorn detective.

The narrow-gauge locomotive and its shabby cars were just pulling into the depot when Bell finally reached town. He'd shaved time from the trip up into the foothills but had paid the price of a battered body from the uneven trails. The dirt streets of Central City felt like freshly laid tar-bound macadam compared to the mountain roads. Bell spotted a young man being assisted by a porter to retrieve a large steamer trunk from the cargo compartment of one of the carriages and place it on a wheeled trolley. He didn't recognize the agent, but the trunk was adorned with the logo of Hecht Marine, an octopus clutching Poseidon's trident.

Bell parked the REO as close to the platform as he could and jumped out, his back stiff and aching from the punishing ride. "Hello. I'm Isaac Bell."

The porter regarded him blankly, but the agent turned quickly and rushed toward him, his hand outstretched like the bowsprit on a schooner. "Mr. Bell. I'm Colin Rhodes. It is an honor to meet you."

Young Master Rhodes must have been an intern because he didn't look a day over eighteen, with a shaggy mop of hair peeking out from under a cap and oversize feet like some overeager puppy not yet grown into its body.

Bell shook the lad's hand, fully expecting him to start wriggling in pleasure at meeting his hero. "And what exactly do you do for Van Dorn?" He tipped the porter a couple of dollars for his continued assistance in loading the trunk from the dolly to the pickup truck.

"I'm the new office boy. I help out with whatever the fellas need. Get coffee, bring in paperwork from lawyers' offices. Take stuff to guys on stakeouts."

"You do a lot of fetching." Bell was irked that one of his requests was handled so cavalierly and entrusted to young Fido in a cheap suit.

"I guess you could say that. They sent me because everyone else is working a major kidnapping case."

"I wasn't aware . . ."

"It's a Chinese lady. She was to be married to the son of a Chinatown big shot, but some rival gang grabbed her from her hotel the night before your request came in. The mayor himself is keeping tabs on our investigation because he's afraid this will turn into a tongue war."

"Tong war," Bell corrected. "A 'tong' is a Chinese gang. This has 'underworld' written all over it. The city is only now rebuilding from the quake. The last thing anyone needs is Chinese thugs gutting each other across half of downtown."

Bell had fresh instructions to give Rhodes before sending him on his way. They finally manhandled the trunk into the rear of the truck. It was balky and weighed over a hundred pounds.

"Okay, here's your next assignment."

"I'm not working with you?" It came out as a whine as pathetic as any dog's.

"No. I need you back in Denver working with Charles Post. You know where his office is?" Colin Rhodes showed Bell his copy of the Van Dorn handbook, which had numbers and addresses for every Van Dorn office, including the ones in Europe. "I want you and Charles to talk to all the mine tool vendors and foundries and find out if they had any large orders in the past few months for a Joshua Hayes Brewster. Write that name down. Or any orders at all that would lead a reasonable person to believe that a small mine was being opened for the very first time, one that is very remote and difficult to reach."

This last deduction came from the realization that if Brewster and the others had faked their own deaths, they would go to such lengths only if their new project had to be kept utterly secret and there would be little contact with the outside world once they commenced.

"Tell them that I found some equipment in the Little Angel Mine and want to see if it lines up with what was sold."

"What do I say if they ask for a list of the equipment you found?"

It was a good question for an average person to ask, but a Van Dorn man should be able to lie his way out of such a question and turn it around so the vendors gave up their lists. "Ask Charles to teach you how it's done. I don't have time now."

Bell hopped into the REO's cab, got the engine ready to fire, and instructed young Mr. Rhodes to crank the starter. The engine caught right away. Bell massaged the throttle and choke until satisfied with the motor's hum and took off out of the depot parking area. The sad-eyed Rhodes watched him leave and made Bell feel like he was abandoning a puppy in the street.

The journey back to the mine took longer, of course, but Bell pushed it as hard as he dared. There was still enough time to get in the dive that day and get back to Central City for a hot bath and clean sheets.

When he arrived back at the Little Angel Mine, the sun was out, though the air remained cold. Tony was seated near the fire, leaning over a wooden box of the booster charges needed to blow the main TNT charges already in place above the adit. Water continued to spew from the dark mine entrance. Bell parked next to the camp, and Wickersham set aside one of the flashlight-sized charges and came over.

"Made good time," the Englishman said as Bell unlimbered his long legs and headed to the REO's bed.

"It's the truck. Thing's as sure-footed as a goat."

Rather than wrestle the trunk to the ground, Bell leapt in the back and sprang open the lid. He removed a thin piece of protective wood that lay just inside and peered at the equipment Alex Hecht had sent along. The rebreather was in a web harness worn over the shoulders like a backpack and consisted of three parts — a square chemical scrubber that bonded the excess carbon dioxide from the diver's breath, a separate copper cylinder of oxygen under pressure that bled into the system via a control knob, and a face mask with an attached hose that fed air to the diver and took away each exhalation.

Alex's work was to make the system as hands-free to use as possible, with different types of valves and pressure-sensitive backflow preventers. Still, there was a great deal more to be done to make the rebreather a simple device to operate. Had he not been properly instructed back in San Francisco, Bell would have never dreamed of making this dive.

He set aside the rebreather carefully. Next came a belt of lead weights. Though the rebreather itself was heavy, the oxygen tank made it positively buoyant, thus the need for additional ballast. He then whistled aloud as he lifted what appeared to be the hide of a man who'd been skinned alive. It was a diving suit unlike any other in the world. This was the other contribution to the world of diving from the mind of Alex Hecht.

Unlike the bulky vulcanized canvas suits worn by traditional hard hat divers, this was supple — pliable, even. It felt waxy to the touch. Bell wasn't sure what Hecht used to coat his suit to make it waterproof, but he had been warned that the suit maintained its integrity for only an hour or so. After that, water would begin leaching through, especially at the joints, where the diver's natural motion would have worn away more of the protective emulsion. Also, the suit needed to be thoroughly cleaned and dried and recoated following every dive. Not knowing how much dive time Bell required, Hecht included a heavy drum of his proprietary sealant.

The suit was heavily padded at the knees and elbows and ended with thick elastic bands at the wrists and ankles. Hecht hadn't yet perfected gloves for his suit, and he figured most divers would wear flippers on their feet. Bell still had the cheap shoes he'd worn earlier.

At the neck was a metal collar with a rubber gasket studded with upright bolts that fit exactly the holes drilled into the matching collar of the rebreather mask. Depending on the depth of the dive, the two collars were fastened together with special lug nuts that could exert countless pounds of pressure on the gasket to keep it airtight. Since Bell wasn't diving too deeply, the nuts would just be tightened by hand and not with the special torque-controlling wrench also included in the trunk. The suit was just baggy enough that Bell's heat would warm the layer of air trapped against his body, though eventually the cold would reach him if this was to be a longer dive.

A final piece of equipment was a dry-cell-battery flashlight that had been made waterproof using layers of rubber. The battery was heavy and had to be worn at the waist, hanging from the rebreather harness, but the lamp was the size of a beer mug, and the connecting wire had been wound in steel to protect it from damage.

Tony helped Bell shimmy and contort his

way into the suit and slid on his shoes and laced them for him. Together, the men carried the equipment up to the mine's entrance. The water sluiced out unabated. Bell first clipped on his belt of lead weights and then Tony held the rebreather so Bell could wriggle into the straps and tighten them so they were snug against his back. The rebreather was heavy, but the detective could still move around without too much difficulty, and once he was in the water he expected to be perfectly balanced. Next came the helmet. Bell had already tested the oxygen flow. Tony lifted it over Isaac's head and fitted the holes over the suit collar's studs and tightened the wing nuts. Finally, Tony clipped on the battery, and Bell turned it on before slipping on some thick leather gloves. Gloves wouldn't protect his hands from the cold water but were necessary to protect them from the stones. He'd regretted not wearing any during his initial trip.

Bell waited a bit, testing that he was breathing the proper mixture of gasses and that the scrubbers were working properly. After three minutes, Bell nodded to Tony, who clapped him on the back, and he waded into the frigid discharge.

He felt the cold, but nowhere near the

savage bite of his first swim. He walked in an awkward, lurching gait because of the gear but was soon deep enough to drop under the surface. He found that it was best to crawl on his hands and feet, making certain his knees didn't scrape the sharp stone floor. This had the added bonus of presenting a most streamlined silhouette to the rushing water and easing the resistance. He flicked on the light occasionally, seeing that the next thirty or so feet were clear, and crawled on in the dark. The resonance of the water gushing past and the hiss and purr of his own breathing were oddly calming.

But after just a few minutes, the darkness felt like it was squeezing him from all sides. His imagination began to work itself into overdrive against his resolve to remain calm. At any second he expected a bloated and waterlogged corpse to come hurtling out of the mine and dash him against the wall or floor. He quickly relit the flashlight and saw that ahead was nothing more than an empty mine shaft. Peering up, he could see that he was now deeper than he'd ever been. The tunnel here was flooded to the ceiling.

He kept the electric torch lit as he forged ever deeper. He could feel the water pressure building against his body, but it was just a mild discomfort.

At last, fifteen minutes into his swim, Bell came upon an obstruction. The ceiling and walls had collapsed into the tunnel and nearly filled it with rubble. Here too the current was strongest, since this was the spot where the mountain's aquifer drained into the shaft. Because there was so much force coming from the artesian spring, Bell wasn't concerned about dislodging rocks and causing further collapse. Whatever loose stones remained following the cave-in had been picked up and carried partway down the mine. Still, he remained cautious as he swam up and over the pile of debris. At the top, he had to fight to keep from getting pinned to the rocks by the jet of water blasting into the shaft. Once he was through, the current abruptly ended. There was no outlet on this side of the divide.

He swam easily in the still water, the cone of light from his lamp receding as he chased after it with long, powerful strokes. He had passed the Little Angel's nadir, its lowest point relative to sea level, and was now climbing a gentle incline. He did pass a few side chambers, as Tony said there would be, but his light was strong enough to show they were relatively small spaces unable to conceal any of the dead.

He came upon yet another obstruction and, unlike the earlier area of collapse, this one spanned the shaft from left to right and from top to bottom. And it hadn't been cleared relatively free like the other one. This was a fractured mass of loose stones, some boulder-sized, others little bigger than his fist. Bell stared thoughtfully at the rubble for a solid minute before tentatively reaching out and moving just one stone from the matrix. As he had suspected, it caused a cascading avalanche of other rocks. It would take weeks of labor — months maybe — to clear enough material away to get to what was beyond this mess.

Bell turned and started swimming back the way he'd come. Another man might have cursed or lashed out in frustration at being denied a definitive answer to the puzzle, but he was wired differently and those differences made him a superior detective. He rarely made his investigations personal, so without an emotional stake, he could endeavor to do his best and be satisfied with whatever answer he found. And then he could simply walk away from the affair.

He was now composing his report to the Brothers Bloeser. His answer as to whether Joshua Hayes Brewster and the other miners actually died in the disaster was inconclusive. However, his intuition, based on a few subtleties, led him to believe that they had not perished in the mine but had faked their own deaths for reasons unknown.

He climbed over the first cave-in, straining once again not to snag his diving suit and potentially rip through the fabric. So far, it had worked flawlessly. He was cold but could still function with little impediment to his limbs or senses. Once he was past the rockfall, the current pushed him toward the surface. He turned himself edgewise to reduce his profile and better control his ascent back to the surface. As before, his exit from the mine was much easier and faster than his entrance. In just a couple of minutes he could raise his head above the surface, and, all too soon, the water became so shallow that he had to walk rather than ride the current all the way out. He eventually saw a corona of weak gray light up ahead. He powered down his electric torch and clipped the lamp to the dry-cell battery at his hip. Just inside the entrance was a bench of rock along the right-hand wall, and Bell noticed that it wasn't empty as previously. A figure lay upon it, utterly still.

Blast at the Little Angel Mine

7

Bell charged like a bull, running through the swift-flowing water in a rampage, needing all his skill not to lose his balance and tumble. He reached the bench in moments, and his worst fears did not come to pass. It indeed was Tony Wickersham, but he wasn't dead. However, he had been shot, his shoulder was a crimson mess and his hands were sticky with the blood he'd tried to stanch. Bell's .45 caliber pistol was at Tony's side, its checkered grip also sticky with blood.

"Tony. It's me, Bell. What happened, man?" Bell slapped him lightly on the cheek.

By force of will, Wickersham roused himself. His eyes fluttered open, then focused. When he finally recognized the detective inside the bulky dive mask, they went wide with fear and relief. "Mr. Bell . . . I was shot."

"I can see that. Who did it?"

"I don't know. I was working in the camp when all of a sudden my arm felt like it had been ripped from its socket. I only heard the shot after the bullet hit me."

"Long gun," Bell said. "Rifle. And then?"

"I grabbed your pistol and took cover here. When I tried to peer outside, the gunman fired again right away."

"So, we're pinned down. When did this happen?" Even as he was talking, Bell worked open the nuts holding his helmet to the suit's collar.

"Not long after you entered the mine. I'd say no more than five minutes."

Holding firmly onto his pistol, Bell dropped to his hands and knees, effectively hiding himself in the swift current. He made it to the mine entrance and anchored himself as best he could so water boiled around him like he was a boulder in a stream. He scanned the surrounding mountains and focused in on those places that he considered ideal for a sniper to cover the mine. He soon spotted movement at one of them. It was a good hundred and twenty yards away, and the gunman would be firing downslope. Not the easiest shot to make. A gust must have pushed the bullet just off enough so it hit Tony's shoulder and not his heart, which was certainly the assassin's target.

Bell considered his options. They were limited. Wait until nightfall and sneak out in the dark. But Tony was in no shape to sneak and very well might be dead by then. Option B was to hunt the shooter himself. Going up against a rifle while carrying only a pistol in somewhat open terrain made option B as unpalatable as option A, but there really wasn't a third option.

He started pushing himself back against the current, moving slowly so he wouldn't alert the sniper, when Bell noticed something out of the ordinary at their camp. Tony said he was working when he was shot. Bell recalled him readying the booster charges and laying them in a wooden box. The log he'd used as a seat was right where it had always been, but the box was nowhere to be seen.

Bell's heart seemed to swell inside his chest cavity as an overdose of adrenaline spurted into his bloodstream. The gunman need only keep them pinned long enough for his accomplice to finish rigging the explosives they'd planted the day before. His helmet dangled past his waist from its hose. He hastily threw it over his head as he strained to get back to the bench where

144

Tony lay sprawled. He tightened only a couple of the nuts to secure the helmet. He grabbed the Englishman and bodily rolled him into the freezing water.

Tony cried out in pain.

Bell ignored the other man's agony. "Take a deep breath."

"What?" His face was awash in confusion.

"Breath. Deep. Now."

No sooner had Tony filled his lungs than Bell dunked him underwater, holding on to him so they were chest to chest, and then he let the current grab them both like leaves in a gutter.

They burst out of the mine in a flash. Bell knew his back was showing above the surface but hoped that such an unusual sight would keep the assassin confused long enough for them to get clear. Instead of shooting at them, he fired two unaimed shots in rapid order. A signal to his partner. Seconds later, the area above the entrance to the Little Angel Mine erupted like the granite rock was no more solid than a bubble breaking the surface of a lake. Tons of rock were lifted into the air and then came crashing back down, grinding and gnashing, collapsing in a smoky, dusty storm.

A house-sized chunk of the mountain slid

down to engulf the mine entrance and stanch the flow of water with one final tsunami-like surge. Pelted by rocks and debris, Bell and Tony suddenly accelerated in the channel the water had cut over the past week as it wended out of the hills. They twisted and tumbled, Tony's bad shoulder doubtlessly taking additional punishment, but they presented such a chaotic target that the gunman couldn't get a bead on them.

Bell clutched the Englishman as tightly as possible, finally taking a moment to poke his head out of the water to see how far they'd come. They'd almost overshot their target. The stream made a sharp bend around some rocks too big to dislodge. They were almost there. Bell braced, and as soon as he felt the stream's flow begin to turn to his right, he stood, still holding Tony Wickersham, and let momentum throw them from the water and over the rocks and into a shallow depression behind them. The maneuver had been so sudden that the shooter fired seconds after Isaac and Tony had landed safely in the boulders' shadow. A pair of bullets hit one of the stones and ricocheted harmlessly away.

It took a moment to straighten Tony's limbs and see that he was still breathing, though no amount of shaking or prodding roused the man from unconsciousness. Bell worked his way out of the rebreather mask and shucked all his bulky gear, much of it smashed by their headlong tumble. His concern was Wickersham. Without proper heat and a change out of his wet clothes, the man would be dead soon, even without the fresh blood oozing from his ravaged shoulder.

The only thing Bell could do now is hunt the gunman and his accomplice and then tend to Tony's needs. He checked the .45's magazine and saw he had six rounds. Tony must have laid down some cover fire for himself as he escaped into the Little Angel. He crawled backward, away from the boulder redoubt and out of the sniper's line of sight.

Bell liked neither his choices nor his odds, but he never hesitated. He followed the shallow curve around the hillside. There was no place to holster his weapon, so he carried it as he moved. He balanced speed with stealth, thinking about Tony lying in a ditch in wet, freezing clothes. There at least remained a little warmth from the sun.

The ground was mostly crushed mine waste, so it was exceptionally sharp and jagged. Soon Bell's suit was in tatters, and the palms of his hands bled and his knees felt like someone had smashed each with a sledgehammer. In time, he reached a point where he was shielded from the sniper's position by the natural slope of the land and he got to his feet and started climbing the steep hillside. He made certain each footfall was precise so he wouldn't dislodge loose rocks and cause a mini avalanche and blow his approach.

Bell, aware of his surroundings, eyeballed a gulley entrance that merged with his own and considered the possibility of the accomplice trudging in the same direction to meet his partner.

And it happened.

The man rounded the corner, walking like someone who hadn't a care in the world because he hadn't seen his quarry emerge from the mine. He hadn't heard the two shots either because he'd stood so close to the blast his ears still rang.

With people willing to protect the secret of the Little Angel disaster, Bell was in a position to need questions answered. Bell had the pistol up and the sights centered on a crease between the man's eyebrows. He had the drop on the guy. "Freeze."

The man jumped at the sound of Bell's voice and went ashen when he realized his predicament. For some reason, he looked behind himself and up the hill.

"Hands up." Bell emphasized the order by flicking his pistol's barrel up and down.

Just as his hands went up, a second man emerged from the gulley. He was large, with a shaved head, and he reminded Bell of a circus strongman but without the charm. There was an aura of menace about him.

The man had his gun cradled low across his hips and wasted no time raising it. He twisted to bring the barrel to bear on Isaac Bell. Bell shifted his aim and fired a fraction too quick and missed, but the rifleman reconsidered his plan. He leapt back out of sight and then fired. But he wasn't aiming at Bell. His bullet hit the first man, his accomplice and partner, just to the left of his spine in line with the heart. The round emerged, the man thrown forward a good five feet by the impact of the heavy copper bullet.

There was no need to check if the injury had been fatal. Nobody could have survived a shot like that.

The man knew where Bell was and exactly where he'd likely show himself. Bell couldn't just charge in. His foe had the high ground, the superior weapon, and all the time in the world. Rather than chase directly, Bell scrambled out of the hillside gulley and atop a ridge that rose up the flanks of the foot-hills. He stayed in a crouched position to reduce his silhouette and started running uphill after the shooter. He could see the man racing back up his own little ravine toward his sniper's nest. For such a big man, carrying slabs of muscle around his shoulders and back, he moved swiftly, eating ground at a pace Bell could barely maintain.

The erosion-worn gulley split into two channels just ahead, and when the man reached it, he spun around and started back down the mountain in the new channel. Bell completely lost sight of him and had to rush back down into the gulley and try to work his way back up the other side in order to emerge above and behind the gunman again.

He'd just started climbing the far bank of the valley when he heard the sound of machinery. Not an engine but mechanical noises, and they grew both louder but also receded.

Bell cursed and redoubled his effort. But it was no use. Even before he reached the top, the assassin had built up enough speed coasting downhill in the vehicle they'd driven here to pop the clutch and force the engine to life. Once lit, the truck roared off, accelerating down the mountain with each second. By the time Bell was high enough on the bank to spot the machine, it was a hundred yards off, trailing a fine plume of dust. He hadn't gotten a close enough look to identify its color, much less its make and model.

He jogged back the way he'd come to check on Tony Wickersham. On the way, he'd check the dead body for clues. He reached the bouldered area where he'd left Tony only to find the young Englishman gone and a stranger in his place. Bell had his pistol trained on the interloper in an instant.

"Easy there, I'm not your enemy."

"Who are you and where's Tony?"

"I'm Buck Tompkins. I'm a miner down at the Satan. We heard the explosion and realized the water had stopped gushing into our camp, so a couple of us came up to check things out. We found your man. The others took him back to our camp and I waited here for you."

"I recognize you now. You helped with drilling the holes."

"Yes, sir, I did." He eyed Bell's strange attire but didn't comment.

"Thank you for looking after Tony. He's in a bad way."

"We'll get him warmed up and into town real quick. Central City has a fine doctor."

Bell thought for a second. The men from the Satan Mine knew nothing of the attack and how the blast had meant to seal them in the mountain for all eternity, and there was no need to tell them. "I need to change and do some things at our camp. If you have transportation out of here, take Tony into town as soon as you can, and I'll catch up at the doctor's office. It's all my fault. I dropped my pistol handing it to Tony. That's how he was shot."

"Don't beat yourself up over an accident. That's part of life. We've got a truck, so it's no problem."

Bell shook the man's hand, thanking him, before turning back to climb up to the camp that had been half buried in debris from the blast. One thing was for certain. Isaac Bell owed his friend Alex Hecht for what had to be a thousand dollars' worth of experimental diving equipment.

Bell rummaged through the mess until he found his clothes. He shed the diving suit and his wet drawers and donned the overalls and work boots. He rekindled the fire to make himself some coffee and wolfed down three prepacked sandwiches.

A half hour after finding Tony in good

hands, Bell returned to the dead man left in the remote erosion channel. He remained facedown, and because his heart had stopped at the instant the shot came, there was very little blood staining the ground when Bell turned the body over.

Bell grunted. He recognized the victim. The man had called himself William Gibbs and said he was a reporter with the *Rocky Mountain News.* Bell had to hand it to the guy — he'd told that lie quickly and convincingly after being discovered tailing him and Wickersham. Though now he was at a loss as to how this man came to be tailing him in the first place.

He went through the man's pockets and checked the labels on all his clothes, including his shoes. None of it told him a thing. It was all nondescript and ordinary, and the only labels were for stores with Denver addresses. The man's black leather wallet initially revealed just a couple of dollars but, on closer examination, he saw a hidden compartment with a photograph preserved between pieces of stiff paperboard.

It showed an even younger version of "William Gibbs," barely out of his teens, with a dark-haired, morose-looking girl of about the same age. They stood on the plaza right in front of the Eiffel Tower in Paris.

Bell had an identical photo, only in it his wife was beaming at the camera.

He turned it. In faded ink was written *Theresa et moi 6/12/99.*

Bell chuckled. On the back of his Eiffel Tower picture he'd written *Marion et moi* and the date of their visit. He realized he wasn't as clever as he'd thought since this guy had added a dash of French to his souvenir too. Bell looked again at the couple in the photograph, and the date once again, and quickly knew why Miss Theresa looked so miserable.

Bell stood and dusted off his overalls. And heard whistling. Close by. He drew his pistol and turned in place. It was a man, and he was walking down the mountain above where Bell stood. He moved casually, hands swinging easily at his sides, though his spine remained ramrod straight. Bell didn't need an introduction to guess this man was current or former military. He'd started whistling so his approach didn't startle Bell, as a sign of good faith. Bell lowered the pistol, though he kept it cocked. He let the man approach, saying nothing.

The stranger said, "I think they would have let you leave unharmed had you not brought that fancy diving gear." He was in his fifties, with weathered skin, a squint to his blue eyes, and silver stubble on his chin and cheeks. He was a cowboy out of central casting, but the real deal and not a Hollywood facsimile. His accent was pure Kentucky honey.

"Who were they?"

"Big one's named Foster Gly."

"And the Frenchman?"

The newcomer cocked his head and his eyes narrowed further. "How could you know that? I saw the shot. Gly shot him dead so you couldn't question him."

"Figured."

"You don't know the half of it."

Bell said, "Tell me who you are, and what this is all about, and I'll tell you how I know he was French."

"I'm Colonel Greggory Patmore, U.S. Army, and you have stumbled onto something you definitely shouldn't have. I've been monitoring this area since we faked the accident, just hoping and praying no one came sniffing around." He paused to survey the forlorn scenery. "I knew the frog-eaters were here, making sure just like me, but I was so high up the mountain they had no idea I was watching them while they were watching you. When all hell broke loose today, I was too far away to do much good. But truth be told, part of me was hoping these men succeeded in punching your tickets because you and your pal just became wrinkles I don't know how to iron out. And if I don't think of something quick, the nine men who pretended to die in that old mine are going to die for real."

Bell was a fast study of situations and people. He knew immediately that Patmore was someone to be trusted. He held out his hand. "My name is Isaac Bell and I am the senior detective for the Van Dorn Agency and maybe I can help you figure something out." Patmore clasped Bell's hand, respect in his eyes, for he knew, like so many, of the fearsome reputation enjoyed by the Van Dorns.

8

Gregg Patmore hiked back up to where he'd spent the past few days watching over the Little Angel Mine to get his vehicle. For his part, Bell was too anxious about Tony Wickersham to wait for the Colonel, so the two men agreed to meet at the Teller House back in Central City. If Patmore was delayed or if Tony needed immediate transport to Denver, they had a contingency plan to rendezvous at the Brown Palace. Patmore said he'd also take the time to bury the dead man.

The sun was going down, and the REO's headlights left a lot to be desired. Adding to his miseries, Bell was still borderline hypothermic, and exhaustion made his eyes feel gritty, the lids swollen and leaden. He was a man who knew his body's limits because he'd asked it to perform beyond them many times in the past. He felt he was coming up fast against a new limit now. It was only his concern for Tony — a stranger yet a friend — that drove him out of the mountains toward the slumping boomtown far down the road. The weight of responsibility was an added burden.

He finally reached town just as the sun slipped over the top of the Rockies, bringing on almost full dark with surprising suddenness. He parked near the Teller House, but left the engine running, and went into the hotel. The manager himself was behind the counter, and when Bell asked the location of Central City's doctor, the man came around and offered to escort him since it was around the block.

Together, the two men strode back out, Isaac invigorated by the manager's obvious concern. He killed the REO's motor on the way past the truck.

Around the corner, the manager rushed ahead to open a door for Bell, saying in a loud voice, "Hey, Doc, I got a patient for you. He looks to be in need of your help."

"Good God, man," Bell said indignantly. "I'm not here for myself but for a friend hurt in a hunting accident."

The hotel manager looked shocked that Bell wasn't in need of medical attention and embarrassed that he'd insulted one of his guests.

"A thousand pardons, Mr. Bell. I just . . . ah . . ."

"Don't worry yourself. I'm sure I look like death's apprentice. Or worse."

A voice from another room called out, "What's the problem? I'm rather busy."

"No problem, Doc. A little misunderstanding."

Bell took over the conversation. "Doctor, my name is Isaac Bell. I'm a detective with the Van Dorn Agency. Mr. Wickersham was assisting me when he was shot accidentally. How is he doing?"

"C'mon back and see for yourself."

Bell followed the voice through a curtained doorway, down a short hallway, and into a brightly lit room with clean tile floors and antiseptic-white walls. A table sat in the middle of the room, with an arc lamp overhead, and there were countless metal tables on rollers covered with surgical devices and other tools of the medical trade. A counter ran along the back wall and had its own washbasin with fresh water. There, a nurse was washing out bloody towels. In all, it was thoroughly modern, and not what Bell expected from a small Colorado mining town.

Tony Wickersham was atop the table while the doctor stood over him wearing a blood-smeared white coat over his suit pants and vest. He wore no tie. Tony was cocooned under a bladder of red rubber filled with hot water held in place by towels swaddled around him as though he were an infant. His color had retuned somewhat, but he was still paler than normal. He was also fast asleep.

"Once he started warming up," the doctor said, "I had to give him a few whiffs of chloroform to keep him from getting up off the table and rushing back to help you. I'm Paul Brinkerhoff, but everyone calls me Doc." He showed Bell the blood on his palm as reason to not shake hands.

"How is he?"

"No ill effects from the hypothermia. Blood vessels all seem to be undamaged, and under that water bottle he's pinking up nicely. The shoulder's another story. The arm can stay, but only time will tell how much function he'll have. The bullet did a lot of damage."

"Is there anything to be gained by taking him to Denver? Specialists? That sort of thing."

"The surgery's already done. The channel of the wound dictated what needed to be repaired, so that's that. He will certainly benefit from physiotherapy. A specialist will work the shoulder using proven techniques to increase motion, mobility, and strength. It's a tough road, but he's young and strong. But that's a little bit down the road. I'll want to keep him here for a few days and then send him back to Denver."

Bell nodded, encouraged. "As soon as we're back at the hotel I'm going to telephone his employers and let them know what's happening." Bell was thinking he'd contribute to the fund for Tony's upcoming rehabilitation, and he felt certain men like the Bloesers would also help pay.

"How about you, Mr. Bell? Are you sure you're physically okay?"

"Nothing a hot bath and a few stiff drinks won't cure, Doc. Thanks for your concern." Bell laid a hand on Tony Wickersham's good shoulder as a good-bye gesture and shook the doctor's hand anyway before heading back to the hotel with the manager.

"I know Tony and I know Ernst Bloeser, Mr. Bell. Would you like me to make the call for you?"

Although Bell was sorely tempted, Tony was his responsibility. "Kind of you to offer, but this is my bullet to take."

The manager set up the call through the various exchanges while Isaac downed a quick shot of whiskey in the bar. When the wires were aligned, the manager motioned for Bell to enter the booth just off the reception desk. Bell did and closed its accordion door. A light automatically flickered to life above him.

"Mr. Bloeser, this is Isaac Bell. Your brother and I met at the Brown Palace Hotel and he hired me to investigate the Little Angel Mine disaster."

"Hello, Mr. Bell. This is actually Hans Bloeser. I am with my brother this evening for dinner, hoping we might get some news from you."

"The news is not good, I'm afraid. Your man, Tony, was accidentally shot in the shoulder." Bell heard a sharp intake of breath over the staticky line. "He's going to be fine. The doc's going to keep him here in Central City for a few days before sending him home."

A few seconds passed while Hans reiterated the news to his brother. He finally told Bell, "When the time comes, Ernst will fetch Tony and keep him at his house until the lad is up and about."

"The doc here mentioned physiotherapy."

"*Ja*, we will find the best in Denver and he will work with Tony every day until he is, ah, right as rain."

"I'm heartened to hear he has such generous support."

"Mr. Bell, what about our reason for hiring you? Were you perhaps successful —"

Bell cut him off before he could finish the question. He cited the fact that this was an open wire, but, in truth, he wanted a fuller understanding of the situation from Colonel Patmore before telling the Bloesers anything. "Why don't we meet tomorrow night at the Brown Palace and I'll give you my full report."

"Very well, Mr. Bell. Until tomorrow."

He exited the telephone booth and asked the manager that when one Mr. Greggory Patmore arrived, Bell was to be told immediately. His room didn't have its own tub, but as it was between dinner and bedtime for most guests, no one disturbed him while he warmed in the large ceramic tub in the shared bathing facility. Afterward, he ate a late supper and had two more drinks. It was nearing ten at night and still no sign of the Colonel. Bell was too tired to consider this a bad omen. He repeated his instructions to the night man and went to bed.

Patmore didn't turn up until an hour after dawn. Bell was in the hotel restaurant, lingering over a coffee and staring idly out the window, when the military man came through from the lobby. He looked a little worse for wear, but, then again, he had been camping for the better part of a week.

"Good morning, Mr. Bell. I thought I could race the darkness back to town, but nights fall like a trip hammer in these parts and it grew too dark. Had to camp on the side of the road."

"Understood. I barely made it to town myself." Bell made a gesture for the Colonel to join him at the table.

Patmore accepted a mug of coffee from a waitress, curling his callused fingers around the earthenware cup to soak up its warmth before taking a sip. "Give me thirty to clean up. Then come up to my room. Number eighteen."

"Take more time if you need it."

"Twenty-five years in the Army drilled a lot of things into me, Mr. Bell, and being inspection-ready as quickly as possible was probably the first."

At the appointed time, Bell rapped a knuckle against the door of room eighteen and Patmore opened it almost immediately. He was now clean-shaven and scrubbed all the way down to his fingernails. His suit was a perfect fit over his well-toned body. His shoes were mirror-shined, and the dimple in the knot of his necktie was precisely centered.

Patmore left the door to his room open. His was at the end of the hall, so only one room abutted it. Bell assumed Patmore had rented that one as well. And now with his door open, no one could sneak up behind the other door to eavesdrop on their conversation through the keyhole.

Bell handed Patmore the picture he'd taken off the dead Frenchman of the man and his girl in front of the Eiffel Tower. Patmore examined it, front and back. "This your evidence he was French? He could have been a tourist."

"My thought exactly," Bell said evenly. "I have an identical picture with my wife. What tipped me off was the date."

Patmore looked again. "June 12, 1899. So?"

"Look at their clothes."

Patmore did as instructed. It took him about ten seconds to see what Bell had seen and he looked up with newfound respect in his eyes. "Glossed right over it."

"I did too, at first, but something didn't read right. They're wearing coats. The date is written out in the European fashion of putting the day first. They were visiting the tower on December sixth. From experience, I know the line to have your picture taken is a long one. The oh-so-unhappy-looking

165

Theresa is freezing. The date thing tells me they're European at the least. Since both are pretty young in this picture, I can assume they don't have a great deal of money, so this is a date or a first vacation. Either way, they won't stray too far from home. Therefore, our dead guy is French, though he can do a spot-on American accent. How'd I do?"

"His name was Marc Massard. He worked for a company called the Société des Mines de Lorraine, now headquartered in Paris. He and his partner — he's a Scotsman, by the way — are essentially company mercenaries. If La Société needs a rival taken out or a strike put down, Massard and Gly were the men to do it. Gly, especially, is a psychopath. Utterly ruthless."

"So what's this all about?" Bell asked.

"A rare element called byzanium."

"Never heard of it."

"It's radioactive, like radium, once it's refined out of its natural ore. Only a thimbleful of this stuff has ever been found, not enough to run any real tests, but enough to leave scientists speculating about its potential."

Bell made a quick mental connection. Marie Curie, though Polish by birth, worked in Paris alongside her husband and was the world's foremost authority on radium. He asked, "Valuable?"

"To call it the most precious substance on the planet is probably not an understatement. An ounce of gold is pegged at $20.67. An ounce of byzanium is estimated at about one-point-four million."

"Dollars?"

"Dollars." Patmore paused when Bell whistled his shock. "And Joshua Hayes Brewster found the motherlode of ore. He left Colorado two years ago to take a position with the Société des Mines de Lorraine, working under contract for the Tsar of Russia to open a lead mine on the Taimyr Peninsula. When the work ended a year ago last July, he was returning to the city of Archangel on the north coast of Siberia aboard a coastal steamer, which became lost in fog and eventually ran aground on the upper island of Novaya Zemlya.

"They were stuck on that hellhole for a month until they were rescued by the Russian Navy. During that time, Brewster did what prospectors always do in a new place — he crisscrossed the island looking for interesting minerals. One outcropping caught his attention, so he took some samples. Under the terms of his contract, he was obliged to turn over any and all geologic specimens. There were others from the Société aboard the steamer who knew he'd been prospecting, so he made sure his employers got what was their due. However, just like any good prospector, Brewster saved one for himself.

"Back in the States, fully two months after leaving the Taimyr Peninsula, he contacted the U.S. director of the Société to see what had happened to the minerals he'd found on Novaya Zemlya. He was told the samples were worthless and had been tossed out."

"He didn't believe them, did he?" Bell asked.

"Not for a second. He trusted his instincts. He gave the sample over to the Bureau of Mines in Washington. A geologist there, as well as another with the Natural History Museum at the Smithsonian, figured out the sample was byzanium ore. Brewster was sitting on a find worth half a billion dollars."

"Do the French know where it was?"

"No. Brewster never told them. What he did do is tell an old friend at the War Department."

"You?"

"My boss in Army Intelligence. They knew Congress wouldn't give them the money to mount an operation to recover the ore, and even requesting funds would announce to the world that there was something valuable on a desolate Russian island. This had to be hush-hush, and it had to be the French who bankrolled the expedition. By this point, the Société had sent teams back to Novaya Zemlya, with no luck. If they wanted a piece of the action, they needed Brewster.

"They agreed to Brewster's terms. But here's the thing. Joshua Hayes Brewster is going to double-cross the men of the Société and make off with the ore back to the United States."

"I get that," Bell said. "But what about the Little Angel Mine disaster? Why the ruse?"

"It was the French who insisted that Brewster and the others must work in complete secrecy. And rather than come up with nine different cover stories as to why the miners vanished from Central City, they cooked up the phony accident. Brewster is convinced that the real reason is the French plan to murder him and his men after they recover the byzanium ore."

"Where are he and his men now?"

"They're arriving in New York on a private train, along with a lot of gear they purchased in Denver. From there, they head to Paris for final briefings and to pick up more

169

equipment. And then the French will return Brewster to the island. He's going to tell them not to return until next June, but he assures us that he can be ready by May."

"How are they going to open a mine off the north coast of Siberia in the winter?"

"It's a tall order, yes, but Brewster told me that to reach the outcrop with the kind of equipment they have, the ground has to be frozen. When he was there in July, he had to wade through a chest-deep bog of melted permafrost to reach the outcrop."

"And you have someone ready to evacuate them off the island?"

Patmore looked away for a moment. Bell thought the man was about to lie to him. However, the Colonel blew out a breath and looked Isaac in the eye. "I'm still working on that."

"I appreciate the candor. And now I see your problem. Because Tony and I were looking into the accident, that we may know the truth, the Société's plan has to evolve, and that focuses additional suspicion on Brewster."

"And I need him to know that fact so he can alter plans as he sees fit."

"You have no way of contacting him?"

"Absolutely none. That was part of our operational security arrangements. From the time Joshua bluffed the French into backing his expedition, he could do nothing to jeopardize the mission. He didn't even know I was on overwatch following the disaster."

"So, what exactly do you want from me?" Bell asked, knowing the answer.

"I'm sure Foster Gly has gotten some warning to the Société, so killing him now won't do much good. Therefore, you've got to make contact with Brewster in Paris and warn him."

Bell had expected the second sentence of Patmore's answer. Not the first, though. Gly was obviously a dangerous man, and these were among the highest stakes he could imagine, but to so casually talk about murdering a man didn't seem right coming from a soldier wearing a West Point ring.

"If Brewster can't find a way to throw the French off their game somehow, they might station guards on the island or make sure their supply ship is in position to preempt our effort to smuggle the ore out of Russia."

"I'm not saying no, but why don't you go to Paris. Brewster knows you and will take your warning seriously."

"Deniability. If it's learned —" Patmore cut himself off, and his eyes shifted from

Bell's face. Isaac turned to look out the hotel room door as a man in an overcoat carrying a cheap cardboard suitcase reached the top of the stairs. He checked his room number off his key fob and turned down the hallway, unaware he'd been watched. The Colonel didn't speak until the man had entered his room and closed the door. "If it's learned I am an active duty officer in Army Intelligence, it could spark a diplomatic incident. Also, it would take a week of fighting bureaucracy to okay such a trip and by then it'll be too late. I first would need to return to Washington, debrief on my time here, and press for additional support. All that takes time. You, on the other hand, can take express trains to New York and hop the fastest ship to Europe."

"Not to sound mercenary, but what about payment for my time?" Bell had already decided to take the case and would do so pro bono, but Joseph Van Dorn would have an aneurism if Bell walked away from some government largesse.

"We have some contingency funds that will more than cover your time and expenses. I'm sure I can draw something up, provided you keep receipts."

"No need for anything formal, Colonel. I'll take it on faith."

"You'll go?"

"Yes. I'm thinking about train schedules. It would be opportune if I can get to New York before they board their steamer, but I can't imagine them laying over in Manhattan for very long."

"No. Your best chance is in Paris. But you need to make your approach covertly. The Société des Mines has a large security apparatus."

"I am versed in operating clandestinely, Colonel."

"Sorry. I tend to overmanage my people. I do want to make you aware that Marc Massard has a twin brother, Yves, who also works in their security arm. Brewster got to know the two brothers. And Gly, to some extent, because all of them were at the lead mine during that time when the nearest village was complaining that their water was being contaminated. The loudest agitators died in a barn fire, and Gly and Yves joked about the sounds they heard during the conflagration."

"Lovely," Bell said sarcastically.

Patmore nodded. "Any talk of contamination abruptly ended, and the three men returned to Paris. Marc Massard tried to murder you yesterday by burying you alive and yet he's considered the kindest of the three."

9

They firmed up details, mostly about how to reach each other, and parted company. Bell now felt the pressure of time bearing down on him. He returned to the lobby to use the telephone. He still had to give Hans Bloeser a report on his findings but wanted to move the meeting from the Brown Palace bar to Union Station. As a frequent traveler, he was well aware of the limitations to transcontinental travel, and, as of now, every second counted. Once things were set, he returned to Doc Brinkerhoff's office to check on Tony Wickersham.

They had moved Tony into a tiny back room with a single window overlooking a grim brick alley. He was lying elevated in bed, his shoulder swaddled under a massive bandage. When he turned from the uninspiring view, his face split into a bright but pained smile.

"Mr. Bell."

"Tony, how are you holding up?"

"Hurts like the devil, to be honest, but the doctor says it's best to wean off painkillers, so I must wait twenty minutes for my next shot. But I can move my fingers and thumb, which is proof there was no nerve damage."

Bell moved closer in order to lay a comforting hand on the Englishman's good shoulder. "That's wonderful. I've spoken with Hans Bloeser and he says that you are to stay with his brother for the entirety of your convalescence. And that they are going to hire a specialist to make sure you retain as much function as possible."

"I guess I can't ask for more than that," he said, looking pleased with the outcome of his ordeal. "Mr. Bell, can you tell me what happened after I blacked out? I don't remember a thing."

"I'm not sure myself," Bell lied. "The hunter who shot you by mistake never came forward. I tried to find the fiend but saw no trace. While I was looking for the shooter, men from the Satan Mine brought you here."

"I kind of recall an explosion."

"That was a little later," Bell bluffed. "As they were getting ready to take you away, the lead miner from the Satan insisted we

176

blow the mine entrance and stop the flow of water into his property."

"That makes sense," the young man said, now that the situation was more clarified in his mind. "What about the Little Angel Mine? Did you find Brewster and the others?"

Bell had considered how he was going to proceed. "Couldn't get all the way to the back of the mine where they were likely working, so I'm afraid the answer is inconclusive."

"What about the hints we found? Did they tell you anything?"

Bell's voice took on a serious, tutorial tone. "In my business, you either have proof or you don't. There is no third option. There is no gray. It's black or white. Period. If I can't absolutely prove otherwise, I have no choice but to endorse the official view."

"That they all died."

"As far as I'm concerned, they're all dead."

"I guess I was hoping for another answer," Tony said.

"That's the other thing about being a detective — never go in looking for an answer you want. It's enough just to find the truth, without personal bias." Bell stepped back. "Wonder if I can ask a favor."

"Of course."

"May I borrow your truck to get back to Denver? There isn't a train until late afternoon, and I will likely lose a day getting back to New York. I haven't seen my wife in quite some time."

Wickersham gave him a little wolfish smile. "Understand perfectly, Mr. Bell. It's no trouble at all."

"I'm meeting Mr. Bloeser at Union Station. He said he'll bring one of his employees to drive the truck to his brother's place so it will be there during your convalescence."

"Not sure how long it'll be before I can handle driving, but . . ." Tony's voice trailed off.

Bell wished he could explain to Tony that he hadn't been shot for nothing and that there was more afoot than he could possibly know. He decided there and then to send Tony a detailed letter when the affair was ended so he would know the crucial part he'd played in its opening gambit.

"You'll be up and about before you know it. For now — and I'm sure everyone has told you this — the best thing is to get your rest."

"I know."

"I'll look you up next time I'm in Denver."

"I'd like that, Mr. Bell."

"And Tony, thank you for all your help."

Wickersham pointed at his bandaged shoulder. "Can't say it was a pleasure, but you're welcome, Mr. Bell."

Isaac caught Dr. Brinkerhoff and asked if there was any payment due and was told that the Bloesers were paying for Tony's treatment. He thanked the man again and went on his way.

The track out of the mountains and on to Denver was much better than the trails up to the mines, so all Bell had to do was top off the REO's fuel tank and make sure the spare can was full too. It was just under forty miles, and mostly downhill, but he didn't want to take the chance of getting stranded. He also made certain he had spare water in a separate can for engine coolant. Tony had extra lubricating oil in a tin, alongside the toolkit, in a hinged box in the truck's bed.

Road travel improved every day, but it was nowhere near reliable.

He asked the barman at the hotel to put together some food for his trip while he repacked his bag and settled the bill. Bell stowed his bag in the back of the truck, took off his hat and wedged it under the seat since at speed it would likely blow off, and left the town of Central City behind him. He had come here to solve one mystery but instead found himself embroiled in international intrigue, facing men who thought nothing of taking another's life. It wasn't the first time he'd found himself in such a situation, but it gave him pause to consider how long it would be before his luck ran out and his opponents had the upper hand.

A little over two hours of driving brought him to Denver. The truck had run flawlessly, but he'd stopped to help another motorist climbing the Front Range Mountains whose radiator had run dry. He parked the truck outside Union Station. He was chilled to the bone but had made it with twenty minutes to spare before Hans Bloeser was scheduled to arrive.

He strode into the tall, echoing main hall and quickly located an idle ticketing agent. Though the man was extraordinarily efficient, it took all of Bell's time cushion to find trains that would get him to New York as quickly as possible. The route out of Denver was straight to Topeka, Kansas, where he'd catch up to the Atchison, Topeka and Santa Fe line's California Limited that had already come through on its way out of Los Angeles. Once he reached Chicago, he could buy a ticket for the eighteen-hour express run to New York on the 20th Century Limited.

Hans Bloeser found him just as he was finishing paying for the tickets. The man with Bloeser was introduced as Stephen, an assistant from the bank who would drive Tony Wickersham's REO to Ernst Bloeser's house in Golden.

They found a booth at the station's lunch counter and ordered coffee from the overworked waiter. They first discussed Tony's condition and future needs. Bell did offer to help pay some of the expenses because he felt guilty over what had transpired. Bloeser wouldn't hear of it.

"So finally we come to what you wanted to know," Bell said. "And, regrettably, I have to tell you that my investigation was inconclusive. A section of the mine shaft had collapsed before I reached the tunnel's end. In all likelihood, Brewster and the others are sealed off behind the wall of rubble, as had been reported by the eyewitness and press accounts."

"No other clues?"

"I am sorry to say, no. There was nothing in what little I was able to find that led me to believe anything other than that the men planned to return from work at the end of their shift. I don't know why Brewster jumped your brother's claim and tried to find ore in a worthless shaft. Because of the massive outlay of time, resources, and especially money it would take to breach the tunnel to its end, no one ever will." Bell laid it on a little thick so the Brothers Bloeser would let the matter drop without further inquiry.

"Mr. Bell, no one can ever accuse you of not doing a thorough job. This has cost us time and money enough, and let's not forget poor Tony's injury. We'll let the matter rest just as surely as those men now rest at the back of the Little Angel Mine."

Bell finished the last of his coffee and stood. He resettled his hat on his head and took up his leather suitcase in his left hand, leaving his right free to shake both men's hands. "I would prefer to stay and chat, but I have a very tight schedule to get back to New York."

"A pressing case?"

"A long-abandoned wife."

Bloeser chuckled. "Even more pressing, sir. Safe travels, Mr. Bell."

"Thank you, Mr. Bloeser. While the task was certainly not a pleasure, meeting you was."

Bell strode across the open concourse and

found his way to the proper platform. He mounted the stairs onto the dark green Pullman car and eased into the saloon from the outside vestibule. He noted immediately that his Pullman was at least twenty years old and woefully out of date. The benches were dark, overstuffed affairs with deep-set buttons that reminded him of a spinster aunt's front parlor. Also, the car didn't have electric lighting but was lit by Pintsch gas globes mounted on the ceiling.

Most of the passengers, he saw, were tired men, returning home from sales calls or meetings, or brighter-faced men heading off to call on potential sales prospects or attend big meetings. However, there were two families. One had a single child in a basket that appeared just months old. The other had two towheaded boys of about six. That was what his eyes took in. His ears told him something altogether much worse. The infant was wailing at the top of its lungs, a high-pitched scream that waxed and waned as it drew breath and protested some outrage that its mother could not appease.

As for the two boys, they were in a full-on argument consisting of the phrases *Are too* and *Am not* shouted back and forth while their mother tried to shush them and the father had his nose buried in his paper and seemingly didn't hear.

"David, do something," the long-suffering wife intoned as Bell threaded past.

"About what, dear?"

"The boys, David. The boys."

"Hmm?"

Bell and Marion knew they wanted children when they could both devote more time to a homelife rather than their current vagabond existence. Isaac vowed that he wouldn't become one of those disengaged fathers who left childrearing to his wife. His own father had been as much a part of his upbringing as his mother, and for that he was grateful.

He was less grateful that this leg of the trip was seventeen hours. The boys would eventually wear themselves out and rest just fine, but the baby was far too young to sleep through the night. Come nightfall, when the porter reconfigured the bench seats into the upper and lower sleeping berths, the child's midnight cries would wake them all.

Bell shook his head, recalling one particular night in his pursuit of the circus thieves. He'd been in the open section of a Pullman car like this with a drunk who snored loudly enough that the porter had to finally roust him from his berth and have him sleep it off in the empty dining car.

During the first part of the journey, Bell left his seat to relax in the lounge car and enjoy a whiskey and soda while he wrote out copious notes about his recent investigation into the Little Angel disaster, the subsequent confrontation, Tony's injury, and the revelations laid out by Colonel Patmore. He ate supper with several single travelers at a table in the twin-unit dining car.

By the time he returned to his car, the porter had converted all the seats for sleeping. Bell at least had a lower bunk. The car was quiet, the gas lamps dimmed to a faint glow. Outside, the moon shone bright silver across the featureless prairie. Bell thanked the porter. He detested the practice of calling them all George, after the founder of the company, George Pullman. If he knew the man from previous trips, he'd call him by his given name. Otherwise, he'd converse in such a way that avoided using a name at all.

He crawled into his berth and then stripped out of his clothes and changed into sleeping attire. The heat had been turned down, so he did this quickly and slid under the blankets. Everything was quiet save for the rhythmic tempo of wheels over rails, a mechanical lullaby that usually put Bell to sleep in seconds.

The baby began crying just before he slid into unconsciousness and didn't relent for the next hour.

And on it went across the country. The locomotive wasn't hauling a particularly heavy load, and the terrain was flat, and this meant fewer stops to take on water and fuel. While the stops themselves were short, and fifteen thousand gallons of water and twenty-plus tons of coal could be loaded in less than five minutes, it took time to slow the train comfortably from fifty miles per hour, and considerably longer to accelerate back up to speed again. Still, they reached Topeka ahead of the California Limited. As before, he slept in an open car since all the private cabins were taken.

Fourteen hours later, the train arrived at Chicago's Dearborn Station. The New York Central Railroad's 20th Century Limited left the city via the LaSalle Street Station. The two were only a few blocks apart, but the distance seemed much more formidable thanks to an icy rain slashing the sidewalks and buildings. It was the kind of storm that lofted men's hats and inverted ladies' umbrellas and led to a lack of available taxis.

Bell had plenty of time — the 20th Century was an overnight express, after all —

186

but he felt the burden of time growing heavier with each passing minute, and his impatience became unbearable, standing outside the station, watching car after car sweep past on the watery road. Just as he was about to toss caution aside and walk the five blocks, a liveried taxi pulled up.

The ride was brief, but he still tipped the driver well, for driving through such miserable conditions, and headed into the next terminal.

He purchased a ticket and was relieved to learn he had a drawing room to himself. Though he was hungry, he put off eating at the station's diner counter. He rode the night train from New York at least once a month, on average, and knew the train's chef was an absolute master. He sent a couple of coded cables to the New York office, updating the staff on his location and making certain someone had booked an express liner to Europe.

As it stood, the major lines — White Star, Cunard, Hamburg America, Dutch-American, and the French line Compagnie Générale Transatlantique — cooperated in such a fashion that there was a sailing to Europe every day of the week, and sometimes more. The trick, Bell knew, wasn't to get on the first ship out of Manhattan but the fastest one to get him to Le Havre, the closest port to Paris.

At last, Bell walked down the now famous red carpet covering the trackside platform along the length of the express train and boarded his car.

"Mr. Isaac," he was greeted enthusiastically by a redcap with a wide, friendly smile. "Didn't know you were traveling with us tonight."

"Short notice and all, Tom," he told the Pullman-employed porter. "I've got the drawing room tonight."

"And I'll take real fine care of you, Mr. Isaac."

"You always do."

"Need help with your bag?"

"No, I'm fine. Thanks."

"Just so you know, the inlet scoop acted up on the run here last night, but the conductor and engineer say it's all fixed up now."

"That's a relief."

Unlike the trains Bell had taken across the country, the 20th Century Limited didn't need to stop in every jerkwater town — so named because the engineer jerked a chain to get water flowing from the towering cisterns — to satisfy the locomotive's unquenchable thirst. This train was outfitted with a special siphon that could be lowered from the locomotive tender. The Limited would need to slow some as they came to special lengths of track that were flooded with water in anticipation of their passing. The siphon would scoop water straight into the tender, and, once the tender was full, the train would speed up again. This ingenious system ensured the rail linking America's two greatest cities had the highest average speed of any long-distance run in the nation.

"Anyone on board tonight?" Bell asked, meaning anyone of significance.

"No, Mr. Isaac. No need for you to be snooping about my train tonight."

Bell laughed. "I'm going to set my luggage in my cabin and head to the observation car for a drink."

"Do you want me to make up your room now?"

"Why don't you. I've been traveling non-stop for three weeks and I am exhausted."

"Well, you'll be with Mrs. Bell soon enough. She'll cure what ails ya."

Bell chuckled. Truer words were never spoken.

Eighteen hours after pulling out of the La-Salle Street Station, the Limited rumbled into Grand Central. Bell had completed a report about his upcoming mission for Joseph Van Dorn. He kept it light on details, which was his usual style. Van Dorn trusted Bell's judgment, so they'd always enjoyed a tight working relationship. He had also managed to sleep well and felt better than he had in days. He'd repacked his case and was standing in the vestibule when the train shuddered to a stop. He tipped his hat to Tom, who was readying steps for less athletic passengers, and began striding the length of the platform. While the urgency of his mission was a driving force within him, when he was so close to home his desire to be with his wife superseded everything.

He crossed the richly appointed Great Hall, where dishwater light filtered through the multiple windows. The Chicago storm had stayed with them across the country, and the sky was leaden. He climbed the stairs for street level and had started looking for a taxi when he spotted a beautiful Rolls-Royce automobile and its even more stunning driver.

Wisps of Marion's blond hair had escaped the leather cap she wore as she stood, clad in baggy jodhpurs, with one foot on the car's running board and her hip cocked alluringly. Her eyes were the green of the clearest emeralds and smiled just as much as her lips. Marion was a classic beauty and spent plenty of time on movie sets explaining to people that she was the director and not a starlet.

She tried to play aloof for a second longer but couldn't. She cried out like a little girl seeing a new doll on Christmas morning and launched herself at her husband. She kissed him openly, social conventions be damned.

"What are you doing here?" Isaac asked when they'd detangled themselves.

"Driving you to Hoboken."

Bell's enthusiasm flagged. "Today?"

Marion nodded, stroking his cheek. "The office called first thing this morning, my poor darling. You're booked on the *Rotterdam* for this afternoon's sailing. I'm going to drive you to the Algonquin Hotel, where we will enjoy a few hours in each other's company, as it were, and then it's off to beautiful Hoboken, where the Dutch-American Steamship Company docks their ships."

Bell saw that Marion had two large suitcases loaded in the backseat of the Rolls. He knew she'd have thought of everything for him, including additional ammunition and a few accessories he usually carried in the field but hadn't thought necessary in pursuit of the circus thieves.

"Wait," he said as Marion slid into the driver's seat. "The *Rotterdam* doesn't make landfall in France."

"Special stop. A funicular railroad engine was too late being delivered here to make it aboard the French line's *La Provence* and apparently they need the little loco right away. The *Rotterdam* has a shallow enough draft for Le Havre Harbor. *Et voilà!* Rather than a relaxing night together, you and I have to tryst like Antony and Cleopatra."

Bell laughed aloud, always loving Marion's turn of phrase. "In that case, my Nile Queen, let's get this chariot in gear."

10

The crossing to Europe aboard the *Rotterdam* was about the worst Isaac Bell had ever experienced. He could place blame on neither ship nor crew but squarely on the shoulders of Mother Nature. The storm that seemingly followed him from Denver, through Chicago, and on to New York, had dogged the Dutch liner across the Atlantic. While Bell had never felt the full effects of *mal de mer,* even he had spent one night in his cabin nibbling bland water biscuits and drinking a cloying pink dyspeptic fluid that was originally marketed for children with cholera but which was finding a market among adults suffering stomach issues.

To his inner ear, the rain-lashed train from Le Havre to Paris bucked and yawed and rolled ponderously even though the tracks were level and straight. It would take a couple of whiskies and a comfortable bed in the new Art Deco–style Hôtel Lutetia to make him right. Marion had made him promise that he wouldn't stay at the Ritz, their customary residence in Paris, without her.

He woke early on his first full morning in France, and when he rolled off the feather-soft bed and stood, he paused to see if the floor was still in motion as it had been the previous night. He smiled at the fact he did not sway. He'd gotten his land legs back. As with so many modern hotels, it had an *en suite,* which made getting ready in the morning so much quicker.

Bell entered the lobby restaurant at a little past eight and saw that his guest was already seated and enjoying a pot of tea. Cigarette smoke coiled from the cut-glass tray at his elbow. He smiled when he saw Bell but did not stand. Bell crossed the room, noting the other patrons, mostly businessmen or gentleman tourists who'd come down early while their wives readied themselves upstairs. Paris being Paris, one does not act the tourist unless elegantly turned out at all times.

The Van Dorn Agency was slowly expanding into Europe. Joseph saw, and Bell heartily agreed, that the world was becoming much smaller due to the speed and safety of the Atlantic express liners and the interconnectivity of burgeoning international trade. It was inevitable that cases originating in the United States would spill over into countries lying across the pond. Therefore, they currently had an office in London, and a one-person contingent in Berlin, but they had yet to establish a formal presence in France. They'd had one man, Horace Bronson, for a short time, but it hadn't worked out. This left Bell relying on a personal contact he'd cultivated on the few trips he'd taken to Paris, always with his wife, who loved the City of Lights more than any other in the world.

Bell and his best friend and fellow investigator, Archie Abbott, had been trying to come up with an appropriate name for such an underhanded business contact. The best they'd managed was "fixer." Bring the person a problem and they fix it for you no matter what.

He missed Archie on this trip. He could have used the help, but Abbott was off tracking a lawyer who'd facilitated bogus contracts for companies doing business in Panama, building the great canal. That case had turned scandalous when it was found the absconding attorney had a young mistress in the family way. Bell had no doubt that Archie was just eating it all up with wolfish delight.

"Henri, old boy, good to see you," Bell said by way of greeting the man at the table. He slid into a chair opposite the Frenchman and, only when settled, reached across to shake his friend's left hand.

Henri Favreau had lost his right arm as a boy during what the French call the War of 1870 and what Isaac Bell knew as the Franco-Prussian War. He had been an unwitting civilian caught in the cross fire of an attempted breakout from the city of Metz, which the Germans had besieged. His younger sister and his mother had been killed. His father, a conscript, died later in the war, leaving young, crippled Henri to fend for himself in a nation afflicted with chaos and strife.

Whatever lessons he'd learned in those early days when the beleaguered country saw so many starving, they had served him well. Henri Favreau was now a man who exchanged favors for a living. He knew practically everybody from every stratum of society, from politician to prostitute — who, in Henri's eyes, were one and the same.

Joseph Van Dorn had written a letter of introduction for Bell years earlier when he and Marion were on a European holiday. Van Dorn didn't know Favreau personally but shared enough mutual friends to give the letter import. Despite their age difference, the French fixer and the American investigator had an instant rapport, one that only grew stronger on their subsequent meetings.

"Isaac, *mon ami.*" Henri smiled with tobacco-stained teeth. His English was much better than Isaac's French. "You are too handsome and refined not to be a Parisian. How is that beautiful wife of yours?"

"Upset that I'm here without her but doing well. What about Claire?"

"If she is not nagging me, she is not happy. So, she is very happy indeed." He laughed at his own joke.

Favreau was a plain-featured man in most all ways. But not when he let his guard down and the intelligence and shrewdness behind his dark eyes shone through. It was in those tiny flashes that his brilliance suddenly made him seem much more extraordinary and gave him a natural charisma that drew people to him without their having the slightest understanding why. Bell once told him it was the beguilement of the cobra.

Bell caught the eye of a waiter in a white uniform and indicated he wanted coffee. No one was within earshot, so the two old friends could talk freely. But they kept their voices well modulated.

"I am delighted to see you again, Isaac, but I confess I am not so pleased at your reason to be here."

One of the cables Isaac had had sent from the Van Dorn office in New York was a request for Henri Favreau to get background information on the Société des Mines de Lorraine and, specifically, where their employee Yves Massard kept an office if Favreau was unable to find the home of his deceased twin, Marc.

"I'm not thrilled either, if truth be told," Bell admitted.

Favreau grunted. "Let me start by saying municipal records show out of a population of two point eight million people, Paris boasts no less than one hundred and twenty Marc Massards and exactly none mention a wife named Theresa."

Bell's plan to reach Joshua Hayes Brewster rested on his ability to find Theresa, the woman from Marc Massard's photograph, and gain her trust. His assumption being they had married, or were at least still together, and she was privy to some aspects of his work.

"I figured it would turn out like that. Even if it's a long shot, you still have to —"

"Pull the trigger," Henri said for him, and held up a discreet hand to pause the conversation while a waiter approached with Bell's coffee and a basket of warm croissants, nestled in fine linen, with a plate of fresh country butter as yellow as a daffodil and some fruit preserves.

When the waiter moved on, Favreau pulled a folded piece of paper from his jacket pocket and slid it over to Bell. Bell opened it and gave it a quick glance, memorizing the address of Yves Massard's office. He slid it back. The scrap was soon turning to ash next to the stubbed-out butts of the Gauloises Henri smoked in an unending chain.

"Okay, that covers the favors you asked for. Now I am going to do you for another by saying whatever this is, Isaac, drop it. The Société des Mines is not a company you want to trifle with. They are like Germany's Krupp. Their tentacles are everywhere, not just in mining but in foundries, shipbuilding, heavy industry, arms. The list is endless, and they did not grow so big by being the nicest or the fairest. The company is run by a ruthless family dynasty. The employees are treated like serfs and live in constant fear. If the company wants something, they simply take it and legalities be damned.

"There was a fire at one of their facilities here in Paris. Eight men were killed. The investigation was inconclusive, though poor working conditions were considered partly to blame."

"Factories are dangerous places," Bell pointed out.

"That's not the whole story. That part wasn't covered up. What came next was. The families of those who died were evicted from company housing that same day. Utter heartlessness. It was a scene of bawling widows and their wailing children. One reporter tried to get the story printed. His editor refused, naturally, because the newspaper sold plenty of advertising to Société subsidiaries. When the reporter complained to others about the deplorable actions taken by the company, word got back and he was visited by two men who broke each of his ten fingers."

Bell couldn't help but swallow involuntarily. He said, "I was told a story about a village in Russia where the elders were burned alive to stop complaints about water contamination coming from a Société lead mine."

"Such a tale does not surprise me. The government won't act against them because they represent such a large part of the French economy. When the socialist Prime Minister, Émile Combes, was in office, he tried to take them on. He was told in no uncertain terms that if the government ever tried to interfere with Société business again, they would immediately fire every employee and shutter every factory and office. Such a move would have toppled the government and crippled the country. Combes backed off, and the Société continues to run its affairs with impunity."

With nothing to be gained discussing their ruthlessness, Bell changed tacks. "Is there a connection between the Société and Marie Curie?"

The Frenchman gave it a few seconds of thought. "Not that I am aware of. I read a news account that she and her team had to process tons of pitchblende ore for mere milligrams of radium. Someone had to be her supplier for the raw material. It very well could be the Société. They are a mining concern, after all. Do you know if there is a link?"

"No. Just supposition."

"Seriously, Isaac, what is this about?"

Bell smiled ruefully. "I wish I could tell you, Henri, but my hands are tied. I can say that I am trying to stop the Société des

Mines from pulling off another of their ruthless operations." He pulled a pint bottle from his coat. In it was a dark amber liquid. On its leaf-shaped label was pictured a quaint wooden shed with smoke pouring from its chimney. It stated that the contents were one hundred percent Vermont maple syrup. "I believe this covers your time."

Henri showed his brown teeth again in another smile and pocketed the bottle. "A certain politician's American wife adores this stuff, and I have someone who needs a favor from him." Favreau stood. "I must take my leave. I have meetings all morning long. I need not tell you, old friend, to be careful. A company comfortable threatening the leader of France will have no qualms silencing an American private detective."

"*Merci,* Henri."

"And if you need anything else from me, just ask. No one here likes you cowboys."

Favreau put his hat firmly on and made for the exit out to the main lobby. Bell remained at the table. He ordered a real breakfast of eggs with *sauce hollandaise,* ham, and fried potatoes with onion and tarragon.

11

One of Bell's skills as a detective was his ability to recall faces in the proper context. Once he saw someone, he could usually remember that person months, and sometimes years, later and the circumstance of their meeting. He didn't need the picture of a young Marc Massard with his girl at the Eiffel Tower to know how his twin, Yves, would appear, but still he studied the old photo, memorizing the young lady's features as well as Massard's.

After his meal, Bell spoke with the concierge. He wasn't familiar enough with Paris to know all its neighborhoods and *arrondissements,* and the office address for Yves Massard was in an unknown part of the city. The hotelier told him that it was a safe neighborhood that abutted some industrial zones. Relatively crime-free, but also an area into which few tourists ventured. He suggested that *monsieur* would be best off not dressing so finely for a meeting in an area like that and to pay the cabman to wait until the conclusion of his business. Just in case.

Bell thanked the man. He took a motorized taxi across the Seine and through half of Paris to drive by the building in question. Like almost every other structure in the city, it was a light gray limestone affair, four stories tall, and probably fifty years old. The mansard roof was sheathed in black iron, and all the windows were trimmed in iron as well. The street was busy, with several open-air markets nearby where trucks and wagons from outside the city were parked and foodstuffs and light manufactured goods were being sold to vendors and then resold to consumers.

The air was sooty — they were not far from a power plant converting coal to electricity — and heavy with the threat of more rain. The streets were washed clean, but dark water bubbled up from one sewer cover from the unseen labyrinth of storm-water tunnels underpinning every corner of the city.

Bell recalled from news reportage at the time that Paris had suffered a severe flood the prior year. The river crested seventeen feet above its normal height, and some city streets were under three feet of water and more. He imagined that with all the recent rain, the authorities must be concerned about a similar catastrophe. He'd spotted several crews working over open sewers on the drive to Massard's address.

There were no nearby cafés, much to his frustration. They made excellent observation posts, once a daily price for a table is worked out with the owner beforehand. Bell would have to watch Massard's office as a street loiterer. He could have rented an automobile and waited in that, but beat cops became suspicious if they saw someone sitting in a car hour after hour. Best to stay mobile and avoid the police altogether.

Bell had the taxi drive him back to his hotel. Directly across the street was the Le Bon Marché department store, some say the world's first such establishment. He entered the store and found the clothing he would need. He bought working-class-style pants and shirt, as well as a black overcoat and a shorter gray jacket, and two different colored hats. He also bought an umbrella, as the one he'd packed was too fine a quality. He figured he'd need to wait outside the building for only three hours, otherwise he would have bought a third coat and hat.

He took his purchases back to his room at the Hôtel Lutetia and changed clothing. He checked himself in the mirror. He could comfortably wear the short jacket under the overcoat and it remained invisible. The brimmed hat completed the picture of a nondescript worker. Once he stripped off the longer coat and replaced the hat for a soft cap, his appearance changed entirely. He now looked like one of the truck drivers from the markets near Massard's address. He had long since trained himself to use different gaits and postures so to the casual observer he would be two different men moving about the street, seemingly both going somewhere but never actually reaching any destinations.

He donned his proper suit for another meal in the hotel restaurant before changing yet again. This time, he had the cabbie drop him a few blocks from his destination. He paid the man and stepped out. A mist chilled the air. He set off walking, taking note of the expressions on the faces around him and adopting a similar vacantness. These people worked long hours, for little pay, and had few things in their lives to make them brighter. Unlike Bell, to them life was something to be lived through rather than celebrated.

By the time he rounded the corner onto Massard's block, he was fully in his role. He settled himself next to a building two down from the large Société des Mines edifice, popped open the umbrella, and waited, occasionally pulling out his pocket watch and scanning the pedestrians on the sidewalks as though waiting for someone. No one paid him the slightest interest.

He changed positions every fifteen minutes, and after an hour he went around the corner and quickly shed the long black coat to reveal the gray jacket underneath. He swapped hats and bundled up the coat and trilby hat and umbrella. One of Paris's many newspaper kiosks sat on the corner, and Bell managed to stash his bundle amid the bundles of old papers not yet hauled away from the establishment. He was back in position in a matter of seconds to watch the building's front door.

For another hour, truck driver Bell paced up and down the block, moving at the same rate as others on the street but showing impatience and irritation as if his afternoon were being wasted. He watched everyone who came in or out of the Société building. A few times, he thought he'd spotted Yves Massard, but a closer inspection revealed his mistake. He was just about to retrieve his other disguise when the wooden door he'd watched so carefully swung open.

Three men emerged in a line and started walking in a group. Bell felt the blood in his veins turn to ice as adrenaline flooded his system. He knew there was no way Yves Massard could recognize him. They had never laid eyes on each other, but Bell's first reaction was to turn away. The man was an exact copy of the man he'd seen murdered in Colorado. He fought instinct and kept moving naturally as Massard and his two companions walked past. One of the Frenchmen said something and they all laughed throatily.

He let them get twenty paces ahead before he turned around to follow. On the way, he ducked behind the kiosk once again and changed on the fly. Even if Massard turned now, the man tailing them looked and moved nothing like the teamster they'd just passed outside his office building.

Bell reconsidered his assessment of Yves Massard. There was a darkness about him that Marc didn't seem to have. Marc had been more open, friendlier. This brother looked tense and ready for a fight. Then, he re-reconsidered. His only interaction with Marc had occurred when he was playing the role of Gibbs, Denver journalist. As he had so thoroughly fooled Bell and Tony Wickersham, the man was a skilled actor and linguist and could probably hide his true nature. Bell assumed he was just as dark-souled as this twin.

The trio went to a worker's café, crowded with tired men quenching a thirst for *une bière.* This street was lined with such establishments. Bell entered a bar across from Massard's, got himself a beer, and worked his way to the mullioned window that was so old he could see dimples where the glassmaker's pipe had been. He figured he had plenty of time. A man with Massard's fearsome reputation would likely be a big drinker. The bar was crowded and the air gray with cigarette smoke. But it was warm, and Isaac's feet and hands had been starting to ice up.

Much to his surprise, Yves Massard stepped out from the café after just a few minutes, time enough for a small beer at best. Right behind him, coatless, came Foster Gly. His bald head was covered with a thin sheen of perspiration. He was huge, with shoulders as wide as a hangman's gallows, a neck like a tree stump, and hands that resembled anvils. He was wearing just shirtsleeves, and Bell could see the muscles of Gly's chest were like slabs of granite. He and Massard spoke for a moment. As Yves turned to head back down the street, Gly looked directly to where Bell stood in the bar. Bell was back enough that he would be little more than a shadow from this distance, but he could see wheels turning in the Scotsman's head, as if he could sense he was being watched.

Bell moved farther from the window. The moment stretched out before Gly stepped into his café again. Isaac let out a breath he hadn't known he was holding. Being this close to Gly was an opportunity to find Brewster and the others quicker than his original plan since, ostensibly, Gly was the Société's liaison with the American miners. However, tailing him on his own wasn't possible. Gly had an animal's instincts, a cunning that would alert him that he was being followed. To do a proper job, Bell would need at least a half dozen people with access to multiple outfits. That would require transportation, a base of operation, coordination. It was all too much.

Instead, he took off the black trench coat, folded it so it resembled a package, and left the bar. From Gly's perspective, he'd been a dark silhouette at best. Now he was a guy in a light gray jacket heading home after a quick drink. It was a precaution.

Massard was half a block away, moving easily through the thickening crowds. The rain had started picking up again, icy. Once Bell was certain Gly couldn't see him from any of the café's windows, he shook out the overcoat and slipped it on. He also unfurled his umbrella.

Ahead, Yves Massard hunched his shoulders against the rain and walked three more blocks, not once turning around or showing any interest in his surroundings. Bell kept a loose watch on him, getting close and then backing off. He also watched his own back, but there was no bald giant coming up behind him, eager to finish what he'd started in the foothills outside of Central City.

They entered a neighborhood of identical four-story apartment buildings, most with stores or cafés on the ground floor and three stories of flats above. The streets were narrow, giving them a certain claustrophobic feel. Bell stepped up his pace, certain that his quarry would duck into one of the buildings, and he needed to be certain which one. He was thirty feet back and could see Massard through the ranks of pedestrians making their way through the storm.

Bell's first big break came in spotting Massard on his first day of observation, so he wasn't expecting to have lightning strike twice. But it did. He had no real interest in

Yves Massard. He wanted to trail the man's girlfriend or wife.

There was no hard-and-fast rule about it, but in Bell's experience identical twins, if they remain close as adults, tend to spend a great deal of time together. Marc and Yves Massard worked out of the same office, so it stood to reason they would live near each other and, by extension, the women in their lives would be close, possibly sisters or cousins, but not necessarily the case.

A woman came out of the building just as Massard was reaching for the door. She'd obviously been waiting for him in the entry vestibule and saw him through the glass. She slid an arm around his waist and tilted her face for a kiss, which he dutifully delivered. She then handed him an umbrella, which he opened and held more for her benefit than his. She had glossy dark hair and was rather tall and slender.

The couple started back the way Massard had come. Bell didn't react. He was just another salaryman on the way home from work. The woman wore a waterproof cape over her outfit that was buttoned up to her throat and she had on practical shoes rather than flat slippers or the increasingly popular heels. Her makeup was artful, accentuating her eyes, which were dark, and her lips, which were generous and strawberry red.

With but a glance, Bell committed her face to memory. Massard had no doubt heard of his brother's death from Gly in a telegram more than a week earlier, and Bell could tell the woman was trying to cheer him up. As they passed, something she said curled his lip into a smile and he tightened his grip around her waist. Bell doubted they were visiting the Widow Massard tonight. Tonight looked like a dinner date, so Bell continued on, leaving the pair in his wake. Tomorrow he'd take up following this woman until she went to console the grieving Theresa Massard. It was she who held Bell's ultimate interest because she was going to be his key to getting a message to Joshua Brewster.

Thinking back to what Colonel Patmore had said about Massard's ruthlessness, it didn't seem compatible with the tableau of domesticity he'd just witnessed. It proved to Bell something he'd witnessed time and time again as an investigator — you never understand anything about a person until you learn everything about that person.

12

From a convenient *brasserie* near the Massards' apartment — Bell had noted she wore a wedding ring — he'd watched her for three days and he felt time slipping away. Mrs. Yves, as he thought of her, did not work, so she spent much of her time in her own apartment. On her occasional forays out into the continuously damp and chilly November air, she went mostly to a market for meal supplies, once to a café for tea with a woman who was not Theresa Massard, and she'd spent part of one afternoon at a cinema watching several one-reelers.

Bell was frustrated that his plan to find Theresa through Marc's twin's wife wasn't panning out. He now had to consider a more direct route, one that risked tipping his hand to Gly, Massard, and the powers that ran the Société des Mines. He could further jeopardize the miners if he was caught.

He couldn't imagine the French consortium keeping the American miners in Paris for much longer. The simple fact was they would never reach their destination once the seas iced over. The window to reach Novaya Zemlya was closing rapidly. So too was Bell's opportunity to give them a warning.

The little eatery's owner was well compensated for Bell's use of the front table, so as a courtesy he kept the detective's coffee topped off. Bell nodded when the man offered to refill the bone china cup in its little saucer but then waved the man away when he saw Mrs. Yves step out from her building. Today was Friday. If she had a standing date to visit her sister-in-law, now was the most logical time and day. Bell stood quickly and gathered his coat and hat. He let the woman get halfway down the block before leaving the *brasserie* and giving casual chase. She was dressed conservatively and her hair was up. She usually wore it down to frame her face. But now it was in a tight bun pinned close to her skull. She was purposefully making herself seem less attractive. Bell suspected he'd finally caught the break he needed.

As he'd predicted, the twin brothers lived just a couple of blocks from each other.

Mrs. Yves entered an apartment building on the corner of a busy street. Cars and carriages jockeyed with one another for space on the congested route. Even from a distance Bell could hear raised voices, horns, and the neighing of frightened draft horses. He made a mental note of the address and retreated to a newspaper kiosk. He bought a paper and moved to a spot where he was partially shielded from view from the building's entrance. He settled in for a long wait but soon found himself in motion again. Mrs. Yves came out of the building with another woman. Bell didn't need to consult the old photograph in his pocket to recognize Theresa Massard.

Marc and Theresa were young enough in the picture to believe in a fairy-tale life together and were probably on their honeymoon. Assuming that, and knowing that most French are Catholic, divorce was out of the question and so they'd still be partners.

He was wrong in thinking Mrs. Yves and Theresa could be related. They looked nothing alike.

Time and Theresa Massard's current circumstance had not been kind to her. Her once dark hair was streaked with dull gray and hung limp to her shoulders. She'd gained weight since she and Marc had posed for the Eiffel Tower photograph, and her posture was becoming stooped around the shoulders and upper back. She was in her early to mid-thirties, by Bell's estimation, but appeared well past her prime, like someone who'd endured many decades of hardship.

Life had beaten Theresa Massard, and Bell suspected her husband had as well. He had stopped thinking of that man as the friendly reporter he'd caught stalking a story and remembered that he'd participated in the burning of innocent villagers. The man was a monster and so were his brother and the Goliath, Gly. He imagined he'd mistreated his wife badly over the years. She moved with the timidity of an oft-whipped dog. Her eyes remained downcast, and she stepped through the crowds with quick, jerky motions so that no one got too close to her. She did allow her sister-in-law to take her arm and thread it through her own.

From a good distance back, Bell could see Mrs. Yves trying to chat up Theresa and lift her spirits but was getting only one-word answers in return. He knew even some whipped dogs missed their masters, and no matter how poorly she'd been treated by her late husband, she was obviously in mourning. The two women ate lunch at an inexpensive café. Bell left them so he could grab a quick bite from a nearby *patisserie*. Upon his return to the street outside the restaurant, he saw, to his horror, that Mrs. Yves was alone now and discussing the bill with a waiter. It could be that Theresa excused herself to use the ladies', but why was the bill there so quickly? It made more sense that Theresa was too upset to even have a meal in public and had run home. Mrs. Yves was in a hurry to pay so she could catch up.

Bell started walking quickly back toward the apartment building where Theresa Massard lived. He cut through the crowds without looking like he was hurrying and soon saw the slope-shouldered silhouette and the jerky, awkward tics. Bell settled his pace to stay behind her. She reached her building before Mrs. Yves caught up. Bell waited across the street at the news kiosk again. When he spotted Mrs. Yves hurrying on the sidewalk, he started back for the apartment building, timing his move so he arrived just a second after the woman. She acknowledged his presence with a look and started up the wooden stairs that rose up through an open shaft in the building's center. Bell gave her a polite few seconds and started up after her. She climbed past the second floor and up to the third. Bell slowed a little more and watched her move down the short, carpeted hallway to apartment C and knock. He continued climbing up to the building's top floor to wait.

He heard the woman knock a second time, then a third, and call Theresa's name. To no avail. Theresa wasn't going to let her sister-in-law try to cheer her up. Mrs. Yves gave up after a minute more. Bell listened to the clack of her shoes as she descended to street level and waited until the building's front door squeaked open and clicked closed.

He descended to the third floor. He took the old photograph from his pocket and slipped it under the door of apartment C. He knocked, and said in French, "Mrs. Massard, I was there when Foster Gly murdered your husband."

For thirty seconds he got no reaction. The door remained closed, the apartment beyond silent. Bell was raising his hand to knock again when he heard the lock thrown. She pulled the door against herself and looked out like a frightened mouse peering from its den.

"Je m'appelle Isaac Bell. Je suis Américain."

"I speak English," Theresa said. "They

told me my husband died in a fight at a bar."

"That isn't true. We were in the mountains outside of Denver, Colorado. They had just tried to kill me and another man. I managed to chase down your husband. He was unarmed. I had this." Bell opened his coat to show the butt of his .45 in a black leather shoulder rig. "I was just about to begin questioning him. Gly couldn't risk Marc telling me anything, so he shot him from a great distance with a rifle."

"You are police?"

"A private investigator." She appeared not to know what that meant. "Like a policeman people can hire for themselves."

She nodded. "Why should I believe you?"

"May we do this in your apartment?"

"*Non.* Until I know what you want, you will remain where you are."

Bell was surprised that she'd refused him. Apparently, her timidity did not make her compliant. "You should believe me because you already know what kind of man Gly is." She shuddered at the mention of his name. Bell knew he'd touched a nerve. "And because I took the time to find that picture and return it to you."

Looking at the photograph in her trembling hand brought her to a conclusion. She opened the door fully and turned back into her apartment so that Bell could follow. The place was nicely furnished and tidy. The kitchen had an ornate ice chest with brass accents, and the stove had two separate burner rings. Bell could see there was a bedroom, though he couldn't directly see into it, and a private bathroom with a porcelain shower.

"I have no coffee," she said. "Would tea be all right?"

"Only if you are making some for yourself," Bell said.

She'd been tracking toward the kitchen, but Bell's answer changed her plan and she shuffled to the couch and wedged herself up against one arm. On the nearby table sat a stack of fresh white hankies and several used ones looking like they'd absorbed so much grief they'd never be clean again. She took an unsoiled handkerchief and absently kneaded it with her thin fingers. The photo she placed on the coffee table.

Bell removed his hat and outer coat and settled into a chair opposite the widow. Outside, the sky was a melancholy gray. Into the quiet he said, "Do you know what your husband did for the Société?"

She didn't answer his question. She said instead, "That pig Foster Gly told me that even though they were in America on company business, the fight was Marc's fault, and so they will not pay me his insurance. We have just a little in savings. I cannot afford this apartment. What am I to do?"

There was nothing Bell could say. He simply watched her hands worry as she worked the hankie as though it were a rosary.

"Gly lied so the Société de Mines didn't have to pay the widow's benefits. He and Yves are the real friends. Marc just went along with whatever his older brother told him to do. Marc is younger by a few minutes and this is something Yves has used their entire lives to control my husband. Late husband," she corrected quickly.

She finally looked up from her lap. Her eyes were glossy, but no tears wet her cheeks. "He was good to me in the early days. He wanted to be a draftsman. He was really very good at it. I was a shopgirl. We met in a park, quite by accident. I knew he was the one for me the very second I saw him. I know now that I was the first girl to ever show any interest in him. It's why we started dating and why he proposed so quickly. It's funny. They're identical twins, but there's something . . . I do not know the English word."

"Yves is the kind of rogue that girls fall

for," Bell offered, thinking of that dark intensity he'd seen.

"Yes. That is it. Yves always had girls around him. Pretty ones. Marc was so shy. Unsure of himself because Yves had belittled him since they were boys."

"Things changed when Yves met Foster Gly." It was a statement by Bell, not a question.

"Yes. Yves didn't really have employment. He spent his nights in bars. He knew people. Did things. Illegal things, you know? I am not sure if Gly knew his reputation and sought him out or if they met through mutual acquaintances, but the two became friends. Gly was an employee of the Société and he offered Yves a legitimate job.

"Yves hadn't been able to recruit Marc for any of his schemes because I would not allow it. But when Yves told Marc he could have a job too, it was too much. Marc had to follow his older brother.

"Up to then, I was able to protect Marc from Yves's influence, but that was no longer the case. Yves won. Marc changed. He would stay out drinking after work. He would just grunt at me when I had questions. The love drained from our marriage, Monsieur Bell. No, that is not true, Marc let Yves and Gly suck the love from our marriage."

Tears finally started down her cheeks and she began sobbing in earnest, deep and gut-wrenching sobs. There were two responses open to Bell at this moment, a choice men must make at their own peril. Either the sobbing woman wants to be comforted or she wants to work through it on her own. There was definitely a correct answer, but the problem was that the solution changed from cry to cry with no clue as to what was now desired.

He figured she'd spent a lot of time alone, so he let her be. He had to give her credit, though. She was crying over a life she'd expected but didn't get. For many people, that was an inconsolable circumstance, but she pulled herself together, dabbing at her eyes and finally giving her nose a good blow.

"Forgive me," she said at last, her eyes and nose red.

"There's no need. I understand. And if our roles were reversed, I see myself crying just as much."

She smiled at that, and there was a shadow of gratitude in her gaze. "Did Marc . . . Did he . . ."

"Suffer?" Bell supplied. "No, he died instantly." Bell returned to his original question. "Do you know what your husband did for the Société des Mines?"

"Not specifically. He had an office here in Paris, but he traveled often."

"With Gly?"

She nodded. "Or Yves. And sometimes both."

"Would you like me to tell you what they did specifically?"

The tone in his voice gave her pause. While she was curious to know some things about her husband's life he'd kept from her, he'd died a violent death at the hands of someone who was supposedly his friend, and her truer self knew that whatever kind of man Marc had become, she was better off not knowing the details. "I do not believe I would like to know, monsieur."

"That is a wise choice."

She asked, "You came here for more than to tell me the truth about Marc's death, yes?"

"He and Gly were in the United States to escort a handful of men to Paris and see them off on a polar expedition."

"I understand." But clearly she didn't.

"I have strong reason to believe that these men will be murdered upon the completion of their mission."

She gasped, now seeing the full picture.

"I need to get word to the team leader to

expect betrayal. I know they are here in Paris getting the last of the supplies they will need. I don't know where, exactly. Did your husband ever mention any houses the company owns?"

"They own a great many for factory workers."

"No, not like that. This would be one where they would lodge visiting dignitaries, heads of other companies, potential clients."

She shook her head. "I am sorry, monsieur, but Marc did not discuss such things with me."

Bell doubted he'd have told her anything, but it was worth the shot to ask. Now he had to go the old-fashioned route. "Did your husband leave behind any keys?"

"No," she said, then immediately amended her reply, a little buoyed by being able to help. "Yes. In his strongbox."

She rose from her spot on the couch and vanished into the bedroom. She returned a moment later with a gray pressed-metal box about the size of an encyclopedia volume. She held it out to him. She took back her place, wedged tightly against the sofa's armrest, and began fidgeting with a fresh handkerchief. Bell examined the box. The lock was a simple clasp type that was better at showing evidence of tampering than keeping contents safe. Bell used the knife he kept strapped to his ankle to work at it, bending the cheap metal until the internal lock snapped in two and the clasp popped open.

Inside was a set of substantial brass keys on a very fine chain of silver. In addition to a snub-nosed revolver and a box of ammunition still in its grease paper, there were bundled stacks of francs. With the lid open so Theresa couldn't see, he thumbed through one of the stacks of mixed bills and quickly calculated the value. He removed the keys and money and closed the lid.

"These the keys he took to work every morning?"

"Yes. They are for his office and desk and the like." She spotted the money. *"Mon Dieu!"*

He stood and handed the sheaves to her. "I'd guess about twenty thousand francs."

"How did —" She wisely reconsidered asking. "No. I do not want to know."

"You're right. You don't. I do not wish to alarm you, but there is also a gun in this box. If you would like, I will get rid of it for you."

"Yes, please. I want nothing to do with any of that."

"I have no advice for your future, madame," Bell said as a way to wrap up their meeting. "Your sister-in-law seemed to pay you kindness."

Theresa dismissed the notion with a wave of her hand, the handkerchief clenched tightly in her other fist. "Bah. She's a former dancer at *Les Follies*. Little better than a whore, and now she is pregnant and only talks about her having a son and naming him Yves after his father. The mere sight of her is a reminder of why my marriage turned out so poorly."

"Then I am truly sorry." Bell stood and slipped into his overcoat and hat. He tucked the box under one arm. "You have been a tremendous help to me and I am grateful. I would not be surprised if Gly and your husband's brother know about the money. They will likely come for it. Hide it some-place outside of this apartment and plead ignorance when they ask. Spend it slowly."

"I understand. *Merci.* I guess I too am grateful, monsieur. I might never have found the money before Gly and Yves came for it. Also knowing the real" — she paused, try-ing to recall the English word — "circum-stance around Marc's death. I suppose it helps a little knowing the truth."

She escorted him to the door. He asked for, and she gave him, the specific floor of the office her late husband shared with his brother and Foster Gly. As he stepped out into the hallway, he said, "I often find knowing the truth helps, Madame Massard. You have my condolences. *Bonne chance et au revoir.*"

13

Bell returned to the environs near the Société des Mines where he had started out. This was not the shiny headquarters in the second *arrondissement* close to the Paris Bourse, the city's fabled stock exchange, but a satellite facility to house the worker bees who kept the hive humming — accountants, copy and file clerks, ledger keepers, and the like.

The building took up the entire block and could probably house a thousand workers comfortably. He circled the block, discovering one of the green iron and glass Art Deco Métro station entrances designed by Hector Guimard that were rapidly becoming as familiar a symbol of the city as Monsieur Eiffel's Tower. The back of the building was punctured by an alley that led to an open central courtyard. The alley was protected by a grillework gate that was chained shut. Bell could see into the brick-paved court.

There was nothing of interest, but he took a moment to note that, in a pinch, he could climb up and over the gate.

He finished his tour, passing the main entrance again and pausing to check out the lobby. It was stark, befitting the lowly workers who toiled within, but functional. A wooden railing bisected the room, with a guard stationed at its only opening. The uniformed agent checked that each person entering had a proper identification badge. If not, Bell saw a reception counter along one wall with three women ready to process visitors.

The hole beneath the doorknob looked right for the largest key on Marc Massard's ring.

He eventually found a taxi and gave an address some blocks from the Hôtel Lutetia. When he was certain the driver's attention was on the congestion, he surreptitiously transferred the revolver to a coat pocket. He'd dump Massard's strongbox in a public trash receptacle and walk the last half mile to his hotel.

Once back at the Lutetia, he ate a light meal and returned to his room. There are two things that keep a body fueled — food and sleep. He closed the curtains to block out the late-afternoon light and made certain the delicate little clock on the bedside table was properly wound and its alarm set for midnight. Bell felt certain of his abilities. He fell asleep right away.

When he woke, he turned on the Tiffany-style lamp and noted it was five minutes before midnight. He trusted his internal clock, but it was always good to have backup. He unset the alarm and rose from bed. He did about fifteen minutes of exercise and stretching before dressing in black slacks and a tight-fitting black turtleneck sweater. While the garment was *très chic* among the leftist elites in Paris, Bell had to admit it was terrific tactical wear. Next, he shrugged into the shoulder holster, clipping its bottom around the oiled black belt at his waist and checking for the two spare magazines. He retrieved the Colt Model 1911 from under his pillow, double-checked the magazine, and rammed the weapon home.

He strapped the stiletto-thin knife to his right calf and slid on silk socks and a sturdy pair of black rubber-soled shoes. He clipped a slim pouch onto the shoulder rig opposite his pistol. In it were lockpicks and other tools of the trade. He finally slipped into his black overcoat.

There was a string of taxis outside the hotel even at this late hour. Like New York,

Paris had a vibrant nightlife seven days a week. He had the driver take him to another hotel about a half mile from the Société's building.

Seeing Bell's attire and destination once they arrived, the cabman asked, *"Une femme?"*

"Une femme fatale," Bell replied, feeding the man's fantasy.

"Bonne chance, monsieur."

"Pas besoin de chance. La chasse, c'est fini."

Bell acted like he was going to enter the mid-level hotel until the taxi's lights vanished around a corner. He then set off walking, as inky black as the deepest shadow. Pedestrian traffic was light once he got off the main boulevard. Unlike the touristy areas near his hotel, these were working neighborhoods, and most people needed the sleep in order to face the following day's grind. The roads here were quieter too. Bell moved quickly but appeared unhurried. Streetlamps lined the road, casting their glow into the fog.

He soon reached the back of the Société des Mines building and, with the street deserted, shinnied up the iron gate, rolled himself carefully over the top. He slid down the other side like a sailor descending a ladder on a Navy ship. He paused, listening, surveying, using his instincts to determine if his penetration had been detected.

He waited three minutes before making his move, certain that no one was in the courtyard with him. He'd scanned all the darkened windows but saw no pale face peering down. He still moved slowly, oozing along one wall, dipping below windows and keeping a sharp watch out for any changes in the night. He reached a set of glass doors he'd noted earlier that lay at the far end of the lobby from the main entrance. He got down low and peered into the dark space. Light from the streets outside the front doors bathed the reception hall in an amber blush — not light, exactly, but enough illumination to tell him if anyone was guarding the building. He could clearly see that the area where the day guard checked in visitors was empty. So too the station where receptionists sat.

Still, Bell had plenty of time and so he waited on the cold stone step for thirty minutes and watched the lobby because there was always a chance a roaming guard would check it on his rounds. Judging by the size of the building and assuming he'd missed seeing such a guard by seconds before taking up his watch, Bell gave a potential sentry ample time to wander from room to room and return to the lobby. He let thirty minutes stretch to forty-five to make sure no one paced through.

Satisfied that the Société didn't guard the bland paperwork shuffled within these walls, he retraced his steps around the courtyard and over the gate and circled the limestone edifice. The sidewalks were still deserted and there was little traffic in the street. As casually as an owner approaches his own house, Bell walked up to the door, slid home the largest of Marc Massard's keys, and turned the lock. He slipped inside and closed the door softly. He looked around the doorframe quickly for any kind of wiring that would indicate an electromechanical alarm had been retrofitted to the door. If this was a new building, he could assume such wiring would be installed during construction and remain hidden from prying eyes. But this was an older structure, and digging through all the layers of plaster and drilling through the rough limestone wouldn't be practical. He saw nothing in the carved woodwork.

Knowing now he didn't need to beat a hasty retreat, he snicked the lock's tongue into the jamb and took a few calming breaths. The hard part was over. He waited a few minutes just to get a sense of how the place felt. To him, it was as quiet as a tomb. He was quite sure he was alone.

The ambient light allowed him to navigate the room, past the daytime guard's station, and reach a large staircase that rose up in right angle flights around a brass-cage elevator within a wrought iron–filigreed shaft. He looked up through a tangle of metal and saw the stairs spiraled up to the fourth floor. Above, all was in darkness. He climbed up past the second and third floors to the fourth, where Marc and Yves Massard shared an office with Foster Gly. He saw and heard nothing. Theresa Massard didn't know her husband's office number, but she told Bell it was on the fourth floor in the far left-hand corner and that it overlooked the street and not the building's central courtyard.

He'd asked if she could remember anything about the room or the building. Of the office, she said it was a plain room with three desks and some other furniture. She said there were blinds over the two windows with heavy velvet panels that sounded to Bell like blackout curtains. The only other thing Marc had shown her was a vault, like a bank's, on the third floor directly below his office. The vault's door was hidden

behind a regular one like all the other offices.

He fished a small flashlight from his
pocket. The lens had been daubed with
black paint so only a mere pinprick of light
escaped. It would be enough. He had his
finger on the switch when he heard a blus-
tery "Ahhh-choo!" Bell froze, as did the
blood in his veins. He'd been certain the
building was empty. The sound had come
from the floor or floors below. It was hard
to be certain, and the man hadn't been on
the staircase but off in one of the wings.
Bell thought it could have been a worker
putting in extra hours, but he hadn't seen
any lights on. He then realized the man's
office could have blackout curtains similar
to Massard's.

The horror sank in. There could be dozens
of people toiling away in offices that gave
no outward indication of their occupancy.

He dismissed the idea. If that many people
worked at night, there would be a few lights
on in the hallways. But there was just a faint
glow coming up the stairway from down
below. The hallways themselves were pitch-
dark.

With one hand on the wall for orienta-
tion, Bell moved down the hall toward his
destination, keeping his stride smooth and

silent on the tiled floor. He reached the corner and after he rounded it he paused for a moment. He heard nothing and chanced turning on his light for just a few seconds. His eyes had so adjusted to darkness that even the little pinlight's illumination was enough for him to see that the walls were lined with identical wooden doors. It was as unremarkable as any office Bell had ever visited.

He got his bearings and continued down the hallway. He heard nothing more from the sneezer downstairs, but knowing the guy was around kept Bell's nerves on edge. A firm with the reputation of the Société des Mines wouldn't bother *Les Gendarmes* with something as straightforward as an intruder. He fully imagined that if he was caught, he'd be tortured to find out why he'd broken in, followed by his weighted body being tossed into the Seine.

He reached Massard's office. He dropped to hands and knees to peer under the door. He could see the faint glimmering of the city's lights passing through the room's windows. Satisfied that the office was vacant — or at least dark — Bell fitted the next-largest key into the lock just below the knob and tenderly twisted it until it disengaged with a click no louder than the lid of a well-made pocket watch. He drew his .45 and disengaged the thumb safety. He pushed open the door in fractional increments so as to not let the hinges squeak.

No one shouted out a challenge. When the door was opened wide enough, he squeezed through and shut it behind him. He locked it as well in case some security contingent was patrolling the halls and checking that all the rooms were properly secured. He shed his coat and lay it at the base of the door so no light could leak through the slim space between it and the tile floor.

It was a large office, and the two windows in the far wall were broad and tall. Bell could see well enough by the light of the streetlamps outside. Two desks were perpendicular to the wall on his right, and one was perpendicular to the wall on his left, with file cabinets interspersed, as well as a long multi-drawer credenza under the windows. A coat-tree stood to the right of the door alongside an outdated wall-mounted telephone.

Bell drew the heavy curtains closed and reminded himself to never let his light point in that direction as further precaution against alerting someone outside that the office was being burgled.

One of the desks had been stripped of lamp and blotter and trays for incoming and outgoing correspondence. Its top was flat and barren. This had to have been the late Marc Massard's station. The others were covered with files, pads of paper, inkpots, a cigarette box in tarnished silver, cups of pencils. By the glow of his little flashlight, Bell scanned these desks without touching a single item. On some level, he was concerned that Foster Gly would know his office had been searched just by the very fact the air might feel different in the morning.

Nothing on the first glance indicated where the Société had stashed the nine Coloradans. There was a black leather booklet on the desk he determined belonged to Gly. Bell recognized it as a day-planning book, with each page earmarked for each day of the year. Bell kept a similar book on his desk in New York. He was about to open it but stayed his hand a few inches from its cover. He knelt so his face was just above the book. He played his light over its surface. Gly either lost all his hair young or, more likely, kept it shaved, so he wasn't the source of the single golden hair sticking out between the cover and the first page. It almost looked like a dog's — a retriever's or Labrador's. It definitely would have fallen unnoticed had Bell opened the day planner.

He noted its exact position and how much of it peeked out before opening the book and catching the makeshift intruder's alert in his palm. He set it carefully on the desk and leafed through the pages until he found the next day's date.

Bell let a smile cross his lips. Gly had a nine o'clock appointment with someone named Gravois at a restaurant on Île de la Cité near Notre-Dame, but at ten-thirty he was to pick up Joshua Brewster and Vernon Hall at the house and escort them to the offices of A. C. Bourgault in a part of Paris Bell wasn't familiar with. He memorized the address. Henri Favreau, Bell's Parisian fixer, would likely be able to give him background on the identity of Bourgault. He checked the next couple of entries in Gly's schedule and saw that he was leading all nine miners to Le Havre in two days' time. Bell knew if opportunity didn't present itself the next day he could always make an approach on the boat train to the port city. Then he saw a notation for a motorbus hire. They were being driven to the docks.

That just ratcheted up the pressure even more. Bell took a breath. Blew it out. Took another. Tomorrow would just have to work.

As careful as a surgeon, he inserted the

long yellow hair back onto the daybook's first page and gently closed the cover on it so it was once again trapped in place. Bell had touched nothing else, but he swept the room just to be certain he hadn't accidentally brushed against a stack of papers or knocked a lampshade askew. Everything was as it should be. If he could make his exit as stealthy as his entrance, he'd be home free.

He opened the drapery to the position it had been in when he'd entered, shrugged back into his overcoat, and gently unlocked the door. Like before, he opened it just enough to squeeze his body through. The hallway was dark and deserted. He retraced his steps down the corridor, ever mindful that someone could be approaching through the gloom. He reached the stairs and paused. All he heard was the rush of blood through the vessels around his ears. He started down. He reached the head of the third-floor stairs when his luck failed him. Coming up from below were two men holding flashlights with red lenses to make them harder to detect in the dark building.

"Je déteste la grippe," one said miserably, and wiped at his nose.

Escape Through Paris Sewers

14

In an intuitive flash, Bell understood the security decisions the company had made to protect the building. They pretended that there was no real security, to lure in unsuspecting thieves — likely, industrial spies from Krupp or some other big European conglomerate. The would-be spies make it inside, but guards silently roaming the darkened hallways with blacked-out lights would eventually find them. This way, the Société could get information out of the captured man and the Metropolitan Police would never know a thing.

Had Bell not heard the flu-addled guard sneeze, he'd have assumed he was alone and been far less cautious. In the end, though, it didn't matter, because the healthy other guard saw him at the top of the stairs in his light's ruddy glow and shouted in alarm.

Bell launched himself at the two, spreading his elbows just wide enough to hit both in the face. The impact knocked the men back down to the landing below, their bodies cushioning Bell's as he fell on top of them. He got to his feet and leapt down to the next landing. Reaching out with his right arm, he hooked his hand onto one of the iron elevator shaft stanchions and whipped himself around before launching himself down another eight-stair flight. This was the second floor. He tore around the elevator shaft and leapt to the final mid-stairs landing, needing to throw up his hands to keep from smashing into the wall. He turned and jumped again, landing in position to whirl around another stanchion and gain the main floor. His shoulder felt like it was pulling from the joint, but his reckless flight had captured him seconds.

The lights of Paris beckoned through the lobby windows, and a curtain of fresh rain fell from the heavens. He could hear the guards rushing down the stairs in his wake. Bell raced across the open space.

Once the guards reported that an intruder had been in the building, someone as paranoid and clever as Gly would suspect information about his project had been the intended target and not whatever was kept in the vault. The Scotsman would immediately change his schedule. No meeting at A. C. Bourgault and no motorbus ride to Le Havre.

He had two options. One was just to shoot the men in cold blood, a thought that was tempting but not Bell's style. These men may work for a ruthless organization, yet that wasn't enough reason for him to just execute them. His second option was to lure them someplace where he could subdue them and keep them stashed long enough for him to make contact with Brewster. It was the more dangerous plan but his conscience would be clear.

He paused just long enough for the pursuing guards to see him at the door before he pushed through the auto lock and out into the rainy night. He turned left toward the Métro station and started running. Behind him, he heard the door crash open and a shout as they spotted him heading down the middle of the sodden street.

A sudden pistol shot blasted the night. The bullet never came close, but the game suddenly changed. Bell drew his .45 on the fly and kept going. Another shot rang out, and this one was close enough for Bell to hear the hot round sizzle its way through the rain. He quickened his pace. More bullets punched the air around him. He was too exposed. His plan had turned from subterfuge to survival.

He veered at the last second and flew down the stairs under the glass and iron awning of the Métro station entrance. He expected to be able to stop at the bottom and shoot both men when they were silhouetted against the shimmering night sky. But when he got there, he saw a train made of stained wooden carriages with plain square windows was in the station. A couple of people were stepping off while a couple of others waited on the vaulted platform to board. The scene had a sleepy quality of commuters going through routines without thought. At the far end of the station, workers in heavy rain gear clustered around an open door that led to a deeper, hellish realm below the streets.

Bell discreetly holstered his weapon and made his way onto one of the electric train's four passenger carriages. A few Parisians sat on the benches, owl-eyed with exhaustion or asleep with their heads resting against the car's interior. One drunk fellow gave him a loopy grin. Bell watched anxiously. The guards would know they'd be vulnerable coming down into the Métro system, so they would be cautious. If Bell had any luck left tonight, the train would glide out

of the station before they reached the platform.

He waited. They didn't budge, even
though everyone who wanted aboard had a
seat. No one came down the stairs from
street level. The car suddenly jolted as the
silent train began to pull from the station.
Bell felt a glimmer of hope.

The two dark figures hit the platform at
full speed and ran along the last car just
fast enough to open the door and leap
aboard. Bell shrank in his seat, peering over
the back as the Société security men began
checking passengers, rousing the sleeping
men and asking questions in short, explosive
bursts. There were only a few passengers in
the last car. Two doors connected it to Bell's
carriage.

They were almost out of the station and
into the dim confines of the tunnels.

Bell made a snap decision.

The boxy Colt pistol materialized in his
hand and he fired three times at the train's
window before rushing at it while the
disintegrating glass cascaded out of the
frame and onto a hapless passenger sitting
below. Bell vaulted over the passenger and
threw himself out the now empty widow,
tucking like an acrobat as he dove so that
his palms hit the terminal's tile floor first

and letting his momentum flip him onto his shoulders, his back, and eventually onto his feet. What he hadn't been able to calculate was the momentum generated by the train's forward speed.

He'd cut it too close. When he came fully upright, he continued to lurch hard to the left and slammed into the station wall with a shoulder that would be five shades of purple and blue the next day. The two men would have to remain on the —

A blast like a sudden thunderclap rocked the terminal at the same instant a vibrant explosion of blue light arced from the tunnel where the train had just vanished. Hot air reeking of ozone and something worse — the charred odor of overcooked meat — belched from the tunnel's mouth. A woman waiting for another train began screaming while white-faced men gazed in wonder down the shaft.

Bell shook off the effects of momentary paralysis. He quickly grasped what had just occurred. The two guards had opened the door at the train's rear and leapt from it before it accelerated away. One or both had landed on the electrified third rail, and its pulse of high-voltage energy had coursed through their bodies, killing as surely as the electric chair at Sing Sing prison. The lights in the station remained on, telling him it was on a different power system.

The workers who'd been clustered around the door leading deeper into the earth ran past Bell to reach the platform edge and peer into the tunnel.

A couple gasped as a man ran out of the blackness, grim and shaken but still holding a revolver in one hand.

The workers were helping hoist the Société guard off the railbed and onto the platform, clutching his belt to lift him free. The man was on his belly, surrounded by kneeling workers who still weren't sure what had happened. The guard fixed his gaze firmly on Isaac Bell, standing no more than a dozen feet away. He started to move his arm up along his body so he could aim the weapon from his prone position.

Bell took off through a dank maintenance doorway that led farther under the Parisian streets. At first he found himself in a brick-work antechamber, with another door opposite the first. Tools lay on the floor next to an open hatch with a wooden ladder rising up through it from below. The air smelled of wet decay. A pair of metal hard hats sat on the floor next to the hatch. Each had an electric lamp on the brim attached by wires to a battery pack in a bag that could be slung over the shoulder like a dispatch rider's haversack. He looped one bag's single strap over his shoulder before clamping the safety helmet on his head.

He went down the ladder. At the bottom he saw lights strung along the far wall of the tunnel that led off in either direction. The shaft was brick lined and consisted of a platform, where Bell stood, overlooking a wide channel roiling at a level just below his feet. The water was dingy brown and laden with debris scoured off the Parisian streets and sucked down into the subterranean system. Now that he was down in the tunnel, the loamy smell gave way to the sharper acrid stench of a sewer.

Behind him, in the far distance where the lightbulbs appeared like distant stars, the farthest from view suddenly went dark.

The next light in the string was so far down the tunnel that he could only perceive its nimbus and yet he could tell when it too winked out like the one before it. Something was coming down the tunnel. Something big and something utterly remorseless. And the deepest part of Isaac Bell's brain, the area honed over eons of evolution, told him to run as fast and as far as he could.

15

The crack of a pistol and the sting of a piece of concrete shrapnel hitting his calf galvanized Bell into action. Whatever was coming from behind him was secondary to the gunman taking potshots from above. Bell whirled, fired once up at the ceiling hatch, and broke into a run. In just seconds his lungs burned from the noxious nature of the air he breathed.

The heavy battery slapped at his hip, while the hard hat was at least sized right to stay on his head. A second shot rang out, but he'd put enough distance between him and the Société guard that the bullet passed by harmlessly. The man was giving chase, and the both of them were breathing hard and amped up on adrenaline. Firing from anything beyond point-blank range was a waste of ammunition.

Bell chanced looking back a few seconds later and almost stumbled at what he saw.

Whatever was barreling down the tunnel was nearly upon him. The dozens of lights he had raced past were all eclipsed by the thing. He could see the guard too, pushing himself, as he also recognized some presence was in motion in the sewer shaft. Bell turned back forward, trying for a burst of speed, anything to stay ahead of the mystery object.

And then it was on him. Bell felt an enormous presence at his side, a surging force that seemed to fill the tunnel. He and it moved parallel for a moment, and Bell finally saw his stalker. It was an enormous wooden ball that rolled along the round channel at the base of the tunnel and it swept past him in mere moments, borne along by a surging slosh of water that washed up onto the platform where Bell was running, soaking him to the knees and slowing his progress. He had no idea of the ball's function, as it continued down the tunnel, now blocking out the lamps ahead of Bell as it had moments earlier with the ones behind him.

The water following in the wake of the rolling ball grew deeper. Its current was swift, and Bell had to be cautious or he'd be yanked off his feet. Another glance back told him his pursuer was also battling the storm surge but was keeping apace. Now it was a test of endurance.

As the ball moved away, more and more of the light fixtures could be seen ahead, brightening the tunnel enough for Bell to note a pair of objects in the water ahead. They were small rowboats, tied to iron rings in the wall. They had been sitting on the elevated platform above the channel but now floated and bobbed like little toys in it.

When Bell reached the closest wooden skiff, he hauled himself over the low gunwale and sprawled onto the bottom boards and thwart seat. He straightened himself and pulled the knife from the sheath at his ankle. He planned on cutting the second boat loose first, yet as he went to reach for it the guard sensed his intention and began firing with not just his own revolver but also the one he'd scooped up from his dead partner. The air around Bell came alive. He ignored the other craft and instead cut the painter holding his own to the wall.

The boat was instantly grabbed by the current and was soon rocketing through the abyssal tunnel, the lamps on the far wall almost turning into a continuous blur of yellow light. He was certain the Société guard would not give up the chase. When-ever the tunnel curved even slightly, the boat would scrape against the wall and dip enough for some fetid water to slop over the gunwale. To protect himself, Bell found two wooden oars on the floor and fitted them through the metal oarlocks and used them like punter's sticks to keep his craft from capsizing against the rough brick walls.

His pursuer remained far enough away that Bell could only detect him as a shape in the distance. After two minutes of headlong rushing through the tunnel, Bell saw ahead that the recessed lamps in the wall came to an end. He found the switch for the light mounted on his helmet and connected to the battery and flipped it on. It cut just a small cone into the inky gloom as he roared past the last lamp and into a differently shaped tunnel. It was tighter, perfectly round, and he realized that the ceiling had dropped. His helmeted head was only a few feet from smashing into the thick iron pipes bolted in conduits along the ceiling of the tunnel.

The tighter confines of the shaft also meant the volume of water rushing through it increased his speed significantly. He was constantly jabbing the oars outward to keep himself from a fatal collision with the walls. He did spare a fraction of a second to look up. The ceiling was closer than it had been just seconds before. The tunnel was filling up with water, and very soon the plucky little boat would be pressed to the top against the pipes and Isaac Bell was likely to drown in a river of stormwater and sewage.

The relentless current suddenly stopped and the crash of water that had filled Bell's ears went silent. Ahead, in the feeble illumination of his headlamp, he saw the mysterious wooden ball wedged tight in the tunnel, and his skiff almost bumped into it as its momentum bled away. And yet the water level continued to rise, pressing him ever closer to the ceiling.

Understanding came in a rush. The wooden ball was introduced into the system whenever there was a clog. It would roll and rumble along with the current, and when it hit a snag, like a knot of tangled branches or a thick shoal of sand, it would form a plug that would cause water to rise behind it. Once enough water had backed up in the tunnel, the tremendous force of its weight would blast the obstruction free. The ball would once again start rolling and would eventually be recovered.

None of that did him any good in the last frantic seconds before he was swamped. He felt something strike his boat. He turned. It was the guard's skiff. The man's face was ashen and his eyes were wide at the inevitability of the situation. Bell ignored him. The rowboat's gunwales were almost pressed flat to the tunnel roof. At the last possible moment, he realized the oarlocks were still slotted in place. They would hit the ceiling first and allow water to pour in. He popped them free and, lying flat on his back, used his hands along the ceiling tiles to orient the boat so that it ran parallel to the roof's slight arch.

The skiff's natural buoyancy pressed the edge of its gunwale tight to the ceiling as the water fully filled the tunnel and began backing up down the passageway. A little water seeped around the sides and into the boat, but the seal was remarkably tight. His fast actions had given him a fighting chance.

The Société guard hadn't been so lucky. Bell heard his scream as his oarlocks hit the ceiling and water overtopped his craft. Buoyancy would trap him in the boat while he drowned, making it his personal sarcophagus until the water pressure was high enough to release the clog.

Three claustrophobic minutes passed. Bell was grateful for the headlamp. Being trapped in such a predicament in total darkness made him shudder. It was the cold water pooling on the little punt's bottom boards that made him shiver. The sewers were filled with the icy rain that had been falling for days, and Bell felt the cold sapping his energy.

A great grinding sound, like the gears of some enormous machine come to life, filled the tiny pocket of air Bell had preserved for himself. The great ball had started to roll. Pressed by hundreds and then thousands of tons of water, the ball moved like a grist stone through the clogged debris, grinding it into pieces that would easily flush away.

As the ball was slightly smaller than the diameter of the pipe, and the onetime tent was no longer acting like a gasket, water began to ooze out ahead of the rolling sphere and the level behind it began to drop. Very quickly Bell's boat came off the ceiling and was again floating freely. He imagined somewhere behind him the guard's water-logged craft would tumble in the wake and eventually spill its grisly contents.

Bell rode the diminishing current for a few minutes until the ball emerged into a wider section of tunnel. There was a platform along one wall and lights. A cross tunnel connected to this main line, and he could see green and black signs at the intersection with the names of the corresponding topside streets spelled out in white letters.

He let it pass, but when he came to another intersection, he pulled on the oars to maneuver upstream and away from the ball. He came to another landing near a set of ascending iron rungs fastened to the brick wall. They rose to a hatch in the ceiling. He steadied the little rowboat against the platform and rather than risk standing and capsizing he crawled out on his hands and knees. He gave the punt an affectionate shove back toward the main channel.

"Fair winds and a following sea, *mon ami.*"

Bell climbed the ladder. With no lock on the hatch, he carefully lifted it. Above was a room. He climbed fully into it and let the hatch lid down softly. The dim headlamp on his hard hat revealed that the room was used for tool storage. There were all manner of wrenches, some the size of baseball bats, and other gear sewer workers might need. He found the light switch by the room's only door. On a rack he discovered cleaned and folded canvas jumpsuits that the men could wear rather than befoul their own clothing. Bell emptied his pockets and thankfully stripped out of his filthy pants and shirt. He also removed his sodden socks and would just have to brave chilled ankles until he returned to his hotel. The ruined shoes wouldn't make it past the discreet trash can just outside the Lutetia's front door.

He tugged on the jumpsuit, buttoning the front up to his neck, and slipped on his wet shoes, making his feet feel like they were being rubbed by the icy hands of a corpse. He secreted his weapons and personal items in the many pockets.

Bell killed the light and cracked open the door. The room beyond was in darkness. He slapped the hard hat back onto his head and shouldered the heavy battery pack. He'd stepped into some sort of operations area. There were large tables covered in poster-sized technical drawings and schematics. There were shelves of hard hats like the one he wore and trays on the floor with ranks of rubber boots. A stairway like one coming out of a root cellar was on the opposite wall. Bell climbed up and came to a metal door painted glossy black. He had to manually unlock it, and when he inched it open, he got a lungful of crisp November air. He quickly stepped out from the stairwell and onto a street. The doorway was wedged into a narrow alley between two buildings. The street was deserted.

The Eiffel Tower loomed large in the

night, an ironwork needle bathed in a warm yellow aura. From its proximity, Bell realized his subterranean boat ride had taken him several miles from the Métro stop near the Société des Mines's building. At this late hour it took him an hour to find a taxi, and the night manager at the hotel, a man Bell had never met, asked for proof of his residency at the upscale establishment. Bell couldn't blame him. A shoeless man in a sewer worker's jumpsuit smelling vaguely of rot skulking in at three in the morning wasn't the Lutetia's typical clientele.

Bell took three separate showers using three different bars of soap, lathering and rinsing until his body was red and his skin wrinkled like a walnut shell. He dressed in a suit, lacing up a pair of shoes identical to the ones he'd discarded.

He knew that if he crawled into bed, he would shut down for a solid ten hours. It was best to soldier on and find a way to make contact with Brewster after he'd been picked up by Foster Gly.

Bell spent the next hour at the desk in his room meticulously cleaning and greasing his Colt .45 — John Browning preferred grease on the slide versus gun oil — and the two spare magazines. He persuaded the night manager to brew him a pot of coffee, which he took in one of the lobby's public rooms. He brought a notebook and took the opportunity to fill out his post-action report. There were so many ways the night could have gone. Ending up in the Paris sewers, pursued by a man who had to have been the most determined night watchman in the city, was not one he would have imagined.

At six a.m., the staff baker brought him croissants fresh from the oven, as light as any pastry Bell had ever eaten. With it was orange marmalade that was the perfect balance of tart and sweet. He ate a proper breakfast at seven in the dining room, peopled at that hour with the most industrious of businessmen and intrepid of tourists.

At seven-thirty, he closed himself off in one of the telephone booths just off the lobby and rang Henri Favreau.

"You had a busy night, *oui*?" the Frenchman said when Bell identified himself.

"Not sure what you're talking about," Bell replied coyly.

"One man fell to his death in the Métro, chasing another man who had just shot his way out of a moving train, and the body of a different man was found in a sewer."

Bell asked, "Has this made the papers?"

"Not yet," Favreau told him. "*Les Gendarmes* are saying nothing of these gruesome finds until they know if there's a connection. Neither man carried identification but they were of a similar type."

"Yes. Société des Mines guards who both deserve posthumous Employee of the Month awards. I am concerned Gly will get wind of this and alter his plans. I have a location where he's going to be sometime after ten-thirty."

"Gly?"

"Foster Gly. He's the lead thug for the Société. I need to get word to one of the men he's escorting this morning."

He could hear the sizzle of Henri's putting match to cigarette and him drawing deeply on the first of fifty he'd smoke that day. "Rest assured, my friend, since I have not heard of this man, he is not tall enough on the ladder to know what I know. Ach, high enough. Not high enough on the ladder. He will read about these deaths in this afternoon's papers just like the rest of the city."

Bell felt reassured by Favreau's reasoning. "Okay. I can buy that. What do you know of an outfit called A. C. Bourgault?"

"They are a large chandlering company. They're based here in Paris, but they operate large warehouses in all the major French ports."

"Do they just provision ships?"

"Mostly, but they've been known to provide foodstuffs and other items to scientific expeditions as well as for wealthy people who want to go on safari. A bit like your Abercrombie & Fitch, but not quite so luxurious."

"That makes sense," Bell said absently. "They'd want the finest hard-rock-mining gear Colorado had to offer, but other provisions could come from France. I bet Brewster and Hall are heading to Bourgault's office for some taste-testing."

"Who are Brewster and Hall?"

"Sorry, Henri, I'm tired and talking to myself. They're two Americans I need to warn about the true nature of the Société des Mines de Lorraine."

"Ah."

Bell asked, "Can anyone just show up at Bourgault's offices?"

"I believe you need an appointment. I can perhaps help. I know a few people in the shipping industry. Someone should be able to get you in as a ship broker of some kind."

"No, the men will be with the expedition side of the business, not the guys who buy groceries for freighters. Get me in as a Serbian naturalist looking to buy provisions for a trip into the Sahara."

264

"Why such a ridiculous cover?"

"It's the exact opposite of who Gly would suspect."

"Gly, the lead thug?"

"He's seen me briefly from a distance, so I don't want him in Bourgault's chancing upon an American looking to go to the Arctic. I don't want him hearing my Americanized French, and it's likely someone in the office speaks German, so I can't pretend I'm from Germany. Serbia is an obscure enough part of the Austrian Empire that few outsiders speak their language. I figure I can fake speaking English with a Serb accent and no one will be the wiser."

"*D'accord.* I see again why you are so good at what you do. I will make this happen. Name?"

"Ah, Dr. Aleksandar Dragović."

"I will get you an eleven o'clock meeting to discuss provisioning a five-man team for two weeks in the desert with native guides who will fend for themselves." Favreau paused for effect. "It will cost you one favor in the future with no questions asked."

That was an extremely open-ended deal, and normally Isaac would have negotiated conditions. That's how these things worked, but he was desperate. The French fixer knew he had Bell over a barrel. Bell closed his eyes and nodded. "Done."

16

At ten minutes to eleven later that morning, Isaac Bell stepped from an elevator and through the door to the offices of A. C. Bourgault. They occupied the sixth floor of a building on the edge of an area called La Villette, where many of the city's stockyards and slaughterhouses were located. The air on the street carried the coppery scent of blood.

He'd bought an appropriately tweedy suit from the Le Bon Marché department store a block down the Rue de Sèvres from his hotel and wore nonprescription glasses he kept as part of a regular disguise kit in his luggage. He carried his body in a round-shouldered slouch that effectively masked his height. Since his hair darkened significantly when it was wet — what Gly might have espied back in the foothills of the Rockies — he let his naturally blond shine brightly on another dreary Parisian day.

A reception desk guarded a large room furnished with two dozen identical desks at which sat two dozen nearly identical clerks shuffling papers, typing, or fielding from the general background drone of ringing telephones. Behind were individual offices with closed doors. There were no windows, so all lighting came from glass domes attached to the ten-foot ceiling. In all, the place had a rather dim, soul-crushing atmosphere.

A heavyset receptionist with poorly bleached hair asked him his name and business in French. Bell replied in a comically accented English, "I am Dr. Dragović. I have appointment with Herr Duchamp at eleven. Please do not disturb, because I am early. I do not mind the waiting."

She merely shrugged and went back to the magazine she'd been thumbing through.

A minute before eleven, Bell heard the elevator chime in the lobby behind the office door and seconds later four men strode into the reception area. Bell kept his face neutral, with a hint of a smile that said he was a man of good cheer. Foster Gly eyed him hard, head to toe and back again, before dismissing him with a scowl. The detective marveled at how Gly could get such a thick neck into a shirt and manage to wrap it with a tie. With him was the twin brother of the man Bell had seen Gly shoot dead.

For a fleeting moment he wondered if there was a way to sow some sort of discord between these two, reveal to Yves Massard that Gly had murdered his brother. Since there was no proof, it was a matter of trust. Who would Massard believe, a longtime compatriot who likely consoled him for several boozy nights following Marc's death and locked in that loyalty or an American stranger with nothing more than his word that he was telling the truth? The mere idea of it was so ridiculous that Bell banished it before it could even fully form in his mind.

The other two men were strangers. One was tall and broad-shouldered, and he was missing two fingers from his left hand. He had dark hair and a farmer's stoic face — the face of a man that nothing and no one ever riled. By sheer size alone, Bell was certain he was Joshua Hayes Brewster. The second was a bantam of a man barely five feet two inches tall, but he did possess a pugnacious thrust to his chin and swagger to his walk.

It wasn't until the small man's gaze swept past Bell that he saw the spark of madness. His eyes glittered with an inner fire that looked like it was about to burn out of control. Bell immediately changed his mind. The shorter miner was Brewster. Only someone with that kind of intensity could convince eight other men to pull off something as audacious as what they were attempting.

Gly informed the secretary of his appointment. His French was accented with a Scottish burr that made it almost incomprehensible. She'd had no qualms leaving Bell in the waiting area, but she rightly decided that making the newcomer wait for even a second was not in her best interest.

She begged her leave and lurched from her desk to fetch the representative assigned to his account.

"Madame," Bell called as she rushed by. "Please, I am to see Herr Duchamp. You tell him I am here. *Da?*"

She made an impatient gesture with her hand, like a bird fluttering its wing, but she also nodded. She worked her way through the bull pen and went first to one office, where she knocked and poked her head inside, and then on to an adjacent office. The same perfunctory knock, the same swinging open the door, announcing the client, closing the door again. She moved with the rote efficiency of an automaton. Soon she was back at her desk, studiously not looking at Gly, Yves, or the two miners, who stood uneasily in a cluster between her and the sofa Bell occupied. Very soon two mid-level functionaries emerged from their vaunted offices. They were older than the young men toiling at the open desks, and were balding and spread-waisted, but with a haughtiness that they could lord over the ranks of drones they themselves had emerged from a year or two previously.

There was a moment of awkward hand-shaking as the two parties sorted themselves out. Bell, playing the hapless Serb, even shook hands with Massard, Vernon Hall, and Joshua Hayes Brewster. Gly refused the gesture with a sneer and pushed past Bell to speak with his rep from the ship-and-expedition provisioning company. Hall did take the detective's outstretched hand without a change of expression. Brewster's eyebrows went up when he felt a square of paper pressed into his palm so subtly that he'd almost missed it. There was a barest pause while Bell mouthed the name Pat-more, which Brewster, to his credit, didn't acknowledge.

Duchamp led Bell back through the bull pen to his office while the others followed their representative to his. Duchamp's office had a window, at least, behind his small, cluttered desk, but the view was of a brick wall no more than a dozen feet away. What light filtered down to the window was anemic and gray.

The Frenchman indicated Bell could take one of the chairs in front of the desk. He was a small man with a pinched expression. "I am not comfortable with this situation. We are a reputable company."

"Pardon me?" Bell said. "I do not understand."

"I know you are not some Serbian naturalist. I was ordered by my superiors to help you with a task concerning the other party that is here now."

Henri had gone for the direct approach in getting Bell this interview. On hindsight, it was for the best. Bell needed to pretend to be someone else only in front of Gly. Favreau had saved him the tedium of playing a role for an hour or two.

"Oh, I see. Good, then," Bell replied, a little taken aback, but he recovered quickly. "You do realize large favors were exchanged by powerful people to secure your cooperation. I do have your cooperation, yes?"

"Of course," the Frenchman replied, his voice softening and his face showing a bit more openness. "In truth, being singled out by Monsieur Michaud, the office manager, for this assignment shows the company's faith in me."

"There you go." Bell smiled, putting the salaryman at ease. "Consider it an honor rather than a burden. Now, how does this process work? For them, I mean. The other party."

"After some preliminaries, my counterpart, Monsieur Gauthier, will take the men to a tasting room, where they will sample some of our canned goods — stews, soups, and vegetables, mostly, plus our popular pastas — and a full assortment of desserts. As you may know, the process for preserving food in cans started here in France at the time of Napoléon."

"I didn't know that," Bell admitted.

"After, they will enjoy samples of cured meats, and porridges that can be reconstituted on-site with a little water. I understand they are bound for the Arctic, so Gauthier will recommend foods that are high in fat and rich with kilocalories. The men will select the ones they deem the tastiest. An order will be transmitted to our warehouse at whichever port they are departing from. Workers there fill the order and put everything on pallets that can be hoisted aboard a ship."

"And this is how you provision a large freighter?"

"More or less. It is usually company representatives who meet here and often they don't sample much of anything since they take on more fresh stores than canned goods. A well-fed crew tends to work harder than ones with poor nutrition."

"I never gave any of this much thought. Amazing how many parts must work together to keep ships at sea."

Bell pulled his pocket watch by its chain and checked the time. He had ten more minutes before the note he'd passed Brewster said to meet in the men's washroom. Though he had plenty of time, Bell got to his feet. He wanted to reconnoiter the lavatory. "I'm sorry to cut you short, monsieur. However, I don't know what level of paranoia I'm dealing with, so it's best I get into position now."

"Oh, *bien sûr.* I understand completely." Far from the dour functionary Bell had greeted just moments earlier, Duchamp seemed pleased to be able to help. Securing quick cooperation from people was among Bell's many talents, one that Marion was forever suspicious of, as she too often found herself doing things Bell suggested.

"La salle de bain?"

"*À droite.* To the right."

Bell saw himself out of Duchamp's office. None of the workers in the outer space paid him the slightest interest. He moved along the wall of doors until he came to one with the proper words on the door versus a person's name. He swung open the door and was stupefied. There was just a sink and toilet. He'd expected to be able to hide in one of several stalls. He fully expected Gly or Massard to escort Brewster to the men's room because that's what he would have done had their roles been reversed.

Though there were dozens of workers, the bath's small size was just one more dehumanizing aspect of this office. Bell poked his head around the door and saw that behind it was a closet. He stepped into the bathroom and let the door close behind him. The closet handle didn't lock, but above it was a dead bolt. Bell dropped to his knees and fished out his lockpicks.

The lock was a sloppy old thing that his slender picks had difficulty engaging. The problem was having too fine of instruments for the job at hand. He'd be better off with a couple of straightened hairpins. Again and again he tried the picks to no avail, pulling them free before another fresh attempt. He was more than aware of time getting away from him. He stood and fished his hotel key from his pocket. The peaks along the top crenellation weren't optimal for what he had in mind, but they weren't terrible either. He unlaced his shoe. Befitting the Eastern European doctor he was imitating, it had a solid thick heel as tough as stone.

He positioned the heavy brass key just outside the lock's slot and wacked it with the shoe at the same time he twisted it. The force of the blow, called a bump in the vernacular of lockpicking, was enough to move the lock's driver pins and create a momentary gap around the shear line. His quick wrist twist had been timed, through countless hours of practice, to exploit this momentary lapse, and the lock snicked open.

"Do not complain again." Bell heard Gly's raised Scottish voice just outside the bathroom. "I am checking it first."

With failure not an option, Bell opened the closet door. The space was smaller than a phone booth and packed with mops, brooms, and other cleaning supplies. He backed in, trying not to jostle anything, and pulled the door closed. The air reeked of ammonia, and in just seconds his nose burned. The bathroom door squealed open. Bell groped for the dead bolt lock only to discover that there wasn't a toggle on the inside. He couldn't lock the door.

He grabbed the regular door handle loosely. If Gly checked, the knob needed to turn freely because it was a simple passage set without a lock. But once Gly tried to tug on the door, Bell had to grip it like iron and pray that the Scotsman didn't put his considerable strength behind the move.

"Empty bathroom, Gly." Even muffled by the door, Brewster's voice was pitched higher than expected.

"Hold up," Gly retorted.

Bell felt the sweat-slick knob suddenly turn in his hand. As soon as it stopped rotating, he crushed it with both fists and tensed the muscles of his arms, shoulders, stomach, and back. He held on so fiercely that it made the door feel as solidly locked as if it had been nailed in place.

"Be quick," Gly said threateningly as he left.

Brewster locked the bathroom and then knocked on the closet door. "He's gone."

Bell stepped out. He stood a full head taller than the miner and had at least fifty pounds on him. For being such a legend of the hard rocks outside of Denver and beyond, Brewster just wasn't at all as expected. He was weak-chinned, with wispy hair, and had such deep wrinkles around his eyes that it was hard to believe the man wasn't yet thirty-five years old. He looked a worn-out sixty.

All except for the eyes themselves. Bell had to admit he had a hard time meeting Brewster's gaze. It was like looking at the sun, painful, and yet he felt compelled to keep glancing back as if to verify that what he was seeing was real. Brewster's look was part madman and part confidence man. Someone daring you to trust him while all the time warning you that you must not.

Bell moved to the sink before speaking and turned on the water. In the small mirror over the basin he saw his face was flushed from the effort of holding the door in position, while his eyes were red from the ammonia burn. He gestured Brewster over to the far corner of the small bath and shook hands. Their conversation was held to a whisper with heads almost touching.

"Mr. Brewster, my name is Isaac Bell. I'm a private detective working with Colonel Gregg Patmore. I've followed you from Central City to Paris with an urgent warning. Gly and Massard are going to kill you and your men as soon as you recover the byzanium ore."

Brewster didn't even blink. "That was

obvious from the beginning. You think I trust any of these frog-eaters?"

Bell was taken aback. "You knew and you're going anyway? Are you" — Bell was about to say "crazy," but he suspected Brewster just might be — "sure that's wise?"

"Gregg and I figured he'd have something sussed out before we're finished tearing into Bednaya Mountain. If not, well, Gly and Massard won't have the element of surprise. Soon as we suspect something, we'll jump them sonsabitches. Say, Gly told us the other Massard got killed. You do that?"

With the world still atilt under his feet, Bell said, "Ah, no. Gly actually shot him to keep him from talking to me." Realizing he'd just made a potentially fatal mistake, he seized the smaller man by the shoulders. "You can't let on that you know that."

"I was born at night, Mr. Bell. Just not last night. I know how this works. 'Twas me that set it all in motion when I realized the Société des Mines had lied about the ore I'd found and I went to Patmore."

"Okay. Let me start again. I know you suspect Gly will try to kill you. Patmore told me that. What you don't know is, Gly is aware that someone — me — is onto him."

"Now I get why he's been on edge. He's cagey on a normal day but hell-bent since we left Denver. I thought it was over Marc's death, yet even Yves isn't taking it all that badly. Marc wasn't a natural-born killer like the other two."

Bell nodded. "I've spoken with his wife. Do they still think you'll need until June to get the ore?"

"That's what I keep telling them."

"But you told Patmore you can do it by May."

"Yes." Brewster grimaced and showed a mouth of tobacco-stained teeth. "If they're suspicious enough, then they'll sail back as soon as they're able and wait for us. Gly knows that I won't allow any of his men to overwinter with us, and the ice gets too thick January through April, so they can't wait offshore. But they will come back as early as they can."

"What do you know about the ship they're using?"

"We saw it when they transferred our mining gear from the ocean liner in Le Havre."

"And?"

"And what? It was a Navy ship converted into a fast freighter, about a hundred feet in length, with extra-long boom arms on its main crane to move cargo ashore."

If it was a Navy vessel, the Société des Mines had secured government sanction for this job. Notable, but ultimately unimport-ant at this time, Bell concluded. "Did it have icebreaking capabilities?"

Brewster shrugged. "I don't know. Wait! It doesn't."

"Keep your voice down," Bell admonished in a harsh whisper.

"Sorry. I remember them saying that it was a good thing summer stayed until so late in October or they would have to use a different ship."

"Okay. That's our advantage. We'll use an icebreaker and get you out before the French leave for the island. What's the soon-est you can finish the job?"

"Mid-April. That's shaving two weeks off the estimate I gave Gregg."

"Not good enough," Bell said quickly.

"You don't know the conditions up there."

"It doesn't matter. If we try to pick you up in mid-April, the French are going to be waiting. We need to go earlier, Brewster, or it's all for nothing. We'll be there on April first."

"Damnit."

Bell could see the conflict in Brewster's fiery eyes. The miner knew just how hard he could push his crew to make the tighter deadline and it was clear he recognized the need for the revised schedule, that he'd have to drive them like a biblical slavemaster. His body was tense, like a cable on a bridge, and he seemed to vibrate, but then he accepted the inevitability of his decision and the muscles of his shoulders relaxed slightly.

A fist banged on the bathroom door.

"Hurry it up, man," Foster Gly growled.

"A minute," Brewster shot back. "The food you're givin' is killing me."

Brewster's eyes drilled into Bell's, and he whispered as quiet and as deadly as a cobra. "If you're not there on the first, most likely my boys are gonna kill me for what I done to them to make the deadline. They're good lads all, but they're facing some hardships no man or beast should endure. And if, by some miracle, they don't kill me for pushing them so hard, Mr. Bell, I'm surely gonna kill you."

Isaac Bell wasn't someone to be intimidated or threatened, especially by a man he towered over, but the glare Brewster gave him suppressed the defiant reply he'd normally give in this situation.

"Understood, Mr. Brewster."

The Coloradan yanked the chain to empty the toilet's cistern. Bell let himself back into the closet in case Gly happened to check again.

"About time," Gly said to Brewster when

282

he stepped out of the small lavatory.

As Bell waited in the dark and cramped closet, breathing ammonia in concentrations not much weaker than smelling salts, he contemplated the only flaw that he could see in his plan — that he had no idea how to get access to an icebreaker or a captain reckless enough to attempt an evacuation of American miners from a Russian island with a vessel from the French Navy possibly lurking nearby.

He had four months.

17

Sandefjord, Norway
March 1912

It was clear early on in Bell's search for a skipper with the right kind of Arctic experience that he'd end up either in the northern reaches of Canada or back in Europe. And the Canadian angle seemed unlikely because most of those experts amid the frozen seas were native hunters in open longboats searching the black waters for small whales and walrus.

That he needed a whaler was never in doubt. They are the only men who are willing to risk both ship and crew on the hunt for the giant cetaceans that migrate around the ice fields at the top of the world. No merchantman need traverse these frozen reaches, save small coastal freighters plying the waters from village to village along the coasts of Norway and Iceland and the Faroe Islands. None had any need to know how to circumvent the mighty floes that drifted down from the Arctic or how to spot and exploit open leads in the ice that were large enough for a ship and navigable.

The fishermen certainly had the bravery for what Bell had in mind, but they were mariners of the open waters where they could trawl their vast nets without fear of them being shredded by an accidental brush against an iceberg's jagged underside. They stayed well clear of bergs and pack ice. And when winter's darkened grip held fast and the ice grew truly thick, they beached the boats and tended to winter chores until the sun returned again in the spring.

The men who chased the whales. That's who Bell was told he needed by sailors he'd befriended during past cases. He talked to the few he knew and they, in turn, led him to seafarers with specialized knowledge of the mariners of the far north. It was at this point a name emerged, whispered as rumor at first but who others claimed to have first- or at least secondhand knowledge of a legendary skipper, a man whose skills and experience and bravery were the stuff of tavern tales. When cannon-mounted harpoons had made whaling so deadly efficient that they'd decimated the populations of minke, blue, and bowhead, he'd been one of the first skippers to turn southward and hunt the vast ice fields surrounding the continent of Antarctica.

The skipper was Ragnar Fyrie, a native of Iceland, and Isaac Bell had tracked him to the city of Sandefjord, which served as the whaling capital of Norway. In reality, the coastal town of six thousand was also the world's whaling capital, as so much of the industry was based here or at least crewed by sailors local to the area.

Situated near the mouth of the mighty Oslofjord, Sandefjord boasted a natural harbor that was well protected from the ravages of the Skagerrak Strait, the section of the North Sea between Norway and Denmark. Unlike the towering fjords in the north of the country, the town was backed by low hills. It consisted mostly of wooden cottages owned by the whalers, but there were some brick structures for the wealthy and a central street dominated by the newly rebuilt Sandefjord church, with its soaring brick tower roofed in dark slate and a suite of bells that sounded every hour.

Bell arrived by train from Oslo. He'd read that in the summer the nearby beaches were popular with the capital city's residents and that there were spas nestled around town. However, when he stepped off the train and onto the platform, a heavy smell hit him like a gut punch and he wondered how anyone could spend even a few seconds in Sandefjord let alone an entire summer season.

The smell was of the whaling fleet at anchor in the inner harbor. The ships were modern, ocean-capable vessels and were regularly serviced by their crews, but, like the slave ships of old, there was no amount of cleansing that could rid them of the noxious odor they carried like the stain of sin for what they were built to do. The particular smell permeated everything within the city and probably carried for many miles. It was the fishy stink of blubber rendered into whale oil, but also the hot copper scent of blood so copious that it would wash the whalers' decks like the slosh of waves during heavy seas.

He imagined it was a stench the locals had grown so accustomed to, they never noticed it, but that outsiders would never find themselves immune from.

It was now mid-March, and his window to reach Brewster and his fellow miners was closing rapidly. It had taken far too long to find the right person for the job, and longer still to develop a plan to secure his assistance. The problem was, Ragnar Fyrie stood accused of illegally poaching whales in an area claimed as the exclusive territory of a concession holder from there in Sandefjord.

For Bell, the legalities seemed a little vague. The concession holder maintained that the Norwegian government gave him the authority to hunt whales over a wide swath of the Arctic Ocean and he, in turn, employed captains and crews to do the actual harvesting. Fyrie maintained that he was a native of Iceland, which made him a Danish citizen, and was therefore not bound by a concession granted by a foreign power. His argument held little sway with the Norwegians. As soon as he'd put into port with nearly ten thousand gallons of whale oil, as well as some more valuable spermaceti oil his crew had harvested from the mammoth heads of several sperm whales, his ship had been impounded and its cargo confiscated.

That had occurred at the end of the 1911 hunting season, and the wrangling between the governments of Norway and Denmark had lasted throughout the sunless Arctic winter and there seemed to be no end in sight as spring fast approached and the great cetaceans' migrations were about to begin anew. Fyrie and his crew were free to leave the ship and enjoy Sandefjord as they awaited their fate so long as their vessel remained tied to the dock with her main engines cold.

Bell knew all of this before he had arrived in the coastal town and had crafted a plan with the help of a marine engineer employed by a wealthy shipping magnate who'd used the Van Dorn Agency on a few occasions when discretion was a must. It was only a matter of convincing Captain Fyrie to go along with it.

It took two porters to wrestle each of the large trunks Bell had stowed in the luggage car for the sixty-mile trip from Oslo. The contents had been purchased at some expense from specialists in New York, Newark, and Philadelphia. Bell's acquisitions had all but emptied the supplies in all three cities. Customs forms declared powdered silica. That was far from the truth.

He shuddered to think what would have happened if one of the waterproofed trunks had failed and its contents come into contact with water. The trunks, as well as two personal bags, went onto a waiting Leyland truck he'd rented that took Bell across town to a small inn that was crowded during the summer season but was empty now except for him on this cold, dark March evening.

He paid extra to have the truck parked in a clapboard barn behind the inn.

Bell changed out of his suit and put on dark woolen pants, a cable-knit wool sweater, and a Navy coat with a high collar.

The docks were easy enough to find. He simply followed his nose and knew he was on the right path when the smell grew progressively stronger. Twenty-odd whaling ships tied up in loose rows. Each sported a raised platform on the bow, usually accessible by a suspended catwalk over the forward part of the ship from the wheelhouse. On the platform was mounted a vicious-looking harpoon cannon capable of hurling an explosives-tipped lance far and with enough force to pierce a whale's thick blubber hide.

He found Fyrie's ship easily enough. Bell knew he had the right ship, the *Hvalur Batur,* or *Whale Boat,* because a small guardhouse had been erected at the foot of its gangplank and a trickle of smoke coiled from the chimney of what he imagined was a potbellied stove.

He strode past the guard shack without a moment's pause or the slightest regard for its occupant and mounted the inclined ramp up from the quay to the deck of the Icelandic whaler. He'd noted she flew a

Danish flag on her jack staff as a cheeky reminder that she wasn't bound by Norway's laws.

The guard didn't emerge from his little metal lodge, and no one challenged him upon reaching the ship's deck. He climbed a steep flight of stairs welded to the superstructure and emerged on a balcony that wrapped around the bridge and extended out to the harpoon some fifty feet forward. The bridge was dark, and when he tugged at a pitted brass doorknob, he found it locked. Back down on deck, he located a watertight door aft of the gangplank, but it too was locked.

He retreated from the ship, and when he came abreast of the guard shack, the door opened. The man wore a blue serge police uniform with bright buttons, but his face was in bad need of a shave, and the bags under his eyes were large enough to be considered ladies' purses. It was obvious he'd been on duty for quite some time and that this wasn't considered a plum assignment.

He spoke a few words in Norwegian to Bell.

"I'm sorry," the detective replied, "do you speak English?"

The guard scratched himself absently.

291

"The crew. *Ja?*"

"Captain Fyrie?"

"*Ja.* They drink at the Lundehund. A tavern. *Lundehund* — is a dog. You see on, ah, sign. Little dog. *Lundehund.*"

"Captain Fyrie and his men are at a tavern called the Lundehund, which is named for a dog painted on a sign outside."

The man flashed nicotine-yellowed teeth and pointed in the direction of the big church that dominated the downtown district. *"Ja."*

Bell thanked the guard and headed out. It was growing steadily darker and colder. He flipped up the jacket collar and crammed his hands into its pockets.

He found the bar at the very end of the main commercial street, closest to the waterfront. As promised, the sign over the front door showed a dog with fox-like ears and a bright yellow coat. The establishment wasn't exactly a wharf dive, but it wasn't much better. Before he mounted the steps up to a wooden porch that ran the width of the building, he noticed a group of men loitering up the street in the light cast by a flickering gas lamp. What piqued his interest was that they shared none of the laughter-filled banter of comrades out on the town for some fun. They stood in a tight circle, hunched against the cold, and with no obvious purpose for idling outdoors on a chilly night.

Bell's natural suspicion went into overdrive.

The long winter was coming to a close and the whaling season would start soon enough. The locals had been patient with the slow grind of justice's wheels over the past months. Now that they were getting ready to leave port again, it was possible some sought extra-judicial retribution against Ragnar Fyrie for poaching whales in their waters.

There were five men clustered around the gas lamp. Bell had no idea how many it took to crew a modern whaling ship, but his estimate was for far more than that and that this lot down the street was likely waiting for reinforcements.

The two quickest ways for men to become friends, Bell had learned over the years, was to either get drunk together or have each other's back in a fight. He'd planned on the former to hire Fyrie for the mission to Novaya Zemlya, but now it looked like it was going to be the latter. He had his .45 holstered at the small of his back, praying it wouldn't be needed. He had his stiletto boot knife at his ankle, and knowing he'd be spending time near the dockyards, he carried brass knuckles in his coat pocket.

Bell climbed up onto the porch and let himself into the bar. The interior was dim, and the air was so full of tobacco smoke, it reminded him of being downwind of a wildfire in Southern California. Under the haze, like the afternotes of a particularly foul wine, lingered the smell of spilled liquor, sweaty men, and the reek of whale oil. Few of the patrons, all male, shot him even a passing glance before turning back to their solo drinks or crowded tables. The floors were bare wood covered with a layer of sawdust so infused with alcohol that some spots were as slick as an ice rink. The plank and plaster ceiling was virtually black with a century's worth of soot.

He scanned the room quickly, making assessments each time his eyes flicked from group to group and person to person. One table stood out immediately. It sat in the far corner, and the men at it all had their backs to the wall, an inconvenient arrangement for conversation but one that was easy to defend.

Ragnar Fyrie had been described to Bell as handsome, blond, younger than expected, and someone who has that certain something.

There was a total of eight men at the table, with Fyrie at the center. He sensed Bell's scrutiny and returned the look with a hint of detached curiosity. Bell had taken the temperature of the room. There was no open hostility toward Fyrie and his men, and there was no love either. Approaching the Icelandic whalers wouldn't get Isaac a shiv in the back, but it wouldn't likely gain him any friends.

Bell strode over and stood before Fyrie, holding the man's steady gaze. The two of them were handsome and blond-haired, yet whereas Bell's looks were classically masculine, Fyrie had a delicacy to his features that didn't jibe with the clichéd image of a salt-toughened seaman. He was already forty, and apart from just a crinkle around his blue eyes, his face was as unlined as a youth's. Bell pictured him at the helm of a sleek yacht out of some wealthy East Coast enclave like Providence or Hyannis Port.

"English?" Isaac asked.

A twitch of a smile lifted the corner of his mouth and made his eyes brighten. "Icelandic, actually, but I suspect you know that. And, yes, I speak English." With his Norse accent, his voice had a lyric quality that didn't conform to the stereotype but somehow managed to convey strength and elicit respect.

"There are five men waiting up the street who I can only guess are looking for a fight. I call it seven minutes before they come through that door."

Fyrie nodded as if this news wasn't unexpected. "It was bound to happen. They're off a local boat called the *Isbjørn* — that means 'polar bear.' They had a terrible season last year and blame us. Thanks for letting me know. What's your interest?"

"My name is Isaac Bell, Captain, and I need you and your crew healthy enough so I can hire you for a particular job."

18

Ragnar Fyrie used a foot to push out a chair on Bell's side of the round table. Bell sat and accepted a mug of beer poured from a half-finished pitcher. The beer was room temperature but richly flavored. "Mr. Bell, apart from the fight we're about to have against a larger crew, there is the problem of my ship impounded and my crew on — let's call it precautionary probation. How can we possibly help you and your, ah, particular job?"

Bell liked Fyrie's style. As described, he was charming yet distant, and he had a certain quality — a sangfroid, perhaps, or just a devil-may-care attitude — that he wore well.

"Are you familiar with the M Line?"

The captain nodded. "Black Jack McCallister. Not personally but by reputation. They're a good outfit. Fast ships on the North Atlantic route. Well-trained crews."

"Their chief engineer and I have come up with a plan to get your ship clear of the harbor without raising suspicion."

"If only that were true," Fyrie said with an overly dramatic sigh before turning very serious. "Did your plan factor in that the *Hvalur Batur* is guarded twenty-four hours a day, that her bunkers were emptied of all her coal, and there isn't a tug within sixty miles that's powerful enough to move her? Oh, and that she and her crew, including yours truly, are the subjects of intense international negotiations, with jail time, or at least a massive fine, as the inevitable outcome?"

Bell took a slow, deliberate sip of beer. "Didn't know about the guard, actually, but that's an easy fix."

Fyrie paused, studying the detective for a moment, before laughing aloud. "You're serious, aren't you?"

"About this? Absolutely."

"Okay. Tell me your plan and I will consider your particular job."

That was as far as the conversation went. The bar door opened. Bell didn't need to turn around to know the crew of the rival whaling boat had entered the room. He knew by how grim Fyrie's crew started to look. As for the captain himself, it seemed the more men entered the bar, the more he reveled in the challenge.

Bell didn't need to understand the words that went back and forth between the opposing captains. He'd heard such confrontations many times before and there was little variation in the verbal lead-up to an all-out fight. So universal was the theme that it was almost a scripted set piece. The only thing he hadn't expected was that the crew from the Norwegian whaler *Isbjørn* was led by a black-bearded captain who stood a solid six feet six inches.

Bell had turned his chair halfway around when the last of the ten sailors entered the Lundehund so he could watch them while keeping an eye on how Fyrie was handling himself. It was the point in the verbal preliminaries when Fyrie got to his feet to signal that it was time they all went outside and settled the affair as immature adolescents pretending to be men that the other crew suddenly launched themselves in a surprise attack.

The move was a total break in protocol. A popular waterfront bar should be given the reverence of holy ground when it came to a fight of this magnitude. A brawl between two or even four men was certainly allowed, but not a full-on rumble, and that disregard for the inviolability of the tavern's sanctity kept Fyrie and his crew a fraction slow to respond.

Bell hadn't expected it either, yet that didn't mean he didn't react instantly and with forethought. He'd watched the big sailors enter the dim bar and fan out in a semicircle with the captain at the center. He'd noted who kept their hands in their pockets to disguise the fact they'd armed themselves with some manner of cosh or cudgel. He graded potential fighting abilities by how they held themselves — who was slouching, who favored a bad leg, who looked like he'd poured himself too many drams of liquid courage. He noted all these things on a subconscious level so that when they sprang into action, he'd already prioritized targets and was moving before Fyrie or his men could extricate themselves from behind the table where the Norwegian whalers had hoped to pin them.

In one fluid motion, Bell grabbed the back of his chair and let his momentum lift it off the floor and swing it in a slashing arc. It was a solid piece of furniture, doubtless a veteran of its fair share of fights. It didn't shatter upon impact with a sailor pulling a baton from the pocket of his peacoat. Instead, the chair legs cracked the man's forearm at the wrist with sufficient enough force to break both radius and ulna. Bell released the chair and followed through by crashing the bottom of his boot into the outside of the man's knee. The man crumpled immediately and instinctively tried to break his fall with his broken wrist. The strikes had been so quick that his brain hadn't yet registered the injury. When the cracked bones took on the weight of his two-hundred-pound frame, the ends came apart like shattered crystal and his scream acted as a distraction for the next man Bell had targeted.

This assailant wasn't as large as his captain, but he had Bell by three inches and thirty pounds. None of that mattered. The sailor pivoted slightly to square himself with the Van Dorn detective and Bell took a fast step toward the man, coming inside what anyone would consider the fighting perimeter. The big Norwegian didn't know how to react. In that moment's hesitation, Bell grabbed the collar of his coat and pulled him forward just enough that his shoulders lost tension and his head dipped.

Bell met the bridge of the sailor's nose with the thickest part of his forehead in a butt that would do a bighorn sheep proud. The crunch of bone and cartilage was accompanied by fountaining blood.

Twenty percent of the *Isbjørn*'s crew was out of commission even before the surprise attack reached its intended target. The four sailors to the right of the captain, and the captain himself, grabbed the thick pine table and put their weight into it, hoping to crush the crew of the *Hvalur Batur* against the wall. The three attackers on Bell's side of the semicircle were shifting into defensive stances, seeing they were now less of a threat and more like the threatened.

Captain Fyrie and his crew had just enough time to set themselves up for the charge and meet brute strength with brute strength, and rather than have the sharp edge of the table crush them into the wall, they managed to hold their ground and then spin the table enough to throw the five men opposite them off balance. The Icelanders scrambled up over the table, kicking aside spilled pitchers and steins, and launched themselves bodily at the rival crew.

The sneak attack turned into a melee of fists and elbows, wild swings, and precision jabs. Bell fitted the brass knuckles over the fingers of his right hand. Around him, the room turned into a kaleidoscope of violence. For every punch the detective took, he gave two right back. He saw Ragnar Fyrie caught in a crushing hold by the captain of the *Isbjørn*. His face was suffused with blood and his eyes goggled from their sockets.

Bell didn't have an angle to hit the attacker's face and didn't want to crack open his skull with the knuckle-dusters, so he threw five rapid, and incrementally deeper, punches into the Norwegian captain's right kidney.

The blows became so painful that the whaler had no choice but to release his hold on Fyrie. When he turned on Bell, the American dropped him with a haymaker he brought all the way up from his shin, a punch with enough force that the monster Norseman was lifted an inch off the floor before collapsing in an unconscious heap.

That was the symbolic end to the fight, but the bartender had reached for the 12-gauge side-by-side kept for just such purposes under the bar and he fired both barrels as the Norwegian captain hit the filthy floor. The men left standing were raked with twin loads of coarse rock salt, a nonlethal way to drain the fight out of anyone taking a hit.

Bell had his back turned to the blast yet felt the wasp-like sting of a salt fragment biting the back of his neck and others peppering his coat.

In the deafening echo that followed the gunshots, men helped comrades to their feet. Patrons started righting overturned furniture, and, most important, the crew of the *Isbjørn* gathered the wounded and slunk from the bar. Two men were needed to drape the unconscious captain's heavy arms over their shoulders and drag him out, while another shepherded the man with the shattered wrist.

Before any protests were raised by the owner and staff, Bell peeled off enough krone notes to cover any damage and slapped them on the bar and then added to the pile, the universal gesture that the next round for everybody was on him. Just like that, all was forgotten.

"You fight well." Captain Fyrie saluted Bell with a fresh mug of lager.

"In your school, was there a group of bullies who terrorized the other kids?"

"Of course. You were one?"

Bell shook his head at the memory. "No. I was the damned fool trying to defend the weaker students. Took my share of beatings before I got any good at defending myself."

Fyrie's laughter quickly faded. "I must tell you, my new friend, that I have considered every possible way of getting my ship out of the Norwegians' grasp. The problem is, the thermal inertia of all that cold water in the boilers and how much energy we need to build up sufficient steam to run the engines. I've worked it out with my own engineer." He nodded at a bespectacled man in his early fifties with a black eye and gold tooth. "Even installing a dozen bypasses and running at supercritical pressure, we still need several thousand gallons of water to clear the harbor. With our system, that will take nearly sixteen hours to bring it up to temperature.

"Even if we had coal, which we don't, we get boarded every morning for an inspection, so there isn't enough time to fire her up. We thought about using kerosene, gasoline, even propane. They all take too much time or will give off enough exhaust to alert the harbor authorities." He saw Bell was about to interject, and added, "There's more than just the gangway guard to worry about. The harbormaster has a particular interest in our case as he will have first dibs to buy the *Hvalur Batur.*"

"The engineer I worked with and I looked at all kinds of alternative fuels too," Bell said, "and came to the same conclusion."

"What do you propose? Magic?"

"To some, I'm sure it'll seem like it."

Bell Takes on the Lorient

19

The Norwegian authorities had allowed the bulk of Ragnar Fyrie's crew to return to Reykjavik because they were simple sailors doing what the captain had asked of them. The six who'd remained behind with him in Sandefjord were officers, senior engineers, and the principal harpooner. They were stakeholders in the *Hvalur Batur* who shared in her profits and were thus considered as culpable as Captain Fyrie.

When it came to implementing Bell's plan, the seven men and the captain worked with an efficiency born of sailors who'd risked their lives for one another so often that a fresh incident no longer required even a simple thanks. Orders need be given only once and were carried out in a timely fashion. None were questioned, no matter how arcane.

Thirty disassembled whale oil barrels were pulled from stores and knocked together in record time. The barrels had been lowered to a waiting motor skiff through a hatch in the starboard hull so that the guard watching the whaler had no idea anything was afoot. They were then transported to the barn behind Bell's hotel, where the owner was being paid to keep a fire lit under a two-hundred-gallon steel tank.

Two men had been dispatched to the railroad machine shop near the station where Bell had, by prearrangement with a conductor on his train from Oslo, secured access to a pile of iron filings waste left over from routine brake cleaning. Another crew member had bought several twenty-kilogram bags of coarse salt from a commercial cannery and begun the laborious process of grinding it down to a fine powder.

By five o'clock in the afternoon following the bar fight, everything was as ready as it could be. Night was falling in the northern latitudes, and the stars and moon were covered by a blanket of high clouds. The harbor itself remained glassy calm, the reflection of the town's lights lancing across its surface in perfectly straight lines.

Bell implemented the last part of the initial phase of the plan personally. At the base of the *Hvalur Batur*'s gangplank sat the little metal guard shack, with its blackened chimney poking through the roof and wisps of fragrant smoke blowing out across the water. The same guard was on duty, and his eyes lit up when Bell approached and pulled a bottle of clear liquid from inside his peacoat. The man quickly stepped out into the chilly night air.

"This is to thank you," the Van Dorn detective said, handing over the liquor.

The guard smiled a little. "I hear you find Captain Fyrie and also captain of the *Isbjørn. Ja?*"

"Any word how he's doing?"

"His mouth, ah, teeth. No, jaw. His jaw is closed for a month with wire."

"Wrong place, wrong time." Bell shrugged.

"Ach, the man is a *raevhål.* Um, a —"

"No need to translate," Bell assured him quickly. "Enjoy your drink. And thanks again." He thrust his hands back into his pockets and ambled off down the street. When he looked back, he could see the guard retaking his seat in the shack and tilting the bottom of the bottle toward the ceiling.

At its strongest, the native drink called *akvavit* is eighty proof. Bell had just handed over a bottle of West Virginia low-holler white lightning flavored with Georgia peaches. It was ninety-five percent alcohol. Three shots of that moonshine and the man would be incoherent and never know what hit him.

When Bell returned twenty minutes later with the truck, the guard was facedown on the desk and the bottle was a third empty. He'd be out until dawn.

In the back of the truck were six of the oaken barrels. Each weighed about three hundred pounds and was filled with water just a few degrees below boiling. They'd cooled some on their journey, and would keep doing so, but Bell's plan needed to start with water well above the near-freezing temperatures of the harbor. The Icelandic sailors had little trouble wrestling the barrels off the back of the truck and rolling them up the gangplank.

Once the first barrel was on deck, the chief engineer was waiting with a hose connected directly to the whaler's boilers. Even as the second and third barrels were being manhandled up the plank, he was draining the first into the propulsion system. Bell had explained his concept by using electricity as an example.

"A good electrician can bypass an active circuit if he's careful enough. It saves time by not having to shut down the power. They call it hot-wiring. What we are going to do, essentially, is 'hot-pipe' your boilers, and the first step is to heat the water as much as we can off-site before I pull the next trick from up my sleeve."

When the last barrel was off the truck, but before it had been rolled up the ramp, Bell was behind the wheel of the Leyland driving back to the barn behind his hotel for the next load of preheated water. This was how he was getting past Captain Fyrie's concern about thermal inertia. It took time. By outsourcing the first one hundred and fifty degrees to the boiler in the barn, they'd need far less energy, and time, to bring the mass of water in the engine's tank to a full boil and produce enough pressure to energize the *Hvalur Batur.*

By eleven o'clock, with no one the wiser that anything was taking place, they had four thousand gallons of preheated water in the whaler's boilers. Once they got the water up to steam, the automatic introduction of additional cold water from the seawater inlets wouldn't chill the system so much as to cause a drop in pressure. The boiler was said to be self-sustaining at this point.

The trick now was to get the water to a high boil because they were racing the clock. Every minute in the icy tanks meant the water was losing another fraction of a degree of heat.

"Okay," Ragnar Fyrie said. They were in the *Batur*'s engine room. "You've taken us this far. Show the men what you demonstrated this morning."

Bell had done a small-scale demo for the captain and chief engineer in order to convince them his plan was viable. Now it was time to make it happen for real. He had worked it all out with the engineer back in New York and had conducted enough experiments to convince them both of the plan's viability, but still so much rode in the balance for the next hour or two.

"Right. Salt, iron, and magnesium mixed together do absolutely nothing. But mix them with water and you create an exothermic reaction." His last words lost his audience, so he said, "The chemicals will produce heat. Lots and lots of heat."

He'd premeasured the chemicals and combined them in the proper ratio. The ship was running a diesel generator to produce heat so the men could live aboard throughout the cold winter, and the electricity it provided had been shunted to the boiler pumps so that about fifty gallons of water could be isolated in a separate tank but still be able to be added back to the steam loops when needed.

Bell used a scoop to pour his chemical mixture through an opening at the top of the tank. The engineer, Ivar Ivarsson, was ready with a hastily made cap with a hose running from it. Inside the tank, the chemicals came in contact with the water and a fast chain reaction took place. Chemical bonds broke down and reformed, and in the end the water was superheated and a cloud of hydrogen gas was forced out through the hose. The tube ran down to the main firebox, where it was paired with a line from a natural gas tank. When the hydrogen reached the air, Ivar lit the natural gas. The blue flame, augmented by the highly flammable hydrogen, amplified the chemical reaction taking place inside the tank.

Moments later, the muffled burble of the reaction inside the steel vessel waned. The engineer purged the tank and added fresh water that Bell quickly laced with the powdered mixture of salt, iron dust, and an oxide of magnesium. It too came within just a couple of degrees of boiling before the reaction abated. It took a couple of hours, and they lost heat in the process, but without producing any discernible exhaust Isaac Bell had been able to bring thousands of gallons of water aboard up to within just a few degrees of operational temperatures.

"So now what?" Ivar asked, wiping grease from his hands on a wadded cotton cloth. "If the boiler was a woman, I'd say you have her attention. But she hasn't said yes yet."

"Ultimate icebreaker," Bell said, and opened the last of his trunks. This was a smaller one, and its insides had been triple-secured against any moisture getting in. "Captain, I advise you get to the bridge because we're going to be up to operating temperatures and pressures in moments. Have men in place to cast off and your harpooner ready to snag our goodies on the way out."

"What's in there?" Ivar asked suspiciously, pointing at the waxed paper bundle contained inside the trunk.

"It's called thermite. This particular version is made of powdered aluminum and some other chemicals. It's a recent German discovery. When I dump this into the main tank, the reaction is going to be swift and violent. The heat will flash-boil enough water to bring your engines up to at least half speed. Also, it should be sustained for twenty minutes at least."

Fyrie grinned like a pirate. "More than enough time. Mr. Bell, I must say I am not disappointed that you came into our lives."

He cast a glance to his crewmen huddled around in the boiler room. "Magnus, get over to the barge and be ready to tie it off. Arn, get to your cannon and make damned sure you don't have an explosives tip on the harpoon. Petr, go find Other Petr and be ready to cast off.

"Once we're clear of the harbor, provided no one is chasing, we'll head to the islands just south of Reykjavik. It's well sheltered, so the transfer should go smoother, but it will in no way be easy. Our next stop will be Denmark for provisions and then Novaya Zemlya, some two thousand four hundred kilometers northeast. Once we drop Mr. Bell and his guests . . . Ah, where do you want us to take you?"

"Norway is out, obviously," Bell said. He thought for a moment, and added, "I'd say Aberdeen, Scotland. We'll find transport to England and sail back to the States from Southampton."

"Right," Fyrie said, and again addressed his crew. "After a quick stop in Aberdeen, we steam for Reykjavik and the loving arms of our families."

"Or in your case, Arn," a crewmate called, "any girl that'll have ya."

Bell gave the crew ten minutes to get into position. He needed to coordinate adding the thermite to the boiler with Ivar because once the reaction kicked in, the steam pressure would build rapidly. He carefully scraped some of the wax from the paper on one spot on the heavy bundle of chemicals. It would take just a few moments for the hot water in the system to dissolve through the unprotected paper. Once that happened, the thermite would ignite, and no force on earth could quench its searing chemical heart.

The Icelander stood by atop a separate ladder next to Bell over an open inspection port that had been unbolted from the tank. In his gnarled hands was a heavy wrench and a fist full of bolts for the platter-sized hatch.

"Ready?" Bell asked, and the man nodded.

The waxed paper bundle was just small enough to fit through the opening, and Bell made sure it didn't rip on its way into the tank, because any spilled powder would ignite while still pouring from his hands. If such an accident occurred, he and Ivar would be cooked down to nothing but charred bones. The package hit the water with a weighty splash. Bell jammed the hatch back in place, and Ivar started hand-threading bolts into position. Bell took a couple of bolts from him so Ivar could start to tighten the bolts that much quicker. The last one was on and being wrenched down when from inside the tank came a hollow whoosh, like a zephyr caught in a tube. The thermite had lit.

Bell and Ivarsson scrambled down their ladders. The engineer went to check on the forest of pipes, gauges, levers, and valves that would convert the mounting pressure of superheated steam into mechanical energy sufficient enough to move the ship. Ivar watched the needle of one master gauge as it wound through the numbers until it quivered at the red "Do Not Exceed" mark and then arced past it. He plucked the battered fisherman's cap from his nearly bald head and ceremoniously covered the dial. "Tell the captain we need to go."

"Right." Bell headed for the bridge three decks up.

Fyrie himself was at the helm, watching as two crewmen cast off the main lines and jumped aboard. There wasn't a light on the bridge except for a faint glow around the main compass bolted to the deck on a chest-high liquid-stabilized mount. Out on the ship's prow, silhouetted against the background lights of Sandefjord, stood the man called Arn. The harpoon cannon next to him looked like something dreamed up by science-fiction author Jules Verne or H. G. Wells.

"Ivar says to get going," Bell said as soon as he entered the bridge. "He's covered up one of the pressure gauges."

Fyrie's eyes flicked over for just a moment. "He does that a lot. Not to worry. The *Hvalur Batur* is a tough ship." His hand reached for the engine telegraph and he ratcheted it back and then forward to quarter speed. At the stern, a single screw propeller linked to the whaler's triple-expansion steam engine came to life for the first time in months. Fyrie worked wheel and throttle to edge the ship away from the dock as smoothly as possible.

Bell stole a glance at the guard shack. The lights were off and no smoke came from the chimney. He imagined the inebriated guard was asleep on the floor, curled around his now cooling stove like an overtired kitten.

Up ahead, a barge had drifted ever so slightly away from the pier. It was fifty feet long and almost twenty wide. Its cargo was mounded up over the gunwales and covered by thick tarpaulins. One of Fyrie's men stood near its bow holding a lantern.

Already, the *Hvalur Batur* was picking up speed. Atop the platform on the whaling ship's prow, Arn Björnsson manhandled the big harpoon cannon into position by pointing its barb-tipped projectile across the barge's center. Satisfied with his aim, he cycled the trigger. The sound came like a brief thunderclap and any whaler in town who heard it would immediately recognize the sound, but it was one o'clock in the morning and Sandefjord slept on. The harpoon blasted from the cannon and sliced through the tarp to bury itself into the mountain of coal Captain Fyrie had been forced to unload — ironically, as a precaution against his escape — when his ship had been impounded.

The crewman on the barge — Bell recalled his name was Magnus — rushed to tie off the thick wire the harpoon had carried across to him in order to secure the scow to the whaling ship.

So confident was he in his crew, Fyrie didn't slow at all or even pay particular attention. He adjusted the helm to get them out of the harbor as quickly as possible. He would take a moment to check to see if more lights were popping on around the town, but so far it didn't appear that their escape had been detected. He chuckled.

Bell was watching astern, concerned as there became less and less slack in the towline, and he said, "Care to share?"

"I think when it comes time to explain how we pulled this off, they might just have to say magic, like you suggested."

Bell grew concerned. The *Hvalur Batur* was up to six or seven knots and the fully laden barge was barely drifting. The shock of the line coming taut could easily snap the wire and ruin the escape before they'd even made it. "Ah, Captain," he called a little nervously.

Fyrie followed Bell's gaze and grinned knowingly. "A bull blue whale weighs a hundred tons. If we make a mistake with the harpoon, he's got enough power to capsize this ship. Which is why —"

The cable running from a special hard-point at the base of the harpoon gun to the barge bobbing in the whaler's wake went taut, not with a jerk but with an elongated series of starts and stops that slowly transferred energy to the line itself. Just like that, the barge was up to speed and following behind the ship like a dog on a leash. There should have been a horrendous crash and yet there hadn't even been a mild jolt.

"— under the prow is a room with a series of springs and pulleys that absorb and dissipate the energy of a charging whale or, in this case, the deadweight of our coal supply."

Bell was impressed. "By doing it this way, you saved ten or fifteen minutes of fumbling around getting into position to take the barge under tow."

The captain said, "I thought it worth the risk of firing the harpoon inside the harbor."

Just then, Ivar popped onto the bridge. He'd recovered his cap and had it pressed down around his ears. "Just so you know, steam pressure's holding nicely. We should get a half hour out of her at this speed, no problem. Neat trick, Mr. Bell. I salute you. That's the good. The bad is, we need coal soon."

"We'll load what we can tonight from the barge and head across the strait for Skagen. We can fill our bunkers there and head north for Russia. It's a delay of maybe fifteen hours, but we don't have a choice. We simply don't have the manpower to load that much coal ourselves."

"And how long to get to Novaya Zemlya?"

"That will depend on the weather. If we get lucky, we will be there two or three days before your deadline, Mr. Bell. If we're not, we could find ourselves icebound until June."

20

The rest of that night went as planned. They slunk out of Sandefjord Harbor undetected and turned west until coming to a secluded bay that kept them hidden and sheltered. What followed was five backbreaking hours of shoveling coal off the barge and into the *Hvalur Batur*'s bunkers. Each man took his turn, including Bell and the captain. And even as the fuel was being tossed through special access ports, Ivar and another crewman were working on the automatic feed system to keep the boilers stoked without wasting manpower, as well as balancing the boiler's need for a fresh supply of water drawn through the sea inlets. Bell had always understood the delicate balance needed to keep a modern boiler properly fed, he'd just never had such an up-close tutorial.

When the sun finally rose and the men were forced to scuttle the two-thirds full barge so it didn't become a navigation hazard, Bell's hands were black with ingrained coal but also split open and bloody with torn blisters. His spine felt like someone had rammed a steel spear between two lower vertebrae, and his shoulders and arms had never ached so cruelly in his life.

"Not bad, for a city dweller," Ivar commented when he saw Bell slumped in the galley over a steaming mug. His face was an anthracite mask, and the dawn light streaming in the little porthole drew attention to the sweat runnels snaking through the grime. "You won't make it as a bluejacket, but you're not completely worthless either."

To Bell, it was about the best compliment he could have been given. "Don't go soft on me, chief."

"Not to worry, Mr. Detective. That was the easy part."

The run across the Skagerrak Strait took less time than expected, but securing enough coal for the round trip to the Imperial Russian archipelago of Novaya Zemlya took longer than anticipated. The extra time allowed Captain Fyrie to provision the ship. News that an impounded ship had escaped Norwegian waters reached the commercial fishing town of Skagen on Denmark's northern tip while a dockside crane equipped with a clamshell bucket was dumping coal onto chutes leading into the *Hvalur*'s holds.

None of the harbor authorities seemed interested in the ship, but the scuttlebutt imbued the captain with a new level of paranoia. Fyrie ordered one of his men over the fantail on a ladder rig with a bucket of marine-grade paint with orders to obscure the vessel's name as a precaution. Even if no one in Denmark cared about them, they still had to cruise up the entire western coat of Norway. They'd stay well beyond shipping lanes, yet as a northern seaman Fyrie believed in prudence above all else.

They departed the Danish port twenty hours after escaping Sandefjord, and Fyrie turned them on a northwesterly course to get around the Norwegian lobe of the Scandinavian Peninsula. Because of the Gulf Stream's continuous wash of warm water, their passage was ice-free and the temperature far more moderate than the latitude suggested. They were about level geographically with Canada's Hudson Bay, and, by way of contrast, those waters would remain under several feet of ice well into May and sometimes June.

A day and a half out, the ship crossed the Arctic Circle, the line ringing the globe above which the sun never rises in winter and in the summer never fully sets. As with other recognized cartographical sites — namely, the equator — the first transect of the Arctic Circle by a sailor was marked with a ceremony. The tradition dated from nearly a century, and while most such commemorations were dedicated to the world's professional navies, some civilians got in on it as well.

Captain Fyrie, Ivar, and the others not on duty didn't have the props and costumes to give the ceremony its air of mock seriousness. They simply rousted Bell from his bed in a cabin he enjoyed by himself since so many of the crew were home in Iceland. A burlap sack was pulled over his head and he was frog-marched to the galley. Bell fought his natural instincts to escape and mete out retribution. He recognized the spirit of what was happening. When the burlap was ripped away, he saw Fyrie and his men, all grinning. Magnus, the third officer, was there with a daub of blue paint for the tip of the detective's nose, and before Bell could protest, Arn, who more resembled an oak tree than a man, hoisted Bell off his bare feet and dunked them into a bucket of ice water.

Just as Bell opened his mouth to protest the shock of his feet and calves going instantly numb, a fair-sized cod was thrust at him so that its lips pressed his for a ceremonial kiss. As soon as this was done, the crew roared its approval.

"Congratulations, Mr. Bell," Captain Fyrie said when Arn lifted Bell from the bucket and set him in a waiting chair. A crewman handed over a towel that had been prewarmed on the stove. "You have been welcomed into the Royal Order of the Blue Nose by crossing into the realm of Boreas, King of the North."

Another crewman thrust a bottle of *akvavit* into Bell's hands and Bell swished a mouthful to rinse away the taste of fish slime while others slapped him on the back.

Isaac Bell had made a successful career of being able to read people without judging them, but for the moment he allowed himself the indulgence of forming an opinion about his companions and found he couldn't imagine a better group.

Eighteen hours later, they came upon the first ice. It was late afternoon and already the sun was almost to the horizon, its light weak and cold. To an untrained eye like Isaac Bell's, the odd angles of the sun's rays elongated distances and made determining position next to impossible. He thought the first bits of pancake ice were well away from the ship when in fact the *Hvalur Batur* passed them in moments. When he looked astern from his spot on the bridge, the ice had been swallowed by the gathering gloom as though it had never existed at all.

"What do you know about ice?" Fyrie asked quietly. He stood at the helm, both hands on the wheel, and the last of the sun shining through his blond hair.

Bell could imagine the captain a thousand years earlier commanding a Viking longboat. "I know too much ruins a good glass of whiskey."

Fyrie cracked a smile but kept his tone serious. "By the time the jet stream reaches these waters, it's lost most of the heat it has carried north and east from the tropics, so come winter the surface can freeze from here all the way over the crown of the planet to Siberia and your Alaska territory. At its edges the ice pack is thin because it melts again each spring. Closer to the center, near the geographic pole, the ice persists for many years and can be several meters thick. At times, though, multiyear ice will migrate outward, and we have masses of floes that stretch seemingly forever, some with ridges, called hummocks, that tower as high as fifteen meters."

Bell quickly converted that in his head and

whistled. It was nearly fifty feet.

"The point is, we never know what we're going to find each spring until the thaw comes and we start probing around the edges of the pack. And, truth be told, whalers are doing it less and less. The big ones have all been taken. That's why some of us tried our hand in the Antarctic below southern Africa."

"How'd that work out?"

"The whales are there, for sure, but it's expensive to reach the best grounds and hard to find a crew willing to sign on for that length of time. This way of life is dying, Mr. Bell. You mark my word, and, honestly, I don't mind a bit."

"Odd statement from someone who makes a living at it."

"It's a living that comes with a price," the captain said in a voice just discernible over the throb of the engines below deck. "A soulless person may feel nothing at the death of one of these magnificent animals, but I remember every single one I've hunted and rendered into oil to light homes for men who think up better and faster ways to perpetuate the slaughter.

"So, Mr. Bell," Fyrie boomed with his normal good cheer, dispelling the pall that had suddenly gripped the bridge, "your fortuitous arrival may well turn out to be the watershed event that sets me on a new path. I have a wife and young son back in Iceland. I will never give up the sea, yet I think it's time I find a better way to balance the priorities in my life."

"I'm married myself," Bell said. "No children yet, but I imagine that when they come along, I won't be too keen to jaunt all over the world looking for criminals and other ne'er-do-wells."

As the night progressed, their pace eastward across the north coast of Norway slowed. They weren't yet in pack ice, but they encountered an ever-increasing amount of drifting sheets, some as small as carpets, others many acres in size. This was the year-old ice Fyrie had mentioned.

While the ship's bow was reinforced to cleave through the thinner ice, she could not do so at anywhere near her top speed, and each time she hit the ice, she slowed and shuddered until the floe split apart and she could proceed, oftentimes with ice bumping along her hull as she passed. Captain Fyrie let Magnus spell him at the wheel just after the watery dawn broke. He lay down on the floor of the bridge under a woolen blanket and didn't stir for four hours, but when he woke he was not only refreshed but clear-eyed as well. Fresh coffee from the galley and a breakfast of soft eggs over shredded beef and potatoes with onion brought him to full wakefulness. He stayed at the helm the rest of the day.

Fyrie had warned there were the ghostly ice castles that calved off the glaciers of western Greenland and eventually drifted southward into the Atlantic shipping channels. These were formed as pressure drove floes into and over one another, mounding up ice that compacted and reformed into new solid blocks that were as hard as iron.

The rigid bergs weren't yet as tall as Fyrie had mentioned, but Bell could tell they were dangerous. A mere brush against such a formation could rip the hull plates straight off the ship's support ribs and sink it in seconds. He also knew from going out on deck for a bit of fresh air that the chill coming off the ocean meant an exposure to such icy water for only a minute or two made death all but certain.

Somehow, Ragnar Fyrie kept them moving in the right direction. They might need to detour north or south, or even backtrack west on occasion, but he always managed to find fresh areas of black ocean amid the twirling tableland of ice and kept them sailing ever eastward toward the distant Russian archipelago.

The sun never rose more than a few degrees above the horizon, so oftentimes the great dome of the sky overhead remained dark. On this night, Bell was treated to a sight of which he'd heard but never experienced. The aurora borealis shone like the most phantasmagorical fireworks display ever. Dancing curtains of green light wavered amid streamers of reds and blues. It was as though the entire sky was pulsing to some cosmic beat emanating from out among the stars. For Bell, it was both awe-inspiring and a little frightening.

"Heavy show tonight," Captain Fyrie commented. "Good for us. I can still see well enough to keep going."

"See?" Bell asked. "What exactly do you see?"

Fyrie shrugged inside his peacoat. Though the engines were running fine, the bridge never felt fully warm because so many gaps under doors and around windows allowed the frigid Arctic air to establish a toehold in the room. "It's a trick my father taught me and one I will one day teach my son.

"I can read the reflection of light off the ice. It's easier during the day and with some cloud cover, but I can do it even using the glow of the aurora. I can see where light bounces back into the sky off the ice floes and I will steer for areas where there is no reflection. That is where we will find open ocean. My father says it is how native hunters and fishermen have survived in these waters for so many hundreds of generations."

Bell scanned the sky, trying to see any difference in the light's properties, but with the aurora thumping and shimmering like a celestial heliograph, it was impossible for his eyes to detect any hint of a reflection.

Fyrie must have noticed Bell's scowl. "Not to worry if you can't see it. None of my crew can either, and some have been with me since we were boys. It's a talent and a gift. It's why I rarely leave the bridge when we're this close to the ice."

Bell said, "I am grateful for the trail that led me to your doorstep, Captain Fyrie. You certainly are the right man for this job."

Fyrie nodded at the compliment and tossed back an assurance of his own. "Not to worry, Mr. Bell. We'll have your miners in Aberdeen before the French ship you told me about has even left the North Sea."

Two hours later, clouds had rolled in that obscured the aurora, and the *Hvalur Batur* was trapped in a black water lagoon surrounded by ice at least three feet thick. She also faced a growing westerly wind that was pushing them away from their destination while simultaneously shrinking the amount of space the ship had before her hull plates were staved in by the floes.

Bell had been asleep in his cabin but had come awake when the engine's lullaby of mechanical rhythms ceased and silence settled over the whaling ship. He'd slept clothed. It took him just seconds to put on his boots and climb up to the bridge. It took just seconds more for him to assess the situation.

"What do we do?" he finally asked.

"Drift," Captain Fyrie replied, "and hope this lead doesn't close entirely."

"If it does?"

"We transfer as much gear as we can onto the ice and pray we get rescued by someone as crazy as we were for coming this far north this early in the season."

21

The area of open water around the whaler stabilized as the mass of ice drifted ahead of the wind. Because the ship presented a larger target to the breeze than the flat ice, she drifted faster than the floe. A crew member had to remain at the wheel in order to keep the vessel away from the lagoon's dangerously sharp edges. It was an endless dance of throttle and wheel because the ice wasn't moving in a uniform direction. It constantly spun and twisted around the *Hvalur* in a jumble without pattern, and even a moment's lapse on the helmsman's part would see the ship founder in the icy sea.

Once Fyrie was satisfied that the ship was safe for a moment he donned thick over-pants and a sealskin parka with wolf pelt hemming around the hood. When drawn tight, the hood practically swallowed the captain's face so that only his eyes shone out from the insulating fur. His mittens were also made of insulated seal and were awkwardly big, but he could still grip a pair of binoculars.

He stepped out onto the bridge wing and then climbed some steel rungs up to the roof of the wheelhouse. From there, he climbed another thirty feet up onto a tiny observation platform at the high point of the ship's rigging tower. This was the whale-watching post, a spot manned during the long hunts where a sharp-eyed crewman would scan for the telltale plume from a whale exhaling the warm air from its lungs into the cold air and direct the boat to give chase.

To Bell, the sky was too dark to see more than a few hundred yards. Fyrie, however, spent two hours standing in the crow's nest monitoring the ice, the weather, and the reflections that apparently only he could interpret. When he returned to the bridge, his breath had frozen into a crust in the wolf insulation. He shucked his outer gear. His face was mottled red and white and his hands shook, as surely his core temperature had dropped despite the extra clothing.

The other changes since his ascent up the mast were the wind had increased its speed and great waves sluiced under the ice, causing the floe to undulate amid a crackle and pop of breaking ice and an occasional blast like a cannon shot when a thick section snapped.

"There's open water about a mile south of us," Fyrie said, his teeth chattering. "Problem is, there's a significant ridge in that direction. This floe will break up with the wind gaining strength, but not where that ridge is holding it together."

"Can we do anything?" Bell asked.

"Not really," one of the two Petrs said from behind the wheel.

"I've got thermite left over," Bell informed them.

"How much?"

Bell grinned. "Enough to bore a couple dozen holes through just about any thickness of ice we encounter. We break up the ridge . . ."

". . . and Mother Nature breaks up the rest," Fyrie finished.

Thirty minutes later, with the thermite prebundled and secure, Bell, Arn Bjørnson, and the chief engineer, Ivar Ivarsson, were lowered down into the water in a small wooden dinghy. Arn's considerable size and strength made short work of rowing to the edge of the floe. Bell wore borrowed cold-weather gear. It was bulky and difficult to move in, but at least everything fit, and the boots were so well insulated that he couldn't feel the ice when they transferred to shore. Arn torqued a screw into the floe to tie off the dinghy, and the three men set off for the large ridge silhouetted by the sun as it made its slow circuit across the horizon.

Arn carried a Model 1898 Mauser bolt action rifle chambered for the new Otto Bock–designed 9.3-by-62-millimeter round. With winter ending, the Arctic's most feared predator, the polar bears, were getting in a last meal before the lean summer season kicked in. A male bear, standing ten feet tall when upright, could weigh nearly three-quarters of a ton and consume a hundred-pound seal all at once. Without a weapon — usually a powerful one like the Mauser — humans rarely survived an encounter with *Ursus maritimus.* Standard procedure when working on the pack ice was for at least one man to be on guard at all times. The polar bear has an incredible sense of smell, and because their fur is actually clear rather than white, they blend into the ice so well they can sneak up on even the most wary prey.

The ridge looked to be less than a half mile distant, its range and size distorted by how the light from the sun reached the surface at such an extreme angle. As they trudged across the ice toward their target, Bell looked behind them. In the uncertain gloom, his shadow appeared translucent, like that of a chimera rather than a man. And when he looked ahead, the solid spine of ice created where two bergs smashed together appeared to be floating several feet in the air. He blinked, behind his dark polar glasses, and the hummock returned to its rightful place.

The other thing throwing off his perception and making him doubt his own senses were the waves passing under the ice and causing its surface to bow and subside. It all looked solid enough, but in fact it was as fragile as a sheet of crystallized sugar that a large enough wave could shatter just as easily. The feeling reminded him of the day six years previous when he was riding out the Great San Francisco Earthquake, when the ground beneath his feet became jelly and the whole city seemed to collapse into fire and dust.

The wind was at their backs, fortunately, and the ice had been scoured of any snow long before, so visibility was good. It took fifteen minutes to reach the fifteen-foot-high wall of fractured and fused blocks of ice. Like scar tissue left after a wound, the ridge was thicker and stronger than the surrounding ice and would keep a huge slab from breaking up when the incoming storm intensified.

With vast knowledge of the Arctic, Captain Fyrie and Ivar Ivarsson figured out the best places to plant Bell's remaining thermite charges. They wanted the chemicals to bore a series of adjacent holes, like perforations in a sheet of paper, in a straight line over the top of the ridge. When the wind accelerated, the weakened rift would crack exactly in front of the *Hvalur Batur* and the whaling ship would be able to steam for open water amid the swirl of collapsing floes.

Ivar found what looked to be a low spot in the hummock. The ice was piled up only ten feet in one section, and the ridge itself was only thirty feet deep. It stretched for at least a mile in both directions. Bell shucked the canvas pack off his back and retrieved one of the glass mason jars filled with thermite and wrapped in cotton scraps for protection during transport. A length of string was tied around the neck of the jar.

He placed the jar on the ground at the base of the ridge near its low point, unscrewed its cap, and backed away, paying out string as he moved. When he got to the end of the line, he gave it enough of a tug that he knocked the glass jar on its side, which allowed some of its contents to hit the frozen surface. Enough residual warmth remained in the thermite powder to melt a small amount of ice. That little bit of moisture, in turn, was enough to spark the chemical reaction with a hissing roar, and, like some runaway display of fireworks, the reaction became self-sustaining. The intensity of the glow forced Bell and the others to look away, while noxious purple smoke billowed from the hole the chemical had bored into the ice. In seconds, the pile of thermite had melted its way down nearly to the bottom of the floe. Bell saw the problem at once. The cavern the thermite produced was tight in circumference, as he'd predicted.

And in just the blink of an eye, the mass of chemicals burned their way through the bottom of the berg, and all the water pooled in the bell jar–sized hole vanished into the sea. Nearby, Ivar laughed aloud. And even Arn, who'd been distracted by the thermal excavation, nodded taciturn approval.

And then Arn was airborne, and his rifle went flying from his grip, twirling like a baton as it pinwheeled aloft. The big man crashed to the ice without trying to cushion the impact. Bell lost a second staring at the prostrate man before he saw the white terror bearing down on him.

The polar bear's mouth was crimson with the blood of a seal it had recently eaten and had been half asleep digesting amid the crags and folds of the ice ridge. Because its belly was full, it had merely bowled Arn Bjørnson aside rather than bitten off his leg at the groin. The noise and smoke and the familiar smell of the only creature capable of challenging its dominance on the ice had it confused and angry. It had incapacitated Arn and now it was coming for Bell and Ivarsson, its jaws open and its two-inch canines gleaming like ivory. It made a sound deep in its throat, a cross between a lion's roar and a locomotive picking up speed. Loping at them, its shoulders flexed and rolled, it kept its wedge-like head down and only a hint of its black eyes was visible.

Bell shucked his gloves. His hands began to go numb the instant they were exposed to the freezing air. Even before the thick mittens hit the ice, he'd pulled his .45 from the outer pocket of his sealskin anorak. He wasn't a hunter himself, but he'd spent enough time with such men in exclusive clubs, railroad dining cars, and private residences to know the bullets his gun fired would do little beyond annoy the charging beast. Bell couldn't hope for a lucky shot, hitting an eye or entering the bear's mouth. The only target it presented was the top of its skull, which for his Colt was as impenetrable as armor.

He'd been working with the .45 for months now and had come to understand that it rose after each discharge and twitched slightly left because the ejection port spit out the spent brass cartridge on the right of the slide. Shooting one-handed required a fraction of a second to recenter the sights in order to accurately fire another round, so he took a two-handed stance.

The bear was thirty feet away, coming hard, its confusion giving way to primal aggression. It had no need to eat the men, but it still wanted them dead.

Bell began firing and cycled through the clip so fast that each shot became an instantaneous echo of the one before it. He didn't aim at the bear at all but at the ice a foot or so in front of its snuffling snout. Each impact gouged a plume of flinty particles that lashed the animal's eyes and sensitive nose.

The first few shots didn't seem to have any effect. The bear came on as implacable as a berserker warrior from the storied

Icelandic sagas. But by the fifth blast from the pistol, the bear's eyes were reduced to painful slits, its nose was bleeding from dozens of nicks, and the rolling force of the shots had eroded its courage. Bell's final two saw the bear veer sharply away when it was only a couple of feet from him. He kept the last round in the pistol in case the animal reached him and he'd at least have the opportunity to fire through the thick blubber and muscle protecting its internal organs in the instant before the bear killed him outright.

He shifted to a one-handed stance as he watched the bear's ponderous backside lope across the floe in the direction of a narrow open lead from where it had hunted the seal hours earlier. Without taking his eyes off the enormous carnivore — the largest land predator on earth, in fact — Bell fished a fresh magazine from his pocket and had it ready so that when he dropped the clip out of the Colt's grip he would be ready to ram home the full one.

Only when the polar bear plunged into the water and began swimming away did Isaac Bell slip the .45 back into his pocket, bend and retrieve the spent magazine, and finally replace the thick mittens on his hands. They shook and were cramping but there was no lasting damage. Nearby, Arn Bjørnson began moaning and pushing himself up from where the bear had so unceremoniously tossed him. Ivar cut short his rant and ran for his crewmate and friend. Bell took a second to recover the fallen Mauser rifle and gave it a once-over to ensure it remained functional.

"Arn, you all right?" Ivar asked, dropping to the ice.

"I think so," the big man said. When he tried getting to his feet, his hip buckled where the bear had plowed into him.

Ivar helped him up and stood with the larger man's arm draped across his shoulders for a moment. Arn took a staggering step. His face became a mask of pain when his leg supported his weight. He ignored it and took a second step, then a third, with Ivar keeping pace at his side.

"I think I will be okay," he said.

"That joint is going to stiffen up," Bell told him over an increasingly loud wind. "We need to work as fast as we can."

Ivar eased Arn back down to the ice and then joined Bell. Together, they marked a straight line over the top of the hummock, placing bits of coal from the ship's bunker as markers for where they wanted to bore through the frozen ridge. At several spots, they had to chip into the ice to create a flat spot big enough for one of the thermite charges. Arn watched them work but also kept an eye out in case the polar bear decided to return. The rifle rested across his knees.

Once everything was set, Bell replaced the first piece of coal with a jar of thermite and, like before, paid out string to give himself a margin of safety from the chemical reaction. Ivar was on the far side of the ridge doing the same thing. Bell tipped the jar and watched for a moment as the chemicals flashed in a blinding jewel of fire and violet-colored smoke coiled away on the wind. In the time it took to place his second jar, the first had penetrated to the sea and the meltwater had drained away.

It took thirty minutes in all to place and set off the thermite charges. During that time, the wind had picked up considerably, scouring the floe and forcing Bell and Ivarsson to work hunched over and with their backs to it. Arn too had to crawl into the lee of the ridge in order to protect himself from the icy gusts but still watch for the bear. The rolling of the waves underneath the floe had also increased and so too had the snap and bang of cracking ice.

The hike back to the boat became a living

nightmare as soon as they started out. They had to march straight into the wind, which had somehow found fresh supplies of snow to whip at any exposed skin with the scouring force of a commercial sandblaster. To make matters worse, Arn's injured hip joint had frozen, as Bell had predicted. He and Ivar had to walk on either side of the big man and support him through each painful step. Arn didn't complain at what had to be utter agony.

The fifteen-minute walk they'd enjoyed from the dinghy to the ridge morphed into a three-quarters-of-an-hour hike back. Until they reached the open water and saw the four-man boat as they'd left it, he'd imagined the ice had already split and their ride had drifted away, leaving them stranded. It was an unfounded fear. The ice still held and the *Hvalur Batur* was only a quarter mile distant. Any stranding would have been short-lived.

It was easier for Arn to crawl into the boat, dragging his bum leg, than to step across the gunwale of the little craft.

"This is no way for a sailor to put to sea," he said stoically.

Ivar retorted, "I've seen you drunk-crawl up a ratline on a bet, Arn Bjørnson, so what's your complaint?"

Bell took to the oars, finding battling a Beaufort scale wind a little more difficult than rowing Marion around the lake in Central Park on a lazy summer afternoon. Very quickly, he felt his body temperature rising at the same time his face was freezing. His lungs were near struggling by the time he positioned the dinghy under the hanging ropes of the *Batur*'s davits. Ivar secured the lines to the lift points while, above them, crewmen waited to haul them up to the deck. With the weather deteriorating further, the men worked swiftly and professionally.

Ivar helped Arn out of the boat once they were safely aboard. One of the Petrs was there to help him to a cabin while Bell made his way up to the bridge, where Captain Fyrie stood at the helm, one eye on the weather off to starboard, the other on the ice floe directly ahead. Despite its drafty nature, the bridge felt blessedly warm. Bell helped himself to some coffee from a glass-lined metal thermos.

"How did it go?" Fyrie asked.

Bell sipped at the steaming mug, and said, "I can scratch facing down a charging polar bear from the list of things I've never done."

The captain didn't so much as glance in Bell's direction when he said, "That's just another rite of passage in the Arctic."

A big gust of wind hit the ship just then, followed almost immediately by a particularly strong swell. The whaler rose up and then dropped into the trough. For a second, they lost their view of the ice floe, but they distinctly heard what happened when the wave passed below it. The crack was as loud as thunder would be from directly overhead, a single deafening sound that hit like a physical assault. When the ship rose up again, the floe ahead of them had been cleaved in two exactly where the thermite had weakened the ridge.

"Congratulations, Mr. Bell, on a job well done." This time, Fyrie cracked a smile.

An hour later, the wind had shuffled the ice enough for the captain to thread his ship between the shattered floes and find an area of open water beyond. After nearly half a day drifting with the pack, Fyrie was again able to turn the *Hvalur Batur* eastward and pour on the steam for the scheduled rendezvous with the Coloradan miners.

22

Fyrie didn't leave the bridge again over the next two days, pushing the ship and crew — and mostly himself — to make up lost time. Bell had impressed upon Fyrie how important it was to reach Brewster and the others by the first of April. He didn't think the miners would mutiny if the ship wasn't there on time, and he certainly didn't fear a physical retribution from Brewster should they be late reaching Novaya Zemlya. The consequences were more personal. What he'd done was give Brewster his word that if he could meet an impossible deadline, Bell would too. And for a man like Isaac Bell, not keeping his word was as dishonorable an act as he could think of.

The weather never improved, which was a blessing because it meant the pack ice continued to break up and they'd have to detour less and less.

On the morning of April first, the ship ran

into icy cold fog. Somewhere ahead, there was an area where the sea's surface was warmer than the air, and the only way that was possible this far north was if they were approaching land. Fyrie slowed the ship and set a watchman up on the mast with a signal bell. By noon, the fog had thinned, and out of the mist rose the massif of Novaya Zemlya, an archipelago consisting mainly of two islands stretching almost six hundred miles in length and separated by a mile-wide channel. By chance they had reached their target abreast of the strait.

The islands were an extension of the Urals chain, so a mountainous spine ran long the centerline. To the north, a thick permanent snowpack hid all but the tallest of the mile-high peaks, while to the south the hilly tundra was emerging from under its winter mantle of snow. It was a bleak, ugly place not fit for human habitation. Bell could well understand how its mineral riches had gone unnoticed for so long. Had Brewster not been stranded here in the first place, who knows how long it would have been before the archipelago was properly surveyed.

"You said a hundred miles due north of the Matochkin Strait?" Fyrie asked. His eyes were bleary and his once-broad shoulders were stooped with exhaustion.

"Yes," Bell replied. "They're on the other side of the islands. We need to transit the strait to the Kara Sea and then head north. Brewster said there's a sheltered bay in the shadow of Bednaya Mountain where he'll meet us."

"Good thing the channel's already ice-free," Arn said. He had just come up from the galley with sandwiches of canned meat on freshly baked bread still warm from the oven and another thermos of sweet coffee. He still walked with a limp, but the bear attack had done no lasting damage. He saw the fatigue in every line and crease etched on his captain's face. "Why don't you let me steer for a bit, Captain. The way's clear, and you look like you can use some sleep."

Fyrie didn't protest. He wolfed down a sandwich and, like before, settled on the floor at the rear of the bridge under a couple of blankets next to a coal-burning stove. He promptly fell into a death-like sleep. Bell ate his lunch a little more leisurely as Arn steered the ship into the narrow strait. At one point, they passed a colony of disinterested walruses sunning themselves on a pebbly beach. Some of the big males had tusks at least three feet long and easily tipped the scales at four thousand pounds.

Dinner that night was a thick and creamy

fish stew, and several extra pots of it were left to warm on the stove. They were nearing the rendezvous. Once again, Fyrie was on the bridge, though a crewman named Gunnar manned the helm. Bell stood a little behind the captain's elevated chair. The sun was hidden by the mountains and glaciers of the northern island of the archipelago. The shadows were long and fixed. The skies were clouding up, and a constant wind rattled the bridge windows and buffeted the ship.

The little vessel was just a speck compared to the ominous mountains and icy glaciers rolling by on her port side. Bell felt a vulnerability in the face of such raw Nature. For the first time, he came to appreciate the task Joshua Hayes Brewster had set for himself.

As if reading his mind, Captain Fyrie said, "Your friend is either fearless or crazy to come here."

"A little of both, I think," Bell replied. "I had no idea how barren and desolate a place could be. This is like nothing I've ever seen before."

"The most forlorn coast of Iceland looks like paradise compared to this heap," Fyrie remarked. "I can't imagine spending the winter here. It had to have been hell."

A half hour later, the ship chugged into a

bay just as Brewster had described. Looming out of an ice field was the naked flank of Bednaya Mountain, a black craggy tor that rose like a shark's fin. The bay was ringed by a rocky beach, but beyond it stretching to the foothills was a bog humped with moss hillocks and riven with frozen ponds and streams. During the summer, it would melt into a soggy morass that would be as impenetrable as any tract on earth.

As they drew deeper into the bay, Bell noted smoke coming from where a river would discharge into the sea once winter relinquished its grip on the landscape. He pointed out the spot to Fyrie, who nodded and adjusted course accordingly.

In the lee of the mountains, the wind became less intense but still tore at the ocean's surface, rendering it into a churning dark mass capped with occasional splashes of white foam. A lone bird glided for a moment just beyond the whaler's windscreen before peeling off, lost in the scudding clouds.

Not knowing the depth of the bay, Fyrie ordered a crewman to the rail with a sounding weight attached to a line marked out in meters. The door to the bridge wing had to remain open for his calls to be heard. When they were two hundred yards from the coast, the bottom started shelving rapidly, and the captain called for the anchor to be dropped. He then ordered the ship's lifeboat to be lowered rather than the smaller dinghy Bell had used earlier with the ice floe. The craft was large enough to fit all the miners and required four crewmen to row it.

Over at the mouth of the frozen river stood the cluster of miners, their backs to their smoky signal fire. Bell expected them to be shouting and waving, eager to be off the cursed rock that had been like a prison these past months. Instead, they stood mutely. The distance was too great to read expressions, but he got an impression of men who'd been so beaten by experience that nothing left on earth could give them joy. They were in a sullen mass like veterans of the Civil War he'd seen at special homes for those who'd been shattered by what they'd seen and done.

Bell made sure he was one of the rowers heading to shore. He needed to be there as a familiar face for Brewster. Seeing Novaya Zemlya, Bell better understood the task the miner had set for himself and his men. Their efforts, no matter if they'd been successful or not, were nothing short of herculean. Bell also wanted to step onto the island as a tangible link to what the Coloradans had accomplished.

Once they got coordinated, Bell and the three crewmen rowed across from the *Batur* to shore quick enough. As they neared, they could hear the slow gurgle of water under the veneer of ice covering the river. The miners broke ranks only when the longboat ran aground on the pebbly beach. Judging by the surf line, high tide was another foot above where the keel gouged into the water-rounded stones. Even with the weight of the extra men, and the crates Bell could see they'd fashioned, they'd be able to float free in a couple of hours if they couldn't maneuver the boat off the shore.

It was only when the men spread out a bit that Bell counted them and came up with eight. Nine men had faked their deaths in Colorado. When he looked closer, he could also see that these were the shadows of men, the bare minimum of flesh remaining to cover the bones. Their beards weren't what he expected. Some had none, but they didn't look freshly shaved, just so gaunt that maybe the skin had no way of producing whiskers. Others' beards were patchy and rough, like half-plucked chickens. The men all wore various types of hats, but only a few had lengths of greasy hair poking out from under them. All had red-rimmed eyes, so distant and dim that they were like walking corpses. All of them were pale too, with waxy skin, again not unlike the dead.

Whatever estimation Bell had concocted in his head of the horrors these men endured was one hundredth of the true depth of deprivation they'd actually suffered. They had all volunteered for the job long before Bell became involved, but somehow he felt responsible, that he'd made these men endure such sickening brutality in the mountainous wastes of Novaya Zemlya.

When he finally gave Brewster his full attention, the man stared at him with the vacancy of the mentally deranged and yet the unbroken hatred of a bitter enemy. The spark of madness he'd seen months earlier had caught fire and was spreading in a growing inferno. It was the most unsettling look Bell had ever experienced and yet he would not turn away. This was Brewster's way of expressing how much this had affected him, and Bell felt obliged to acknowledge it. After ten or fifteen more seconds, Brewster's expression didn't exactly soften, but it became less focused.

"You made good on your word, Mr. Bell," Brewster said while Isaac Bell jumped over the lifeboat's gunwale in borrowed rubber boots and splashed into a receding wave.

Bell pointed to the ten wooden crates. "And you yours, Mr. Brewster."

"Thousand pounds of high-grade ore. The cost was one man killed, but I don't think the rest of us are too far behind, to be honest. We're all walking dead men. Only, none of us has the sense to settle into the grave just yet."

None of the men reacted to their leader pronouncing such a grim fate.

"What happened to your man?"

"Jake Hobart? He got lost in a storm in early February and froze to death. As for the rest, we think it's the food that's killing us."

Magnus interrupted. "Mr. Bell, maybe we should go to ship now and talk later. *Ja?*"

"You're right. Yes."

Brewster and his men were so thoroughly exhausted they needed help just to crawl over the lifeboat's gunwale and left the work of loading the crates to Bell and the three sailors. Once loaded, the boat was heavy but the tide was swift. Bell and the two biggest seamen pushed with everything they had and soon slid it off the beach. The wooden craft floated free, though sluggishly. They scrambled aboard and got to the oars, having crawled around the sprawled forms of the ghastly looking miners. Bell noticed a couple were missing most of their teeth. This in and of itself wasn't uncommon, but these men's mouths were bleeding, making him believe their tooth loss was something recent.

Because of the tide, the *Hvalur Batur* had swung around on her anchor chain so that she was a bit closer, but the oarsmen had to fight the rising waters and a ponderously loaded boat. It took twice as long to reach the whaling ship, and Bell was grateful when Magnus clipped the ropes to the davits and the lifeboat was cranked aboard.

No sooner had the keel settled onto the chocks welded to the deck and the anchor chain started rattling up the hawsehole than a heavy gout of smoke shot out the ship's stack. Captain Fyrie was wasting no time getting them headed for home.

Magnus oversaw several other crew members off-loading the wooden chests to store in an unused cabin while Bell shepherded the exhausted miners down to the warm mess hall, where the aroma of fish stew filled the air. The odor was too rich for one of the men and he rushed for a corner trash can to dry-heave his pitifully empty stomach.

As the miners shed hats, heavy gloves, and thick parkas, another odor permeated the cozy room, the smell of eight men who'd spent months holed up in a poorly ventilated mine shaft lit by sooty fires without any way of bathing. They reeked of stale smoke and old sweat. Their skin was veined by dark lines, and dirt-encrusted joints and wrinkles. Hair lay flat and lifeless, and Bell noted most of the miners had lost significant patches of it so only odd tufts remained.

But it was their eyes that he noticed the most. More than the smell or the filth, it was the haunted and haggard look of the eyes, the look of men who'd been driven to the edge of insanity and had not yet stepped back from the precipice.

A few of the miners slurped the rich stew while the others seemed to enjoy cups of steaming coffee laced with Scotch whiskey Bell had purchased during the layover in Denmark. Like Banquo's ghost in Shakespeare's *Macbeth,* the men's silence seemed accusatory.

Bell sat opposite Joshua Hayes Brewster and waited patiently until he'd partially finished a bowl of stew, washed it down with coffee, and gingerly set a plug of tobacco from a pouch of Mile-Hi.

"Ain't much more to tell ya, Mr. Bell," Brewster said at last. "After the Frenchies dropped us off, we hauled our gear up the mountain a ways and set to blasting our way in. Lived in tents until we'd tunneled deep enough to wall ourselves in and only go outside for the facilities or when we set off a charge of dynamite. We stripped the earth of every trace of byzanium. Then we set about to erase all evidence we were there and camouflage the tunnel entrance and tailings dump."

"But . . ." Bell wasn't sure how to broach the subject of the men's appearance.

"How we all look," Brewster said for him. "Started just about when the worst of the winter hit us. We were already holed up in the mine but still bitter cold. No night in the Rockies could compare to the wind shrieking off that ice.

"We were doing all right for a piece. Then we all started feeling sickly. Stomach issues. Hair and teeth started going bad. We worked through it, mind you, but it was bad."

"Are you sure it wasn't some type of gas leaching out of the rock?" Bell asked.

"Nothing like I've heard of, and it wasn't our fire causing it neither. We kept proper ventilation the whole time. It had to be the food. The cans were contaminated. Charlie Widney said he'd heard about something like it taking place on a ship. And the food had all been tainted when they sealed the cans with lead or some such thing."

Bell had heard similar tales, and while he wasn't too knowledgeable about the lead poisoning, he had to defer to the man suffering its effects. He tried to sound upbeat for Brewster's sake when he said, "We've got fine stores aboard the ship and a first-rate cook. In a few days it'll pass out of your system and you will all start feeling better."

"Not so sure about that, Mr. Bell. I'm no doctor, but my insides feel so tore up they ain't never gonna be right."

"We'll reach Aberdeen in a couple of days. I'll get you and your men to a hospital. And, I'll see your ore transported to the dock at Southampton."

Brewster didn't seem capable of holding his head straight, and yet at Bell's words, he lunged across the table and grabbed the detective by the collar, holding on so close their faces were only inches apart. The voice he dredged up came from a place deep and dark. "I will not leave that ore to another living soul! Do you understand me?"

Brewster's breath was foul from months of cheap tobacco and neglect, and his eyes were wide and crazed, but Bell was still able to fight the urge to defend himself and lay the much smaller man out on the deck with a well-placed punch. He didn't even bother wiping away the foamy spittle that had hit his face. He said calmly, as if to a child, "If that's what you want, Mr. Brewster, that's fine with me. No need to get yourself upset. Okay?"

The fiery little man remained tensed, his jaw working wordlessly and his black pupils darting from one of Bell's eyes to the other, searching for something — betrayal? Reassurance? Bell had no way of knowing. Brewster finally sat back down on the bench opposite. Bell noted that not one of the other miners had shown the slightest reaction.

He shuddered because for a split second he almost believed what Brewster had said on the beach, that the men really were already dead.

23

Not long after, Arn Bjørnson entered the mess to announce there was enough hot water for each of the men to take a five-minute shower. Brewster had been silently glowering at Bell, and the unexpected intrusion broke the spell. Bell stood and left the room without a backward glance. Any doubt he had concerning Brewster's sanity had evaporated. He didn't know what madness had driven him to take on and ultimately succeed at mining the byzanium ore, but the price he'd paid was obvious. He wondered what sort of life the man would enjoy once he'd turned the samples over to the Army. None of the options that came to mind seemed agreeable.

He retired to his cabin and didn't bother removing more than his shoes before rolling into bed and falling into a dead sleep.

Bell woke with a throttled gasp and threw aside his mass of blankets and sheets. He was covered in a sheen of slick sweat. The dream remained vivid for a few more moments before it faded into a vague, unsettled feeling. Something beyond the dream had roused him. He listened for a moment. All seemed as it should be — the ship's mechanical heart beat down in the engine room, water hissed smoothly along the hull, and at the very stern of the whaling vessel the steel screw whirred like a muted aeroplane propeller.

Then he heard a metal door squeak closed on its rusty hinges. He quickly lit a match to check the time. It was a quarter of two in the morning. Unless someone was visiting the head, there was no reason for any of the miners or crew to be out. A man walking by his cabin door had awoken him. There was no reason that should have roused him unless it piqued Bell's subconscious.

He swung his legs out of bed and toed into his loose-laced boots.

The dim hallway was deserted. There were six cabins near enough that he would have heard their doors squeal. Most of them had just a single occupant. Brewster and Vern Hall were quartered in another section of the superstructure. Bell ignored them and headed aft to one of the two communal washrooms. It contained a commode and sink, and its walls were a jumble of wires and pipes and conduits. There was no porthole, but there was an electric lamp. Bell left it off and lit a match in the pitch-blackness. The light and sulfur made him squint his eyes. He reached up and touched the glass sconce around the single lightbulb. It was cool to the touch.

A normal person would have concluded that the light hadn't been used and therefore neither had the bathroom, but Bell was cautious and thorough. He unthreaded a set screw that held the fragile globe in place and lifted it enough to feel the actual bulb. It too was cool. Now he was satisfied and checked the second lavatory. The light hadn't been on there either, and in both rooms the seats were up. Neither had been visited by anyone in the past few minutes.

Intrigued, Bell went down to the galley. It was deserted, and its electric lamps were also cold to the touch. But possibly someone had spent some time alone in the dark. His answer wasn't here. He climbed two decks to the bridge.

Red lamps glowed softly, to preserve the watchstander's night vision. It gave the space a warm, intimate feeling, while beyond the broad windscreens the ocean's vastness quickly shattered any illusion of amiability. He recognized the big shape of Arn at the wheel.

"Good morning. How's the leg?"

"Is good. Thank you. You can't sleep either?"

"Either?" Bell said. "Someone else up?"

"One of the miners was just here."

"Do you know which one?"

"No. In this light, everyone looks the same."

"Did he say anything to you?"

"Not really. He said he just wanted to watch the ocean for a while. He sat in the radio room so he would not be in my way."

The bridge was big enough for a half dozen men to stand without overcrowding. The fine hairs on the back of Bell's arms tingled. "How long was he up here?"

"An hour or so."

"Be right back."

The radio room was at the very back of the bridge, enclosed and insulated by shelves containing rolled-up charts and reference books on celestial mechanics and navigation. Bell stepped in and closed the door so he could turn on the overhead lights. He rolled up his shirtsleeves and pressed his elbow against the leather swivel seat, it being among the most thermally sensitive parts on a human body besides lips and cheeks, and there was no way he was going to press his mouth to a scabrous chair in a whaling ship's radio shack.

It was still warm. Body heat had transferred down to the metal frame and was now slowly radiating back out. Bell felt the metal box containing the ship's crystal wireless radio. It was cool. The keypad for the Morse encoder was cool as well, but that wasn't a surprise.

He thought through the scenario. One of the miners woke in a cabin without windows and was feeling a little queasy. The seas weren't bad, but some men have no stomach for any kind of ocean roll. He dresses and comes up to the bridge. There's no place to sit except the captain's chair, and he knows enough not to use it. There's a stool in the radio room. The porthole is small and requires a wrench to open, but he can see the horizon and the faint sun clinging to it through some clouds. An hour later, he's feeling better, and so he heads back to his cabin, passing Bell's to reach his own and awakening Bell by merely walking past.

It all made sense, and Bell had no reason to suspect otherwise, and yet he found himself opening drawers in the desk under the radio set, until he located a toolkit rolled up in a piece of cloth. He unfurled the bundle of equipment and found an appropriate screwdriver. The wireless transceiver wasn't particularly powerful, but an antenna only needed to be close or exceptionally large to receive a signal. There was no reason for him to investigate this any further — nothing, that is, except a lifetime of trusting hunches that oftentimes never made sense at first.

There were a dozen screws holding the outer cover to an inner frame surrounding the radio's internal parts. Bell carefully lifted the shell and placed it on the floor. He touched the exposed crystal. Heat dissipates from the outside inward. The radio's case was cool, and so was the framework protecting the device's innards, but at the very heart of the crystal, which vibrated at frequencies powerful enough to traverse the ether, a tiny amount of warmth remained.

The other scenario that Bell had considered when Arn had told him a miner had sat in the radio shack for an hour was far less plausible but no less true. He'd come in here to transmit a message — coded, no doubt, to be short and to the point — and he'd waited for the set to cool down on the off chance Arn or another crewman came in to check. The traitor had waited until the outer case was as cold as the desk and the shelves and the metal walls themselves and then slunk to his cabin, his dark deed done.

The fact he was trying to sneak back to his bunk and was not walking normally like someone returning from the head is what had penetrated Bell's sleep and woke him with a start.

Bell narrowed his choices to the six miners bunked near his own cabin. Made sense that it wasn't Brewster or Vernon Hall, who Brewster had been friends with for years according to reports he'd heard back in Central City. Who the message had been sent to was also pretty easy to deduce. There was only one other group of people interested in the byzanium.

As he set the last screw in place and twisted it home, he considered the will it took to work so closely with these men, day in and day out, laboring under truly hellish conditions, sharing untold deprivation and hardship, and knowing all along you were going to sell them out. For as insane as this job had driven Joshua Hayes Brewster, the miner who was going to betray them all had been a psychopath long before he ever set foot on Novaya Zemlya.

Bell said good night to Arn and headed to the forward part of the ship, where Brewster was quartered in a cabin reserved for two harpooners who'd been lucky enough to return to Iceland when the *Hvalur* was impounded. He didn't knock and he turned on the light as soon as he entered. Brewster was on his back under a blanket, only his face showing, and for a moment Bell thought he was dead. He was deathly pale, and it looked like he wasn't breathing at all, but then his eyes reacted to the light filtering through his lids and they fluttered open, confused and teary.

"What's going on? Where am I?" He spotted Bell standing at the cabin door. "Who are you?"

"It's me, Brewster, Isaac Bell. You're aboard a whaling ship. We picked you up yesterday from the island."

"Isaac who?"

"Colonel Patmore sent me. You and I met in Paris just before the French shipped you and your men to the Arctic to mine the byzanium for them."

Brewster struggled up into a sitting position and began a coughing fit that only ended when he spit a glob of blood into a trash can. "I'm sorry. My mind wanders now. I have a hard time concentrating."

Bell asked, "What's the last thing you remember?"

"We'd closed up the mine. Yeah. That's it. We'd done it and we closed it up and headed for the cove to wait for . . . you. That's right. You promised to get us off that rock on April first."

"I kept my word," Bell told him. "Do you remember now? We came aboard, and I took you down to the mess. You ate some chowder, and we talked about how the food was poisoning you."

"Right," Brewster said absently, scratching at what little remained of his beard. "The food."

"What happened to Jake Hobart, Joshua? How did he die?"

"I told ya, didn't I?" Brewster said, suddenly angry now. And suspicious. "I had to have. You need to understand, Bell. You have to know what could happen."

He could sense that Brewster was on the verge of a full mental collapse. He needed to calm him down or he'd have a stroke or his heart would simply stop. "Easy, Joshua. You told me already," Bell lied smoothly. "It's okay. I just want you to tell me again. All right?"

"What? Yes. Okay. Um." He coughed again, and foamy blood appeared at the corner of his mouth. "I've, ah, kept the secret so long I guess it's gotten to me."

"You told me he got lost in a storm and died of exposure. Is that what happened?"

"No. That's what we were supposed to believe, and I didn't let on that I knew."

"Knew what?"

"Jake was murdered, Mr. Bell. Not sure which one of 'em done it, but someone rammed a steel rod into his ear and killed him dead."

24

Bell was in motion even as Brewster's words still hung in the cabin's cold air. The passenger he first considered to be merely a traitor to his fellow miners he now saw as a murderous fiend willing to kill to protect his secret and escape with whatever reward the Société des Mines had promised him. For three months he'd toiled side by side with Jake Hobart and then had rammed a shiv in his ear and ended the man's life on the most inhospitable spot on earth so that his body would forever remain frozen in time and place and go unmourned.

He rushed to the aft section of the superstructure, where there was another hallway of cabins. More were located one deck down, inside the hull, but they were empty, since the *Hvalur Batur* was running with a skeleton crew. He entered his own cabin, noting for the first time that his door also squealed on its hinges as it came open. His

.45 was under his pillow. He cleared the chamber and checked the magazine before quietly reracking a round into the firing position. He vowed to remain armed at all times until this affair was settled.

He tucked the pistol behind his waist so the icy metal was against his lower spine, kept in place by his belt. Back in the dim corridor, he reached for the handle of the cabin door closest to his. It was locked, so he rapped on it with his knuckles until he heard a mechanical snick and the door creaked open.

Upon hearing the grating squeal, Bell went for the pistol at his back but stopped himself before drawing the weapon clear. Barely able to keep himself from swaying, the miner named Alvin Coulter regarded Bell with wide owl eyes under a furrowed brow and a completely bald pate. His complexion was a sallow yellow, made more sulfurous by the hallway's muted lighting.

"What?" he asked, knuckling sleep from his eyes.

From inside the cabin came a weak voice from the middle berth of a three-bed bunk. "You okay, Al? Ya ain't gonna be sick again?"

"Rest easy, Johnny. It's the man that came to fetch us off the island."

"Have either of you left your cabin in the

last twenty minutes?" Bell asked.

"Aye, Al did just a minute ago," John Caldwell wheezed from his bunk. "Poor sod's been heaving up his dinner."

Al Coulter stepped from his cabin and closed the door partway so his bunkmate couldn't hear. "I was sick just after we left the mess. Hours ago. Mr. Bell, Johnny's in a bad way. Delirious with fever, and he can't keep down more than a few sips of water. That's why I agreed to sleep two to a cabin, so's I can keep an eye on 'im. We're all in a bad way, but Johnny's the worst of us."

"What was his specific job back in the mine?"

"Assistant blaster to Jake Hobart. When Jake died, Johnny took over as head driller and chief blaster even though he's so young. Jake had taken the boy under his wing a while back, you see."

"And you?"

"I usually run ore trains in the mines, but here I do tool repair and sharpening and general labor."

Bell nodded. "Sorry to have woken you."

"Is there something wrong?"

"I heard someone moaning as if in pain," Bell lied. "Thought it was coming from here. I'm going to check on the others."

"Could be any of us."

Coulter slid back to his cabin and locked the door.

Bell checked the next cabin's door. It was unlocked, and like his and the previous it came open with a noise not unlike nails clawed down a chalkboard. The amber light cast by the hallway lamps shone across the bearded face of Walter Schmidt as he slept on his bunk. He was a large man, and his feet in their threadbare socks showed at the foot of his bed. The white sheet near his head and pillowcase were speckled with a dark fluid. Bell didn't need to see any clearer to know it was blood.

He closed the door without rousing the sleeping miner and checked a third cabin. He opened the door only a crack before closing it again. Like his door and the other two, it creaked as if the hinge points hadn't seen oil since the *Hvalur Batur* took to the seas.

While not destined for the stage, Bell considered he had a pretty good ear and could hold his own in any front parlor sing-along around a friend's piano, but he was damned if he could discern the difference between various door creaks. He was sure that someone out there possessed such perfect hearing and pitch that they could tell one squeal from another and pinpoint the door used by the clandestine radio caller, but he was not that person.

For a moment, he bemoaned his particular lack of ability but then chided himself for being utterly foolish. Dupin and Holmes were conjured up in the minds of fiction writers and thus could be infallible, while he had to contend with a real human's foibles and failures and could not be.

He allowed himself a small chuckle. It was one thing to accuse someone of a crime because of a squeaky door hinge, but such evidence would be laughed out of court. He needed something far more solid, and for the time being he'd have to make do without help. Bell knew better than to rely on Brewster. The man was so far gone mentally and physically that adding one more burden to the weight already pressing down on him might be the proverbial final straw.

In truth, Bell didn't know how much more any of the men could stand. The coughing, the bleeding, the vomiting, the lethargy — these were all symptoms of a great many illnesses, and food poisoning couldn't be ruled out. But Bell felt a darker presence, something more insidious than merely contaminated meals. He surely was no doctor, but, looking at the eight remaining Coloradans, he couldn't help thinking back to Brewster's description when they met on the beach. His exact words were "We're all walking dead men."

Bell hurried to Captain Fyrie's cabin, located just under the pilothouse and next to the stair that led to the bridge. His fingers had no sooner made contact with the cold steel door than the whaler's voice called out, muffled but clear, "Come."

Given the readiness of the summons, Bell expected the man to be seated at his desk, going over a report or making notations in the ship's log, but the cabin was dark, and Ragnar Fyrie was just swinging his legs free from under a thick polar bear pelt he used as a blanket. A lifetime at sea had taught him to come fully awake at the slightest disturbance.

"Sorry to bother —"

With a strong belief that if it's important enough to wake him for, it's urgent enough to skip the pleasantries, Fyrie snapped, "What is it?"

Bell wasn't put out by the gruff tone. "One of the miners used the radio and tried to cover his tracks. I suspect he contacted whatever French ship they left lying in wait in these waters."

"Skit." He pulled a pair of breeches off the floor and legged into them before ramming

his earlier-stockinged feet into calf-high rubber boots. "Don't suppose you know which one?"

"I lack the ear of a good acoustician."

"Huh?" Fyrie shinnied into a bulky roll-neck sweater the color of old whale bones.

"Your doors all squeal the same, so, no, I don't know which. Only that it's not Brewster or Vernon Hall, and likely not Alvin Coulter or John Caldwell."

Thirty seconds after Bell's initial knock, he was trailing Captain Fyrie up to the wheelhouse. The big harpooner, Arn, still had the con and nodded a taciturn greeting to his captain and guest. The seas were as black as slag heaps and capped with jagged white lines of foam that wriggled and twisted like living creatures or fanned across the surface like pale bolts of electricity. The sun was a distant smear against the horizon behind them, not yet powerful enough to inject any color into the sky except for a blue just one shade lighter than the deepest obsidian. They were traveling south and west toward the north coast of Norway and making sixteen knots, as they had passed below the ice limit.

"Mr. Bjørnson, course correction, please."

"Captain."

"Take us north-northwest at three hundred degrees. Reduce speed to ten knots, and I'll get Other Petr to act as an additional lookout."

"Yes, sir. Making my course three hundred degrees and reducing speed to ten knots." Arn first worked the spoked wooden wheel until the *Hvalur Batur*'s prow was cutting through the waves on the proper course and then ratcheted the engine telegraph to reduce speed until it read ten knots on the retrofitted pitometer log gauge mounted on the wall next to the pendulum inclinometer that showed the ship's roll. "Captain. Speed, ten knots. Course, three hundred degrees."

Fyrie regarded Isaac Bell. "There's ice to the north of us. With some luck, we can hide among the hummocks and keep moving west."

"Outflanking the French ship?"

"If she's out here. Our radio doesn't have a lot of range, but if they have a big enough antenna, they could still have heard a call."

"But knowing we've left Novaya Zemlya isn't the same as knowing where we're going to be," Bell said.

"Right. It's a big ocean. We just need to keep all our passengers from knowing our direction and speed and then we should slip by their picket without them ever knowing it."

"Confine them to the cabins, you mean?"

"I'll get someone to black out the port-holes outside the mess and paint over the small ones in each cabin. That way, they can roam a little bit but not try to get a fix on our position."

"Why not just take the crystal out of the radio?" Bell suggested. "They can't help their allies if they can't communicate."

With a chagrinned look on his face, Fyrie said, "I'm still getting used to even having a radio aboard my old *Batur.* I should have thought of that in the first place."

Bell shrugged good-naturedly. "My wife thinks I'm too clever by half. Anything else we can do?"

"In a few minutes, the light will be strong enough to show our smoke trail. I'm going to have Ivar vent steam out an auxiliary exhaust mounted to the stack. It's a terribly inefficient use of the engines, but the steam will help dissipate the black coal smoke faster and make us less visible against the ice fields. I can talk to Ivar over the voice tube, so please roust the two Petrs and have them come up here."

Bell left the bridge and strode back down to Brewster's cabin. He opened the door without knocking. The miner was dressed and sitting on his bed, his elbows resting on his knees and his head hanging low. He'd been coughing, because there were spots of blood on the deck. Next to the splatters were bits of hair and beard that had fallen by themselves from his head and face and drifted down.

"Mr. Brewster. It's me again. Isaac Bell."

The man looked up. His face was as pale as a full moon, and the bags under his eyes were bruised the color of eggplants. "I know who you are, Mr. Bell. I'm forgetful, not stupid."

"Right. Tell me about Jake Hobart. Do you know who killed him?"

"Whoever smuggled a radio onto the island with him," Brewster replied.

"A radio?"

"Yeah. Smallish thing powered by a hand crank. I found it after Jake's body was found. When we found him, see, he was out by the mound of tailings we'd already mined. It was after a bad storm, but that wouldn't have bothered Jake. He was a bull of a man. Nothing could stand in his way, least of all a little bad weather."

"Who found him?"

"Charlie Widney."

Bell pictured the man. He was a gentle giant with a prominent Adam's apple and scars on his face from some childhood pox.

He recalled that Widney's job was master of the draft horses and mules used in the mine. Therefore, his presence at the tailings pile wasn't an unusual event. "Go on."

"It was after we carried Jake back to the mine that I discovered he'd been stabbed in the ear. I hid that from the men and wondered why someone woulda killed him. Made sense that old Jake saw something someone else didn't want him to see. Something near the tailings, since no one but Charlie could have moved Jake's body alone and even then it would have been a struggle. You see, Jake liked to —"

"Please stick to what's relevant, Mr. Brewster."

"What? Oh, sure. Sorry. I ramble sometimes. What was I talking about?"

"Charlie Widney discovering Jake Hobart's body. You wondered why someone would have killed him and you surmised that Jake saw something the killer didn't want him to see."

"What was it?" Brewster asked, as if this was now Bell's tale to tell and not his own.

For his part, Bell kept calm despite his raging sense of impatience. "You tell me. You mentioned a radio."

The man's face lit up in recognition. "Right. The radio. I wondered what got Jake

383

killed, you see. So I went back after we brought in his body and looked around some. And hidden in the pile of waste rock and debris I found a metal box. I vaguely recalled it from when we off-loaded the equipment and animals from the French ship, the *Lorient,* but had no idea who brought it or what was inside. And inside was a radio set and a small hand-cranked generator to provide electricity."

"You're sure no one paid it special attention during your journey?"

"Yes, damnit!" Brewster snarled, obviously upset at being second-guessed. "One of my men was dead, Bell. Murdered. I've racked my brain over this every day since."

"Sorry . . . What did you do?"

"I didn't want whoever was behind the murder to know I was onto 'em so I pulled the magnet from the little generator, and when I went back in the mine, and no one was paying me any attention, I heated it in the forge we'd fashioned to repair our tools and such. The heat demagnetized the metal, and I put it back just like I found it."

Bell was impressed. "He could turn the crank all day and not generate one volt of electricity."

Brewster grinned at his own cleverness. "Yup. I watched that spot as best I could over the next weeks but never saw anyone nosing around. I think he'd been spooked by having to kill Jake Hobart and decided it best to not radio his French buddies."

"Until tonight," Bell said, for his benefit rather than Brewster's. "If you think of anything else — and, I mean, anything no matter how trivial — you need to tell me straightaway. Okay?"

"I will. I promise." Now the man looked to be on the verge of tears. "I'm sorry I forgot to tell you this earlier. My mind plays tricks on me."

"With luck, it will turn out to be an omission without consequence." Bell didn't believe that even as he said it. He left Brewster to whatever thoughts rattled around in his increasingly distraught brain.

Three days passed. Three days of monotony tainted by a nervous anticipation that kept the crew on edge. The ship handled well, and the pack ice was left behind, but they were discovering a great many small and midsized icebergs that had calved from east Greenland ice sheets or migrated from the west coast around Greenland's southern tip and now drifted in the straits between Norway and the Svalbard archipelago.

The miners spent most of their time in the mess or in the cabins. They weren't allowed on the bridge, the captain citing safety concerns, although Bell was there as a regular fixture. No one seemed to care. Bell spent time with each of the men trying to learn what he could about them without seeming too nosy. If anyone did think his questions were becoming too personal, Bell would immediately back off, saying it was his nature and no offense was intended.

He made certain that all the Coloradans knew he was treating each of them more or less the same so as to not arouse suspicion. He operated on the hope that the traitor in their midst didn't know Bell had been alerted to his presence, but at the same time accepted the possibility the man knew the Van Dorn detective was already suspicious. It was a fine line he trod but one on which he'd walked a thousand miles.

The miners seemed to regain some vigor, if not their health. They all had various aches and pains and complaints, but none seemed to be getting worse, and those who could eat more solid food regained some strength.

25

It was just after dawn on the third day since someone had sent a radio call, and Bell was on the bridge about to go below to eat breakfast with the miners. He tried to dine with them as often as possible. If he wasn't engaging with any of them, he was always watching, alert to any idiosyncrasies that might betray his quarry.

Ragnar Fyrie was in the captain's chair, a pair of binoculars to his eyes, watching a berg shaped like a lesser noble's castle slide by a mile off the starboard side. Magnus was at the con, his mop of blond hair contained under a tight woolen cap. His attention was on the coffee he'd just spilled down the front of his cable-knit sweater, so Bell was the first to see it. There was an odd, undulating movement, unrelated to the ship's roll, near the prow. Bell watched for a moment, unsure what he was seeing. But as soon as Magnus noted it, he gave a panicked cry.

"Captain. Fire!"

And then Bell realized that what he was seeing was smoke, boiling up from under the wicked-looking harpoon cannon.

Fyrie dumped the binoculars into a canvas sling dangling from the wall and leapt for the stairs down to the main deck. He used his elbows to slide down the polished brass railings so that his feet never touched a tread. Bell followed as best he could, his feet slapping at the stairs in a vain attempt to keep up. He well knew that fire, more than any other danger, more than even sinking, is what a mariner feared most.

One of the two crewmen named Petr was just coming from the galley with thermoses of freshly brewed coffee, and Fyrie almost bowled him over. "Get up to the cannon. The cover for the harpoon fairlead came off. Watch yourself. There's fire in the mechanical room below the firing platform." The man's eyes went wide at the word *fire,* but he wordlessly rushed off.

"Should have confined them," Fyrie said tightly as he raced forward.

Bell knew he meant the miners and knew he suspected the fire was deliberately set, an arson attack to slow their escape to Scotland. He stayed on the captain's heels, wholeheartedly agreeing.

They raced past the main deck cabins and into a mechanical space with even poorer lighting than the rest of the ship. Greasy machines hulked in the gloom, and the fishy stench of whale oil was overwhelming. They came to a forward bulkhead with a waist-high hatch rather than a traditional doorway. It was secured with dogging latch. Next to it were brackets holding three copper dry-chemical fire extinguishers. The copper was dull and pitted, but the mechanisms looked workable.

"This is where the springs and tensioners are located for the harpoon line," Fyrie explained, popping the safety ring off one of the extinguishers and handing it to Bell while keeping a second for himself. "There's a lot of wheels and pulleys, and everything is coated in grease. If we can't contain this quickly, we're in trouble."

Bell nodded grimly.

Fyrie ducked below the bottom edge of the hatch, Bell staying upright but well to the side. When the captain swung open the hatch, he'd braced himself for a rolling wave of fire to billow from the room as a new source of oxygen was introduced. Nothing so dramatic occurred, and both men chanced looking into the burning space.

The room was rectangular and low-ceilinged and filled with machinery as complex as an industrial loom's. The smoke was as dense as cotton and black, and it was drawn up through a hole in the ceiling as though by force of a powerful vacuum.

"Petr hasn't sealed the harpoon line fairlead," Fyrie shouted, and he jumped into the room, holding the extinguisher low with its rubber nozzle held at chest height.

Moving through the space required the skills of a contortionist, but Fyrie knew his ship so well he could maneuver by muscle memory alone. Bell needed to grab for handholds to keep his balance, which slowed him and left him smeared with grease up to the elbows.

The fire finally caught a taste of the additional oxygen reaching it from the open hatch and grew like an overinflating balloon. Fyrie was forced to bend over backward until his shoulders were almost level with his hips as flames licked and rolled along the ceiling just above his face. He recovered and went to work with the extinguisher. He ignored the river of fire dancing along the ceiling and directed a stream of white powder at the base of the fire. The chemical blanketed burning ropes and globs of molten grease. Bell reached his side and added his extinguisher to the battle.

With the fire intensifying, the heat inside the low chamber began to skyrocket. And still smoke was sucked up through the vent in the ceiling as though it had been designed as a chimney. The crewman Petr hadn't yet done the simple task set to him.

For a moment it seemed they would get the best of the fire with just the two extinguishers, but then it found some old oil-soaked oakum left in a basket. The oakum ignited with a searing whoosh that forced both men back and gave the blaze a fresh toehold amid the machinery. The flames swelled and seemed to grow more confident as they enveloped more of the space, like an animal probing its freedom after being penned.

Bell and Fyrie exchanged a swift glance that affirmed for the detective what he sensed — the fire had just taken the upper hand and it was time to concentrate on saving their lives rather than the ship.

"Captain," a crewman behind them called out over the mounting roar of the flames.

Fyrie turned to see Arn Bjørnson carrying two heavy metal pails through the tangled maze of ropes and wires and hydraulic pistons. He handed one to his captain as though it were empty, but in fact it was filled to the brim with clean white sand.

Fyrie grabbed it from his hands and with a deft touch flung its contents in a sweeping arc that smothered everything beneath it in a perfectly placed half-inch layer. What flames it smothered it killed. Arn had set the second pail on the deck so he could go get more. The captain snatched it up and wafted another spray of sand into the fire.

"Will there be enough?" Bell had to shout this to be heard.

"We keep tons of sand aboard for just this reason," Fyrie shouted back. "Don't know if we have enough crew to get it to us before the fire's too big."

Bell backed away from the captain. The man was trained for this kind of work. Bell was not. Instead, he met Arn halfway across the smoky room and took the two pails of sand Arn had returned with from him, adding himself as another link in a bucket brigade that stretched from here to a sand bunker located outside the main hold.

Each bucket weighed forty pounds, and the thin metal handle dug into the meat of Bell's fingers like a wire garrote, but he dutifully took them from the harpooner and rushed back to Fyrie's side. The pain suffered by the men who'd worked to get those two buckets of sand was for nothing, because just as Bell was passing the first to Fyrie, the whaling ship hove hard to starboard. The deck canted so quickly that Bell lost his footing and dropped both buckets, and their contents spilled uselessly.

Before either could react further, the unmistakable iron patter of machine gun bullets striking metal plating filled the chamber and drowned out the hellish din of fire. One round punched a hole through a thinner piece of plate and ricocheted between the two men.

Bell spoke first. "You fight the ship, I'll fight the fire. Go!"

Fyrie needed no further encouragement. He raced from the room even as Arn struggled under the burden of two fresh pails. Bell took one from him, hunching down for fear of another raking attack by the unknown machine gunner, and tossed sand at the fire like it was a bucket of water. His technique lacked Ragnar Fyrie's finesse. And did little to quell the flames.

"No," Arn said. "Like this."

He fanned the bucket sideways almost like he was swinging a baseball bat, and the arc of sand that spilled from it beat the fire back a few inches.

Knowing the Icelander had practiced tossing buckets during countless drills, Bell knew he'd best serve the effort by becoming a mule. "You pour," Bell shouted, "I'll haul."

He left Arn's side and raced over to the low hatchway. He was able to draw a few deep breaths of relatively fresh air. Lars Olufsen, the ship's second engineer, rushed at him from down the hallway, lugging two buckets. Bell caught a glimpse of Vernon Hall turning back to descend the staircase from where he'd carried the pails up handed to him by some other crewman or miner. It seemed that everyone was in on the attempt to fight the blaze.

Another burst of machine gun fire raked the ship's prow, but it hit with less fervor, as if coming from a greater distance. No new holes appeared in the hull plates.

Bell moved buckets as fast as they were brought to him, ignoring the strain on his shoulders, arms, and especially his hands, as well as the heat and the fact his lungs burned and his eyes streamed channels of tears through the soot caking his face. Each bucket he brought to Arn, Arn threw with the surety of a farmer sowing seeds on his land. He maximized the distribution, and thus the efforts of all the men, so that the fire was slowly being beaten back into the corner where it had been set.

Then something curious happened. The noxious smoke that had been rushing up to and then out the ceiling vent as though being pulled by a bellows suddenly began to amass in a roiling billow that grew until it was soon invading every corner and niche within the chamber. Arn backed out swiftly, turning and pushing Bell ahead of him and leaving two buckets still filled with sand behind. They staggered out through the hatch opening, each falling to the deck at Lars Olufsen's feet, their chests convulsing with great, racking coughs that were forcing up tarry balls of phlegm from deep inside. The second engineer slammed the hatch closed. The smoke rising from Arn's and Bell's clothes made them look like they'd just escaped the Underworld.

"What happened?" Bell wheezed. Someone handed him a canteen of water and he drank from it greedily.

Bjørnson was also guzzling water from a canteen, so Lars answered, "The fairlead under the cannon was finally sealed. That room's airtight so long as it and this hatch here are closed. The fire will put itself out. We can enter in twenty or so minutes with water hoses and cool everything so the fire does not re . . . ah . . ."

"Reignite," Bell offered. The men all had such a good command of English that he sometimes forgot it wasn't their first language.

"*Ja.*" Lars was unreeling a two-inch canvas hose from a wall-mounted firefighting station.

Isaac hauled himself to his feet. He was unsteady for a moment but found his center. "You don't need me, then. I'm going to see who the hell was taking potshots at us with a machine gun."

From the floor, Arn offered his hand to shake. Bell did. The two men nodded. No words were necessary.

"Mr. Olufsen, I advise you round up all the miners and confine them to the mess until we get everything sorted out."

The man looked at him with incomprehension.

"Don't let on that we suspect, but this fire was likely deliberate."

At that, the man gaped.

Bell took just a second to rush to his cabin. On his way, he passed weary miners and mariners, each seemingly paused mid-stride since no one ahead was asking for more sand. The bucket brigade had come to a halt.

"We did it, men," he told them as he

passed, patting Tom Price on the shoulder in recognition. "We beat the fire." The cheers were ragged, exhausted, but heartfelt.

In his room he soaked a cloth in water left in the basin from that morning and wiped the worst of the smudges from his face. He stripped off his sweater to don his only spare. He still felt grimy, and his eyes would be red for hours. And his chest ached. But at least he could stand his own smell.

"Report," Captain Fyrie snapped from the helm as soon as Bell stepped onto the bridge. He hadn't turned toward Bell but had detected him coming up the stairs in his peripheral vision.

"We had the fire three-quarters out when the room was sealed. Arn's waiting twenty minutes before moving in with the hoses. He seems confident. I've instructed Second Engineer Olufsen to keep all the miners in the mess for a while."

Bell studied the ship's surroundings. The sky was streaked with purple clouds, the sea remained inky. A towering berg cut off his view starboard. The mass of ice stretched at least a mile, and ahead was another berg, only slightly smaller. Others sat stolidly to port and more loomed in their wake. Of the ship that had attacked earlier, he saw no trace. What dominated his attention, however, was the long, coiling finger of smoke that rose from the ship to a height of several thousand feet, proclaiming their location as surely as if they were an island marked on a nautical chart.

"Who was it?"

"No flag, but it's got to be the French you warned me about. Hundred feet long. Painted dark gray. Looked like military surplus. Machine gunner was on a platform aft of the bridge. On her foredeck is a cannon turret. Don't know if it works. Aft, she carried twin cranes with extended-length booms."

"How'd they find us so quickly?" Bell asked, more of himself than actually seeking an answer.

Fyrie replied anyway. "I made a mistake. I expected them to remain east of us when I believed we were flanking them, but the French captain is smart. He came west immediately and set a picket for when we turned south along the Norway coast. I thought we were farther offshore than we are. I turned right into where he was waiting for us. The smoke pouring off our bow was all he needed to zero in."

"Damned bad luck, is all," Bell said, trying to ease the captain's guilt. "We'll figure something out."

"Will we?" he shot back. "They've got a machine gun, Mr. Bell. Magnus saw the whole thing. That initial barrage we heard? It hit Petr first. He had just reached the pulpit. Magnus said he came apart like he was made of wet red straw. I managed to get some distance on them so Mags could finally seal the mechanical room, but if they find us again in all these bergs, I'm surrendering the minute he gets his sights on us."

Bell let a moment pass so Fyrie could get his temper under control.

"They won't leave any witnesses, Ragnar." He deliberately used the captain's Christian name. The man was reeling from the death of a crewman, the fact that a saboteur had tried to burn his ship, and that he was now being actively hunted, the irony of which couldn't be lost on a man who himself hunted across all corners of the ocean. "I am sorry about your man. But the truth is, if we surrender, they get the ore without having to fight for it. It won't change our fate."

"Are you saying we're dead either way?"

Bell shook his head, a devilish glint in his bright blue eyes. "I'm saying we take control of our fate. They picked the fight, Captain. I say we end it. And I know how."

26

The explosion came a few moments later, while Bell was outlining his plan, and was followed almost immediately by the boom of the French ship's bow cannon hurling a solid projectile over their heads. The shell had struck a hundred feet up the side of a large berg they had sought shelter in the lee of, and chunks of its ice, some the size of refrigerators and larger, were blown from the berg and crashed into the sea. Smaller bits raked the side of the *Hvalur Batur* like a fresh barrage from the machine gun.

Before the echo had a chance to dissipate, as it rattled through the field of ice, the French fired again. This time, the shell landed lower, just above the smokestack, but also a good hundred feet behind them.

Straight off the port beam, about a half mile distant, was another berg that resembled a flat-topped mesa from the American Southwest. Steaming around it, and headed right for them, was the French ship *Lorient,* its bow still obscured by white smoke from the brace of shots it had just fired.

Captain Fyrie cursed and jerked the engine telegraph to emergency full power. Bell plucked the binoculars from their canvas sling and glassed the approaching ship. The *Lorient* was swinging to port in order to keep her bow pointed straight at the *Hvalur,* and Bell suspected he knew why. The whaler wasn't quick or maneuverable, so coming up to speed took time. This allowed the prow of the French ship to track her progress across the face of the big berg as though it were the barrel of a shotgun swinging around at an escaping bird.

"Captain," Bell said urgently, "turn us toward them."

"What? Why?"

"Just do it!"

Fyrie swung the wheel, and the whaling ship drove her shoulder into the sea and she came about far sharper than she ever had in her career. She heeled over hard, forcing the men on the bridge to clutch handholds. The sound of something crashing to the deck below came up the stairway.

An instant later, the French fired a third time. The shell crashed into the nearby berg exactly where the wheelhouse would have been had Bell not shouted a warning. More ice cascaded down into the sea.

"Their turret doesn't swivel," Bell said. "They have to aim the cannon by turning the entire ship."

"How do we take advantage of that?" Fyrie asked, turning his ship once again so he could duck around the back of the berg and take refuge amid the enormous field of floating ice islands.

"For one thing, don't let him get directly behind us. We need to keep moving unpredictably. Zig when he zags."

Arn bellowed up the stairwell, "Captain, we need to vent the mechanical room."

"One moment." Fyrie turned his attention to Bell. "You go out and open the fairlead plug. It twists a quarter turn into position, and it's secured to the ship with a chain. Take gloves because it's going to be hot. Same with the deck. Out and back as fast as you can."

"On it," Bell replied. He found gloves on a shelf above some hanging parkas. He pulled on the thickest pair, and a hooded anorak, before sliding open the bridge wing door.

The temperature was tolerable, maybe a dozen degrees below freezing, but it was the wind rushing across the deck that numbed

Bell's face and made his eyes stream. Down below, below his waist, he could feel warmth radiating from the deck above the place the fire had raged. He raced along the raised catwalk connecting the bridge to the pulpit, where the harpoon cannon stood empty. Even at a fast jog, he could feel the hot metal through the soles of his boots. He saw the round plug used to cover the hole that the wire of the harpoon was attached to, on its deadly arc, rise from within the ship.

The plug had expanded due to the extreme heat, forcing him to use both hands to twist with all his strength. It finally loosened, and the pressure of overheated air down below blew the plug upward like a champagne cork. Bell fell to the deck, but then the heat meeting the seat of his pants forced him back to his feet in a comical bit of acrobatics.

From the hole spewed a solid column of black smoke, followed by dense white steam, as the fire team belowdecks began to cool the metal machinery with the two-inch hose. In the pristine Arctic air, the smoke was a dark stain.

Bell needed time. He needed time for the hull to cool, the smoke to dissipate, and for the captain of the *Lorient* to make a number of tactical mistakes. Otherwise, they were going to tear the *Hvalur Batur* apart, steal its cargo, and murder its crew. Luck, skill, and sheer audacity had worked so often for Bell in the past that sometimes he forgot fortune may favor the bold, but oftentimes it punished the unaware.

He admitted, as he dashed back to the bridge, that he knew little of the ship's capabilities, less of naval tactics, and nothing at all of the chances of pulling off his plan.

Over the next hour, the two ships played a game of cat and mouse amid the towering ramparts of ice. When the French found the whaling ship in its sights, it fired off several shots, but the hastily aimed shells never came close. And then Captain Fyrie would hook them around another berg and make a quick retreat. The trick was to keep moving so the *Lorient* couldn't come at them directly and bring her deck gun to bear. And for much of the day, that's exactly what kept happening. Even if the French caught a glimpse of the whaling ship, it was at such an angle or distance that they couldn't engage with the big cannon.

Luck seemed to be on their side until it abandoned them without warning.

The *Hvalur* was racing west, hoping to hook around the back of a berg, when suddenly the *Lorient* burst out behind them from around another drifting mass of ice. Her cannon fired, but before its thunder rolled across the Icelandic vessel its solid steel shell slammed into the rear of the pilothouse. It tore through the radio room, before screaming across the bridge and finally exploding out one of the windows overlooking the foredeck. The round landed unseen out past the bow.

Inside the bridge, the kinetic energy shed by the five-inch shell as it transited the space had been transformed into heat and shock waves that assaulted the men's senses like they'd been thrust inside a whirling kaleidoscope of light and sound and motion. A fire started growing in the radio room, and the temperature dropped fifty or more degrees as the cold Arctic air gusted through the broken window.

Bell's ears rang like church bells and his vision was blurry for many long seconds. His head felt as though it had been worked over with a pneumatic rock hammer. A little blood dripped from his forehead where a piece of shrapnel had embedded itself. He winced as he pulled the shard free of his flesh and tossed it aside in order to unclip a fire extinguisher from the wall and douse the burning books atop the shack's desk.

The radio set was a sparking ruin, which he soaked for good measure.

Fyrie was trying to talk to him, but Bell couldn't hear the words, only see his mouth moving soundlessly. He held up a hand to forestall any conversation and worked his jaw to equalize the pressure between his ears and sinuses. When things cleared up with what to him was an audible squeak, his head felt instantly better and his vision normalized. Fyrie's voice was nothing more than a monotonous buzz for now, but it was an improvement.

A second shot followed the first, but it went wide and streaked past the bridge wing like a meteor. A moment later, the French lost sight of their target as the *Hvalur Batur* motored around the trailing edge of another iceberg.

After another few moments, Bell was finally able to hear Captain Fyrie lighting off a string of curses in English, Icelandic, a little French, and quite possibly Swahili. No sooner had he caught his breath than Chief Engineer Ivarsson climbed up the stairs from the main deck, his expression grim. He looked around at the destruction and nodded, accepting the mess as just one more thing gone wrong that day.

"I'll get some plywood from stores to

cover the window, Captain," he said when he had Fyrie's attention. "But we've got a real problem. It's cool enough to check the bilge below the mechanical room. Some plates are buckled and we're taking on water."

He held up a quick hand to prevent the inevitable barrage of follow-up questions. "We've jammed the holes with oakum mats and caulked them in place as best we could. The pumps can stay ahead of the water, but we must reduce our speed by one quarter at least."

"The crew's okay?" Fyrie asked.

"Some smoke inhalation. Arn got the worst of it, but you know him. Indestructible."

"Send him up here," Fyrie ordered. "Now that we know we can't outrun the French, it's time we put an end to this. Bell, are you sure about your plan?"

"No, but it's the best we have."

The captain bit at his lip in worry, not about himself but about his crew.

Two crewmen arrived on the bridge with Arn, who'd changed out of his smoke-infused clothes but whose face remained streaked with soot. They fitted a sheet of plywood already cut to size over the broken window. The relief from the cold and wind was almost instantaneous. They also used a couple of magnets to secure some thick paper stock over the hole blown through the back of the radio room. Arn stoked the potbellied stove until it was almost glowing. When the work was done, Bell and Fyrie went over their plan and made certain the big harpooner understood the risks. If he was concerned, he gave no indication.

Two tension-filled hours later, they were still working to get into the proper position. It was a game of chess, with each ship playing the role of queen, and the expanse of icebergs as the board determining which moves were possible. Twice the French ship had appeared from around a berg and opened fire with its cannon. They weren't trying to sink the whaler — otherwise, they'd lose the prize — but the shots roared by the pilothouse close enough to burn off paint and singe the metal. The scream of their passage rattled the windows and left the men temporarily deafened.

To make things worse, a fog had descended, lacy and a-swirl, deadening noise so that everything sounded muffled and oddly distant, the groaning of the ice became a haunting lament. The hunt was slow. Each time they thought they spotted the *Lorient,* it turned out to be a small berg.

The occasional crash of ice cascading off the face of a taller berg sent jolts of adrenaline through Bell's body. At one point, as the afternoon wore on, a big iceberg lost in the mist calved enough that its center of gravity shifted and it flipped entirely over in the water, splashing and thrashing like a drowning victim.

The fact that they were being hunted in a ship that was taking on water without any visible means of defending itself made the experience just one degree more unnerving. But Captain Fyrie acquitted himself well, in Bell's estimation. He was making the best of a horrendous situation and remaining in full command and calm, even when artillery shells were falling around his ship.

During what seemed like a lull in the hunt, the sun suddenly burning through the fog and the air turning crystalline, Bell went below to check on the miners. They were growing resentful of being forced to stay in the mess. Bell explained that because of the pursuit by agents of the Société des Mines, staying in the dining area was for their own safety. As he talked, he couldn't help but think one of them had deliberately set the fire without knowing how large the blaze could grow. He'd risked a conflagration that could have killed them all. That the arsonist was a native Coloradan, a man well known to the others, made his act of sabotage especially fiendish. He had no compunction about seeing his fellow miners dead so his French conspirators could take possession of the byzanium ore.

Such reptilian disdain was chilling.

27

Bell felt a renewed tension as soon as he climbed back to the bridge. In the chasm between two towering icebergs ahead of them, the converted French warship was steaming away from the whaler. They'd surely spotted the quarry, but in the confines between the pair of bergs there wasn't enough room in the sea to turn the ship and launch another attack.

"This could be our chance," Fyrie said.

"Not if they reach the end of the bergs and come about," Bell countered, putting the binoculars to his eyes. "We'll be trapped like a rat in a sewer pipe."

"Then let's hope Ivar's plug holds." The captain ratcheted the engine telegraph, asking for full power.

Down in the engine room, Ivar Ivarsson and his men began adding their own labor to the automatic feeding system, shoveling bucket after bucket of crushed coal into the firebox so the heat swelled and the pressures rose. The ship's acceleration wasn't very dramatic, but it did come.

Fyrie's attention never left the French ship. They knew the prey was behind them because they had increased speed, if the expanding plume of smoke belching from her stack was any indication. He was judging angles and relative speeds, committing to one final gamble. Because if the *Lorient* managed to turn in time, their range meant the pilothouse could be scythed off the *Hvalur* with just a couple well-placed shots and the fight would be over.

Several minutes elapsed. Bell struggled not to ask the captain if they were going to make it.

The two ships kept accelerating down the gap between the miles-long icebergs. As night approached, the air temperature between the bergs dropped and yet another fog began to coil off the surface of the sea. It wasn't thick enough to be dangerous, but the effect was eerie.

The French were a half mile ahead and approaching the point where the berg on the left ended in a tall, spiked peak resembling a miniature Matterhorn. The *Lorient* began to turn to starboard to swing around and race back at the whaler before she broke free of the gap herself.

The captain's hands remained loose and relaxed on the wheel, his eyes squinting just a fraction. The engine's thrum was like a heartbeat, rhythmic and powerful. Aft, her wake was a creaming white line that spread in a V and lapped at the base of the icebergs.

"Well?" Bell asked when he could stand it no more.

"She's faster than I thought. They might get a shot off, but not two."

Cutting as tight an arc as she could manage, the French vessel continued to turn while the *Hvalur Batur* charged down the gap at her best possible speed.

"You'd best get into position, Mr. Bell. Good luck."

Bell had donned a coat and had the equipment he needed. "To us all, Captain."

He went down the stairs and out onto the deck via one of the hatches. The wind slammed into him, forcing him to take a few staggering steps before gaining solid footing. The ship was cutting through the sea at better than fifteen knots. The fog was clammy and diaphanous, and Bell felt disoriented by it and the sight of the massive walls of ice streaming past him as they raced after the French warship. The icebergs felt close enough to touch.

He found cover at the stern rail behind one of a pair of winches used to haul in the carcasses of the massive whales the ship so doggedly hunted. He could look ahead and see the enemy had almost completed the turn. The ship had looped wide to port in order to come around parallel to the larger of the two bergs. Had she not been able to turn so tightly, she would have slammed bow first into the wall of ice. As it was, the *Lorient* came dangerously close to sideswiping the iceberg and that would have torn her hull open like she was made of paper. Bell could only wish to be that lucky.

The French steamer completed its turn and was barely a thousand feet from them and charging hard under a pall of coal smoke. The two vessels were now coming at each other like jousting knights racing down the lists. Only one of the knights sported a lance, in the guise of a five-inch gun. The other appeared defenseless.

Bell watched a silent gout of white smoke explode from the cannon. The sound of the blast took a moment to reach him, but the scream of shot was near instantaneous. The shell struck one of the tall derricks on the aft deck, severing the steel column halfway up. The crane crashed down in a tangle of lines and pulleys and ruined metal, forcing

Bell to hurl himself over the winch capstan to avoid being crushed. He immediately had to leap back as the mass of debris didn't settle on deck but rather was dragged over the side of the ship by its own weight. It vanished into the foggy wisps and inky sea as surely as if it had been swallowed.

On the bridge, Fyrie spun the wheel to get them out of the direct line of fire and called for full reverse on the telegraph to slow the headlong rush toward the French.

Another blast from the cannon sent a projectile flashing past them. It hit the berg off the starboard side. Bell was showered with bits of ice and snow but was otherwise unharmed. He crouched. The two ships were about to come abreast of each other with little more than fifty feet separating the hulls. The enemy machine gunner was about to enjoy the best hunting of his military career.

From his concealed position, Bell could see the gunner, who was wearing a long khaki greatcoat and a fur hat. He stood behind a pintle-mounted Hotchkiss M1909, fitted with a small armor shield. Bell recognized the weapon by its distinctive brass feeding strip inserted on the right side of the receiver. As the gun was fired, the strip slid through the mechanism until it fell out as the last round left the barrel. Each strip held thirty 8-millimeter bullets, and the gun could fire at nearly six hundred rounds per minute.

At this range, the majority of the bullets would rip right through the wheelhouse's thin steel skin.

"Arrêtez-vous!" someone called out from the other ship but gave no time to have his demand heeded before the gunner racked back on the Hotchkiss's charging handle.

Bell rose up from his hiding place. The ships were side by side, passing each other at a combined speed of twenty knots, but there was more than enough time for the gunner to wreak such devastation that the Icelandic whaler would be all but dead in the water. The gunner didn't see him. He was crouched behind his weapon, sighting in to unleash a barrage on the superstructure.

Arn had to be watching all of this from where he was hiding, and Bell knew the man would instinctively react because his captain was in danger. Bell would have done the same. But the plan called for the harpooner to remain unseen until Bell engaged the machine gunner. If Arn made his move too soon, then he and the rest of the crew were going to die.

Shouting at the top of his lungs, his voice echoing off the towering ice massif in front of him and sounding like the banshee wail from mythology, Bell took aim with his .45 and started firing.

The machine gunner too opened up with quick, controlled bursts that reverberated like an autocannon, the plink of lead against steel lost in the din of exploding powder and dropping brass. Bell kept firing with one hand, holding steady, until a few rounds hit close enough to the French sailor to draw his attention. The sailor stopped firing at the pilothouse and swung the heavy machine gun around to direct his aim toward the armed threat at the whaling ship's stern.

Bell saw the muzzle coming toward him and still he kept pulling the trigger. He dropped the box magazine from the .45's grip when the last round was still in the chamber so he wouldn't lose time pulling his aim off target to recock the pistol. The French gun was almost on him. Bell had played it out as long as he could, but his definition of bravery wasn't being the target of an automatic weapon. He managed firing one more round, and was about to drop behind the capstan, when the French gunner suddenly ducked low behind his little armor shield. That last bullet had hit close enough to make him seek cover. Bell tightened his grip, rummaging in a pocket for his last magazine, while he fired shot after shot.

Unseen on the bow, and totally ignored, thanks to Bell's efforts, Arn Bjørnson tossed aside the stained canvas sheet he'd hidden himself under and rose up behind the big harpoon cannon. Had he moved a single second sooner, the French gunner would have seen him and he would have been cut down as easily as his crewmate Petr. The harpoon cannon had been primed and loaded. All he need do was grab the trigger grip and muscle the barrel into position. He'd done this a thousand times on targets not much smaller than the French ship. And, for the first time, he'd take some satisfaction in the hunt.

The harpoons were fired using an explosive charge in a breach chamber much like a conventional cannon. Only, these projectiles were heavily barbed and tipped with an explosive to kill their quarry as mercifully as possible. Prior to the engagement, and at Isaac Bell's urging, he'd double-loaded the harpoon with a second grenade. And now he swung the cannon over and down until the *Lorient*'s lower hull showed in the aiming reticle. Aft of him, the French shooter had paused, and he could hear the steady *crack, crack, crack* of the American's handgun.

Arn pulled the trigger, and the big cannon thundered. Unburdened by the rope it normally trailed behind it, the harpoon flew straight and true and struck the French ship just above the waterline at just about where Bjørnson had estimated the engine room would be. It hit with a heavy clang, and half of the three-foot projectile buried itself in the steel side of the ship, meaning both grenades were inside the hull when they exploded.

The blast sent a shock wave racing across the waters almost faster than the eye could track, and the *Hvalur Batur* began to heel onto her port side even as fire and smoke erupted from the French vessel in a vision straight out of hell. The explosion tore a hole in her side big enough to drive an automobile through. Water began sluicing down the rupture in an unending surge. It took just seconds to fill the spaces below engineering and climb high enough to envelop the boiler.

The thermal shock of ice water quenching the red-hot firebox and massive steam tanks blew the aft section of the ship into oblivion.

Bell had sought cover behind the windlass as soon as he heard Arn fire the cannon but still cringed, as if to make himself even smaller, as the concussion and spray of shrapnel rolled across the whaler. He chanced looking up to see the bow of the Société's warship slow to a stop and then get pulled under the waves in a sucking maelstrom of bubbles and debris.

Already weakened by the warming spring temperatures, the iceberg looming over the Icelandic whaler shuddered at the reverberating onslaught of such a nearby explosion. Chunks weighing many times that of the ship dropped off the sheer face of the berg. The ship itself was just out of range, but the swells created when they collapsed into the sea would have swamped them had the captain not spun the whaler to take them on the rear quarter rather than broadside.

Afterward, nothing of the *Lorient* remained on the surface of the sea but a few bits of flotsam and some smoldering wreckage no larger than steamer trunks. It was all that marked the grave of the men sent to murder the Coloradans.

Suspended above the awful destruction, the discharged cloud of superheated steam from the boilers had transformed from gas to solid in the shape of shimmering particles of ice that filled the air as enchantingly as fairy dust.

The *Hvalur Batur* bobbed like a child's toy in a bathtub, and Bell was forced to totter drunkenly back to the bridge. He lurched up the stairs, dread rising in his chest at what he'd find when he reached the bridge. He knew Fyrie was alive — he'd steered them out of harm's way following the icy avalanche — but that didn't mean he'd survived the autofire unscathed.

"Ragnar. It's Bell," he called halfway up the steps. "Are you okay?"

He reached the bridge. The portside wall was peppered with a dozen holes, and the window glass in the bridge wing door was missing. Arctic air whistled through the holes and gusted through where the glass was missing. What little decorative wood-work the bridge had possessed was now so many splintered shards. Fyrie himself stood among the destruction without any outward sign of being attacked. He turned to Bell with a slight shrug as if to convey a recognition of the absurdity this trip had become.

"Upon further consideration, Mr. Bell," he said at last, "I believe it would have been in our best interest to remain in the custody of the Norwegian authorities back in Sand-efjord."

Bell saw out on the prow that Arn Bjørnson had finished securing the harpoon cannon and was making his way back from the pulpit. "And I wouldn't blame you for that assessment one bit," he said.

They shared the laugh of men who'd cheated death by the narrowest of margins. But then both remembered that one of the crew had paid for the escape with his life, and the laughter died on their lips.

Like a harbinger of ill omens, the chief engineer climbed up from the main deck a few minutes later. He had some crewmen with him, who got busy patching holes and boarding up the window.

"How does she look, Ivar?"

"We might make Aberdeen, Captain, but I don't see the old girl steaming back to Reykjavik without a long overhaul in dry dock. The hull plates are buckled a lot worse than I first thought. I had to reset my plug, thanks to you running about like a madman, and I realized the damage is bad. The keel itself might even be compromised. I've got a few new leaks on the boiler system from blown fittings. That will keep us slow enough to protect the plug since I have enough steam pressure for ten knots."

"Anything else?"

"All the arresting gear in the mechanical

room is so much charred junk now. None of it's salvageable. We lost the aft deck main derrick. It's just gone. And you can see what a mess they made of the bridge. Radio's shot dead, charts are ruined. Only a few panes of glass remaining."

Fyrie moved the handle of the engine telegraph. It flopped uselessly, obviously ruined by the Hotchkiss. "And this."

Bell was shocked and saddened. He had no idea these men had lost so much. They'd lost everything, in fact.

Rather than giving in to gloom, Fyrie said rather agreeably, "It's a good thing this tub's insured for double her value and that we were able to convert our whale oil to gold kroner before the Norwegians threw us into impound." He looked to Bell. "I guess this is when we shift away from whaling. Like we talked that night when we first hit the pack ice."

"Double insurance?" Bell asked.

"The man from Lloyd's insisted two years ago when we sailed to Antarctica. They never figured we'd survive to collect it if we had a claim. They also never reduced the coverage once we got back, and I wasn't going to remind them of their mistake. We'll put a little aside for Petr's parents, since he wasn't married, and the rest should set us up nicely with a couple of trawlers. And an idea I have for a fish-processing ship at sea."

"Or . . ." Ivar said with a raised eyebrow as though he had a better idea.

"Forget it, old friend. We're not going to dredge the coast of Africa looking for diamonds. We're sailors of the blue water, not coastal flat wallowers playing in the mud."

28

It was a three-and-a-half-day journey from where they sank the French vessel to the Port of Aberdeen on Scotland's northeast coast. Bell wasn't concerned that the saboteur would strike again. He'd gambled that his allies were close enough to see the smoke from the fire he'd set below the harpoon gun and that they'd reach the whaler before flames consumed the ship. With the *Lorient* destroyed, the man had no means of escape until they reached land, so Bell was sure the Société des Mines's agent would play nice until then.

With the ice far behind them and the weather pleasant enough, for the far North Atlantic, Bell had more time to resolve which of the Coloradans was his man. He had to be honest and say that little distinguished the remaining eight miners from one another apart from a few superficial attributes like size and build.

At the best of times, they were mostly taciturn and unsmiling. None were married or had children, and, apart from Brewster, none were educated beyond a functional level of literacy and some math. They knew little, other than mining for gold and silver, but all agreed that signing on to Brewster's crazy scheme would net them more money than they ever could among the slag heaps and mine shafts of their native Rocky Mountains.

Add the horrific experiences on Novaya Zemlya, the acute food poisoning they'd all suffered, and it made for this truly sullen group.

Bell observed and interacted, asked questions and doled out answers, but as they entered their last night before reaching port, he admitted defeat. He was no closer to identifying the perpetrator than when he started. His frustration was like ash on his tongue. He could have forgiven himself had his adversary been a trained operative, an agent provocateur of some sort who'd been schooled in the arts of espionage, but that wasn't the case. He'd been foiled by a rough-hewn laborer with no tradecraft or experience.

He called a meeting of all the miners prior to dinner in the mess. Fifteen minutes before addressing the men, he stopped at Joshua Brewster's cabin to outline his plans. Brewster hadn't left his room much except to take a little food around noon each day. He had always been a slightly built man, but his countenance now was that of a skeleton. All spare flesh had been melted off his frame. His cheeks were sunken and cadaverous, and the bones of his hands looked like they were about to erupt from under his skin. His eyes were haunted by demons that drew closer and closer each day.

Bell felt certain that if Brewster's health didn't turn the corner soon, he'd be dead in a fortnight.

"What is it?" he rasped when Bell entered his cabin. The room smelled of unwashed clothing and fever.

"I've decided to leave you all in Aberdeen, as I'd first suggested."

The haunted look turned instantly to one of rage. "Like hell you will."

"Be reasonable, Brewster. We land in Scotland tomorrow, and I haven't been able to determine which one of your men is a murderer and saboteur. I can only safely eliminate you and Vern Hall from my suspects list because of your cabin location."

"You're the detective. Figure it out. I am

427

not letting the byzanium out of my sight until I hand it over to Colonel Patmore in Washington, D.C. Vern'll demand coming along too. Hell, they all will." His defiance softened, and he spoke candidly, raw emotion barely in check. "You don't understand what it means to us. We left our hearts and souls back in that mine. It broke us, Mr. Bell. I can admit that to you. It broke every man jack of us. Delivering the ore is going to be our final act. Our reward. Knowing it's in safe hands means more to me than whatever miserable time I have left on earth."

Bell took a breath. Foster Gly and Yves Massard were doubtless expecting their agents on the *Lorient* to have successfully hijacked the precious ore and be on the way to Paris, so there was little chance of violent reception in England, yet Bell wasn't taking any chances. He wanted armed guards to accompany the byzanium until it set sail for the States. It would have been better if he could go straight to the authorities and request help, but of course that was impossible.

He could just imagine the diplomatic implications of American miners transporting illegally obtained Russian minerals that they'd stolen from the French company that hired them in the first place. And then he considered that they arrived on a ship that had been snatched out of impound due to a dispute between Iceland and Norway. He wasn't sure if there was enough of them to go around for all interested parties getting the proverbial pound of flesh. It was best to keep everything in-house, so to speak.

His plan was to hold the ore on the ship until he could cable Joel Wallace at the Van Dorn office in London. It was a small operation, but Wallace would have locals he could hire, men he trusted with odd jobs. He would order Wallace and a few English cohorts to travel up to Aberdeen and rendezvous in the harbor. Then they, with maybe Brewster and Hall, would escort the byzanium by rail to Southampton.

Bell hadn't yet made arrangements to ship the ore back to the States, but that was an easy enough task. Freighters and liners crisscrossed the Atlantic with the frequency of New York taxis cutting through Central Park. He lamented the loss of the wireless set, as some of these details could have been handled while they were still at sea. For his part, Bell had a promise to keep, so he already had tickets for the trip home.

He was certain Brewster wasn't the murderer, and neither was Vernon Hall. Other than the fact both men should be in a hospital and not traveling the length of the British Isles, there was no real downside to them coming along again. If they were healthy enough, the two could even accompany the crates of ore on the journey back to America if they didn't entrust them to a freight forwarder, as was the custom with such cargo.

His decision wasn't a difficult one. "Fine. You and Vernon can come with us. I get it, I understand the sacrifice your men made. But one of the others didn't bust his gut in that mine — for glory or whatever you promised to pay him. He was there to collect whatever the French promised him too. And it's clear he'll stop at nothing to get what he wants. So the rest of your men remain in Aberdeen. Agreed?"

Brewster stroked the bridge of his nose with a bony finger in a nervous gesture. "They won't like it none."

"I don't care. They stay behind or you all stay behind. Those are the choices."

"What do I tell them?"

"Nothing!" Bell snapped with more ire than he'd intended. "We don't tip our hand until the last second. When we dock, I'll have Captain Fyrie make up some story about a quarantine — no one leaves the ship. Only when my people arrive from London do we transfer the ore crates to a truck and eventually the railroad. If we can, we'll sneak off the ship at night, and they'll be none the wiser. If not, I'll tell your men there isn't enough room to transport them. It doesn't matter, so long as they remain here. I'm sure Fyrie and his crew can keep them until our train's out of the station."

"It ain't right, leaving them behind like that. Not after what they've sacrificed."

Bell was unmoved. He said, "Ask Jake Hobart what he thinks."

Bell spent the last evening at sea with Ragnar Fyrie in his cabin playing chess on a metal board with wooden pieces embedded with magnets in their bases so that no matter how rough the sea, they remained in position. He'd gone over his plan with the whaling captain and had even written out what he wanted sent by telegraph to the Van Dorn office in London. Fyrie had no problem with keeping the miners aboard with a deception and said he'd have one of his men slip away to deliver the telegraph dispatch.

"There is one thing I would ask in return," Fyrie said without taking his eyes off the board on his desk.

Bell, always reluctant to agree to terms

before hearing them, asked, "What would that be?"

"I've seen you writing in a journal. I assume it's for an official report you will turn over to your employer."

"Mostly, it's my personal observations, but some of it will make it into Joseph Van Dorn's hands if for no other reason than reimbursement of money I've spent on this mission. It is not an inconsiderable sum."

"I believe you would call that an understatement."

"And then some."

"I would ask, Isaac, that you do not mention me, my crew, or this ship in your report. I've seen Brewster scribbling in a diary too, and I ask that you review it and make certain he doesn't describe his time aboard the *Hvalur Batur* either."

"I believe I know the reason why, but would you mind telling me?"

"We sank a French ship. It doesn't matter that they fired first. We put them on the bottom with significant loss of life. There will be repercussions. I don't know what the spy managed to convey that night on the radio, but I doubt it was detailed enough to name the ship or crew. There is no need to identify this ship in anything official if the spy failed to identify it himself. Our anonymity remains intact."

"That's what I thought."

"I can see reasons to mention us but plenty of reasons not to. I'm sure there's a Lloyd's office in Aberdeen or even Edinburgh. I'll have Ivar fetch their agent to the ship so we can make plans to have her scrapped. It's a clean slate after that."

Bell nodded. "Perfectly reasonable, especially considering the cost you and your crew have paid on this journey. I'll edit my report to my Army liaison and Old Man Van Dorn. Whatever story I fashion, I will make sure that Joshua Brewster's diary jibes with it. Fair enough?"

Fyrie was visibly relieved. "An outfit like the Société des Mines has a long memory. And an even longer reach. I wish to avoid both, thank you."

"Least I can do." Bell made his move on the chessboard. "Check. Mate in three."

Fyrie saw his king was trapped with no means of escape. He ceremoniously tipped it over. "I am glad this is our last night at sea," he said with a wry smile as he deposited the pieces in a chamois pouch. "I grow tired of losing to you."

"Chess is a lot like what I must do to earn my living — think two and three steps ahead of my adversary."

29

Aberdeen was one of the busiest commercial fishing ports in Great Britain, and no matter how often they increased the size of the anchorage at Victoria Dock or Albert Basin, there never seemed to be enough room for all the ships and boats. A smoky pall hung over the city because the normal sea breeze that blew pollution away from its center had stalled. The smell from the town's paper mills was as ripe as sewage, and the normally bright gray granite of the city's main buildings looked funereal under streaks of soot and ash.

Bell was accustomed to London reeking and being dim from coal smoke and factory pollution, but a coastal town like this usually enjoyed a more agreeable atmosphere. He supposed that after he'd been sailing the pristine Arctic, any sign of man's intrusion in the natural world was bound to be a shock. That thought made him grin — at himself. He'd been aboard so long, he no longer noticed the whale oil stench that permeated every inch of the ship and every fiber of his wardrobe.

The *Hvalur Batur* was forced to lay at anchor beyond the breakwater and out of the way of the flow of traffic coming down the River Dee. Following a visit from a harbormaster to confer with Captain Fyrie, the chief engineer had managed to leave with Bell when he did without the miners becoming aware. He had several telegrams to send on behalf of Isaac Bell and orders to get word to the Lloyd's representative that a claim was going to be put in for the whaler.

It wasn't until after nightfall that a different harbormaster approached in a motor launch to tell them that berthing had been arranged. Fyrie was allowed to take his ship in without need of a professional pilot. He'd left it to Bell to tell the miners that the ship was under a quarantine temporarily due to a consumption scare.

"I don't care if the docks are teeming with diseased leprechauns," Walter Schmidt griped. "I've had enough of this."

Schmidt was descended from German immigrants, so his speech was accented with his native tongue. He was a general laborer, and while not particularly big, he had unimaginable stamina. Everyone agreed he'd worked harder than anyone at the mine. Also, at night he would sit in the mess and entertain the men with a handheld concertina. He sang such haunting songs that it didn't matter if the words were in German, the sense of love and loss rang clear.

"I know how you must feel," Bell said placatingly. "I want off too, and I wasn't stuck in Russia for four months. But it's out of my hands. The Scottish authorities aren't going to release any foreign crews or passengers without a quarantine and a follow-up health check. This is nonnegotiable, you might as well relax. Captain Fyrie is arranging to have some fresh food brought down, so at least we have that. Okay?"

Warner O'Deming was the smallest of the men. He was Irish-born, with a lilting voice and puckish demeanor, and it was usually up to him to find the humor in any situation. The men called him Warry. "Fresh Scottish food means haggis straight from the slaughterhouse. No thanks to ya, if ya please. I'll take soup made with Tom Price's boot before ya feed me that tripe."

They all laughed at the comment because among a great unwashed mob of men, Tom

Price's foot odor stood out as particularly vile.

"In fact," the little Irishman continued, "I'd knowingly eat the poisoned grub the French gave us than choke down what the Scots consider food. Fer the love of all that's holy, they make sausages in squares like a bleeding packing crate lid. And they're not half as tasty."

This got a fresh burst of laughter. Bell could see the men were relieved just to have made it as far as port. They wanted the odyssey to be over, surely, but a few days longer really made little difference. They were safe, and, in their minds, they'd soon be under way again with the ore they'd plundered from the depths of Bednaya Mountain.

Bell took a mental snapshot of the moment, the pinpricks of harbor lights piercing the darkness that showed in the mess room's single porthole, the dull sheen of old kitchen equipment in the scullery seen through a pass-through opening, the wooden table with its indecipherable jumble of carved initials and phrases. Paint was peeling from spots on the metal walls, and the linoleum tiles on the deck were worn through to bare metal in all the high-traffic lanes. The light was low and kind to the eight miners there who'd cheated death to pull off something extraordinary. As they laughed at Warry's witticisms, they looked healthier than when they'd boarded the ship. They were ill, for certain, but in Bell's estimation each looked like he had a little more glow to the cheeks, a little brighter spark in the eyes.

All except Joshua Hayes Brewster. No merriment reached past the protective veil he'd pulled over himself. He sat, unmoving and glum. And then Bell recalled that this snapshot wasn't at all what it seemed. One of the laughing men was a betrayer and murderer on a par with Judas Iscariot.

The image he'd just tried to capture took on much darker overtones. In truth, he'd rather leave them all behind once fellow Van Dorn agent Joel Wallace arrived, but at least he wouldn't have to watch his back around Brewster and Hall when they went south with him.

He heard his name being shouted from down the hall outside the mess. "Bell? Damnit, man, where are you?"

"In the mess, chief," he yelled back, recognizing Ivar Ivarsson's voice. He assumed the urgency was related to a message from the London office. Perhaps Wallace was indisposed for some reason.

"There's trouble," the man said as he

burst into the mess.

Bell was on instant alert. He got to his feet. "What sort of trouble?"

"There's men harassing the drivers of the food delivery wagon just down the quay."

"What men?"

"I couldn't tell," he said. "Just men. But given the trouble you've caused us since Sandefjord, I can't imagine their intentions are to our benefit."

Bell looked across the table at Brewster. There was such fatalism in his tired eyes. He recognized the situation as surely as Bell did. Bell pulled the .45 from the kidney holster at his back and racked the slide with a mechanical finality that cut the last of the laughter.

"Be ready," he said to Brewster, but the others took it to mean them as well.

He ran out of the mess, down the short hallway, and raced up the stairs to the bridge. Bell needed the height advantage to get a better overview of what might be coming their way. He thrust all speculation aside. Now wasn't the time to worry about who or how someone might be coming after them. The important thing was to be ready to respond. The wheelhouse was dark and abandoned. He stepped quietly out onto the bridge wing to survey his surroundings.

Under the glare of dozens of lights, the dock was littered with all kinds of equipment — bundles of coiled-up net, buoys and floats, all manner of crates and boxes, and barrels by the dozen, as well as carriages uncoupled from their horses. There was also a pair of open-bed trucks — what the English were calling lorries, after the verb "lurry," which meant "to haul."

To the stern and the bow of the whaler were local fishing boats tied up for the night. A few fishermen appeared to be doing maintenance on a net beside one of the nearby boats, while the remainder were quiet. There was enough light from the lamps dotting the pier to see an approaching wagon drawn by two exhausted-looking horses. At the back of the carriage was a dark wooden box stenciled with lettering. The horses' shod feet rang rhythmically against the concrete, adding a complementary beat to the lap of the waves and the ringing of rigging slapping masts.

There was nothing unusual about the two men sitting at the head of the wagon. The driver was hunched over the reins, sporting a rough jacket and a cloth tam-o'-shanter on his head. His mate was dressed similarly. The pair looked legitimate, and their plodding pace had the air of bored workers going about business as unhurriedly as possible. Whoever Ivar had seen bothering the drivers must have backed off.

Bell relaxed. He was being paranoid, and Ivar was jumping at shadows. What he'd seen was probably a dispute between local drivers — a union beef, most likely. These men were working extra hours to accommodate the *Hvalur*'s crew, after all. He silently decocked his .45, resafetied it, and slid it into the holster at the base of his spine. Below, he heard a hatch open, and Captain Fyrie and Arn speaking quietly in Icelandic as they prepared to meet the grocer's dray.

When the wagon drew closer, almost abreast of the whaling ship, Bell noticed the horses' ears. Both animals were on alert, their pinnas swiveling left and right. A million years of being prey gave horses heightened senses, and these two were definitely spooked. Bell looked closer and saw the driver's hands on the reins were stiff with tension. He was holding back the draft animals with considerable effort.

What Bell was seeing could have a hundred explanations, or none at all, and should have made him pause to see how events unfolded over the next few seconds. That would have been what most people would have done — hesitate for another moment or two. Bell didn't. He acted on pure instinct.

He grabbed his pistol again, racking the slide even as he brought it to bear, and fired one round into the strip of water between the pier and the whaling ship. Down on the dock, the old horses whinnied in fright, and the driver had to redouble his effort to keep them from bolting. The man unleashed a string of Scots-accented oaths that could be heard over the frightened animals and echoing shot. Bell knew the voice immediately. And the blood in his veins went icy as the picture below became clear.

Foster Gly was driving the team, while next to him, dressed as a regular deliveryman's assistant, was Yves Massard. The five fishermen, who Bell had noted a minute earlier, had been watching the approaching wagon much too keenly than just out of mere curiosity. They dropped all pretense of repairing the net and started rushing toward the ship. It was a full-on assault, but Bell had disrupted the timing. Gly should have been leading the charge, yet he was still trying to rein in the team of draft horses. Massard struggled to maintain his seat as the wagon skidded around a pyramid of wooden crates. The horses' flanks were slick with the sweat of fright, while their eyes were white and their tongues lolled grotesquely.

The "fishermen" were quickly pulling weapons from belts and behind backs. Bell saw the glint of knives and the silhouette of clubs not unlike baseball bats. One pistol shot reverberating across the harbor was unlikely to bring police attention, as the sound could be discounted as any number of things, but a sustained barrage from the .45 would have brought the bobbies coming at a run. Bell holstered his pistol and ran for the catwalk leading to the harpoon cannon, where there was a set of metal stairs back down to the main deck.

He could only hope the miners heard the gun's crack and were coming to meet the charge.

Gly was fifty yards down the dock by the time he'd muscled the horses to a stop. Bell ignored him and Massard and concentrated on the five men rushing the whaler. They came fast and silent. They appeared to be disciplined fighters and held weapons with easy familiarity. They had just about reached the gangplank when a roar erupted from inside the ship and out spilled a ravaging army of Colorado hard-rock miners bent on protecting a stake. They brandished clubs and cleavers and the awful-looking bladed pikes used to flense blubber from a whale's carcass. They came like berserkers lost in the lust of blood and violence.

The five men Gly had either brought from France or hired locally didn't stand a chance. They had just started up the gangplank when the counterattack was launched. The confines of the narrow ramp were too tight to turn quickly, so they were forced to fight it out against a horde nearly twice in number. The miners went at them without mercy, blades sinking deeply into flesh, bones cracking under the swings of men whose bodies, though racked with pain and afflicted by weakness, were still honed by lifetimes of crushing labor.

By the time Bell got to the melee, Charlie Widney was heaving the last of the attackers over his shoulder and into the black waters of the harbor. Captain Fyrie and Arn Bjørnson had remained on the ship but seemed prepared to join in had the fight gone differently. Farther down the pier, additional men were spilling from the back of the grocer's cart under the direction of Gly and Massard.

In the other direction were the two open-bed Leyland trucks. Bell pointed at one, and shouted to Brewster, "Move that to the gangway." He looked back at the Icelandic captain. "Can your men load the ore onto the truck?"

"We've got it. Go!"

"And please grab my travel bag from my cabin." Bell pulled the knife from its ankle sheath. "Follow me."

He ran to the end of the gangway and dodged left toward where Gly and Massard's men were gathering. The numbers seemed evenly matched, but these men were big, healthy-looking, and eager to get at it, while the Coloradans were a little bloodied from the first round. And yet they didn't hesitate. Except for Brewster, who was turning the truck's engine crank so they could steal it, the miners rushed after Isaac Bell like a pack of baying hounds.

The two groups crashed together like opposing football teams, only the idea was to maim and kill rather than merely tackle. Bell managed to stab one man in the arm before ducking out from under a swinging club. That man was struck in the shoulder by Walt Schmidt, brandishing the flensing knife like a halberd. The blood looked black in the murky dockside lighting.

Men scrambled and fought, throwing punches and heaving weapons when the confines were too tight to swing. Bell looked for Gly or Massard. For them, he'd risk pulling the .45 and ending this now, but neither man showed himself. Someone swung a length of chain at his head. He threw up an arm, and the links coiled around his bicep. He clutched at the end of the chain, and both he and his adversary pulled at the exact same instant. The tension as they pulled made the links as taut as an iron bar, and each man strained to best the other.

Knowing how to end the stalemate, Bell willed himself to relax and let the man yank him forward. He couldn't get an angle with the knife, so he whipped past his opponent and then planted a foot and swung his body with everything he had. His extra momentum yanked the attacker backward, and Bell was able to swing him hard enough that when he released his grip on the chain, it rattled free of his arm and the man went plunging off the dock and into Aberdeen Harbor.

Around him, bloodied men fought desperate battles. On the filthy concrete, those who lost the melee lay moaning or dead. Bell still couldn't find Gly or Massard. He tried to reach the grocer's wagon to see if they were hiding behind it, but one of the men ran at him with a bat. Bell ducked back and the man held his ground, a smug look on his unshaven face. Another came to join him at his side, and just as quickly as the two groups of men had attacked each other, they separated to take a breather, as if this were a boxing match and the round had ended.

The *Hvalur Batur*'s whistle suddenly blew during the lull. Bell hadn't set up a signal with Ragnar Fyrie, but it sounded like the crew had finished loading the byzanium ore and the ride out of this trap was ready. Like schooling fish or a flock of birds that change direction as one entity, the miners wheeled and started running back toward the ship. Their attackers, winded by the fight, were still game and were about to give chase.

Bell pulled his .45 from its holster and held it in such a way that the brawlers saw its silhouette. "First man to take a step gets one in the heart."

30

Bell's action had the desired result. The fighters stopped in their tracks, giving him a chance to race after his people. He heard Gly behind him and stopped to look back. The bald Scotsman had been behind the wagon. He was now on the seat, cajoling his men to pursue. Bell took aim, but he was already too far away for an accurate shot. He was also down to just six bullets. He turned to follow the miners, the heavy pistol swinging from one hand while the other held his blood-smeared knife.

The ten wooden crates were settled in the truck's flat bed and the engine was purring. Arn was sitting behind the wheel and had his hand on the gearshift ready to wrestle it into drive.

"What are you doing?" Bell asked, panting.

"I've been to Aberdeen before. I know how to get out of the city."

Not about to pass up local expertise, Bell stepped onto the running board while the others piled atop the treasured crates. "Let's go."

With a thousand pounds of ore, and two thousand more of men, the Leyland was grossly overloaded and had barely started creeping forward when Arn engaged the transmission. The heavy links of its chain drive slipped a few cogs as the machine tried to overcome so much inertia. Bell, Charlie Widney, and John Caldwell — the youngest of the miners at nineteen — all jumped from the vehicle and started pushing it to build up some speed before clambering aboard again. Well behind them, Foster Gly had managed to turn the team of horses and was starting to give chase, his men hanging from the sides of the wagon or clinging to its roof.

Bell watched them come. It took him just a few seconds to see that the old horses were actually faster than the Leyland, at least until the truck could build up more speed. The problem would come when they hit the streets of Aberdeen. It was late enough that traffic had thinned, but there were certainly going to be delays. Further impeding them was the necessity of slowing to a crawl in order to make a turn. And then acceleration, once they were clear, would be painfully slow.

The only thing keeping Gly from pressing his attack was Bell's .45 pistol, yet he knew a missed shot would put any late-night pedestrians at unacceptable risk. If Gly had been able to bring weapons from France, Bell doubted he'd have qualms about firing indiscriminately into the crowd. He was grateful the thug had arrived without firearms.

There was a night watchman at a guardhouse where the dock ended and the city streets began. He might have heard the pistol shot had the fight not taken place too far down the quay from him to detect. He looked alert as the lumbering truck approached, while a hundred yards back the grocer's wagon was coming like it was a sulky in a harness race. The guard carried only a flashlight and he waved it like a train conductor to get their attention and compel them to stop. He would certainly know the truck's rightful owner and recognize that none of the men hanging from it were he. Behind him, a chain-link gate was pulled closed across the road but didn't look like it had been padlocked.

"What do I do?" Arn asked.

"Ignore him and keep going," Bell said.

He and Arn drew their bodies tight against the truck's cab as they raced past the astonished watchman and slammed into the swinging gate. The impact didn't slow the truck but left the wire gates bent and quivering and emitting an odd metallic warble. The guard shouted after them as they motored on.

"With luck, he'll face down the horses," Bell said, "and buy us a little time."

Just a couple of blocks from the dock was Aberdeen's fifty-year-old train station, a crumbling affair soon to be replaced with a modern building. The truck's motor was working doubly hard trying to move its ponderous load, and Bell realized there was a better way to do this.

Bell said, "Drive past the station and turn left along the outgoing tracks. We need something faster than this truck."

Before they made the corner, Bell looked back. Just before the guard shack went out of view, he saw the watchman had placed himself in the middle of the exit, and the horses, so well conditioned, had stopped at the gate and no amount of urging by Gly would get them moving again. In moments, the guard would be manhandled aside, but Bell was getting the additional time he needed.

The truck went extra wide through the corner and almost plowed headfirst into an oncoming car. That vehicle had to cut sharply to the inside of the truck at the last second, the ashen-faced driver recovering his wits enough to curse them out. The maneuver didn't cost them as much speed as it would have if Arn had stayed in his own lane, and they were accelerating again almost immediately. Beyond the passenger terminal, along College Street, were the freight yards. They were mostly hidden from the city by a corrugated metal fence, but there were gates leading into the secured depot. Farther ahead, the road had been torn up in preparation for the construction of the new Aberdeen rail station. The over-burdened truck wouldn't stand a chance through this area where the macadam and cobbles had been dislodged.

Bell had Arn stop next to one of the gates and made short work of the lock with his pick. Beyond, he could hear the huff and snort of locomotives and the clank of rail couplings. Like before, men needed to hop out of the Leyland to get it moving again once Bell swung the gates open. Because they were metal sheets, Bell couldn't rese-cure the lock from the inside, so he found some proper-sized stones to use as ballast from a nearby railbed and wedged them on either side of the gates' roller wheels so they couldn't move.

"What are we doing, Bell?" Joshua Hayes Brewster demanded from the back of the truck, where he sat atop the crates like a Near Eastern potentate.

"Our truck doesn't have the power to out-race those two nags hauling the meat wagon."

"So? Gly won't get too close. You've got a gun, and it doesn't look like he could smuggle any into England."

"I have less than a full magazine. After that, my pistol's just a fancy paperweight."

Brewster didn't respond, and Bell concentrated on his surroundings. There were a half dozen rail spurs that led out of the yard and progressively merged until becoming a single track running parallel to the passenger line as it followed the River Dee out of Aberdeen. A string of freight cars sat idle on the far track and appeared to be abandoned. On another spur, a small shunting locomotive was backing in a row of slat-sided wagons used to move livestock.

Closer was a more modern train, with metal freight carriages. The locomotive, a 0-6-2 from the Stoke Works, was attached, steam streaming around its six tall drive wheels, while brakemen and the engineer performed visual checks. At the rear of the train was the guard's van — what in the States was referred to as the caboose. There were gravel crossings over the rails for vehicles, overhead platforms with stairs for workers. Halfway down the depot was a tower with an observation platform for the yardmaster to coordinate freight handling and switches when the yard was busy.

Bell didn't see any security, as he might at an American depot, and wondered if England didn't have the need, as no one tried to illegally ride the rails. He was glad for it. They didn't have time for a confrontation with a bunch of thick-necked railway bulls.

He pointed to where he wanted Arn to park the truck. It was a spot just behind the locomotive's coal/water tender and next to a boxcar with an open door and room enough for the byzanium ore.

"Who are you and what's all this?" a brakeman, in smudged overalls, asked when the truck's engine shuddered to silence. He had a working-class accent that was almost too thick to understand.

Bell ignored the question and asked one of his own. "What train is this?"

"The ten-ten to Glasgow. What's it to you?"

Bell leapt from the truck's running board and approached the train's engineer, the confused brakeman following in his wake and muttering to himself, "This is the ten-ten to Glasgow. Right?"

"Aye," the engine driver said, eyeing Bell suspiciously.

"Mr. McDougal asked that we load these ten crates and accompany them to Glasgow Station." It was pure bluff.

And it didn't work. "I don't know any Mr. McDougal. And I don't care if the King himself asked ye to put them boxes onto me train. It isn't gonna happen. Now, who are ya and what's yer business here?"

"So much for the easy way," Bell muttered. He moved so that the brakeman and engineer were in front of him and pulled the .45 from behind his back. Both men's mouths turned into matching round holes and the color drained from their faces. Their hands went up instinctually. "My men are going to load our cargo, and then you're taking us to Glasgow."

"Easy there, mate," the engineer said when he could find his voice. "We don't want any trouble."

"Nor do I want to give you any," Bell said mildly. "Yet here we are. Is the train ready to leave?"

"It is. But, we've another fifteen minutes until we depart."

"No one ever complains when a train's early, only when it's late. Get aboard and let's get going."

"You don't understand. The track may not be clear. Our railroads run on very tight schedules."

"We can slow down once we're out of Aberdeen, but we are leaving now."

"I won't do it," the engineer said defiantly, feeling that since it was he who knew how to drive the train, he had some leverage with his would-be abductor.

Bell shouted over to where the Coloradans were loading the crated rocks into the goods wagon. "Can any of you men help me run a locomotive?"

Alvin Coulter poked his head out of the boxcar. "In my sleep, Mr. Bell."

Seeing his leverage disappear, the engineer started blubbering. "Please, don't shoot us, mister."

Bell rolled his eyes. "I'm not going to shoot anyone."

The blast from the gun was like standing inside a thunderclap.

An instant before Bell's ears registered the noise, obscene pits appeared on the brakeman's face and neck as a dozen pellets from a shotgun at full choke raked his body as well as that of the engine tender behind him.

Bell lost a fraction of a second to shock and horror and then leapt sideways while the gore-spattered engineer just stood there paralyzed with fear. Bell rolled when he hit the stony ground so that he was facing back toward where the blast originated, his .45 brought to bear. Around him, as though trained by professionals, the Coloradans went into action like soldiers. The last of the crates were heaved into the railcar while Alvin Coulter, John Caldwell, and Vern Hall raced for the locomotive cab by first climbing over the tender's coupling and using its bulk as cover.

Knowing how few rounds remained in his pistol, Bell held his fire until he had better situational awareness and fully understood the scope and press of the attack. Near the gate they'd entered, he saw the upper half of several men just outside the wall. They had to be standing atop the delivery wagon. Yves Massard was there, holding a smoking shotgun pressed to his shoulder as he prepared to fire another shot. Other men were trying to find a way over the coiled barbed wire that topped the fence.

Bell didn't know why Massard hadn't

used the gun back at the dock unless he and Gly thought they could get the job done with muscle alone or they didn't want to draw undue attention. As he'd thought at the time, his single shot had been ignored, but a protracted gun battle would have brought the police.

Two thoughts struck him as he ran under a pull cart loaded with quarter-ton hogsheads of distilled Scotch whiskey. The first was that the shotgun had to be an expensive model to fire such a tight grouping at the range Massard had engaged from. The other was that the Frenchman wasn't a very good shot, because he'd pulled it to the left and killed the brakeman rather than firing the double-aught straight into Bell's back.

The shotgun roared again, and the gravel in front of Bell's position turned into so much shrapnel when the lead pellets raked its surface. His eyes were spared the worst of it, but they teared up from a faceful of grit. His skin burned where sharp stone chips bit into his flesh. As the Frenchman was reloading, Al Coulter, who'd reached the locomotive's cab, vented a shrieking blast of steam from the boiler that enveloped the train in a dense white cloud. Unseen in the mist, the engine began to creep forward, causing the string of mechanical couplings to clank taut.

Under cover of the cloud of steam, Bell scrambled out from under the cart and climbed up into the moving locomotive's cab. It was a tight fit, with all four men, but the labor of shoveling coal from the tender into the firebox would be better shared with him present.

Massard fired two more times. For the most part, the pellets pinged off the rolled-steel boiler, but a couple found their way into the cab and ricocheted for a couple of terrifying moments before falling harmlessly to the floor. Massard's men were unable to find a way through the concertina wire without tearing themselves to shreds, and the gate remained impassable despite the unseen efforts of more hired thugs trying to force it from the outside.

For good measure, Alvin sounded the whistle as the train gathered speed out of the rail yard. Bell watched the wall, where Massard's men were coming to the realization that they'd failed and were giving up their struggle to breach the wire. They watched bovinely as the train continued to pull inexorably from the depot. Massard was ready when it drew abreast of his position. It was his best angle from which to fire down on the locomotive. The door to the boxcar containing the ore and the remaining miners was closed on the Frenchman's side, so all his rage was focused on the cab.

Unwilling to risk Massard's getting off a lucky shot, Bell fired off three rounds just before both barrels of the Purdey 12-gauge thundered. From a moving vehicle, and at well over eighty paces, one of Bell's shots still managed to strike one of Massard's men and spin him into the tangle of razor wire. It was enough of a distraction to throw the Frenchman's aim off. The tight spread of pellets peppered the engine's tender.

And then the train was past the danger zone. The relief at making such an audacious escape made Bell laugh aloud. The others — Coulter and the two acting stokers, Hall and Caldwell — joined in.

31

The depot's six rail spurs merged into a single track out of the yard, and, by necessity, Coulter kept the speed down so the train didn't derail. They were also hauling at least a dozen cars, and the weight slowed the locomotive.

Bell holstered his weapon.

"How'd they find us, Mr. Bell?" Alvin Coulter asked.

Bell could safely remove Coulter from his list of suspects. He could have said nothing about knowing how to drive the locomotive and potentially strand them at the yard or, had he been the saboteur, he could have jammed up the controls once he was in the cab. The fact they were under way and almost clear of the freight depot meant he wasn't Jake Hobart's murderer. The same logic didn't hold true for young John Caldwell. Volunteering to shovel coal put him in a better position to help the French agents than had he remained with the ore. He was glad Vern Hall was the second stoker because he was one less unknown variable.

"I'm not sure," Bell lied.

He believed that the night the saboteur had informed the French the miners had been picked up from the beach by an Icelandic whaling ship, Bell recalled mentioning in the mess, before he'd been informed of the nature of Jake Hobart's death, that they were heading to Aberdeen. That information had obviously been passed on as a contingency in case the *Lorient* failed to detain the *Hvalur Batur.*

After learning that one of the men was a murderer and had secretly used the radio, Bell should have changed the destination. Once again, he'd underestimated his opponent. So far, the cost of his mistake hadn't been high, but, given the stakes, he expected that to change at any moment.

He said, "If I were to guess, I'd say the French ship that attacked us in the ice floe got word back to the Société des Mines before we sank them that we were steaming to Aberdeen. When they couldn't reach the *Lorient* after a day or so, Gly and Massard crossed the Channel with a bunch of their heavies to meet us."

Alvin and the other two seemed satisfied

with Bell's answer, and none saw the glaring hole in his hypothesis and asked the logical follow-up question of how the crew of the *Lorient* could possibly guess the whaler's destination.

Bell leaned out of the cab's open side just before they cleared the freight depot's perimeter fence. He looked back along the length of the train. It appeared that the gate he'd wedged closed was now open. It didn't really matter. They were accelerating smoothly and soon would be on the main line to Glasgow at a comfortable forty miles per hour.

"What about an oncoming train?" John Caldwell asked. His baby face was already streaked with sweat and coal dust from his labors shoveling. Tom Price sat on a spare stool ready to spell Caldwell when his strength waned.

Bell pointed to the telegraph lines. "They'll cable ahead and make sure the line's clear. At some point, they might try to stop us with a barricade, but not for a while. I doubt anyone's ever stolen an English train before, so they'll take time to get organized."

"Can we get all the way to the south coast?" Coulter asked.

"No," Bell said emphatically. "Glasgow's

a big city with a lot of train traffic. If we go that far, they'll shunt us onto a dead-end spur. We need to leave the train before then."

They soon left the lights of Aberdeen as the tracks took them along the coast. The sparsely populated farmland was as dark as the ocean surging off to the left side. Thankfully, the moon was high and full, bathing the landscape in a silvery aura that made the fields glow but turned shadows stark and impenetrable.

Bell believed that Gly and Massard's next move was to race to Glasgow ahead of the train and steal the crates during the inevitable confusion of a mass arrest for — he considered the proper charge — grand theft railroad.

To counter the move, Bell had to get the men and ore off the train sooner and find a bigger, more powerful truck. He needed to telephone the Van Dorn office in London. He knew Joel Wallace was on his way north with additional men but hoped the local station chief had left someone behind to man the phones. Bell needed to know what ship Wallace had booked passage back to the States. He assumed they would sail out of Southampton, yet any number of other ports were possible.

Johnny Caldwell finally stepped back from

heaving shovelfuls of coal into the hungry firebox, and Vern Hall, perhaps the most recovered of the sickly men, took his place. Caldwell crossed to the open window to let the chilled April air dry some of the sweat from his face and hair. No sooner had he draped himself over the sill, he came upright as if yanked by wires.

"Mr. Bell!" he shouted over the roar of the fire and the clang of the locomotive's steel wheels. "You need to see this."

Bell had to dance around Vernon Hall to reach the teenage Caldwell. Dread was like a stone in his stomach.

On the track running parallel to theirs, a small shunting locomotive was racing along the length of the train pushing a flatbed car. At the front of the car was a hand-operated crane used in repairing damaged sections of the rails. Suspended from its hook, and bobbling because of the speed, was a fifteen-foot length of track. Several of Massard's men were crouching behind the crane as cover from Bell's pistol. They were waiting to get into position to swing the boom in front of the stolen train and release the cable. If the locomotive didn't immediately derail and plow into the earth, at the very least the rail would act as a massive brake and the train would grind to a halt.

Massard was there to oversee them and he had his shotgun cradled in his arms. The man was no more than fifty feet back and he spotted Bell immediately. He fired both barrels from the hip and this time the pellets spread wide because he'd unscrewed the barrel chokes. Bell wasn't hit, but the hard patter of shot hitting steel so close was unnerving.

At the relative speeds the trains were moving, the little engine, with its single car, would be ahead of the larger freight in mere minutes. Bell had to act fast or they were all dead men.

In the seconds it took the Frenchman to break open the expensive weapon, replace the two spent shells, and snap it closed again, Bell had jumped past Tom Price and climbed atop the coal tender behind the locomotive. From the cab's aft bulkhead, he'd grabbed a heavy-duty bolt cutter. He was familiar enough with English trains to know its purpose.

"Pour it on with everything you've got," he shouted to Alvin Coulter, and continued down toward the back of the tender.

He kept low on the opposite side of the train away from the second set of parallel tracks where Massard couldn't see him. Though lighter and faster than the freight locomotive, the shunting engine Massard had commandeered had a critical disadvantage. It didn't carry a tremendous amount of coal or water, as it was designed to never leave the cargo depot and its immediate area. Massard had a finite window in which to implement his plan to derail Bell and the Coloradans or he would literally run out of steam.

If Bell could increase the speed enough, eventually Massard would be forced to abandon his attack.

Bell was safe on top of the tender, but once he reached its end, and the gap between it and the boxcar carrying the men and ore, Massard might be able to get off a shot. Slowly he crawled across the tender's roof in order to get a fix on the other train. Massard had no way of communicating with his man in the shunting locomotive, holding its engineer captive, so they couldn't work out the timing. And yet the front bumpers on the flatbed railcar were aligned with the gap between the tender and the boxcar — exactly where they needed to be for Massard to be able to cut Bell to ribbons.

Bell couldn't afford to wait and let them get farther ahead. He slithered back and then crept toward the locomotive for a bit before turning once more to face the back of the car. He jumped to his feet and ran in a stooped position, trying to minimize himself as much as possible. The heavy bolt cutter made the maneuver awkward.

Massard saw him and wheeled to fire. Bell leapt the gap between the tender and the two-foot-taller boxcar. A shard from a splintered bit of birdshot tore a groove in the nape of his neck and burned as though a red-hot poker were laid against his skin. He sprawled across the roof in a disjointed pile yet stayed down so Massard couldn't see him.

Bell heard the boxcar's sliding door roll open beneath him and tried to shout a warning, but it was drowned out by another blast from the shotgun. This one had been more carefully aimed, and the scream of a mortally wounded man keened above the wind whistling past Bell's ears. The door rolled shut immediately. Massard fed another pair of shells into the gun and fired again, but the shot wasn't powerful enough to penetrate the railcar's metal side.

Bell stayed on his belly as he crawled aft. The quest to strip Bednaya Mountain of its byzanium ore and return it to the United States had taken its second life.

32

Yves Massard was still in a position to fire at Bell if he tried to uncouple the car he was splayed across. He needed to get farther down the train. He crawled for most of the way and then leapt up to jump the gap to the next carriage. Like most British trains, the ends of the cars had a set of steel bumper bars for three link chains to be attached. A turnbuckle system kept the cars locked together, so that as the train sped up or slowed, the slack in the chains wouldn't cause the cars to slam together. At times, being a passenger on English railroads was rougher than riding a bucking horse.

Glancing over at the shunting engine, Bell saw Foster Gly in the open cab. He didn't appear to have a weapon, but he towered over the engineer, as well as another of his own men. When Gly saw Bell, he moved so that the train's driver was between them in case Bell decided to open fire.

Bell thought Gly needn't have bothered. It was too tricky of a shot to waste one of his few remaining bullets on. He climbed down the ladder bolted to the rear of the goods wagon.

The faint chirp of a whistle caught his attention. It wasn't a blast from one of the locomotive's horns but instead a single puff through the sort of whistle a policeman typically carried on a lanyard around his neck. Keeping the bolt cutter in hand, Bell climbed up the front of the next car and looked over its tarry top. Two men were running at him from the rear of the train. The more distant one was dressed in a blue serge uniform. He had the whistle to his mouth and a wooden baton in his left hand. The closer man Bell recognized from the fight on the dock back in Aberdeen. He'd been the smug hoodlum who'd taken a swing with the baseball-style bat, though he didn't appear to have it now.

Bell wondered how the man had managed to board the freight train and then he recalled the pedestrian bridges over the tracks back in the yard. A leap from one of them to the train wasn't much more than stepping down from a carriage. Alerted by the unusual appearance of a shunting engine out on the main tracks, the guard back in the caboose must have come out on the roof to patrol the train. Seeing the French agent, he'd blown his whistle and no doubt saved Bell from certain death when his focus was on separating the cars.

The Frenchman stopped and turned to look back, his shoulders hunched against the wind generated by the train's headlong rush through the night. His greatcoat flapped around his form like a luffing sail so that in the moonlight he looked like a demon. He spread his arms in a placating gesture, and the guard came toward him until they were mere feet apart. The distance was too great and the wind too loud for Bell to hear what was said, but the exchange lasted mere seconds. The agent had whipped a knife from a scabbard up his sleeve and plunged it into the poor guard's belly, turning and twisting the blade to do maximum damage as the guard fell into him.

The man might not have died instantly, but his fate was sealed. The Frenchman let him fall from his arms onto the roof. He turned back to Bell and kept coming, his face now a mask of savagery and bloodlust.

Bell didn't have time for this. Every second's delay meant Massard and Gly were that much closer to getting ahead of the train and dropping the section of rail across the track. He pulled out his .45.

"Ha!" the Frenchman said derisively. "I saw you at the dock. You did not use your gun. I think you are out of bullets."

"And you'd be wrong." Bell gut-shot the agent in the same spot the agent had just stabbed the guard. The man's eyes goggled in surprise, confusion, and ultimately pain. He fell just a few paces from what became his last victim.

Bell raced back down the ladder, stepped over the coupling to get himself back onto the ore car, and went to work with the bolt cutter. One part of the handle was a tool that could be worked into the turnbuckle to release its tension even when the train was moving. An expert trainman could have done it in his sleep, but the cars were in motion, swaying just enough to make inserting the awkward handle all the more difficult. Bell felt more time slip away. He looked to his right. He was abreast of the shunting engine's cab again. Gly wasn't there. He was on its roof instead.

Without need of a running leap, the Scotsman launched himself from the cab and soared through the space between the trains. Bell looked around the boxcar's forward edge to see Gly had crashed into the side of the next freight car high enough on its side to grasp the railing that ran along its roof. It was a superhuman effort and yet he wasted almost no time catching his breath. By the time Bell had his pistol out again, Gly had climbed up and slithered from view.

Bell stabbed at the turnbuckle again and this time managed to find his target. He rotated the apparatus and it released all at once. The other two lengths of chain came taut as they took up the full weight of the trailing boxcars.

He reversed the bolt cutter and fitted its hinged jaws over the first of the chains. The force needed to bite through the hardened metal was mechanically augmented by the cutter's design, but still Bell had to strain to shear the link through. He kept glancing up, expecting Gly to appear at any moment. He attacked the second chain, cinching the jaws around the link and muscling the tool's arms closed.

The knife came from above, thrown with tremendous force and near-deadly accuracy. The only thing that saved Bell's life when the weapon hit his neck was that it wasn't designed to be a throwing knife. It hit him handle first, and while painful, it wasn't the fatal blow Gly expected. The knife clattered down past Bell's boots and vanished on the railbed.

Gly leapt after the knife before Bell had time to recover. He crashed on the detective's back hard enough and at such an angle that it actually helped Bell snip through the remaining chain. The dozen trailing cars were now released. Unburdened by an additional two hundred tons of weight, Alvin Coulter should be able to keep the train ahead of Massard's.

There was no room for Bell to pull his weapon. And no time. He merely let himself fall over the bumper and let Gly's momentum toss him over his shoulder and onto the ground. For such a large man, Gly had incredible reflexes. Just as he was about to tumble onto the ribbon of ballast stones between the tracks, he got a hand on the chain dangling from the receding railcar and was yanked clear. He fell so that only the heels of his shoes hit the ground, the rest of his weight being supported by the chain as he dangled beneath the slowing boxcar. He'd just barely kept himself from falling under its wheels and was now hidden from view under the car itself and safe from Bell's now drawn automatic pistol.

Bell watched the gap between him and Gly grow as the locomotive put on a burst of speed. He hoped distance would give him an angle under the boxcar's leading edge. However, he quickly realized that by the time he would be able to see Gly, Gly would be too small of a target.

He holstered his weapon and climbed atop the car carrying the miners and the crated ore. He had just gotten his footing when he felt the train dramatically slow, and he nearly toppled off the car. It appeared that Massard's men had almost gotten into position to swing the crane boom over and drop the rail in front of the freight train when Bell had loosened the remainder of the cars and his locomotive began to outpace Massard's.

Now the train was slowing of its own accord, and soon Massard would have them trapped. And God only knew what would happen when the string of cars that Bell had just cut free slammed into the rear of this boxcar carrying such a destructive amount of kinetic force.

And that's when Bell noticed broken Alvin Coulter lying in the gap between the two sets of tracks just before the train flashed past his inert body.

33

Bell let the wind carry away the oath he muttered. He was in motion even before the plan was fully formed. He dropped flat to the roof just above the sliding door. Massard was far enough ahead that he couldn't get a good angle to fire back, so that wasn't a concern.

"Can you hear me?" he shouted. "It's Bell. Open the door."

The door slid open smoothly. Looking up at him was big Charlie Widney. He said, "Tom Price is dead."

"We might all be too. Really soon. Give me that long flensing knife."

Just seconds later, the eight-foot-long pike-like weapon was thrust up into Bell's hands. He said nothing further and ran for the coal tender. He leapt, landed in a forward roll, and came up with the long shaft of the knife still at port arms. He ran over, slid down the face of loose coal just behind the cab. Vern Hall and Johnny Caldwell were both sprawled on the floor, both bleeding from the skull, both as likely dead as not.

Bell ignored them. He saw the throttle had been closed and immediately cranked it to full open. The engine responded like a horse on the final turn of the Belmont Stakes. The rocker arms attached to the wheels became gleaming blurs as a burst of steam pressure sent them shuttling back and forth. The acceleration was immediate.

He looked ahead and saw Massard's men had almost succeeded in cranking the crane over so that the end of its boom, and its dangerous payload, were almost directly in front of Bell's train. The shunting engine was giving it everything it had, but it was no match for Bell's more powerful locomotive. The front of their boiler smacked into the crane boom and swung it back so that it was pointing straight up the tracks once more. The section of rail swung like a pendulum. Bell kept low. Yves Massard must have realized his prize was again out of reach. He'd be desperate.

And still the freight train kept moving faster and faster. The clack of the wheels on the rails became as frantic as the staccato clatter of a typewriter. In a minute, Bell was level with the leading flatbed and pulling ahead with every yard of track they covered. He stayed to the far side of the locomotive cab and crouched. Out the window opposite, he saw the gears and pinions of the crane. The men tried to crank it over again, trying to wedge the dangling rail into the big drive wheels like a spiteful child might do with a length of pipe through a rival's bicycle spokes.

Bell judged his timing and yanked his .45 free of its holster. He moved cautiously and took careful aim and fired off three shots. He wasn't trying to hit anyone, wanting instead to cause enough confusion for the second part of his plan. As it was, he hit one man in the throat, and the spray of blood as he corkscrewed to the deck was all the distraction that was needed.

Bell thrust the flensing knife out the cab's glassless window, leaning as far as he could, his arm quivering with the strain. The weapon was more than long enough and, more importantly, sharp enough. The blade was no match for the braided steel cable that wound around the crane's main take-up drum, but it sliced cleanly through the hemp sling that let the rail dangle from the hook.

The rail hit the tracks in front of Massard's train with a clang like an out-of-tune bell. It rolled and rattled for a few seconds before wedging under the flatcar's front wheels. Friction built quickly, as did the crescendo of noise that was so high-pitched it was painful. The engineer back in the shunting engine must have understood what had happened, and no amount of threatening by the man Gly left with him could get him to maintain the pursuit. The train began a swift deceleration, the engineer fearing the wedged length of metal would get under the wheels and derail the first car and likely the entire little train.

Bell allowed himself a single nod to celebrate his feat and at that very moment the world echoed with the scream of a massive steam whistle. Bell hadn't been paying the slightest attention to what was ahead of the dueling locomotives and so he never saw the train barreling down the same track as Massard and his men.

Wreathed in steam and smoke, the train was pulling a long string of coal hoppers headed north to keep the people of Aberdeen warm and their factories churning. It was so heavy, it required two locomotives, even though the run from Glasgow was relatively level. Its horn continued to wail. Its driver slammed closed his throttles and engaged full brake.

Bell had time to see Massard's men leaping from the flatbed like rats abandoning a sinking schooner. What he didn't see was Massard himself making it off. Just before Bell's view was blocked, he spotted the Frenchman propped up against some rail ties on the flatbed, his jacket off and his shirt pulled open. Bell's imagination added the bloodstained skin. Apparently, he had also hit Massard with his three-shot barrage.

And then came the impact. The two flatcars folded like hinges to the point where they coupled together and were suddenly thrust thirty feet in the air and then tossed aside. They were followed immediately by the small locomotive. It plowed into the ballast stones, rolling and shedding piping, so it was soon hidden amid jets of billowing steam. Steel wheels still screeching, the big coal train remained on the track.

Bell eased back on the throttle of the train and finally turned to check Caldwell and Hall. The teenager was dead. There was a dent in the back of his head the size of an orange. His blue eyes were wide and unblinking. Vern Hall was still alive but comatose. He had a contusion on his forehead that looked as though he'd been struck with an iron skillet, but other than that he was unmarked. Bell took down a lantern left by the engineer's seat and raised the flame. He checked Hall's eyes by lifting his lids. The pupils constricted normally, but he gave no conscious sign he was aware of Bell. Bell laid him out a bit more comfortably and draped him with an old coat that had been hanging on the bulkhead next to the bolt cutter.

Alvin Coulter had ended up dead and tossed from the train like dregs from an old cup of coffee. Bell gave the cab his critical consideration, trying to determine a logical sequence of events. There was little in the way of clues, as the cab was made of steel formed in hard edges and sharp corners. He did find blood on a steam line control knob that was the right size for the dent in Caldwell's head. There was no way of knowing if he'd tripped, been pushed intentionally, or was pushing in an act of self-defense.

Bell asked himself if he'd been wrong dismissing any misgivings about Coulter because he'd volunteered to run the train. Had he tried to stop the engine as soon as Bell was otherwise occupied? Had Hall or Caldwell tried to stop him? Or did one of them kill the driver in order to slow the train and allow the French to claim the prize?

Vern Hall was Joshua Hayes Brewster's best friend and nominal second-in-command of the expedition. It didn't follow that he'd be the turncoat, but Johnny Caldwell was young and impressionable. The French had had plenty of time to find one of the miners with a weakness and exploit it to turn him into a saboteur and ultimately a murderer.

Bell recalled finding a small silver picture frame in Caldwell's room back in Central City. One without a photograph in it. He wondered if it had held a snapshot of a sweetheart. Love was a powerful motivator. Bell had seen men do incredibly brave things, as well as incredibly stupid, while in its thrall. He found Caldwell's wallet in his back pocket and inside, among some American dollars and French francs, Bell found a photograph of a sloe-eyed woman. The photo was smaller than the frame Bell remembered, but when he flipped it over he could tell by the way the name had been cut off — all that remained was the final *tia* — that it had been cropped.

He shook his head at the wastefulness of it all but could understand why Caldwell would consider taking the French up on their offer to be their man on the inside, as it were.

He replaced the picture and stood, not

sure what to think anymore. For the time being, none of the other stuff mattered, including the deaths of Tom Price, Johnny Caldwell, and Alvin Coulter. Getting the ore onto a ship bound for New York was the priority. The authorities would be rightly enraged about the theft of two trains and the ensuing deadly wreck. Bell needed to abandon the locomotive as soon as possible, but the quiet towns they passed through were so sleepy and rural that he knew he'd never find the right kind of truck to replace it. His best bet was the outskirts of Glasgow.

Seeing the steam pressure falling, Bell went to start shoveling coal into the hot mouth of the firebox. He had finished up when he heard a clatter above him. Bell looked up just as Yves Massard leapt from the coal tender and crashed into him. Both men fell to the steel decking.

34

Bell's mind was reeling even as his body took a boot to the ribs. But Massard was prepared and had executed the move with total surprise. He recovered quickly and went berserk, kicking and shouting about his brother. It was all Bell could do to protect himself from the savage attack. Remaining curled up on the floor wasn't an option. Massard wasn't going to stop until Bell was battered beyond recognition. Bell launched himself from the floor, taking a kick to the stomach that drove the air from his lungs, but he was free of the initial onslaught.

"He was my twin," Massard screamed. "And you killed him."

Bell was unable to go for his gun as Massard charged him again. Bell had to bring up both hands to ward off the next punishing round of blows.

"Gly killed him," Bell said as they were

chest to chest, grappling to get an advantage and room enough to throw an effective punch. "He was weak, Massard. He wasn't like you."

"But he was still my brother."

"He surrendered to me outside the Little Angel Mine. I had my gun drawn on him, and he just quit. Gly couldn't risk him talking, so he shot him at long range in the back. It's true. You know your brother and you know Gly. I didn't kill him."

"Foss did it?"

Bell had hoped the revelation would take some of the fight out of the Frenchman, and for a second it looked like it would work.

"No!" Massard screeched. Instead, it sent him into an even greater rage.

Bell had perhaps perpetrated a heinous act against Massard's family or he'd borne witness to its greatest betrayal. For either crime, Bell had to be destroyed. Spittle flew from Massard's lips like a rabid animal's, his eyes glazed with hatred, as he tried to get at Bell with fingers curled into claws.

Massard managed to hook a foot around the back of Bell's leg and trip him and he fell. The Frenchman tried to dive onto his prone form, but Bell levered his legs at the last second and landed the soles of his boots against Massard's chest.

"In case you went looking for it," Bell snarled as he had Massard defenseless for a moment, "Marc's widow did have the money. I made sure she hid it."

Massard wasn't a small man, but Bell's legs were strong, and when he uncoiled them with an immense grunt of exertion, Massard was thrown across the cab. His head and torso flew out the open window, but his legs caught on the sill, and he flipped in the air as he fell. He landed so that his head and chest hit the rail a fraction of a second before the locomotive tender's leading wheel cut across him as cleanly as a guillotine.

Bell was left panting.

Massard wanted revenge against the wrong man for his brother's death. Bell didn't want vengeance, but he had more than enough reasons to see the real murderer, Foster Gly, dead.

Thirty minutes later, the train reached the outskirts of Glasgow. Bell let it ease slowly past tall brick factories and warehouses until it was approaching a spur off the main line. He stopped and ran ahead to lever the switch to the secondary branch. By the time he got back to the locomotive, the boxcar door had been rolled open and four owl-eyed men were peering out.

"What's happening, Bell?" Brewster called.

"I'll explain in a minute." He pointed up the track to the switching lever. "Someone throw that back to the main line after we're clear."

He climbed up into the cab while Charlie Widney jumped down from the boxcar and ran ahead to wait by the switch. Once the stolen train was safely on the spur, Widney muscled the lever to its original position and trotted after the slow-moving train.

Bell drove the locomotive as deep into the industrial park as he could. The engine's front bumpers finally kissed buffer stops at the end of the line, and he opened valves to vent steam from the boiler. He was exhausted from the twin duties of driving the engine and feeding its boilers. His hands were raw with split blisters, his clothes were stained through with sweat and shimmered with ingrained coal dust.

He climbed down for a final time. The Coloradans got out of the boxcar but protectively stayed close to it. Bell joined them. His throat was raw with thirst.

"Where's Vern and the others?" the impish Irishman, Warner O'Deming, asked.

"Vern Hall's badly injured. Head wound.

He's unconscious. Caldwell and Coulter are dead. Johnny's body is in the cab. Alvin either fell or was most likely thrown from the train."

That sobering statement ended any bit of satisfaction they felt for putting the French opponents behind them once and for all. Bell's next statement left them rethinking everything they thought they knew. "Either Vern or Johnny killed Alvin and is likely the murderer of Jake Hobart too."

In the silence that followed, a train whistle could be heard in the distance coming from the direction of Aberdeen. The rail authorities were in pursuit of the stolen engine and boxcar and were gaining on their quarry.

Bell said, "That's our cue to keep moving. We can talk about all of this when we're very far from here. Walt, Warry, go find us some transportation. There's bound to be some trucks around here. Make sure they've got fuel. Charlie, give me a hand. We'll put Johnny's body in the boxcar with Tom Price's and get ready to transfer Vern to the truck."

The men went into motion, leaving Josh Brewster standing alone, his eyes glazed and his mouth working but no words coming from his lips. The very idea that his best friend could have betrayed them all was too horrible to contemplate. His mind had gone blank.

Seeing him so utterly distraught, Bell muttered as he walked past on his way to the locomotive, "Circumstance points to young Johnny Caldwell, not Vern Hall. I'll explain later."

Brewster stopped jawing and gave Bell what passed for a smile. "Are you sure?"

"Not court-of-law certain, but close enough to inform my opinion."

Bell couldn't bring himself to simply abandon the bodies. He opened the small travel bag of essentials Captain Fyrie had fetched from his cabin and tore a blank sheet of paper from his journal. On it he wrote the names of the two men as well as the approximate location of Alvin Coulter's remains. He didn't have any pound banknotes, so he pulled the last hundred-dollar bill from his wallet with instructions that each man be given a proper burial.

The miners were unmarried and had died far from where they were thought to have, so marking their graves was of no real import to the world, but Bell felt it was the right thing to do for men who had sacrificed so much and ended as heroes.

Moments later, two Leyland trucks rumbled into view from around one of the warehouses. Warner and Walt had more than succeeded. The men were all exhausted and yet wanted to be on their way, so moving the crates from the train to the lorries took little time and was done with a minimum of conversation. They placed the unconscious Vern Hall onto the bed of the truck with Josh Brewster, his back against a crate, holding Vern's head in his lap to protect him from the worst of the bumps they were going to encounter.

"We should take him to a hospital," Charlie Widney suggested.

"Like hell we will," Brewster fired back, cradling his friend. "He's staying with us."

Bell didn't want to abandon him in Glasgow. The authorities would eventually check hospitals for survivors of the train theft once the locomotive was discovered. Upon regaining consciousness, Hall would surely be arrested and questioned intensely, cutting the odds of the rest of them making it out of the country.

"All they'd do in a hospital is exactly what we're doing, which is nothing," Brewster added. "They can't treat a head wound like this. Either he wakes up or he don't."

That wasn't far from the truth either, Bell conceded. An X-ray would show the severity of the skull fracture, but there were no surgical fixes. Bed rest was certainly preferable to rattling around in the back of a truck, yet, as Brewster had said, it was up to Hall alone. He'd either regain consciousness or he wouldn't.

It was the early-morning hours of April the fifth. Bell needed to get the men away from Glasgow before police were able to cordon off the city. Once he was past their dragnet, his next step was to get them out of Scotland. Only then would he worry about making contact with the London branch of the Van Dorn Agency. And no matter what arrangements Wallace had made, Bell knew he had an option of his own, but one that entailed performing an utterly unforgivable act.

Best not come to that, he thought as he led the two-vehicle caravan out of the factory complex. The gate watchman was tasked with monitoring people entering the sprawling facility, so he gave no thought to men leaving on what looked to be a delivery.

Hours later, when workers arriving for the Friday shift reported the abandoned train and its grim contents, the guard was able to retain his job by giving the police a fair description of the vehicles and men.

35

The next twelve hours for Bell and his few men were spent on the grueling drive to Newcastle upon Tyne, a soot-covered coastal city on the English Channel. They stopped only for fuel for the trucks and made do with hastily bought food from whatever pub was nearest the garage that had petrol to sell. For cash, they used the proceeds from the sale of a gold coin Bell had stopped and offered to a jeweler in one of the larger towns they'd sped through. The man paid only half its value because he could tell Bell was desperate and in a hurry.

In a country steeped in history dating back to the days of the Roman Empire, the roads were surprisingly bad — rural, rutted, and in some places so muddy that the men had to unload the trucks and carry the crates by hand to get them to dry ground. To Bell, so used to living in America's burgeoning cities, it was like stepping back a hundred years.

It was nearing dark when they came to a village several miles north of the industrial center of Newcastle. There was a garage with a full gas storage tank on a tall trestle to refill the trucks and the couple of cans they'd bought. There was also a small inn with a large barn in back out past an open plot planted as a vegetable garden. Bell wasn't much interested in the amenities offered by the inn, except that it had a private telephone. The owner rented them three rooms and let them store the trucks in his barn. They snuck Vern Hall into a ground-floor room when the proprietor and his wife were in the kitchen preparing a meal for the men.

There was a single, shared washroom. Bell let the others go first, as he wanted to use the phone. His call to London went through remarkably quickly and he was soon speaking with one Davida Bryer, an East End girl, who explained that Joel Wallace hired her from time to time when he had need of a secretary. He'd left with strict instructions that she wait by the phone for a call, especially one from Isaac Bell.

"He speaks very highly of you, Mr. Bell," Davida Bryer cooed. "I do hope I have the chance to meet you."

She was trying to sound sophisticated but couldn't hide the impoverished roots in her accent. Bell said, "Probably not this trip, Mrs. Bryer."

"Oh, it's Miss," she corrected quickly, as if Bell didn't know what she was up to.

"Did Joel leave any messages for me?"

"He did. He called earlier to let you know that he had arrived in Aberdeen and met the captain of the" — she paused as if reading — "um, the *Ha,* ah, *va* —"

"Hvalur Batur," Bell supplied.

"Cor blimey, that's an odd name now, isn't it?"

"Miss Bryer . . ." Bell said with a tinge of frustration in his voice. He doubted she could type, sort, or file, but he imagined she was quite the looker.

"Right. The captain told Joel — um, Mr. Wallace — all about what happened with the fight and how you ran off in some lorries and stole a train. He said to tell you Arn made it back and that he'd been asked to mail a postcard by Mr. Hall and hoped it was okay."

"Whose postcard?"

"Mr. Wallace thought you'd ask that. It was for Mr. Hobart to his wife."

Bell wasn't sure if he'd heard correctly. "Wife?"

495

"That's what he said. Her name is Adeline and she lives in a boulder."

"I suspect she lives in Boulder," Bell corrected absently, his mind running through implications, "not in a boulder. It's a town in Colorado."

"That makes more sense," the girl said so brightly that he suspected it had been a truly perplexing issue for her.

"Was Wallace able to book passage for us back to America?"

"Oh, that. Yes. Yes, he did. It's right here. Hold a tick." Although the wire was static-charged, he could hear her searching through papers on a desk. "Found it. He has you on the SS *Bohemia,* a freighter owned by Bougainville Shippers."

Bell wasn't familiar with the line, but it mattered little. "When and where?"

"Um, next Wednesday at two from Southampton. Berth 26. That's away from the Ocean Dock. And, besides, the hullabaloo should be long over by then."

Bell wrote the date and time in his journal, ignoring her prattle, and said, "When Joel checks in next, I want you to tell him to meet me at the docks with at least ten men who should be expecting trouble. Can you do that?"

"I sure can, Mr. Bell. Joel will be calling

in the morning. I mean, Mr. Walla—"

"That's fine, Miss Bryer. Just make sure he knows to meet me and bring some guys. Okay?"

"Okay, Mr. Bell." She paused, calculating. "Maybe I can come with them and we can meet."

"That's not a good idea. It could be dangerous, and I wouldn't want you to get hurt."

"Wow. You sound so sure of yourself. Have you really done all the things Joel says you've done?"

"Not even half," Bell said. "Good night, Miss Bryer."

He found Brewster in the room he'd share with Vern Hall. It was a quaint space with smoky oak furniture, hand-stitched bedspreads, and portraits of Queen Victoria and the nation's current monarch, George V, on the walls. Brewster was working on his journal. Hall was tucked under a mound of quilts and as still as a statue. Or a corpse.

"How's he doing?" Bell asked.

"Same," Brewster said as he glanced at the frail figure of his oldest friend. "Not a peep out of him."

"We should leave him here," Bell said softly, as if he were musing to himself rather than making a suggestion. He was testing for a reaction.

"Maybe we should," Brewster said. "He's not looking good, and we have a ways to go."

"We do," Bell agreed, "and we have a destination. The freighter *Bohemia,* Southampton Dock, Berth 26. We sail on Wednesday at two."

"Can we make it?"

"Shouldn't be a problem. And I'll have men there waiting in case there's trouble."

"Think there will be?"

"Gly's no fool," Bell replied. "He was smart enough to ambush us in Aberdeen, and I suspect he knows we've come south and are likely here in Newcastle since it's England's largest northern city. He can guess our next moves because he knows we want to leave for the States."

"And that means he knows we're heading to Southampton?"

"That's the most logical port."

Brewster went quiet for a moment before asking, "Are you going to tell me what happened back on the train with Alvin and Johnny and Vern?"

"The boys are all heading next door for a few pints at the pub before we eat. I'm going to wash up and I'll meet you there. And explain everything."

"But it wasn't Vern. Right?"

"No."

Fifteen minutes later, the five men were around a table at the corner pub, pints of good English beer at hand. The air was ripe with smoke, and the room buzzed with good cheer. The fire in the stone hearth was cherry red and crackled with warmth. Bell allowed himself to relax just a notch or two.

"So tell us," Brewster said impatiently.

"Johnny Caldwell was in love with a woman he couldn't have."

"What's that mean?" Walter Schmidt asked.

"He carried her picture. She could have almost passed, but she's a Chinese girl, Walt, and while we live in an increasingly progressive society, that's something a lot of people won't understand or tolerate." Bell let that sink in for a second. "I think someone in Paris discovered her picture and, knowing the social situation in America, explained to Johnny that there would be no legal barriers for him and his girl if they moved to France. I think they offered to set the young couple up in company housing with a company job. Johnny saw this as his chance to live happily ever after with the girl he loved."

"And the price?" Charlie Widney asked,

although they all understood what it was.

"Betrayal," Bell said flatly. "He had to act as their agent in your midst, reporting back by radio when you were finished clearing that mountain out of its byzanium ore. That's why the *Lorient* was so close by when we snuck you off Novaya Zemlya. They'd been waiting for Johnny's message from the island that the job was completed. Because Joshua disabled the radio he'd found after Jake Hobart's murder — a murder Johnny committed, by the way, because Jake had discovered the secret transceiver — Johnny bided his time and used the one on the *Hvalur Batur.*"

"Wait. What? Jake was murdered?" O'Deming cried before the others could raise the point.

"It's true, fellas," Brewster said. "Stabbed through the ear, he was. No doubt at all. I knew but said nothing, hoping I could catch the killer. I hope you can forgive me for not telling you all."

"Joshua told me about the murder the night I heard footsteps outside my cabin on the ship and confirmed with Arn Bjørnson that one of you guys had spent time in the wireless room. I checked myself, and the set still retained some residual heat."

"What's that mean?" Warry O'Deming said.

"It's proof someone used the radio on the whaler," Charlie told him. "And that Johnny was willing to kill to keep everything a secret."

"I'm just guessing here, but I don't think Johnny planned to kill Jake Hobart. I believe he panicked."

"Jake and Johnny were real close," Joshua Brewster said. "Jake was showing the boy how to be a blaster, like an apprenticeship. Hell of a thing killing your mentor."

"That bothered me most," Bell admitted. "In talking with you all, I knew how tight those two were, so it had to have really eaten at John's conscience to do what he did. But back on the train outside of Aberdeen, it was different. He must have seen we were escaping from the French and he was losing his chance at happiness with his girl. He saw his opportunity when I went back to unhook the cars. He threw Alvin out of the cab and then turned on Vern Hall. Vernon gave better than he got and he's alive while Johnny's dead."

"Awful," Walt Schmidt said.

"The truly awful part is, Gly would have likely killed Johnny the first chance he got, only the lad was too naïve to know it."

"What happens now, Mr. Bell?" O'Deming asked, wiping the foam mustache from his upper lip and setting his pint back on the table.

"We make our way to Southampton, where there's space aboard a freighter bound for New York, and somehow we find a way to put this mess behind us."

Brewster suddenly laughed in a tittering falsetto that was completely unlike him. "It's only the past we can put behind us, Bell. This will never be our past. This will always be our present. We can't escape it, you see, because we chose it in the first place." He looked at his remaining men. "We made a pact with the devil. We wanted that ore and we made a deal with him for the stones and now we have to live up to the bargain. Right?"

He covered his face with his hands and rested his head on the table. His voice was a hoarse croak. "We all have to pay the price."

Bell caught the embarrassed eyes of each remaining man. They knew all too well into what depths of madness the leader had sunk. They finished their beers in silence and went back to the hotel, Brewster walking like an automaton supported by Charlie and Bell.

36

Bell woke late the following morning and was immediately annoyed. Knowing his level of exhaustion, he'd left word with the hotel owner to wake him at seven. It was almost eight-thirty. They'd lost precious time.

Charlie Widney was asleep in the other bed. Bell called his name to wake him and dressed quickly. The inn was quiet. He knocked on the door for the room Schmidt and O'Deming shared and went down the stairs to rouse Brewster.

"Let's go. We've all overslept."

"What time is it?"

"Eight-thirty." Bell checked on Vernon Hall. He looked a little better this morning yet remained unresponsive.

"I'm sorry about my little outburst last night," Brewster muttered. He focused his attention on lacing his boots. "I get these wild ideas sometimes. Don't know where they come from, but it feels like I have to say it out loud or it'll only get worse in my head."

"Nothing to apologize for," Bell said, checking Hall's eyes. They were reacting normally to light. "We're all feeling the pressure. You most of all, since this is your crew."

Brewster shook his head dismissively. "Some leader I am. Four men dead, one injured, a traitor living among us for months."

Bell said, "You succeeded, Brewster. Keep that in mind."

The miner just looked at Bell, his face wrinkled beyond its years, sunken and sallow, and framed by long gray hair as wispy as spider's silk. There were stains on his chin from him coughing up blood in his sleep.

There was no sign of the innkeeper or his wife. Bell let himself into the kitchen to see what he could rustle up. He heard the back door open and guessed Charlie was heading out back to check on the trucks the way he'd checked on the draft animals back at the mine in Russia. On the table was a local newspaper.

Bell picked it up to see if there was news about the train theft. It was splashed across the front page, with details about the dead men found on the train and a description of the men and trucks that left the factory outside of Glasgow. Below the article was a separate box with a plea to the public to help apprehend the thieves and a telephone number to call with information. A reward was offered.

Bell's heart slammed into his ribs. That's why the hotel was quiet. The police were on their way. The innkeeper had read the article and called the number and was told to vacate the premises because the renegades were dangerous. He fought the stab of panic and read the newspaper's plea for information again. Something bothered him. He read it a third time. It didn't mention the police specifically or who posted the reward. The telephone listing meant nothing to him. Just numbers preceded by a three-letter exchange.

Then he saw it. The exchange was the same as he'd used the night before to speak with Joel Wallace's assistant, Miss Bryer. The exchange was for London, not Glasgow or Aberdeen.

"Fellas, get moving!" he bellowed, and raced for the telephone. He got an operator and had her put the call through. It was Saturday so there were free lines. After a moment of clicks and hisses, a male voice answered.

"Allô?"

Bell smashed down the earpiece so hard that its cord whipsaw-danced. The English *hello* and the French *allô* sounded close enough that many bilingual speakers never bothered to translate the word. They just pronounced it as they always had. Like the man who'd answered the phone just did. Bell would bet anything that call went straight to the French Embassy, near Hyde Park.

Bell was fully expecting to encounter Foster Gly again, but he had to admit Gly was craftier than just about anybody he'd ever faced. He'd placed an advertisement in the paper and had it look like it was from the police when in actuality it was a direct line to agents acting on behalf of the Société des Mines. He'd had all the previous day to set this in motion, and Bell was certain the ad ran in other cites as well. Foster Gly had turned the entire nation into his own private spy network with just a few inches of ad space. Even as he felt disaster descending, Bell had to acknowledge his own grudging respect for the strategy.

He rushed for the back door, meeting Walter and Warry as they came down the stairs. With Joshua Brewster close behind, they ran out into the backyard. The morning was cool and still, with just a few clouds in an otherwise blue sky. The industrial pall of Newcastle was still some miles to the south.

Charlie Widney had just reached the doors of the distant barn and didn't hear Bell's shouted warning. Nor did he hear the roar of the Leyland truck's motor just before it slammed into the doors from the inside. Charlie was struck first by the swinging door and went flying back some feet, landing heavily on the hard-packed earth and lying there quite still. The driver could have swerved at that moment and maybe given him a fighting chance, but he deliberately ran over the prone miner. The truck's narrow tires and heavy load made sure the pressure across Charlie's body crushed his internal organs.

Bell roared incoherently at the senseless murder and ran doubly hard. He gestured to the others to head for the barn to prevent the second truck from being stolen. Pushing himself as fast as he could go, Bell couldn't cut an angle to reach the truck before it was past him without risking the driver running him down as well. The vehicle shot the alley between the inn and the neighboring building with Bell in pursuit.

The Leyland had to go wide as it turned

onto the unpaved street and brushed up against a parked delivery wagon. The mild impact barely slowed the vehicle, but the two draft horses yoked in the traces reared, their hooves pawing the air, their neighs like the screams of frightened children.

Bell made up some ground, as the driver had to work the gears, but he knew it wasn't going to be close. Once the truck came up to speed, the road was open enough to outpace him easily. Half the byzanium would be gone, and if the miners failed to prevent Gly's men from stealing the other truck, then the whole mission was for naught.

To the uninitiated, the contraption parked in front of a store just down the block resembled a long, robustly built bicycle with an engine slung on its frame. To Bell, it looked like the fastest Thoroughbred he'd ever ride. It was a Norton 16H, a nearly 500cc single cylinder motorcycle that Bell had read was about to take the race world by storm. The engine was running, while the rider was down on his knees adjusting something on the motor.

Bell was astride the bike and had the clutch popped by the time the owner knew anything was amiss and was down the street fifty feet before the man got to his feet. The truck had gained some more distance, but when Bell cranked back on the throttle, the Norton came alive between his legs. He had to slit his eyes against the wind, while his hair was blown flat across his skull.

In seconds, he'd cut the distance to the truck. The problem was, the man in the passenger's seat had heard the motorcycle in pursuit and alerted the driver that they were being followed. Bell didn't recognize either of them from the dockyard fight. Gly had brought in more muscle from Paris. His supply of heavies seemed limitless.

When Bell tried to pull up alongside, the driver would swerve into his path, forcing him to ease off the Norton's accelerator to avoid being crushed beneath the lorry's wood-spoked wheels. Three times he tried it and three times he was beaten back, the third sending him on a wobbly trajectory that almost forced him to crash into a sanitation wagon used by workers to clean manure from the streets.

Bell was well aware their antics were likely to attract attention. He had to end this quickly, and reached behind his back for the .45, hoping he could place an accurate shot. Before he tugged it free, he saw another opportunity. A tip wagon drawn by oxen was on the side of the street, lowered so its trailing edge was on the ground and the rest of it elevated in a perfect ramp. Next to it, some workers had just unloaded a dozen fat, oak-staved barrels.

The angle and timing had to be perfect, but Bell had confidence in his machine and his abilities to ride it. It was similar to the Indian cycle he enjoyed back home. He came up almost to the rear bumper of the truck. In anticipation, the driver swerved to the left to block him. It put the Leyland exactly where Bell wanted it. Bell peeled away farther to the left so that he was approaching the trailer at a diagonal and he cranked the throttle.

The front wheel rattled the rig, but the oxen that had dragged it there remained motionless and kept it from sliding forward. The Norton rocketed up the ramp and off the edge at close to forty miles per hour. The bed of the Leyland was under the bike as it came back down to earth. The bike slammed into the crates of ore, slicing its drive belt, which ripped free like a snapped whip. Bell was jolted by the Norton's stiff suspension but kept enough control so that he had the bike stopped before it rammed into the back of the truck's cab.

Moving fast, he let the motorcycle spill onto the bed and stepped up over the side of the truck and around to the passenger's side of the cab. There was no door, so he merely reached in, grabbed a handful of the co-driver's jacket, and heaved him from the moving vehicle. The man tumbled across the dirt road like a stringless marionette and lay there, not moving.

The driver reacted fast, swerving the big lorry in an attempt to make Bell fall from the truck. Bell clung tightly to the truck as his legs swayed out into space for a moment. As soon as they came back and he could plant his boots on the running board, he pulled the Colt and shot the driver in the left shoulder. A bloody mist filled the cab for an instant. Bell lunged at the driver, punching him twice where the bullet had impacted and reaching across to the low, windowless door beyond. He levered it open and shoved the injured driver to the road. The lorry kept right on going as Bell seamlessly took control. He eased off on the speed and took the next corner.

The village didn't have Manhattan's easily negotiated north-south grid, but it didn't take him long to make his way back to the inn. The second truck was in the courtyard outside the barn, three surviving Coloradans sitting grimly in its bed, and the fourth, Vernon Hall, still unconscious, under a blanket. Bell jockeyed his truck around in the tight space until the nose was pointed back out to the street beyond their Tudor-style accommodations.

"The thieves?" Bell asked.

"There were four of them. Frenchies. Two are dead in the barn. Innkeeper's wife is taking the others to the hospital," Warry O'Deming replied, his normal lilt muted to a throaty growl. "One of the bastards might live. Other's a goner for sure. Walt here took a knife to the belly."

"It's nothing," the German émigré said. "I've cut myself worse shaving."

"Charlie?"

Brewster answered, "We laid him out on the sofa in the front room."

Bell nodded. "Get the motorbike out of the truck and leave it here. I'll be right back."

He entered the inn. It had been an inviting space just hours earlier. Now it was shadowed with the gloom of a funeral parlor. The innkeeper was tied to a chair next to Charlie Widney's body. Brewster must have figured the proprietor had ratted them out, even if he didn't know how, but he wasn't taking any chances. The man had been gagged. The man's wife would have been too concerned with saving the Frenchmen to involve the police until after she'd reached the hospital. By then, Bell and the others would be miles away.

Bell took two twenty-pound notes from his wallet and tossed them into the terrified man's lap.

"His name was Charles Widney." He spoke deliberately, ensuring the innkeeper understood every word. "He was a good man who deserves a Christian burial. The men who killed him are French mercenaries who we'd escaped from. Your call put them back on our trail and cost Charlie his life. I will be back someday to make sure he's been buried properly. If he hasn't been, I will find you and I will beat you to within an inch of your life and then I will beat you two inches more. Are we clear?"

The man could only sob in fear.

"I'll take that as a yes." Bell turned and left the building. Moments later, the trucks pulled out and vanished down the road.

37

Burdened by even more death, the men continued south, compelled to finish their quest and as unable to deviate from their course as migrating birds from theirs. Bell sold the other two gold coins he kept sewn into his travel bag for contingencies. He used some of the money to buy paint to disguise the trucks. They covered over the red bodywork and smart gold lettering with a shade of dreary green. They also worked out routes that maintained some miles between the two vehicles so that they no longer were traveling as a convoy.

Bell drove the lead truck, and every fifteen miles he would wait at a discreet spot by the side of the road for Warry O'Deming to appear in the second Leyland. O'Deming would pause, servicing his lorry, while he waited for Bell to pull ahead once again.

They averaged just twenty miles per hour. Walt Schmidt sat in the cab with Bell while Brewster remained in the bed of the second truck with Vern Hall.

As the day wore on, Walt spoke less and less, and whenever Bell looked over at him, his face was drawn and ashen. He was in pain, and the jostling he was taking along the rutted roads was making it worse. Bell decided that they would stop in Stafford, a large town north of the massive sprawl of Birmingham. They were far enough removed from the train theft that there was no danger in leaving Walt and Vern behind. He would make Brewster see the necessity of it.

When the sun sank over the distant Irish Sea and darkness filled in the spaces between shadows, the trucks' headlamps did little to cut the gloom. Still, Bell could see a faint glow in the night sky ahead that foretold their destination.

"How are you doing over there, Walt? I think tonight we'll find you and Vernon some warm hospital beds with a couple of rosy-cheeked English nurses to look after you. How does that sound?" Schmidt said nothing. He just looked ahead, his body bouncing and swaying with every movement of the truck.

Bell knew, but still he called Walt's name a little louder. "Walter? Are you with me, buddy?"

He reached over to touch Walt's shoulder and the slight pressure upset an equilibrium that had been in play for some time. Walter Schmidt's lifeless body tipped sideways and would have fallen from the truck had Bell not clutched onto him tight and brought the vehicle to a stop. They were in the middle of the road. There was no traffic, and the only sound was of the breeze rattling leafless branches.

"Typical German," Bell said with affection. "Stoic 'til the end."

Fifteen minutes later, Warry arrived in the second truck. He parked and approached on foot. When he saw something was amiss, he ran the last few steps. There was enough moonlight to see his friend slumped in his seat in an unnatural pose.

"You damned kraut," O'Deming cried, letting his grief express itself as anger. "Why wouldn't you even let us look at the wound? We might 'ave saved ya. Twenty years I knew him, Mr. Bell. Twenty years, and he never complained once. About anything."

He stepped back so he could direct his next comment at Brewster, sitting dejected in the rear of the truck with Vern Hall's head cradled on his lap. "See that, Brewster? Walt's dead. And Alvin and Johnny. And

Jake and Charlie and Tom. And Vern might as well be. And for what? Eh? Why are they all dead?"

"Easy, Warner," Brewster said softly. He was affected by this latest death but appeared coherent. "You know why. This is more important than us. Walt could have asked us to stop at any time and we would have. But he knew we needed to keep going. There's no stopping until we get the byzanium home. This ore represents an opportunity we can't even comprehend because science hasn't caught up to its potential. We all agreed to that back in Central City. And it still holds true right now."

This seemed to calm O'Deming. "You're right. It's just . . ."

"I know," Brewster agreed, not needing to articulate anything further.

They moved Walter's body to the rear of the truck and drove onto a crossroad that led into utter darkness. It was still close enough to dusk that people might be around, especially as the Leyland drew closer to bigger towns, so they waited in a meadow until midnight. It was cold, and they huddled the best they could around the small fire Bell had built in the lee of his lorry. There was nothing to be done about hunger or thirst.

At the head of a grassy square in a village a few miles from where they'd stopped sat an old stone church with a bell tower on its side and a heavy slate roof. It was so ancient, it made Bell think it had been sculpted by Nature rather than fashioned by the hands of man. He used his picks on the door's simple lock, and he and Brewster and Warry O'Deming carried Walt Schmidt's body inside. The nave was pitch-black, but they made their way down the aisle and laid him carefully on the steps leading up to the altar. As with the others, Bell left a note on the man's jacket with his name and a request that he be buried with a proper marker, as well as some money to cover the costs.

Warry crossed himself as he turned away and wiped at an eye when they made for the exit.

Bell had the morbid thought of how someone could mark their progress from Aberdeen southward by following the trail of headstones.

Believing that Gly's advertisement had run in Birmingham's newspapers and that a segment of its population was on the lookout for the convoy, Bell decided it was time to dump the Leylands and find another mode of transport. His first thought was consigning the crates of ore on the railway and shipping them to Southampton.

On the outskirts of the manufacturing city of seven hundred thousand, Bell hid one of the lorries behind an abandoned cotton mill. The stream that had once provided power to the looms and other machines had become a silted-over quagmire that stank of chemicals and decay. It was a victim of the Industrial Revolution's second phase, wherein coal and steam and, increasingly, electricity took over from streams and rivers. Beyond the mill were modern factories studded with chimneys that seemed oddly idle even though it was a weekend night.

They off-loaded Bell's truck, and he told the two men he was leaving and promised to return sometime after dawn with food, water, and news. Before he left, Bell was encouraged to see Vern Hall tossing and turning a bit in his sleep. It was a sign he was struggling to breach the surface of consciousness again.

Bell found the New Street Station about two hours before sunup. He parked the truck a good distance away and approached on foot. The building, like all rail terminals in major cities, was huge and never fully quiet even on a Sunday. At the front doors were porters and drivers making arrangements for the day. Vendors were arriving to provide breakfast for early passengers on their way to London or Bristol. The great hall was smartly lit, and already a few ticket booths were open. Beyond, covering over a dozen platforms, was one of the largest arched roof spans on earth. The sound of steam under pressure echoed along it, punctuated by whistles, horns, and the raised shouts of conductors readying the trains.

Bell used a few coins to purchase a cup of tea — he would have preferred coffee, but this was England after all — and an early-edition newspaper. It headlined news of a coal miners' strike entering its third week, which was crippling industry and explained the quiet factories he'd noted outside the city. The only other item that caught his eye was continued coverage of the death of polar explorer Robert Falcon Scott some weeks earlier. Everything else was the local stuff found in any hometown paper.

What he didn't find was any mention of the Aberdeen railroad heist or any advertisements offering rewards for the apprehension of those responsible.

He wasn't sure what this meant or if it was significant at all. Had Gly only targeted Newcastle? Or had he been so certain of it working quickly that he'd only paid for a single day's advertisement in multiple papers? Given the depth of Gly's resources, Bell imagined him throwing as wide a net as possible and keeping it out until he'd caught his fish. There was meaning to this, Bell felt certain, but he didn't know what exactly it was.

He was certain about something else as well. He wasn't the only person staking out Birmingham's principal rail terminal. He spotted four definites and three possibles. Two of the definites were a couple sitting on a distant bench. The man's head swiveled as he scanned faces and doorways and anything else he could see. The woman's head was on his shoulder, and Bell knew from experience that she would have told him to hold still if she was really trying to get some rest but that she was just a bit of cover. The other two definites were a couple of men pacing the perimeter of the station like they were soldiers on patrol. Bored walking while waiting for a train wasn't that unusual. The fact that they studied — as in leered uncomfortably close to — anyone they crossed gave them away. Not bored but on alert. The three possibles were single men, each waiting contentedly, like Bell, with the paper and a cup of tea. Two appeared legit but the third spent an inordinate amount of time looking about.

There was no way he and the others were going to wheel a thousand pounds of rock through the station without drawing attention. And once aboard the train, they were trapped. Gly's men could watch them until a moment of his choosing to strike, probably down the line a ways when additional men could be brought in to better the odds.

Bell found the telephone exchange office as it was just opening. He gave a deposit and had them open a line to London. He hoped to get an update from Joel Wallace, or at least some news from his assistant, Miss Davida Bryer. Bell let the telephone ring a dozen times, hoping it would wake whoever was watching the office. He finally canceled the call on the fifteenth unanswered ring.

There would be no help from that quarter until they reached Southampton Dock, and only then if Miss Bryer did her job. Bell had his doubts.

If the rails were out, they would have to switch vehicles, and now that they were down to just four men, Bell had an idea of how they could blend in a little better.

"Mind if I wait with you, *ami*?" It was the passenger Bell had singled out earlier as a possible lookout. The Frenchman had approached on Bell's blind side and had taken him unawares.

Bell knew the man was putting out feelers about who he was and why he was at the station so early. Rather than get drawn into a conversation, Bell uttered a sting of angry, consonant-heavy syllables that sounded like some Slavic language. He then plastered a scowl to his face.

"I'm sorry?"

Bell repeated the performance, pointing to himself and repeating the name Korczynski.

The Frenchman held up his hands, retreating. "My mistake. Thought you might enjoy some company while you waited."

Bell watched him go, glaring like a statue of a Chinese dragon in case he turned back. When the Frenchman went in to use the restroom, Bell dumped the rest of his tea and stuffed the newspaper in a wastebasket. He was out of the station door and gone moments later.

He drove the city until he found what he needed and bought some food and several thermoses of tea and returned to the abandoned mill. Brewster and Warry appeared especially gray in the early light of day. Both looked like they hadn't slept in weeks. Warry had developed a muscle tic that made his wrist flinch every few seconds. Both complained of nausea but managed to eat some of the bread and sausage and mashed-up fried potatoes he'd bought on the outskirts of Birmingham. The tea seemed to settle their stomachs.

"How's Vernon doing?" Bell asked while they ate. Hall remained in the back of the other lorry under a mound of blankets.

"Better," Brewster said. "He's muttering in his sleep. I take that as a good sign."

"I agree." Bell inspected the crates they'd off-loaded from his truck. The men had knocked them together back in the mine. Much of the wood had been repurposed from larger crates of drilling equipment, blasting caps and fuses, and explosives. Bell saw they could be taken apart and reassembled with relative ease.

Once they had finished breakfast, he said, "We've got three days to make our two o'clock sailing from Berth 26 on Wednesday. That's plenty of time, as we're about a hundred and fifty miles north of the port. Our problem comes every time we get near a city. Gly has people out looking for a couple of trucks carrying heavy crates."

"Not much we can do about that, is there?" Warry remarked.

"There is. We're going to hide the ore in

plain sight. We just have to make it through Birmingham and we'll be okay." Bell didn't lay out the rest of his plan just yet. Instead, they unloaded the second truck and mounded dirt around the cache of boxes.

"Why aren't we taking them with us?" Brewster asked, sweating heavily even though the morning remained chilly.

"Gly has the train station staked out, so he has to suspect we'll come through the city. In case there's trouble, we can ditch the trucks easily enough and not lose the byzanium ore."

"Makes sense." Warry looked little better than Brewster. His mouth was surrounded by weeping sores, the inside awash with cankers.

Both men had to stand opposite Bell in order to lift a crate and, even then, they struggled. Five months earlier, even little Warry O'Deming could have manhandled one of the chests on his own.

38

Back in the city, Bell drove the lead truck to the garage he'd found earlier and whose owner had agreed to a trade. The building was in a rougher part of town, which was why Bell had chosen it. Around it were row upon row of worker tenements and pubs doing business despite it being the Sabbath. The streets were filthy and teeming with dirty-faced boys, roaming like packs of wild dogs, searching for anything of interest. The men had the dullard look of overworked draft animals, while the women appeared decades older than their years.

The lookout posted at the larger of the commercial garage's two entrances had been told to expect the convoy and swung the doors open. Bell drove straight into the cavernous space with Warry right behind. On the concrete floor sat several trucks and motorbuses in various states of repair, in addition to a row of autos fitted out as taxis and a tarp-covered touring car that had likely been boosted from the streets of London. Its front fender was exposed and gleamed like polished silver.

The garage owner, a thickset man with a few days of stubble on his chin and a gin blossoms nose, had been in a glass-enclosed corner office when Bell rumbled in. He wore loose-fitting khaki pants held up by a dark belt and over-the-shoulder braces that he was just snapping back across his meaty deltoids. His shirt was so oft-laundered, it appeared gray rather than white.

"What's this, then?" he asked in a thick Midlands accent. He squinted at Bell through the smoke of a cigar.

"We talked."

Behind the owner was another man, whip-thin and dressed in black. He had hard, unflinching eyes and the look of a killer. He was clearly the garage owner's enforcer for all the criminal enterprises he dabbled in besides stolen vehicles.

"Right, but you said half eleven. You're early, mate. Hold on." He pointed to one of the workers loitering in the bays, a young boy used as a runner. "Joey, do that thing I told you or I'll tan ya hide. Right?"

"Sure, Mr. Devlin. I's on it." The urchin scampered through a judas gate set inside one of the main doors.

"Bell! Bell!" Brewster was still in the back of the second truck. "Vern's awake."

"About time," Bell muttered, and indicated to the garage owner he had to see to his people.

The owner, George Devlin, made a harried, dismissive gesture and turned back to his subordinate, while Bell boosted himself on top of the truck's rear tire to peer into its bed. "Welcome back," he said.

Hall was owl-eyed and disoriented. "Where are we?"

"Birmingham. More than halfway between where we started and where we need to go."

"What happened?"

"You need to tell us that," Brewster said to his old friend. He gave Hall some tea from one of the thermos flasks. "You were in a nasty fight in the locomotive cab when we left Aberdeen."

"A fight?" Hall didn't seem to recall.

"Aye. You and Johnny and Alvin."

"Who were we fighting?"

Bell knew it was common for people with head injuries to have short-term memory loss. He told Hall, "Each other, it would appear. Alvin Coulter was thrown from the train, and Johnny Caldwell died from a blow to the head."

"Oh, God. No."

"They're all dead," Warry said. "All of 'em but us three and Mr. Bell."

"What?" Hall moaned. "How is that possible? Tell me what happened. All of it."

"We don't have time for that," Bell said. "Being here is a hell of a risk, so the quicker we finish, the better."

He stepped back down from the truck, but kept close to it, while Devlin and his henchman ambled over. "It doesn't matter that we're early. You have what I need and I have two perfectly good trucks to trade. Let's do this and we can be on our way."

Devlin scratched absently at the bald spot atop his bullet head. "My sources tell me the coal strike ends tomorrow. I have to sell my stockpiles before the price drops back to normal, so I need to keep my truck."

Bell felt rage boil to the surface.

"And," the gangster continued, "I have this other deal brewing."

"What other deal?" Bell growled.

"Seems there's a thousand-pound bounty on your heads, payable by an old son of Scotland named Foster Gly. Benny!"

Devlin's enforcer pulled a two-barreled derringer-style pistol from his jacket pocket and held it steady to Bell's stomach. The gun was an antique, at least fifty years old, but it was no less deadly now than it had been in some riverboat gambler's waistcoat or up his sleeve.

A flash of silver. A jet of red and a high-pitched shriek. The derringer, along with the hand holding it, hit the concrete floor with a meaty smack. The enforcer grabbed at the gushing stump with his left hand so that blood spurted through his fingers. Joshua Hayes Brewster stood on the bed of the Leyland truck and swung a follow-through with the flensing knife they'd kept since the escape from the docks. The blade struck the gunman in the chest and sank almost to the handle. His chuffing screams of pain ceased in a wet wheeze.

Bell recovered his wits and scooped up the fallen pistol by first shaking loose its grisly adjunct. The room had exploded in motion. Most of the mechanics and hangers-on scattered after witnessing the barbarity of Brewster's assault. A couple of others, the largest of the men, were hired for their brawn, not their mechanical skills, and they came at the truck in an all-out attack. Bell cocked the pistol and let fly the ammo in one of the barrels. The weapon was woefully inaccurate, even for a marksman of Bell's abilities, and the bullet grazed a thug's shoulder so softly that he didn't even flinch.

A blackjack appeared in his hand even as he swung a heavy fist at Bell. The lead-filled satchel missed Bell's head by a hair's breadth. Bell weaved out from under the guard and fired off a straight right to the man's nose that left the man's knees wobbling. From the truck's bed, Warry O'Deming finished the job with a tire iron to the crown of the man's scalp.

A mechanic with more bravery than sense threw a hammer at the little Irishman. It missed, and O'Deming leapt from the truck, screaming like a madman, the tire iron cocked and ready. The mechanic yelled and started running, with Warry gaining on him rapidly.

Joshua Brewster had squared off with another guard, brandishing the flensing knife like a scythe and keeping the man well back. A guard tried to take Bell from behind in a hold around the shoulders, as if this were going to be a wrestling match rather than a rumble. Bell rammed down on the man's instep with his boot. And when the tension went out of the hold, he snapped the attacker's head back and broke his nose. The man released Bell to stanch the flow of blood and Bell unceremoniously kicked him at the juncture of his legs. As he went to the ground, another kick, this one to the face, took the last of the fight out of the man.

In the opening seconds of the fight, George Devlin had rushed to his office and closed the door behind him. Bell saw him throw the lock and scramble for a telephone hanging on the wall opposite his desk. Devlin was calling in reinforcements in case the runner he'd sent earlier couldn't find Gly's agents. Bell raced across the garage for the glass-enclosed space. He torqued in midair so that he hit the mullioned panes with his back with his fingers laced behind his neck and his elbows clamped to his sides to protect them from the glass.

He burst through the glass in a cascade of tinkling shards, landed on his side atop the gangster's desk, and rolled to his feet, his right hand now extended so the pistol was pressed between the stunned Englishman's eyes.

Bell flicked his attention back to the garage floor. Brewster and O'Deming were in the thick of it and holding their own, but they were outnumbered three to one, and Bell knew Gly had people on the way. He needed more time, though.

"Drop the phone," he ordered the English mobster. Devlin complied, and Bell motioned him back to the shattered window.

"Tell your people to stand down."

"You're dead, Yank," Devlin sneered. "Only you don't know it yet."

"Harder men than you have died with that threat on their lips," Bell said, watching the brawl and the cowering mechanics, including one near the rear bumper of his Leyland truck. He watched a moment longer. It was done.

Bell returned his attention to the gangster, his eyes cold, and cocked the second of the derringer's barrels. "Call them off now."

Devlin nodded so much that the pouch of fat below his chin squished against his chest. The mobster's bellow echoed from every corner of his garage. "Enough, lads. Let it be."

The guy facing Brewster and his flensing knife seemed relieved by the truce, though the Coloradan looked ready to keep going. Warry O'Deming was bleeding from the arm, and his face was a mass of contusions, but at his feet was a bruiser twice his size who would need an eyepatch for the rest of his life.

Bell forced Devlin to step through the shattered glass wall and remained behind him with just enough separation that the hood wasn't tempted to try to disarm him. "Joshua, Warry, help shift Vern over to the black truck that's parked behind the bus. It's our ride."

Brewster saw the heavy-duty vehicle and understood Bell's plan. "Clever man. Using a dump truck to haul rocks. No one'll look at us twice."

"Right."

Once they helped Vern Hall shuffle over to their new truck and they had the engine cranked to life, Bell motioned with the pistol for a mechanic to open the main doors out to the street. Only when that was done did he begin backing up, never taking the handgun off George Devlin.

Like when facing down a dangerous animal, Bell put as much distance as he could between himself and the gangster before turning on his heel and running for the dump truck. He jumped up into the cab and had the chain drive rattling before Devlin could shout for his man to close the doors again.

At that moment, another vehicle raced through the partially open doors, knocking the mechanic back against a bunch of barrels, upending one and sending its mixture of oil and gasoline sloshing across the floor. The newcomers had arrived in a four-seater Austin tourer with the top up. Through the big windscreen, Bell could see the front passenger was armed with a sawed-off shotgun. He was sure these were local thugs hired by George Devlin to help Gly secure the crates of ore.

He gunned the dump truck's engine but left it in low gear so it had maximum torque when its front fender staved in the Austin's grille and ripped the engine right from its mounts. The front passenger was jerked so hard by the impact that the gun went off in his hands. The inside of the windscreen went instantly red, sparing Bell from seeing what horror the blast had done to the driver's head.

Bell kept the truck going until he'd rammed the Austin into a wall with enough force to collapse the frame and tear the fuel tank. Smoke belching from the engine compartment quickly turned into a whooshing conflagration that saw flames shooting to the iron rafters twenty feet overhead.

Jamming the truck into reverse gear, Bell backed away from the flaming wreckage only to realize with mounting apprehension that the car was tangled up on the truck's bumper and wouldn't release. He mashed down on the gas, backing blindly in the cluttered garage and then throwing the wheel hard over. The centrifugal force of the maneuver ripped the wrecked Austin free and it slid like a burning meteor across the floor and into a group of rolling toolboxes and barrels. The oil-soaked scraps of cotton ticking that filled one of the barrels went up in another gout of smoky flame, while one of the four-hundred-pound metal boxes fell over on the man hiding behind it, breaking both his shoulders.

Pandemonium erupted throughout the garage as the fires spread. The sludge that had dumped out when the Austin first arrived ignited and turned the building's entrance into a sea of flame. Smoke condensed along the ceiling in ever-thickening clouds that were rapidly mushrooming down toward the floor.

Bell's eyes streamed tears. They had to get out.

The main door was inaccessible behind a lake of fire, and the smaller one next to it, though large enough for the truck, was closed. It could be opened only by a person pulling on a chain that mechanically raised it along tracks that curved under the ceiling.

Bell considered ramming the roller gate, but it was made of heavy-gauge steel and looked impervious. The other option was to drive through the flames, but Brewster and Hall were in the back and they would have been burned alive.

He looked back across the garage. Through the deepening smoke, figures scurried in hopes of finding a spot where the flames weren't growing higher and more fierce.

There was no other way.

Warry O'Deming opened his door and had to shout over the roaring chorus of the fire when he said, "I know what you did for the others, Mr. Bell. Just make sure I'm buried in a Catholic cemetery or my sainted mother will make heaven hell for me."

He ran across to the closed door, forcing himself to stand mere feet from the flames. The chain dangling from the hoist mechanism had been exposed to heat for many long minutes and doubtless burned the Irishman's hands as he yanked on it to open the door. No sooner had the door risen a few inches than the influx of fresh oxygen caused the fire to expand in nearly every direction as though the air itself was combustible.

Bell was protected by the dump truck's enclosed cab, and Brewster and Hall were afforded some protection by the high sides of the truck's body, but Warry took the blast of flame full force. His hair burned off like a flaring match and his clothes were alight, yet he didn't stop working the chain, sacrificing himself so the others could live and complete their mission.

Isaac Bell had never witnessed such an act of bravery in his life.

Even before the door was high enough, Bell put the truck in gear and started gunning for the exit in the vain hope that somehow Warry could be saved. But welding tanks near the gate just then reached critical temperature and exploded with the force of a bundle of dynamite.

Warry O'Deming ceased to exist.

Bell slammed on the brakes as blinding white flame rolled over the truck's cab and rocked the vehicle on its suspension. The mechanic Bell had seen earlier had been fortunate enough to be sheltered from the blast by the truck's steel body, but the concussion wave left him dazed, and he started walking back toward the center of the building rather than picking his way through the burning debris toward the exit. Bell opened his door enough to grab the man's arm and guide him up onto the running board. He then raced through the inferno and out onto the street, the truck trailing smoke from where the fire had burned off some paint.

He braked a half block from the fire, and

looked the mechanic in the eye. "I just saved your life. Do what you were told to do in there but don't mention the dump truck. Understand?" The man was too frightened to speak. "Nod your head if you understand."

The man nodded, and Bell released his grip. The mechanic stepped down onto the road. Bell yelled for his companions. The two men, sooty but unharmed, climbed down from the back of the truck and joined Bell in the cab. They accelerated away while crowds of onlookers began to gather to watch the fire consume the local crime boss's garage.

39

No one spoke during the ride back to the abandoned cotton mill where they'd stashed the byzanium. Rather than empty the crates into the dump truck so the ore looked like so much gravel, Bell decided to load them filled and just bury them with more dirt from behind the mill. The truck was more than powerful enough for the extra weight. Vern Hall was no help with any of the physical labor, and while Brewster was willing, he was too weak and wasted to be of any use either. It fell on Isaac Bell to load the hundred-pound crates and shovel a few hundred pounds of dirt on top.

They were back on the road around suppertime. Bell circled as far around Birmingham as he could before turning south. The men kept their own counsel while they drove. The only sound in the truck was the growl of the engine and the hiss of the tires on the pavement. They stopped for food and fuel once, but then kept going. It was only when they were about ten miles north of the Port of Southampton that Bell turned the truck off the main road and followed a country lane into the rolling farmland. The truck's headlamps barely cut through the darkness, forcing Bell to drive at a walking pace. Ancient rock walls lined parts of the road and divided some of the pastures.

"Where are we going?"

"We have thirty-six hours before we need to board the ship. I have a healthy aversion to anyplace Foster Gly might lay an ambush, so I thought we'd wait it out in the country-side. I saw a sign back there for a little town. They'll hopefully have an inn. Or at least a pub for a meal and a barn where we can sleep."

As it turned out, Southby wasn't much of a town at all and had neither inn nor pub and barn. The place was all but abandoned, with only a few thatch-roofed homes showing any light. They passed a church and were back out into pastureland. A half mile later, Bell spotted a gate that had been left to rot. He turned onto a narrow track that led to a house with a collapsed front wall, but the barn behind it was intact, if not a little run-down. The silence when Bell killed the engine was soon filled with the sound of a gentle breeze moving through the tall grass and rustling the leafless trees.

"We'll try to get food in the morning," Bell said, knuckling kinks out of his lower back.

The barn door only closed partway, and most of the floor was bare earth, but one stall was packed with hay bales left from the previous autumn. They had hardened over the winter, but a little pulling and twisting loosened enough straw to make them comfortable enough for exhausted sleep.

When they were settled in, Vern Hall said, "That was a hell of a thing Warry did for us back there."

"Aye," Brewster replied, but in such a way as to indicate he didn't want to talk about it.

Bell changed the topic by asking, "Do you remember anything about what happened on the train with you and Johnny and Alvin?"

"Some," Hall said. "It was Johnny. When you went back to uncouple the cars, Johnny hit Alvin with the blade of the coal shovel without warning and shoved him right off the train. He swung at me and did a good number on my head, but I think I got ahold of the sledgehammer they use to break up bigger chunks of coal and swung it back just before my legs went out from underneath me."

"So, it was Johnny who was working for the French," Bell said.

"Must be," Vern said.

"I wonder why," Bell mused.

"I've been thinking about that, Mr. Bell, and there's something I've kept secret."

"What's that?" Brewster asked with suspicion. "What secret?"

"Jake Hobart was married, and I think Johnny had fallen in love with his bride and killed Jake over it."

"What?" Brewster cawed.

"It's true. Jake knew about how you didn't trust working with married miners, Josh, so he never told you. He confided in me, and even asked that I send some postcards on his behalf when we were in Paris. I mailed some when we went to the tasting session at the food company, and I had Arn send a final one from Aberdeen that told her Jake had died back in Russia."

Bell said, "I did find evidence that Johnny had a girl he couldn't be with."

Vern Hall nodded in the darkness. "He spent a lot of time with Jake Hobart because Jake was teaching him how to be a blaster. That's how Johnny met the wife, who's much younger than Jake. Maybe even younger than Johnny. I think what happened was Johnny fell in love with her and wanted to get Jake out of the way. He must have seen an opportunity on the island, committed the murder, and made it look like Jake had died in a storm."

Bell seemed intrigued by Hall's theory, and asked, "How do the French play into this scenario? We know someone contacted them from the *Hvalur Batur.*"

"Not sure," Hall admitted. "I didn't know about that. Must be they promised him a job with them and a home for him and Adeline."

Bell got up and felt his way over to the truck. He reached in and flipped on the headlamps. Though they appeared dim while driving, they gave off more than enough light to fill the small barn.

"Why'd you do that?" Vern Hall asked peevishly.

"Because," Bell said, "it's time to put an end to this charade."

40

Bell's words hung in the air for a long moment.

Vernon Hall looked from Bell to Brewster and back again. He somehow managed to sound defiant when he asked, "What charade?"

"What's going on, Bell?" Brewster asked.

"I needed Vernon to pass on to Gly the name of the ship we've booked passage on and when it sails."

Brewster's eyes went wide and his mouth slack.

"You haven't figured it out? Johnny Caldwell wasn't the saboteur. He was a victim. Your old friend Vern was the one who sold you all down the river. I realized a couple of days ago but needed to keep him around to pass the information on to Gly. I've got to hand it to you, Hall, you had me going for a long while. And pretending to be concussed since that night on the train was a brilliant move."

Hall made like he was going to get to his feet.

Bell had his .45 in hand before Hall had moved even an inch. Hall relaxed again, but his eyes glittered and darted like a trapped rodent. "What threw me initially was the squeaky door I heard on the whaling ship. You hid your identity from Arn well enough when you used the radio, but you couldn't risk his reporting your visit without finding a way of deflecting suspicion onto someone else.

"When you were finished calling your people on the *Lorient,* you came down to my cabin, made a noise outside of it loud enough to wake me, and then opened and closed one of the other cabin doors to make me think it was one of the six men sleeping near me who'd just been up. I went to the bridge, where Arn told me about one of the miners in the radio shack. I tested the set and found it was still warm. But I never once thought it was you because your cabin was on a different deck than mine."

Bell looked to Brewster. He appeared unable to grasp the level of betrayal. Bell had no choice but to plow on. "I realized after I found you unconscious on the train that the blow to the head — self-inflicted, no doubt — was the only mark on you. The rest of us were banged-up from the fight on the dock, but you didn't have a scratch. It's because you didn't participate. You were hoping the French would beat us there and you'd get whatever reward Gly had offered you.

"But the two times I checked your eyes, they didn't react like someone with a head injury. So I was suspicious. When it appeared we might give Gly the slip permanently by switching trucks in Birmingham, you suddenly woke up. You had to get word to Gly."

Bell looked again at Brewster. Brewster still stared at Vern as though he'd never seen him before. The detective continued his narration. "Vern couldn't reach the French from Novaya Zemlya because you'd secretly disabled the radio, forcing him to make the clandestine call from the whaling ship. From that, Gly knew we were headed to Aberdeen and he had an ambush waiting for us. What follows after that — I really have to hand it to Gly, he's as smart as he is evil. By putting that telephone number and mention of a reward in newspapers, he turned everyone in central England into his personal spy. The innkeeper made the call and the French almost got away with the ore.

Next, Gly correctly figured we needed to change vehicles and couldn't do it through any legitimate means. That led me to the next major city, Birmingham. And Gly had already put out word to the local underworld to be on the lookout for us. I practically handed us to George Devlin on a silver platter."

Bell paused for a reflective moment. "Had it not been for Warry O'Deming, we'd all be dead and the ore lost behind an abandoned cotton mill for all eternity.

"But Gly's not a mind reader. He could have guessed we'd head to Southampton, but he didn't know our ship or sailing time. During the initial stage of the fight in the garage, I saw Vern speaking to one of the mechanics. I had gone over the travel arrangements my agent in London made for me again this morning so there would be no confusion when he passed on our itinerary. That's why I saved the man as we were leaving the garage. I had to make sure Gly had that information." Bell turned his attention back to Vernon Hall. "Now that that task is completed, I no longer have any use for you."

"That's nothing but pure fantasy, Bell," Hall said. "None of it's true. Johnny cracked me over the head with a shovel and I've been unconscious until just this morning."

Bell ignored him. "There's two things I don't have an answer to. One, I don't know why you did it. I assume you were offered a tremendous amount of money and you believed — wrongly, I suspect — that Gly would let you live. You're a loose end to him. He'd just as soon put a knife into your belly as honor his bargain. The second thing I don't know is, how you planned to pin this on someone else if I ever got suspicious. Blaming a lovelorn Johnny Caldwell and claiming ignorance about the radio equipment and the call from the *Batur* was good."

"I almost believed it myself," Brewster said in a dead monotone. "I wanted to believe it."

"You two have been friends for a long time, so I can't blame you," Bell told him. "You see, Hall, Johnny probably did know Jake Hobart's wife, but it wasn't her picture he carried. When concocting lies, it's best to keep them as vague as possible. Naming Adeline Hobart as Johnny's love was a mistake. I'm not sure of his girl's name, but it ended in *tia,* and Johnny couldn't be with her because there are laws on the books and prejudice in men's hearts over people of different races being happy together. You took your lie one step too far. I've known about

549

your being the mole for a while now, but I needed you to reveal yourself in front of Joshua. Otherwise, he never would have believed me. Right?"

"That's why you told us about Johnny and the girl when we were back at the pub."

Bell nodded. "Because of how the fight turned out aboard the locomotive, Vern had no choice but to say that Johnny was the saboteur. Tonight, I fed Hall a line about Johnny having a girlfriend he couldn't be with and he went with it, embellishing the story as he went. He spun a narrative that dovetailed with how Jake Hobart was secretly married and thought he was convincing us with every word."

"Only, he was digging himself deeper."

"That he was." Bell shot Vernon Hall a mocking smile. "I can't tell you how many confessions I've gotten over the years because criminals are too stupid to keep their mouths shut."

"What happens now?" Hall asked. "Are you going to kill me?"

Bell said to Joshua Brewster, "There's some rope behind the seat in the truck. Could you get it for me?"

"Yeah." Brewster got to his feet and lurched over to the truck. He was at his breaking point, physically and mentally.

Returning his attention to Hall, Bell said, "I'm going to leave you tied up here until Wednesday afternoon, when there's nothing more you can do to interfere in this mission. Afterward, I'm going to turn you over to the Army liaison officer at the American Embassy and see to it you're shipped back to the States in irons."

Brewster came back, walked up to where Hall lay on the straw. He hesitated for just a second. Standing only a few inches above five feet, Joshua Hayes Brewster managed to look like he towered over his old friend. He gave that same disturbed tittering laugh Bell had heard in the pub back in Newcastle.

"No," Bell shouted, but it was too late.

Brewster had fallen upon Vernon Hall with a rusty screwdriver that Bell had overlooked when he'd inventoried potential weapons in the dump truck. By the time Bell got to him and pulled him off, Brewster had sunk the tool into Hall's chest a half dozen times. Brewster didn't struggle. In fact, he was quite passive, considering the savagery of the attack.

He looked at Bell, his face streaked with blood. "Sorry about this little outburst. I get these wild ideas sometimes," he said, repeating what he'd told Bell after the pub incident. "Though this time I know exactly where it came from."

A few minutes passed. Brewster said, "It doesn't matter to me why he did it. Maybe he was crazier than me. I'm going to tell myself that he had no choice. I'm going to believe the French had him in such a jam that he had to do this to us and that he'd been told we'd all be spared. I can't live thinking it was any other way. That said, it's still important to me that this stays between us. I'm not going to write about Vern's betrayal in my notes and I'd be beholden to you if it stayed out of your official report."

"I never lie in my personal journals, but I'll make sure this stays out of my write-up for Colonel Patmore."

"Thanks. So what now?"

Bell studied the corpse for a moment. "We make the best of this tragedy and bury one last Coloradan on British soil. The town of Southby has to have a church and cemetery. We need to also find a stonecutter for a special headstone. Vernon Hall is going to take a secret to his grave."

41

The SS *Bohemia* was roughly three hundred feet long, black-hulled, with a single smokestack as tall and as straight as a chimney. She had two forward holds, with a mast derrick between them, and a third hold aft that also had its own crane for slinging aboard cargo. Bell estimated she was at least a decade old, and while someone had taken care of her in the early years, she seemed to have hit a rough spell of late. Her paint was peeling in places, and there was a massive dent in her bow where she'd slammed into a pier or possibly another ship. A placard on her pilothouse just aft of the bridge wing said she was owned by Bougainville Shippers Ltd. It was one of the smaller of the twenty-three steamship lines that used the port.

He had wanted to keep the ship under observation since her arrival in the bustling Port of Southampton, but making arrangements in Southby had taken a great deal longer than he'd anticipated. They'd barely arrived in time for the scheduled sailing.

The afternoon was fair, with the sun dancing around the clouds overhead. The temperature was nearing sixty degrees, which made it the warmest Bell had experienced since long before this case had begun back in Denver all those months ago. He was a man of dogged persistence, and there was no question he'd see this through to a satisfactory conclusion, yet it had taken a heavy toll.

He had watched the *Bohemia* on and off since before noon, but with all the commotion around Berth 44, it had been difficult. There had been thousands of passengers and well-wishers, as well as dozens of trucks carrying luggage, and more trucks with the last of the perishables, and barges loading coal that the recent strike had made so expensive, many ships had been left idle in port. While he hadn't spotted Foster Gly, by the time he began a serious stakeout from the roof of a nearby warehouse with a ridiculously easy lock to pick, Bell had counted no less than six men moving about on the ship who didn't act like sailors and another four loitering in the area that weren't stevedores.

"What do you think?" he asked softly.

"I think if your plan doesn't work, we didn't bring enough guys."

Joel Wallace looked almost as travel-worn as Bell, but he was back from a useless jaunt to Aberdeen, and Miss Bryer had done her job and told her boss to gather some troops. Sadly, he'd only managed to get four additional men, English lads eager for a few extra quid and good with their fists. They were waiting in a car out of sight behind the warehouse.

Bell checked the time. "We'd better get down there. The taxi should be here any minute. Don't do anything until I give the signal."

"Which is?"

"If I shoot my pistol or Gly's thugs swarm me on deck, get up there and save me."

"Got it. Gunshot or swarm."

Bell and Wallace descended to the dock. Wallace went to get his boys, and they took up position hidden behind pallets of machine tools. Bell hung back too, checking his watch. Finally, a taxi appeared. He stepped into the open and it was as if he'd upended a beehive. The four heavies on the pier rushed toward him, fists clenched, intimidating scowls in place. On the freighter, several more of Gly's men moved to the head of the gangplank, while another vanished into the superstructure. Even before Bell had made it ten paces, Gly appeared on the ship's deck with a slovenly dressed man with a peaked hat. It had to be the captain, René Bougainville.

The taxi eased to a stop at the foot of the gangway. Bell was ready to watch the reaction when she exited the vehicle. This was going to be one for the ages, he thought.

The rear door opened, and a slender Asian girl with a rope of black hair dangling down her back jumped out. Bell was expecting someone else and was startled. She regarded him languidly. She was pretty but had too much self-possession for one so young. She had a cynic's eyes in a schoolgirl's face.

"Min," the captain yelled. "Get up here and go to the cabin."

Two men grabbed Bell from behind. His plan had gone sideways before it had even launched. What were the odds of a second taxi arriving at the allotted time of the one he was expecting?

The girl scampered up the ramp and disappeared, the captain giving her a disquieting look. Bell was frog-marched up after her. Gly sported a Navy peacoat that looked like it had been fitted by tentmakers. His shoulders and arms strained at the wool cloth. He had a cigar going in the corner of his mouth, and his eyes were slitted against the smoke.

"Where's the ore?" he asked, and stepped forward and rammed a fist so deeply into Bell's gut it felt like Gly had punched the inside of his spine.

Bell would have collapsed had the two men not been holding him up. Gly backed away, pacing like a caged animal awaiting its meal, while Bell tried to reinflate his lungs by taking agonizing sips of air.

"Gone," he finally wheezed.

"What do you mean gone?"

"What it sounds like, you ape." Bell straightened as best he could. "Gone. I was onto Vern Hall from the beginning. I fed him false information so he'd pass it on to you. See that dark cloud way down the Channel? That's the ship carrying the ore, Gly. It left dock at noon as scheduled and should arrive in New York to much fanfare on the seventeenth."

A terrible blackness descended over Gly's eyes as the realization struck home.

Captain Bougainville sensed it and stepped forward. "No killing on my ship, Gly." His accent was an odd mash-up of French and something else. "You want to tear each other apart, do it on the dock."

The huge Scot ignored him and ran at Bell with a full-throated roar of hatred. Bell kicked both legs up since his arms were being supported by Gly's henchmen and struck outward just as Gly came into range. The dynamics of the strike saw Gly stagger back and the men holding Bell stagger back and lose their grip. In the confusion of the sudden reversal, Bell lifted the .45 from its holster and shot the closest man.

He swung right to line up on Gly, but the guard on his other side barreled into Bell at the last second and he was thrown against a tall, tuba-like air intake scoop. He leveraged an elbow free and slammed it into the man's nose, breaking it.

Joel Wallace must have been watching much closer than Bell gave him credit for. He and his guys came up the gangway like a flying squad even as the echo of the single gunshot was fading to nothing.

Boots and fists flew in a mad scrum. Bell just saw flashes of it, like some stroboscopic effect. Faces leered at him and he struck out at them, punching with abandon, kicking where he could. For each time he was shoved, he pushed back twice as hard. All the while he was looking for Gly amid the tangle of bodies. He had one round left in the Colt and he didn't want to waste it.

But then he was taken from behind, arms with the strength of boa constrictors pinning his arms to his sides and beginning to crush his chest. Gly lifted him from the deck so that Bell's feet wheeled uselessly. He tried to ram his head back into Gly's face, but the Scotsman absorbed the blow as though it were a tap.

The crushing force seemed to double. A little air escaped Bell's mouth, and Gly was there to make sure he couldn't replace it with fresh oxygen. Men bumped into them, fighting around them, and yet the two stood still in the melee, Bell's life slowly ebbing from his body as the pressure on his ribs doubled again.

He had just enough of an angle to shoot the two smallest toes off Gly's right foot.

Gly released him out of surprise more than pain. Bell fell to the deck but didn't remain still. He pulled his boot knife free and was rising fast to jam it up under Gly's ribs when there was a shout of such command that he stopped. They all did.

"Arrêtez-vous immédiatement!"

A woman stood at the head of the gangway flanked by two men in overcoats carrying revolvers. She was stern-faced, with a nest of dark hair, and dressed severely in all black. Even had she not been one of the

559

most famous women in the world, her presence would nevertheless command a room.

"What is the meaning of this?" demanded Madame Marie Curie. "Gly, what is going on here?"

The natural-born killer actually looked like a contrite schoolboy for a moment. Bell moved away from him as the two groups of fighting men also separated themselves. Most of the faces were bloodied and deeply bruised, though Joel Wallace's boys seemed to have enjoyed themselves, judging by their newly gap-toothed grins.

"They tried to steal the byzanium, madame," Gly said.

"And this gives you permission to act like an animal? Mr. Bell phoned me at my friend Hertha Ayrton's in Portsea yesterday with news of how you've comported yourself. Is it true?"

Gly said nothing. Even he was no match for the Polish-born Laureate.

Bell had discovered, from a small article in the Birmingham paper he'd spotted that morning in the train station, that the famous chemist was in England recuperating from kidney surgery. The city council had extended her an invitation to speak at a symposium. He'd deduced early on that she was the logical benefactor of the Société des Mines's mission to find the ore, so informing her of the lengths taken was the best course to get her to intervene.

Curie's righteous anger came off her in waves. "I cannot bring myself to fathom that men have been killed on account of the byzanium. What were you thinking?"

"I had my orders," Gly said, falling back on the excuse used by monsters for their actions since time immemorial. "I was told to get the ore at all cost and that's what I did."

"Human life, Mr. Gly?"

He showed a spark of defiance. "What gives you the right to question my tactics? You wanted results and I made it happen."

"Then where is the byzanium now?" she demanded haughtily and quelled Gly's moment of bravado.

Bell said, "Ma'am, I oversaw all ten crates being stowed in the hold of the *Titanic* not two hours ago. The last surviving miner that dug it out of that Russian hellhole, Joshua Hayes Brewster, is sailing back to New York with them. He'll be met by representatives of the War Department at Pier 59 next Wednesday when they dock."

"Ten crates you said?"

"Yes, ma'am. Nearly a thousand pounds of rocks. They stripped the mountain clean."

She was quiet for a moment, then finally said, "I would have loved the opportunity to refine the byzanium like I did when I discovered radium, but I suppose it is not meant to be."

"I assure you, Madame Curie, my government understands the importance of this find and will treat the samples accordingly."

She took his arm and led him to the *Bohemia*'s starboard rail with a view of the shipping channel and the warehouses and piers on the opposite shore. "Perhaps it is for the best, Mr. Bell. I fear war is coming to Europe again. Soon. All these tangled alliances mean one tiny spark will ignite the Continent and all the generals are eager to use their shiny new weapons and prosecute a war on an industrial level."

Up close, there was a melancholy to her that went beyond her being widowed. She had knowledge — deep knowledge — and it scared her.

She turned back to him and said, "We know from Albert's work that a distillate of uranium can produce an explosion that could flatten a city." Bell assumed she meant Albert Einstein, although he'd never heard mention of such a doomsday weapon. She continued. "As terrifying as that is, we have no idea what earth-shattering effects may be derived from this new elemental specimen. If the byzanium remains in Europe, some fool will exploit it in such a way that might destroy us all."

"We'll keep it safe," Bell assured her. "What about Foster Gly?"

"Based on everything you told me yesterday, I arranged for him to be returned to France, where he will stand trial for his crimes."

Bell looked back across the deck. Gly stood a full head taller than the others. The two men locked eyes, and Bell knew at that moment they were fated to meet again. And next time they met, he promised himself, he would put a bullet in the mercenary's skull.

42

Four days after seeing Brewster off on the *Titanic* and the confrontation with Foster Gly, the chill hadn't yet thawed. Bell rattled the morning paper while closing it properly and peered across the breakfast table at his wife. If there was a look colder than glacial, she was still giving it to him. And it didn't appear he'd be forgiven anytime soon. Other guests in the Savoy Hotel's dining room could certainly feel the icy hoarfrost and kept their distance.

"Marion?"

"Don't you 'Marion' me, Isaac Bell."

"Please, be reasonable."

"When in the history of couples arguing," Marion snapped, "has a man saying 'be reasonable' ever, ever worked?"

"Well . . ."

"Well, indeed." Her voice softened, though her posture remained erect and distant. "How could you? We'd planned this for months. I picked out the perfect cabin, rescheduled not one but two movie productions. I bought new dresses for the passage, and some special frilly things for your benefit, and for what? So you can give it to some smelly old miner."

"Marion, I wouldn't have done it if it wasn't important."

"Important?" Her eyebrows arched impossibly. "As in 'Gosh, I think it's important to keep promises to my wife so she doesn't divorce me or maybe just murder me.' Important like that?"

He changed tack. "The ship will be back in ten days. We have the same cabin reserved. All we've lost is a little time."

"Oh! You are such a man."

"I should hope so."

"Don't you get it? A maiden voyage means beds that have never been slept in, glasses that haven't been sipped from, plates that have never been used. We had use of a tub big enough for two, and now some sow from Fifth Avenue has already befouled it with her wrinkled carcass."

Despite himself, he had to chuckle at her phrasing. Even Marion had to give that one a bit of a laugh, and her eyes did finally soften. "It's the newness of it all that we lost. That's why I'm mad. And I know you wouldn't have switched places with him if it weren't crucial. But sometimes I wish you'd —"

She stopped in midsentence when someone walked into a serving cart and upended the entire thing. It crashed to the floor in a clatter of metal dishes and a splatter of eggs Benedict and coffee. The patron remained on the floor, obviously in terrible distress. Isaac and Marion both got to their feet to see if they could render aid when they heard a disturbance starting out in the lobby. Like a wave, word spread through the hotel. It came in whispers, then sobs, then long moments of utter silence.

Bell grabbed a passing busboy, a lad who looked like he'd just seen a ghost.

"What the devil is happening?" he demanded.

"It's news just come from America, sir. The *Titanic.* She struck an iceberg last night."

"Was anyone hurt?" Bell would forever remember asking such a stupid question on that historic morning.

"She sank, sir. They're saying half the passengers and crew drowned." The boy pulled free and vanished into the kitchens.

Bell and Marion exchanged a look, a look that only married couples could understand.

In that single glance, they apologized for arguing, reaffirmed their love and commitment, and thanked the Fates that they hadn't been aboard. Neither would have left the other or taken a seat in a lifeboat that could have gone to a stranger.

Bell sat heavily, his chin sunk to his chest. Marion came to his side and rested a protective hand on his shoulder. He knew Brewster wouldn't leave the crates. He'd have gone down with the *Titanic* as surely as her captain must have. The last of the Coloradans was dead.

Bell had spent that previous few days tidying up some details of the case. He'd anonymously paid for the funeral of one of the victims of the Devlin Garage fire. Warry O'Deming now rested in the Catholic section of Birmingham's Handsworth Cemetery. He'd also reworked Joshua Hayes Brewster's journal, expunging any mention of Ragnar Fyrie and substituting a piece of fiction about an American gunboat under the command of one Lieutenant Pratt. Bell got that name from a childhood friend back in Boston who'd died of diphtheria. He made sure his own report contained the fictions he'd agreed to with Brewster concerning his closest friend. Vernon Hall might have died as a traitor, but history would record him as a hero.

One detail he couldn't sew up was the derringer pistol he'd taken from the garage. He'd planned on tossing it into the waters off Southampton following his meeting with Marie Curie only to discover he no longer had it. He assumed Brewster had taken it with him on the *Titanic* and could only hope he hadn't done anything foolish during the pandemonium of the great liner's sinking.

Bell never once considered it would all end like this. Thinking about the sacrifice and the hardship, the deprivation and ultimately the madness, he wanted to rage against the injustice of their deaths but knew there was no solace to be had in that. It had gone wrong from the very first, and no matter how hard he tried to make it right, the outcome seemed inevitable. He supposed all that remained was to submit his report to Colonel Patmore at the War Department and hope they did the right thing.

Nine good men went into the Russian wilderness to pull off the impossible and not one survived to tell the tale. It was all a senseless waste, he thought, and said under his breath, "Thank God for Southby."

EPILOGUE

Dirk Pitt reached the bottom of the staircase and strode down the platform. To his right was an empty set of tracks. At his left sat the gleaming silver body of an Amtrak Acela high-speed train.

He smiled at the porter as he stepped aboard the first-class car and found his seat. He stowed his bags in the overhead but kept the copy of Isaac Bell's journal. Despite his best efforts the previous night, he'd been unable to finish it before being overtaken by exhaustion.

He accepted a bottled water from the porter and read the last pages of Bell's saga while there was a delay pulling from the fluorescent-lit tunnels below New York's Penn Station for the run down to Washington. Ten minutes later, he turned the last page. He rested his head against the railcar's window.

Pitt was a man of few regrets, but one he

was beginning to feel was that he'd never get the opportunity to meet Isaac Bell. What an extraordinary man, he thought.

Straightening the pages of the journal and slipping them back into the envelope, he saw that a piece of paper was stuck to the back of the last page of text, something he hadn't noticed earlier as he'd perused the journal.

It had been torn from a notebook. Dated October 15, 1953, and signed by Isaac Bell, it read

Writing out this story brought back many memories and one burning question — what did the government do with the information I provided? Following my return to New York with Marion and presenting my notes to Colonel Patmore, I never once followed up on the affair, thinking that it would remain classified. I made some calls this week and learned that Patmore and his immediate superior were killed in a training exercise days after my meeting with them. To the best of my knowledge, the government dropped all interest in byzanium following their deaths. In light of what Madame Curie told me, and what I saw firsthand in Nagasaki and Hiroshima, I believe it is for the best.

Pitt knew from speaking firsthand with one of the last *Titanic* survivors, John L. Bigelow, that Joshua Hayes Brewster had insisted on being led to the vault that ill-fated night. He wanted to be taken to where the crates were stored and then asked to be locked inside. He'd even pulled a pistol, the one Bell had lost track of, on the junior officer to compel his assistance. Brewster's last words, according to Bigelow, mirrored the final handwritten line of Bell's tale. At the bottom of the notebook page were scrawled the words *Thank God for Southby.*

BELL

Isaac
1880-1968

Marion
1886-1968

Together Forever

POSTSCRIPT

Under a light mist that fell over the nation's capital, Pitt walked between the rows of headstones and family mausoleums until he came to a red granite stone with the name Bell across its face that simply said

BELL

Isaac	Marion
1880–1968	1886–1968

Together Forever

Pitt's fondest wish was to approach this man he admired. To express his admiration for a man lost in the mist of the ages. He stood silently as his mind traveled into the past, recalling their parallel dangers, with death a constant threat. He reached into his pocket and pulled out a small stone, one of several he had picked up when he had visited the graveyard in Southby a few years earlier, and laid it at the foot of the granite marker.

The mist was dissipating when Pitt walked away after paying his respects to a man separated by time.

Clive Cussler

ABOUT THE AUTHORS

Clive Cussler is the author or coauthor of more than 50 previous books in five best-selling series, including Dirk Pitt®, NUMA® Files, Oregon Files, Isaac Bell, and Sam and Remi Fargo. His nonfiction works include *Built for Adventure: The Classic Automobiles of Clive Cussler and Dirk Pitt,* plus *The Sea Hunters* and *The Sea Hunters II.* They describe the true adventures of the real NUMA, which, led by Cussler, searches for lost ships of historic significance. With his crew of volunteers, Cussler has discovered more than 60 ships, including the long-lost Confederate ship *Hunley.* He lives in Arizona.

Jack Du Brul became a #1 *New York Times*–bestselling author by cowriting Clive Cussler's Oregon series, which has become a fan favorite. Du Brul is also the writer of the bestselling novels featuring Philip Mercer. Du Brul lives in Vermont with his wife.